"Hornsby handles the diversity of cultures—gangs, barrios, homeless, cops, filmmaking—adeptly as Maggie's probing stirs up a toxic residue of unsolved killings that again proves fatal. It's good to see Maggie back in action."

—*Publishers Weekly* [on *In the Guise of Mercy*]

"This novel rocks. The action slides from page to page, never breaking the suspense. Just when you think you can take a breath, another surprise pops up and you're off and running again. Hornsby has mastered her genre.... This is a very good read."

—*BookLoons* [on *In the Guise of Mercy*]

"Smart, tough, and idealistic, Maggie MacGowen is an appealingly unorthodox heroine in a fine series. This one belongs in every collection."

—*Booklist* [on *A Hard Light*]

"Maggie's convictions about issues that really matter make her a true idealist."

—Marilyn Stasio, *New York Times* [on *Bad Intent*]

"...Edgar Award winner Hornsby's fourth Maggie MacGowen novel [is] a tour de force. Hornsby's powerful writing and her equally thought-provoking story blend to make this one of the most gripping, compelling mysteries of the year."

—*Publishers Weekly* [starred review, on *77th Street Requiem*]

W9-BNU-500

The
Paramour's
Daughter

—A MAGGIE MACGOWEN MYSTERY—

Wendy Hornsby

2010

PALO ALTO – MCKINLEYVILLE

PERSEVERANCE PRESS • JOHN DANIEL & COMPANY

The interior design and the cover design of this book are intended for and limited to the publisher's first print edition of the book and related marketing display purposes. All other use of those designs without the publisher's permission is prohibited.

A Perseverance Press Book
Published by John Daniel & Company
A division of Daniel & Daniel, Publishers, Inc.
Post Office Box 2790
McKinleyville, California 95519
www.danielpublishing.com/perseverance

Distributed by SCB Distributors (800) 729-6423

Book design by Eric Larson, Studio E Books, Santa Barbara, www.studio-e-books.com
Cover design and illustration by Peter Thorpe, www.peterthorpe.net

10 9 8 7 6 5 4 3 2 1

LIBRARY OF CONGRESS CATALOGING-IN-PUBLICATION DATA
Hornsby, Wendy.
The paramour's daughter : a Maggie MacGowen mystery / by Wendy Hornsby.
   p. cm.
ISBN 978-1-56474-496-8 (pbk. : alk. paper)
1. MacGowen, Maggie (Fictitious character)--Fiction. 2. Women motion picture producers and directors--Fiction. 3. Los Angeles (Calif.)--Fiction. 4. Normandy (France)--Fiction. I. Title.
PS3558.O689P37 2010
               2010006360

Paul—Encore!

─THE FAMILIES─

IN CALIFORNIA

Maggie MacGowen

Casey MacGowen, her daughter

Detective Mike Flint,* LAPD, her husband

Elizabeth and Alfred* Duchamps, her parents

Mark* and Emily* Duchamps, her brother and sister

Max Duchamps, her uncle, lawyer and agent

IN NORMANDY

Élodie and Henri* Martin

Isabelle Martin, their daughter

Claude Desmoulins, Isabelle's ex-husband

Freddy Desmoulins, son of Isabelle and Claude

Lena Desmoulins, Freddy's wife

Gérard Martin, son of Élodie and Henri

Louise Foullard Martin,* Gérard's first wife

Antoine Martin, older son of Louise and Gérard

Kelly Martin, Antoine's wife

Bébé (Charles) Martin, younger son of Louise and Gérard

Gillian Martin, Gérard's second wife

Jemima Martin, daughter of Gillian and Gérard

deceased

— THE PARAMOUR'S DAUGHTER —

—|—

"MY DEAR GIRL!"

The woman, a phantom clothed in shades of gray, rushed toward me out of the shadows at the edge of the parking lot, her arms outstretched as if she expected me to fall into her embrace. I took a quick glance at her, in case she was someone I might know or should be worried about, didn't know her, also didn't see any of the primary reasons to flee: blood, weapons, or the clipboard of some fanatic looking for signatures on a petition.

She was too well dressed, clean and expensively coiffed to be a homeless panhandler—even in the rarified environs of the Malibu Colony, where we were, the homeless don't wear cashmere sweaters.

It was ten o'clock, the night before Thanksgiving. Whatever her issues, I didn't want to hear them. I'd had a long and brutal day and all I wanted was to get some groceries and go home. I hurried toward the market's lighted windows, hoping to find sanctuary among other cranky, late-evening shoppers, doing my best to ignore her.

Normally, I would not have parked so far away from the market, but the lot was packed. There are only three supermarkets within the twenty-seven-mile-long oceanfront snake of land that makes up the City of Malibu. Beyond this market in the Malibu Colony, the next was eight miles up Pacific Coast Highway at Point Dume. So, for any local like me still in need of a turkey or any of the trimmings, this was the place.

I dodged a car backing out of its space, the spikey-haired driver distracted by his conversation via hands-free telephone. Or with voices only he could hear; the effect is the same, either way.

"Please, my dear," my pursuer called, slowed by the same car swerving into her path, then picking up her pace when it was past. She seemed to be in pretty good shape for someone I guessed to be at the upper end of her sixties. "Just a moment, please."

I kept walking. She appeared to be benign enough, but the pure delight in her face when she looked at me, as if she were the birthday girl and I her entire party, set off my alarms. Never before had anyone, not even my dear mother, ever been that happy to see me. Frankly, the happy sparkle in her eyes scared me.

Maybe she just had a snootful of holiday cheer. If so, I didn't want to share her joy. I was not feeling the rise of holiday spirit, did not want to. I had lost my husband, the notorious and wonderful Detective Mike Flint, Robbery–Homicide Division, LAPD, to cancer the previous spring and absolutely dreaded going through the holidays ahead without him. With all the Ho-ho-ho junk all of a sudden popping up everywhere again, it took a lot of effort for me to keep up a façade of composure, and this annoying old girl hovering at my elbow was pecking away at fragile edges. I wanted to brush her off, get my groceries and go. But, because I was brought up by a proper Bostonian who taught me to respect my elders, instead of letting loose with any of the colorful, blistering versions of "Piss off" that occurred to me, I turned toward her, smiled blandly and asked her, "Do you need me to call 911 for you?"

The question seemed to confuse her for a moment, made her step falter. Then she shook her head and resumed her pace again. "No, no."

"Then please excuse me." I turned from her and kept walking.

"I need to speak with you." She began to lope along beside me. "My dear, please, wait, just a word."

I knew better than to stop. Now and then I am accosted by strangers because of my line of work. I produce pithy documentaries, "Maggie MacGowen Investigates," for one of the big television networks. The series not only bears my name but also frequently shows my face, and that sometimes makes me a target. The people who are happy about my reports occasionally send me nice notes, addressed to the studio. But people who are angry about what I dig up have on occasion come gunning for me, usually verbally, a few times literally. I have learned to be wary. And, of course, a parking lot at night is not a place where a normal person would go hoping to initiate some chipper conversation with a stranger glimpsed on television.

"Do you not know who I am?" she implored. She had a pretty little accent that became more pronounced the more agitated she became. "Please, just for a moment, look at me."

I glanced at her, saw not one scintilla of familiarity. I said, "Sorry, I don't know you. Please excuse me." And walked on.

"This is not where I wanted for our meeting to take place, my dear," she persisted, taking the lead and then walking nearly backwards so that she could watch my face, or maybe, I, hers. "But this is where I find you. So…"

"Please," I said, leaning away from her.

"You must know me in your heart." She grabbed my forearm and pushed her face up close to mine, so close I could smell her shampoo. Stunned, I put my hand over hers to pry away her fingers, and as I did I glanced from the hand to her face, saw tears in her eyes.

She gasped, imploring, "Marguerite, I am your mother."

Obviously, the woman was what the LA police call a fifty-one–fifty, a mental incompetent. Someone's crazy aunt out on the loose the night before Thanksgiving.

"Two mistakes there," I said as I shook my arm free from her grip and backed away from her. "First, I spoke with my mother ten minutes ago on the phone. She's at her home, setting the table for dinner tomorrow. And two, my name is not Marguerite."

She wagged a finger at me, smiling in the wry yet gleeful *Caughtya* way that my old dragon of a teacher, Sister Agnes Peter, would when I proffered a wrong answer. "They call you Maggie, but that is not the name on your birth certificate."

True enough, but the name on my birth certificate was not Marguerite, either. I looked around for some help, got a nod from a checker who had been watching this scene unfold from inside the store. He had a phone to his ear; I hoped he had called Security.

If things got ugly, I knew I could push my way free of the old dear, but, again, that proper upbringing made me hesitant to deck a senior citizen. Better to let the pros do it for me, I thought. I knew from experience that, out of necessity, the market plaza kept a good security detail so that its local patrons could pick up their groceries and dry-cleaning unmolested. Malibu is a strange alternate universe where paparazzi, fans, Hollywood wannabes and stalkers abound. All of the above are on the lookout for celebrity prey because, in Malibu, if the guy behind you in the check-out line holding a carton of Häagen-Dazs looks like George Clooney, he probably is George Clooney.

I am not a big-name celeb like Mr. Clooney. Off screen and out of makeup, I am rarely anything more than a vaguely familiar face to anyone except my near and dear, an unlikely target for paparazzi, wannabes, or fans. But stalkers can fixate on anyone; it has happened to me twice before.

The market entrance was only a few yards ahead. I picked up my pace. Sternly, I said, "Good night, ma'am. I hope you find whomever you're looking for."

"I have. It is you. And I have waited for this moment for a very long time." She sounded exasperated, scolding; not a good development.

As a reflex, for protection, I pulled a shopping cart from the end of a rank in front of the market and wedged it between us as a shield while I closed in on the entrance. Whatever the woman's issue, I was not going to wait around to hear about it. I didn't want to be rude to her, I didn't want to start a scene. All I wanted was for her to go away and let me get about my business. Not only was my larder bare, but that night I was also running short on the milk of human kindness.

My day at work had peaked in the morning with the completion of a film project, on time even. It was the second installment of "The Legacy Series." Each episode we produced this season featured a different retired police investigator presenting that one unsolved case that he or she most regretted never closing. We weren't doing "Cold Case," or even trying to solve these old crimes. Instead, we examined the cases as pieces of social history, focusing on the culture of law enforcement and the culture of the city at a particular moment, and looked at the reasons why a particular case touched some deep place in even the most hardened of investigators.

Usually, at the project hand-off there would be huzzahs from my studio bosses, general back-patting, followed by celebratory drinks and dinner somewhere posh with my small staff and some of the people we met during the production. But this time the hand-off occurred at a private meeting, just me and the bosses. After truncated congratulations, the meeting segued into a bruising budget session where I was threatened with staff and funding cuts for my unit that could be so deep I did not know how we could do justice to the remaining episodes on our contract. And by the way, I was told on my way out, the completion date for the next project had been moved up.

Instead of an evening swapping tales and gossip over martinis and steaks-frites at Morton's, I ordered in pizza and beer for my little crew and let them know that they should take time during the upcoming Thanksgiving weekend to revise their résumés, a task I intended to work on myself. Then I called my agent and filled him in on the meeting.

My agent and lawyer is Max Duchamps, my Uncle Max, AKA the Shark, my late dad's younger brother, the offspring of my grandfather's second marriage. He told me we'd talk after dinner tomorrow at my mother's house, or sometime during the weekend. I did not hear abundant optimism in the tone of his voice.

Tough times all over, I thought, risking a glance at the woman in gray as a new notion occurred to me. Was she trying to provoke me into doing something that she could sue me for? In Malibu it happens all the time. Paparazzi and litigious others push and provoke people they assume have deep pockets, hoping to be rewarded with a potentially million-dollar punch in the nose. If a lawsuit was this woman's intention, she had chosen a damned shallow pocket to go after. For God's sake, I had a daughter in college and an uncertain work future.

"Wait, please, just a moment." The woman grasped the far end of my cart and tried to move it out of her way. A car pulled up alongside us, the driver's window went down, and our little scene was suddenly illuminated by a camera flash. We both turned toward the flash, a reflex, and were hit by a second flash as the car sped away. I thought, Goddamn paparazzi, always lurking, ever hopeful of catching the shot that will launch the next celebrity scandal and earn themselves a nice paycheck. Thinking this guy would be sorely disappointed when he discovered that his pix caught no one marketable and had only called attention to my dance with a stranger, I let go of the cart and made a dash through the market's automatic doors, with the stranger close on my heels.

Two enormous, well-muscled men with SECURITY discreetly embroidered in gold over the pockets of their black polos, swept in through the big doors right behind us. I could feel the air they displaced as their bulk moved into position to barricade us from moving further into the market. I relaxed right away; they both had necks as thick as bulls, biceps like the trunks of mighty oaks, chests that challenged the knit fabric of their short-sleeved shirts. From the look of them, these rent-a-cops came from the high-rent end of the security spectrum.

"There a problem here?" one of the guards challenged, sotto voce, looking between me and the stranger. He had dark, short-cropped hair and jaws so gnarly he could munch boulders for breakfast. I felt better, certainly safer, immediately. Either of them could have picked up the woman with one hand and carried her away.

"This lady seems to have lost someone," I said. "Maybe you can help her."

"You don't know her?" Gnarly Jaws asked me, eyes narrow, skeptical. I shook my head. "Never saw her before."

"Yes." She nodded vigorously, agitated, anguished even, shaking as she looked from one mountain of a man to the other. "She simply doesn't remember."

I raised my hands, shrugged: I didn't know what she was talking about, didn't want to know; your problem now, fellas.

Gnarly Jaws put himself between the woman and me, facing her. She tried to see around him, to keep track of me.

She pleaded with him. "I have been searching for my Marguerite for so long. And here she is."

He looked over his shoulder at me, asking a question with a bobble of his head in her direction. When I shook my head no, he turned back to her, crossed his muscled arms over his bulwark of a chest, an intimidating gesture that should have made her cower. It didn't. She kept up her plea.

I turned to the second man, a blond, azure-blue–eyed version of Gnarly, who was keeping an eye on me. I pointed to myself and then toward the back of the market, a request to be excused from what promised to be an ugly meltdown. Azure Eyes nodded assent and I started to walk away. The woman made a desperate lunge for me, but the security men blocked her.

"My dear," she called out to me, loud and distraught, as I retreated farther into the market. "Please. I don't mean to frighten you."

Gnarly never raised his voice to her: "Ma'am, you need to leave the premises."

"You don't understand," the woman protested, weeping now. "I need to speak with Marguerite."

"Yes, ma'am, but the lady doesn't want to speak with you. And *you* need to understand this: you will leave on your own, or you will be escorted away, but you are leaving, right now."

I was so grateful to be rescued from watching any more of that poor woman's desperation and grief, and was so genuinely fatigued and had-it-up-to-here, that I nearly wept. As I said, it had been a rough day. But I managed to pull myself together enough to go about gathering the things I had come for. I wanted to get home, have a glass of wine, something to eat with my daughter, Casey, a hot bath, and to bed. But first I needed to get the ingredients for sweet potato mousse and the fixings for Friday's breakfast. Early Thanksgiving morning, Casey and I would be in the car, headed over the river and through the woods to my mother's house in Berkeley, a minimum eight-hour drive if traffic wasn't too awful.

I was at the back of the store by the dairy case reading yogurt labels when a box boy I had known for a couple of years, a kid named Nick, brought me a replacement shopping cart. He was a good-looking young man, a sophomore at Pepperdine University just up Pacific Coast Highway from the market plaza. He was polite to everyone, but I usually got special attention from Nick because of his interest in my daughter, a dance major at UCLA.

After Nick inquired about Casey, he asked, "You okay, Miss Mac-Gowen?"

"Yes, thanks," I said.

"See what happens when you get your face in the tabs?" he said, teasing, as he turned to walk away. "Now all the nuts know where to find you."

What he said gave me pause. A few weeks earlier, out in the same market parking lot, I had been mowed down by a paparazzo when I inadvertently walked between his viewfinder and his target, a notoriously misbehaving multi-bazillionare hip-hop princess named Tiffy. In the photographer's forward rush I got knocked on my ass with Tiffy, obviously sans underwear and apparently a natural blonde, sprawled across my lap, miniskirt around her waist. Someone took a picture that instantly became a worldwide media flash, seemed to be everywhere at once, briefly. I seriously doubt, however, that anyone who saw that picture paid the slightest attention to me, not with the exposed privates of that particular young woman at the center of the frame. But, as I said, stalkers can fixate on anyone.

My daughter called when I was in Produce trying to figure out how many raw ones it would take to make one quart of cooked, whipped sweet potatoes.

"Mom," Casey greeted me with her usual exuberance. "Is it okay with you if my roommate, Zia, comes with us to Gran's?"

"It's fine with me, but you need to ask Gran," I said.

"I did, she's fine with it."

She told me she and Zia were already on their way from their campus residence hall to my house and had picked up some Indian food for dinner, as arranged. Asking for my approval was only a courtesy, a point of information for me; they were adults, over eighteen, and didn't need permission for most things.

Casey, a sophomore, my ballerina since she was a very little girl, had stretched up to a full six feet in height by the beginning of the fall school quarter, an inch taller than she had been at the end of her freshman year. During the summer a much-shorter male partner failed to assay a lift and dropped her, and Casey's ankle was broken. The fracture healed quickly, but her future plans had not yet re-knit, as it were. There aren't very many six-foot ballerinas for good reason; male dancers tend to be small. I hoped she was seriously rethinking her major.

I was headed toward checkout when Gnarly Jaws came looking for me. He introduced himself, Ray Valdez, told me that he was a Los Angeles County Sheriff's deputy moonlighting by doing private security. He said he had known my husband, Mike. Valdez offered his condolences. Everyone seemed to know Mike, or had heard about him. Eight months after Mike's passing, I was still getting sympathy cards.

Valdez took the handle of my cart and walked beside me. He was Hollywood–dark-and-handsome, could have been recruited for the Sheriffs straight out of Central Casting. Quite a few local cops, LAPD and Sheriffs alike, have part-time gigs in Hollywood as actors, extras, screenwriters, advisors and security because they are buff and smart and willing, and the pay can be good. Most have some sort of college degree or certificate, and they take seriously the local police culture of fitness; I have yet to meet a doughnut-eating young cop.

"Sorry you were bothered, Miss MacGowen," Valdez said. "That lady's been hanging around the plaza off-and-on for about a week now, mostly just sitting on the patio drinking coffee. You're the first person I've seen her accost."

"Lucky me," I said.

"Yeah." He had a worried furrow between his heavy brows as he studied me. "You said you don't know her?"

"Correct, I don't," I said. "Never saw her before."

"She says she's your mother."

"So she does," I said, smiling up at Valdez. "I hope she isn't expecting me for Thanksgiving dinner tomorrow because I already have plans. At my mother's house."

He nodded, relaxed visibly when it was clear that the parking lot dustup hadn't been a family squabble, smiled enough to show his dimples. "Holidays always seem to set off the wackos. I think 'Jingle Bells' channels secret messages to them."

Indeed, Christmas music was already streaming through the market's speakers, an endless loop that would last through New Year's Day. Drive a sane person over the edge after a while.

"Woman just had a notion." He actually winked at me. "Somewhere out there, there's a fruitcake missing one of its nuts."

Valdez helped me unload my groceries onto the checkout conveyor.

Too obviously casual about it, he said, "She called you Marguerite. Is Maggie short for Marguerite?"

"I suppose it could be," I said. "But that isn't my name."

"But Maggie is short for something else?"

"It is," I said.

He was thoughtful for a moment before he asked, "So, what *is* your real name? You know, like your whole name."

"My *whole* name?"

He nodded, watching me intently, as cops do, always looking for the "tell."

"Keep it between us, but my real whole name is Margot Eugenie Louise-Marie Duchamps MacGowen Flint." I caught him grinning. "You said, the whole name."

He laughed softly. "Margot, then, not Marguerite. That's where you get Maggie."

"Yep." I put a quart of non-fat milk on the conveyor. "Margot."

"That's a lot of names for one little baby," he said, just being conversational, or a typical nosy cop. Who knew?

"I wondered if my parents had planned to have a big family, stopped with me, and just gave me all the girls' names they had left over."

"You an only child, then?"

"No." I'd had to pause before answering the question. "Older brother and sister, twins actually. But they're both gone. My brother died at the very end of the Vietnam War—I was just a little kid when it happened. My sister, Emily—"

"You said, Duchamps." He froze clutching a head of lettuce in his big hand, and stared at me, studied me. I nodded. "Emily Duchamps? Dr. Emily Duchamps?"

I looked up into his face. "Did you know her?"

"No, not really. I met her. The Doc spoke to my Academy class about some things to watch for, to protect ourselves against, when we went into people's houses, different diseases. She'd go into the projects looking for kids with measles and TB, all alone. The worst of the hell holes, Jordan Downs, Nickerson Gardens—cops won't go in there alone, but she did. Unarmed." He relinquished the lettuce to the conveyor and picked up a bag of apples. "I was a rookie when…" He paused, wouldn't look at me. Seemed at a loss for the right words.

"When she was shot," I said. "No one in the projects ever bothered Emily. But an old friend, well, that was different."

"I remember." He nodded. "That's the way it usually goes down, someone you know. God, Dr. Duchamps was your sister? I hadn't put that together."

Was I an only child? No. Last one standing? Sadly, yes.

Seemed Valdez was going to stick close to me until I made it safely out of the parking lot. If that was the case, we were going to talk about something other than my sister Emily.

"Thanks for your help," I said, running my debit card through the scanner. "What's going to happen to that woman?"

"Nothing." Valdez shrugged one beefy shoulder. "We removed her from the premises, and that's all we legally can do. She didn't show a weapon or threaten anyone, so that's it. We'll escort you to your car when you're finished here and make sure you get out of the lot."

I thanked him again.

He took the handle of the cart and walked me outside. Making small talk, ever nosy, he asked, "So, who is MacGowen?"

"Ex-husband."

He seemed to take note of the answer.

Incident over, crazy woman banished, groceries safely loaded in the car, I drove out of the lot onto the side access road, Webb Way, named for Jack Webb I was told once, and stopped at the intersection with PCH for the light to change so that I could cross. I planned to continue up Webb Way, the first leg of the locals' secret back way to access Malibu Canyon Road, my route home.

The night was clear and chilly, almost wintery by Southern California standards, maybe fifty degrees. On the far side of PCH, in a vacant corner field, workers were stringing up lights for a Christmas tree lot that would open on Friday morning. A truckload of trees had already arrived and was waiting to be unloaded.

Seeing the trees, this opening salvo for the holidays ahead, I was surprised by a sudden welling of sadness; maybe it was only fatigue, let-down from the day. And I missed Mike. I even missed his feigned Bah-humbug routine. Mike loved the holiday season, no matter how hard he tried to pretend he didn't.

I took a deep breath, flipped on a Diana Krall CD, *Live in Paris*, as a holiday antidote, and opened the moon roof so that I would be able to see the stars as I drove away from the glittery, crowded coast and up into the wilds of the Santa Monica Mountains to the canyon where I lived.

I averted my eyes from the tree lot. And that's when I saw her again, standing knee-deep in dry scrub at the edge of the vacant field directly across the highway, watching me. She took a step toward the road when our eyes met. I saw a narrow gap in the oncoming traffic between a delivery van and a Maserati, put my foot on the accelerator and blew through the light, slipped through the hole, squealed into a left turn and sped away.

— 2 —

CASEY AND ZIA had brought home enough Indian food to feed a regiment. Potato *samosas*, *murgh makhani*, chicken *tikka*, and vegetable *korma*, all of it seasoned to *vindaloo* heat. We tamed the fire with sweet, milky iced tea and cold beer.

We ate in the kitchen to keep an eye on the sweet potato mousse baking in the oven. Listening to the girls talk about classes, friends, end-of-quarter finals that were only a few weeks ahead, I felt like a spectator at a tennis match, head turning from Casey to Zia and back again. Now and then I chimed in, but was thoroughly happy to just listen to them deliver snapshots of their life at school. Casey and I had always been very close, and suddenly she was having a life separate from my own except around its edges. I was happy that she had adjusted so well, and I missed her very much.

Children grow and develop in spurts. They seem to go to bed one night a scuffed-knee kid and wake up in the morning an emergent, gazelle-like adolescent. Casey suddenly, and recently, seemed to have made another of those leaps, this time fully into adulthood. Altogether, it seemed to me, she was more substantial than she had been when I deposited her at her dorm in October, six weeks earlier. I had seen her several times since, but I hadn't noticed the change until that night. The contours of her face had new definition, her body seemed sturdier, less elfin. Less ballerina.

But there was more to it. Casey's conversation with Zia, a junior, an economics major, was sophisticated, informed, inquisitive, as any parent of a university student would hope it would be. She was still my baby, but when I wasn't watching, she had become a grown-up.

I put my hand on one of the well-defined biscuits of her biceps. I said, "You pumping iron?"

She nodded with some enthusiasm and quickly swallowed a mouthful of something so she could speak. "The physical therapist I've been seeing since I got the cast off my ankle got me into weights to build strength again in my legs, but I've also been working on core strength and shoulders."

"She has a crush on her therapist," Zia offered, grinning wickedly as she mopped up yogurt sauce on her plate with a piece of *naan*.

"Who wouldn't?" Casey's face brightened, but she didn't blush. "He's amazing."

"But he's like, thirty," the roommate added, winking at me, teasing.

"Old," I said, passing the chicken *tikka* to Zia.

"And very married," Casey added, and with a wave of her hand aimed in Zia's direction, she dismissed the man as a romantic possibility. "He introduced me to one of his other patients, a setter on the women's volleyball team. He says I'm a natural for volleyball."

"Oh?" My straight line.

"Let's face it, Mom." She leaned toward me. "I'm too tall for ballet. But I'm perfect for volleyball. I'm strong, I'm quick, and Lord knows I can jump. I met the women's volleyball coach and she invited me to work out with the team. I'm not eligible to play this season, but I can get ready for spring tryouts."

"What about dance?" I asked, thinking about the scholarship that was helping with tuition.

"I'll always love dance—it's been my life since I was a little girl—but I can't make a career out of it. I've always known that."

"Have you?" The word "always" was a surprise to me.

"You keep telling me I need a backup plan." She grinned at me, a wiseass grin. "I listen to you, Mom, I listen. Really."

"What is your backup, assuming that it's other than volleyball?" I asked.

"I've been thinking maybe sports medicine."

Zia turned to me. "Told you the therapist is good-looking."

"Oh, he's gorgeous," Casey affirmed. "And he's also really, really smart. He says that sports medicine and physical therapy have been built around the male athlete, and that model doesn't always serve women athletes. There are so many more women athletes all the time. I'm thinking about aiming for medical school."

"Have you considered the coursework?" I asked. "Anatomy, physiology, biology, chemistry."

"She aced all her gen-ed science courses," Zia said. "Straight A's. I hate her."

"They aren't that tough," Casey said.

"You're your grandfather's girl, after all. He'd have been awfully proud to have another doctor in the family." We clinked glasses. Casey told Zia about her Aunt Emily, a public health physician.

I was reminded how much alike Casey and Emily were in both build and intellect. As I listened to the girls' conversation, in my head I was doing some rough math. A minimum of six more years of college tuition. I kissed off any notion I might have harbored after my meeting at the studio earlier in the day of returning to independent film production. I hoped Uncle Max, my agent, could pull something out of a hat for me if necessary, if my current gig crapped out on me.

"I've had the cast off my leg for three weeks," Casey said. "Reggie says that if I keep up physical therapy and keep my ankle taped, it's safe to work out with the volleyball team."

"Reggie?" I asked, looking with wonder at this metamorphosed creature sitting at my kitchen table.

"Oh, Mom," Casey said, shaking her head at my naïveté with good-natured tolerance that bordered on patronization. There are times when parents, too, grow older in spurts.

Before dawn, my bedside clock radio, set to the local morning news station, stirred me from a beautiful, deep sleep. I lingered under the warm comforter long enough to hear the weather and traffic reports: roads were clear, skies were clear, all systems were go for our drive north to Berkeley.

When I walked downstairs, I could hear Casey and Zia talking in the kitchen. I dropped my duffel of weekend essentials beside the front door and, before joining the girls, stopped at the tall living room windows to wait for the first light of morning to reach the mountainside on the far side of the canyon below us.

My house was in a small enclave that jutted like a thumb of habitation into the open lands of the Santa Monica Mountains Conservancy. There were twelve houses built up the steep face and nestled among the folds of a craggy mountainside. We were about halfway between Pacific Coast Highway in Malibu and the Ventura Freeway that bisects the San Fernando Valley, an acceptable commute to my studio in Burbank, but light years away from the clatter of greater Los Angeles that surrounded us. Coyotes, owls and red-tailed hawks kept the rodent population in check; deer ate my roses. It was a magnificent, unspoiled oasis only a few miles from the wilds of the big city and its own set of predators.

Out in the yard, our trail horses began to stir in the corral we shared with the neighbor, Early Drummond, a co-worker of mine. I could only see their outlines against the dark as they moved about: Rover, my quarter horse, a rodeo circuit washout; Red, Mike's big old roan; and Early's feisty gelding, Duke, argued over access to the water trough, position at the rail, and anything else that occurred to them to fuss about. When the lights on Early's front stairs snapped on, they suddenly went still, hopeful that he was coming down to feed them.

For one moment, the living room was awash in the soft blue glow that immediately precedes dawn. The sky gradually turned rose and then, suddenly, as I watched, the first flames of sunlight lit the ridgetops on the far side of the canyon; the deep canyon bottom would remain dark for another hour. Heavy coastal fog spilled over the tops of the jagged peaks, white and puffy and beautiful like the foam on the face of breaking ocean waves. The dawn alone made the challenges of living perched in an aerie worthwhile.

I looked up at the sky, deep blue now, and thought about the beautiful life Mike and I had worked so hard to make for each other.

"Mom?" I turned and saw Casey framed in the light from the kitchen. "You okay?"

"Yes, of course."

"You were so still."

"Morning ritual," I said, shrugging off a sudden chill as I walked across the room to accept the mug of coffee she held out to me. "You ladies ready to rumble?"

"We are." She was watching me closely, as she had since Mike died. Looking for what, evidence of my imminent collapse? I'd been through some very rough passages over the past eight months, but I thought the worst was over. My real concern was for Casey. She had shouldered too much loss already for someone her age. Some years ago, her father left us to start a new family—that order isn't accurate; the new family was already started before he announced his departure—and never made room for her in his new life. Then, in short order, she lost her beloved grandfather and Mike. I thought that she kept her eye on me because she was afraid she would lose me, too.

Zia, leaning against a kitchen counter hunched over a mug of coffee, stifled a yawn before she said, "Good morning. God, it's early."

The kitchen radio continued the weather and traffic reports I'd been listening to upstairs. It is foolhardy to head out onto Southern California freeways without first locating the hazards and mapping alternate routes, especially on a holiday. There was a report of a fender-bender on the Hollywood Freeway near Cahuenga Boulevard, a big rig overturned somewhere in Orange County; our route was still clear.

As I took the sweet potato mousse out of the refrigerator and bent to put it into the ice chest we were taking with us, through my own morning fog and something Casey was saying about plans to meet friends in San Francisco on Friday, I heard the radio announcer say the word "Malibu" and paused, held up my hand to interrupt Casey.

"The body of an unidentified woman was found late last night near the intersection of Pacific Coast Highway and Cross Creek Road in the exclusive Malibu Colony area, an apparent hit-and-run victim." There was no description of the victim given, or any further details, except that the coroner had been called. There was a request for witnesses to come forward, and the number of the LA County Sheriff's Malibu substation was recited. I punched the button for another news station, heard the weather repeating, tried a third, hoping for more information about the hit-and-run, found none.

"What is it, Mom?" Casey asked, always attuned to me.

"Probably nothing," I said as I dialed the Malibu substation. The man who answered identified himself as Sergeant Ho. After identifying myself, I asked him, "The woman who was killed on PCH, what time was she hit?"

"Between ten-thirty last night and two this morning," Sgt. Ho said. "Do you have information?"

I told him about my encounter with the woman at the market, and suggested that Deputy Ray Valdez might have more information about her; perhaps she had shown him some identification.

Sgt. Ho asked me for a description. I told him, Woman in her sixties, wearing well-cut charcoal wool flannel slacks and a smoky gray cashmere pullover sweater; medium-length, medium-brown hair, probably tinted; blue eyes, shorter than me—I am about five-six. No handbag that I saw.

"Why do you think this woman you describe could be the victim?" Ho asked.

"She was out walking near PCH at about the right time," I said. "She obviously had some big problems. But even if she isn't the victim, maybe she saw something."

"Exactly where was she when you saw her?"

"She was standing in the vacant field at the corner of PCH and Webb Way, across from the tree lot." That is, almost directly in front of the Sheriff's substation and a long block from the intersection of Cross Creek and PCH.

"What time was that?"

"A little after ten," I said.

Ho took my phone number, thanked me for the information, and wished me a Happy Thanksgiving. He didn't seem the least excited about what I told him, indeed, had given me precious little information except the probable three-hour window for the time of death. If I had identi- fied myself as a reporter—I carry a legitimate press pass—he probably would have given me more information, but she wasn't my story and I had no reason, nor any real desire, to know more. Anyway, I thought, it was a long shot that my woman was the victim, but just in case...

"What was that about?" Casey asked after I hung up.

I told her and Zia about the woman, in brief.

"Look at your face, Mom. She scared you, didn't she?"

"Yes. A little. You never know what people might do."

"Lucky you," Zia said, tears suddenly rolling down her cheeks. "You have two mothers who want you."

The stranger at the market was forgotten as Zia, who always seemed so pulled-together, had a mini-breakdown over her divorced parents, neither of whom had included their only daughter in holiday plans. One said that travelling across the country over the Thanksgiving week- end just wasn't worth the effort. The other had recently remarried and wasn't ready to "blend"—his word—his new family with his old, that is, his nearly grown daughter. Poor Zia, dumped off at a huge university on a far shore from family, felt abandoned, motherless. Parentless.

I watched Casey comfort her roommate, and decided that one day, in some distant future, my daughter, most precious daughter, would be a lovely mother.

For the first time I felt true compassion for that poor woman at the market who seemed to have lost her child. What could be worse than losing a child? I should have been kinder, more patient with the old girl, I thought. And I vowed to be more patient with my own mother over the weekend, even if she launched into an endless verbal ramble about some long-ago and best-forgotten event from her nearly eighty years of experiences. The pre-holiday dose of guilt rose from the pit of my stom- ach along with the *vindaloo*-hot residue of Indian food.

I haven't been to church for a very long time, but I remembered the confessional plea, Forgive me for what I have done and for what I have not done, got hung up on that last part and vowed to be more attentive to my mother than I had been during the year since my father died. I was forty-three years old. I hoped there was time left for atonement. Would atonement require committing no further sins? Dangerous to aim too high. I vowed, then, to just do my best, to be patient at least through the weekend.

I took a deep breath. As Mike always said, in life, there is no re-do. We make decisions based on the information we have at the time. And then we live with those decisions.

— 3 —

MOM WAS SITTING on the front porch of her big, old Craftsman house—the house where I was born, where I grew up—when we pulled into the driveway. She waved as she rose, hesitating a bit as she straightened. Her knees seemed to feel stiff lately, but she never complained.

My mother is a tall, sturdy New Englander who transplanted brilliantly to Berkeley where, as a faculty wife with old-fashioned leftist sensibilities and a gift for entertaining, she truly found her niche. She is genuinely dear, but no one could ever call her sweet. Maybe she cuddled me on her lap when I was little, as she had held my daughter, but I don't remember it. Instead I remember clinging to her hand as she marched for open housing, voting rights, free speech, equality for women, saving the redwoods, and an end to nuclear testing—a gutsy stand when my father was chair of the university physics department, the same one where the father of the American atomic bomb also once taught. She also played cello in a string quartet, taught piano to her friends' children and accompanied university dance classes. What she did not do was tie ribbons in my hair, tolerate fools, or coddle anyone. If she had flinty edges and could seem formidable, she was also unfailingly honest, pure in her motivations, and funny as hell.

"Here are my girls." Mom held out her arms and Casey rushed to her, enveloped her grandmother in a hug, lifted her off her feet and gave her a little swing. For as long as I can remember, Mom has worn her hair twisted into a loose, gravity-defying knot held in place by a single long tortoiseshell skewer. It always looks as if it is about to come apart, but, one of the mysteries of physics, it never does, not even when Casey twirled her. Maybe that was part of my father's attraction to Mom, her defiance of the laws of gravity.

"Good to see you, Gran," Casey said when Mom again had both feet safely planted on terra firma. "You remember my roommate?"

"Zia, dear, how nice." Mom held out her arms to Zia, who shyly returned the embrace. "Lovely to see you again. So glad you've come."

"Hello, Mom," I said. I slung my weekend bag over one shoulder and wrapped my free arm around her; she was bonier than I remembered. "How are you?"

"I've decided I'm old, Margot. So, considering the options, I'm just fine." She kissed my cheek; she is the only living person who calls me Margot, my given name. "The important question of the moment, my dear, is, how are you?"

"All things considered, I'm okay."

"That's not what your darling daughter tells me. She says you're a wreck waiting to happen."

"Hah!" And not subtle. No one ever accused Mom of subtlety. "The truth? I feel like I've been caught in the undercarriage and dragged along."

"Atta girl." She patted my back firmly. "Here we are, two old widows starting anew. I cherish the prospect of spending some good time this weekend with my girl." She glanced at Casey and Zia, who were unloading the car. "With all my girls."

"Oh, lordy, Mom." I took one handle of the ice chest and helped Casey carry it up the front steps. "You're the first person to call me a widow to my face. I'm a widow. Damn."

"It's just language," Mom said as she picked up the canvas bag that held Casey's laptop and walked up the steps. She held the front door open for us. "The Widow Flint does have a certain antique ring to it."

"So, Mom." Time for a new subject. Casey and Zia went through to the kitchen carrying the ice chest between them. "How's your garden?"

"Hired a yardman." She led me upstairs, where we would check on sleeping arrangements. "The garden was more your father's interest than mine. I enjoyed working alongside him because he was always such good company, but without him it's just hoe and prune and pinch and stoop. I love flowers in the house, but the flowers I buy at the farmer's market are perfectly lovely." She smiled brightly. "I've handed the backyard over to the neighbor boy for his 4-H project. He's going to raise a sow."

"In your backyard?"

"He put up a nice wire fence out where you used to have your pony."

"That's where your herb garden is now." The house seemed unchanged to me, except that things looked a bit frayed around the edges. A big house for Mom to maintain, and live in, alone, I thought, and not for the first time.

"The market sells fresh herbs, and they're perfectly lovely, too," she said pointedly. "I had the boy pull up everything except for the rosemary hedge."

"Pork and rosemary, a natural pairing," I said, smiling at the logic that is particular to my mother.

"I thought so, too." She laughed. "It'll be nice to have some activity around the place."

"Even if it's a sow?"

"A sow and the boy tending it," she said, opening the door to my old bedroom and leading the way in. I put away my bag and looked around the room as she told me about the neighbor boy and his pre-occupied professional parents.

At her core, my radical mother is remarkably traditional where children are involved. She believes they need peace, stability and the constant presence of two involved parents. I know that her true affection for Mike, even though she detested his politics, was established when she learned that he had a very fragmented childhood: alcoholic, mostly absent mother; alcoholic petty-chiseler father who ran an automobile chop shop. My mother, the universal mother, took Mike into her heart, and so had my father.

The fuss Mom had made preparing my room made me feel like a visitor. For one thing, it was far tidier than I ever had kept it. There were fresh flowers on the nightstand, a feather comforter inside a white duvet cover on the single bed, big pillows with starched cases, an Amish quilt folded at the foot; my mother's beds always looked like clouds.

"When did that happen?" I asked, looking up at a water stain on the ceiling.

Mom followed my gaze. "During one of the storms last winter."

"You never said anything about it."

"Margot," she said pointedly, "last winter you had more important issues on your hands than my leaking roof." A reference to Mike's illness. Last winter, there was no other issue for me than Mike.

"Did you get it fixed?" I asked.

"Hal Carter went up and did some patching," she said, invoking the name of the old family handyman. "We need a new roof—your dad was looking into it—but the cost is just prohibitive."

"How much?" I wanted to say, Whatever the cost you need to bite the bullet and get the roof fixed ASAP because the rainy season is due to begin very soon, but the expression on her face as she looked at the stain stopped me. Did she have money issues?

I had never thought about my parents' finances, and they had never felt a need to share the details with me. They always lived comfortably and carefully. Dad retired with an excellent California teacher's pension.

He regularly received royalties from some patents he held that were never a fortune, but were always a steady supplement. And Mom had a little family income of her own. I assumed those income streams were infinite. And maybe I was wrong.

Mom hadn't answered my question, How much? I made eye contact, pointed up. "Mom?"

She told me. A five-figure estimate that was more than they originally had paid for the house fifty-some years earlier.

"Do you need some help?" I asked.

"Let me think about it," she said, and changed the subject to the rest of the guest accommodations.

We decided that the girls could share the guest room that had twin beds. It was obvious that Mom had taken some effort to make it up, polishing the wood, bringing in flowers, making the beds with lots of feather pillows and comforters and crisp linens. The *en suite* bathroom gleamed.

She left me in my room to freshen up. Before I went back downstairs to join the others, I peeked into the other rooms on the second floor. My parents' friends called the old house Hotel Duchamps because there were plenty of bedrooms available to offer visiting colleagues, friends, family, friends and family of friends, and occasional graduate students. As a kid, I never knew, when I got up in the morning, who I might find waiting their turn for the big upstairs hall bathroom—old house, lots of bedrooms, not so many bathrooms—or might wander down the stairs for breakfast, or show up for dinner. But I always knew there would be great food and lively mealtime conversation. Sometimes it was chaotic, but it was never dull.

Now, as I looked from room to room, it was clear that Mom hadn't hosted many visitors during the year since Dad died. Except for the room my Uncle Max used—it had been made ready for him—what I saw was a lot of dust, disuse, more water damage. I thought back over the last year, trying to remember when I had last been upstairs.

Mike and I had built a cottage up on the far northern coast, in the redwoods of Humboldt County. Whenever we visited the cottage, we would spend a night on the way up and another on the way home with Mom and Dad in Berkeley. But Mike had been under treatment or too sick to travel for a long time. Mike loved the cottage, and it broke his heart to stay away. It still broke my heart just thinking about going up without him.

After Dad died, Mom flew down to see us about once a month.

I realized I had not been to Berkeley since my dad's funeral fourteen months ago. I suffered daggers of guilt: Elderly mother, elderly house, had both been neglected too long?

Just like Casey, Mom had made one of those leaps when I wasn't paying attention. Indeed, suddenly, as she had said, she was old. Clearly, she would need more help if she were going to remain in the house, and, I knew, she would fight every effort to get it for her.

The kitchen was abuzz with meal preparations when I joined the others; it smelled like Thanksgiving, turkey roasting in the oven. Mom always spent long hours planning and preparing so that her guests would see none of the effort. Stuck to the refrigerator with a magnet was the master game plan: the menu, listing who was bringing each dish, and the preparation schedule for dishes she was preparing, times that hot dishes were to go into the oven then come out, and when cold dishes were to be assembled and set on the dining room table. No football coach could have devised a game plan as complex as this meal-prep plan.

The table itself had been set the night before, the silver polished during the week, the crystal and china—Mom set her table with the remnants of various sets she had accumulated over the years, an assemblage every bit as interesting and eclectic as her guest list—made to sparkle, tablecloth and napkins starched and ironed. I noticed, on my way through the dining room, that she had sent the linens out to the laundry instead of doing them herself. A good sign.

Casey and Zia were at work filling relish trays and condiment bowls in the butler's pantry—in the east this room between the kitchen and the back door would be called a mudroom; we certainly never had a butler. Mom handed me a bowl of risen bread dough and some muffin tins and instructed me to form the dough into cloverleaf rolls.

"Heads up, ladies." Uncle Max came through the back door, snitching olives from Zia's carefully arranged relish tray as he walked through the butler's pantry. "Roosters in the henhouse." Close behind him was a surprise visitor, my film production partner, Guido Patrini.

Max kissed Mom on the cheek. "Hope you don't mind, Betsy—I should have called—brought you one more mouth to feed."

There was an instant of hesitation before Mom gave Guido her Welcome smile. I knew from my tour of rooms upstairs that she wasn't prepared for an additional overnight guest.

"Guido, what a wonderful surprise," Mom said, leaning into a cheek kiss. "So nice to see you."

I looked behind Guido, expecting to see the graduate film student we had brought onto our last project as an intern. The young woman had become Guido's shadow, the latest in his long string of intern love interests. He taught a graduate seminar at the UCLA film school, which provided an endless source of young talent, any way you want to define that word, to work with us. Guido is handsome, a face carved from Italian marble, big brown Bambi eyes. His body is trim. But he's a year older than I am, and his latest girlfriend was exactly half his age.

As Guido hugged me, I asked, "Where's whatsername? I thought you two had plans for today with her parents."

"Shasta. Her name is Shasta." He shook his head, crestfallen. "She made other plans."

"Poor bastard," Max said, popping more olives into his mouth. "Called me last night after you did, Maggie. First he gets word from you that his job may be in jeopardy, then his girl dumps him. On a holiday weekend, no less; heartless cow. I told him he might as well come along with me today. He didn't say no, so I swooped by his house on my way to the airport this morning and fetched him."

"Good." I gave Guido a wet smooch on his cheek, tickled him under his ribs—he says he hates being tickled, I know he loves the attention—made him smile.

Uncle Max was as round and dark as his brother Alfred, my dad, was angular and fair. But somehow there was a strong family resemblance: their voices, mannerisms, some intangible qualities rather than appearance. When I was with Max, I always felt my dad's presence, and felt comforted.

Still chewing olives, Max wrapped me in a bear hug. Then he held me by the upper arms and looked into my face, which meant he was ready to deliver a pronouncement: "Maggie, the three of us, you and me and Guido, will put our heads together sometime this weekend, go over some of the fine print in your network contracts, and work out a strategy to get what we want out of the network bastards. If going to the mattresses becomes necessary, we'll be armed and ready."

"How nice, then," Mom said, smiling prettily at Guido as she untied her big chef's apron and headed for the swinging door into the dining room. "You'll be staying the weekend. Margot, if you'll keep an eye on things." She tapped the master plan on the refrigerator door as she looked me in the eye, a warning to pay heed to the plan. "I'll just get Guido's room ready upstairs. Won't take a minute."

"Don't bother," Guido said, embarrassed to have caused additional work for Mom. "A couch will do. Or a warm corner by the stove."

"Not at Gran's house, it won't do," Casey said. She took her grandmother by the shoulders, turned her away from the door and tied her big apron back on her. "I'll go, Gran. Which room?"

I saw a look of panic cross Mom's face. She obviously was not prepared for the rest of us to see the condition the unused parts of the house had fallen into. And cleaning an additional room would take far more than a minute.

I said, "Mom, put Guido in my room. If it's okay with you, I'll bunk with you. We'll eat popcorn under the covers and stay up all night talking; a regular slumber party."

She sighed, truly looked relieved. "I'd enjoy that. Good idea."

"Guido," I said, wrapping an arm around his shoulders, "upstairs, second door on the right. Don't go looking in drawers for my old diary; I burned it. Max, you're in the usual. Casey, Gran put you and Zia in the room with twin beds."

"Woo-hoo," Casey said. "We get our own bathroom."

Sleeping arrangements settled, the kitchen crew went back to work. Guido was given the jobs of filling water glasses, opening the red wine on the sideboard to breathe, and then, later, serving chilled, bubbly *Prosecco* wine in tall flutes to guests as they arrived. Max was designated *paterfamilias* and given charge of removing the turkey from the oven when it was ready and carving it. With essentials prepared, the kitchen crew was dismissed to go upstairs to dress for dinner.

Guests began to arrive, each of them bearing a contribution for the meal.

Gracie Nussbaum, the widow of my dad's best friend who was our longtime family doctor, Ben—the doctor who delivered me—arrived first, bringing her special no-mushroom-soup green bean concoction. Jane and Jake Jakobsen, the next-door neighbors—Jake had taught in the math department for years, but was the graduate dean at the time he retired, Jane aided and abetted my mom's political activism—came bearing pies, a fat double-crust apple and a pumpkin.

"Lyle, Lyle, crocodile," Casey exclaimed when she opened the door and found our former housemate, Lyle Green, and his partner, Roy, on the porch. Until the last big earthquake, Lyle was our across-the-alley neighbor when Casey and I still lived in San Francisco. California earthquakes are capricious things. They show up without warning and destroy randomly. During the last quake, our house came through intact, a few new cracks, but still standing. Lyle's house was reduced to rubble. We took him in, just until he could rebuild. He quickly became our

resident *mensch*, and we became his family. The arrangement worked
for all of us.

We stayed together until Mike and his son and Casey and I became
a new family, in Los Angeles, and Lyle found Roy. Lyle and Roy bought
the house from me, and they are still there.

Lyle's meal contribution was an assortment of cheeses to accompany dessert. Some of the cheeses were fairly stinky; I could smell them
halfway across the room as I approached to greet him.

Jane Jakobsen, elegant in cranberry velvet, her steel gray hair cut
into an assertive bob, took the cheese tray from Lyle's hands and looked
it over, searching for something. "Did you remember to bring sharp
cheddar to go with my apple pie?"

"Of course, Janey, dear." He pointed out a thick, dark orange wedge.
"An aged Vermont, sharper than a farmer's long-johns come spring."

And so on, friends old and new and a couple of strays arrived; each
was handed a flute filled with *Prosecco*, and swept into the fold. The final
seat count was eighteen, and the table was so laden with food that it
truly was a groaning board.

Mom seemed to be in her element. Happy, relaxed once the food
was on the table. But toward the end of the meal, I thought she began
to flag.

After lingering over dessert, Casey, Zia, Guido and I claimed kitch-
en clean-up duty and left Mom to relax with friends in the living room
with coffee and a decanter of very good port that Max found at a winery
in Paso Robles.

The food was all put away and the dishwasher humming through
its first load, and we were almost ready to rejoin the others, when the
telephone rang. I reached for the kitchen extension, but stopped before
picking it up. Mom's house, Mom's caller.

"Margot, dear." Mom pushed through the swinging door. "Call for
you. That nice friend of Mike's, Detective Longshore."

"Rich?" I said into the receiver. Rich was a sergeant with the LA
County Sheriffs, assigned to the Homicide Bureau, and had been one
of Mike's closest friends. "Nice to hear from you. Happy Thanksgiving.
Did you have a good meal?"

"Not yet," he said. "Happy Thanksgiving to you, too."

Mom took a glass out of the cupboard and filled it with water, but
then left it on the counter. Was she hovering? Snooping? It wasn't every
day that a homicide detective called her house.

"Sorry to interrupt your party, Maggie," Rich said. "I got a message that you called the Malibu substation this morning with a possible tip about a hit-and-run victim."

"I did. Have you identified the victim?"

"We have. It would have taken us longer if you hadn't called in with information. Thanks."

"Oh, dear." The twinge of guilt I had felt earlier descended, a weight on my chest. "It was her? That woman?"

"Mom?" Casey looked up from the silverware she was drying. "Is the dead woman…?"

I nodded. My mother, brow furrowed, wanted to know: "What dead woman?" As I tried to focus on what Rich was saying to me, Casey filled in her grandmother about my encounter the night before at the market.

I heard Mom say, "My Lord," a couple of times. For good reason, when in the course of my work I get into a dust-up, I don't usually tell my mother about it.

Guido and Zia came in from making a trash run and Casey explained to them what was happening.

"You alerted us to Deputy Ray Valdez," Rich said. "Valdez was off duty this morning, hadn't heard the news yet when I called him. He filled me in on the market incident. Last night, the woman told him her name and where she was staying, the Surfrider Beach Club in Malibu, a funky little hotel less than a quarter mile up PCH from where we found her. Her purse with her I.D. was in her room."

"Who was she?"

"Isabelle Martin. Did you know her?"

"Isabelle Martin," I repeated, writing the name on the message pad beside the phone, in case seeing the name jogged something. It didn't. My mother pulled out a chair and perched on its edge, chin on hand, blatantly eavesdropping right along with Casey, Zia and Guido. Mom looked pale. Exhausted, I thought; time for company to go home. I set her glass of water on the table in front of her and watched her take a sip.

I told Rich, "I meet a lot of people. Most of them, I don't pay very much attention to, but if I see them again there is at least some glimmering of recognition. But the woman's face, her name, they just do not ring any bells."

"She had a French passport, arrived about a week ago, Paris to LAX via Virgin Air. No scheduled return," he said.

"Visiting family?" I asked.

"No, Maggie," he said. "Visiting you."

"What makes you think so?" I heard the skepticism in my voice; what he said simply did not make sense.

"In her room we found a map with your studio's location circled and a French tabloid that had a picture of you on the front page."

"Oh, shit." I leaned against the counter and rubbed my eyes with my free hand. "Let me guess. The picture of Tiffy sitting on my lap?" This also was explained to Mom by Casey.

"That's the one," he said. "My high school French isn't so good, so I rounded up a translator. The caption says something like, Filmmaker Maggie MacGowen gives bad-girl rock star Tiffy a soft landing outside a supermarket in the mega-star nest of Malibu, California. And then there are some comments about her lack of underwear and hopes that you delivered a much-needed spanking to her bare bottom."

"The box boy at the market last night warned me. He said now the nuts know where to find me." Mom took Casey's hand and held it. "So, this Isabelle Martin who said she was looking for her daughter Marguerite sees a tabloid photo of someone named Maggie and flies across the Atlantic to stake out the photo's location, hoping her daughter will come by. You know what Mike would call her?"

"A fifty-one–fifty," he said.

"That's the short form." I tore the page with the woman's name off the message pad and crumpled it into a ball.

Uncle Max pushed through the swinging door, leaned in. "Betsy, guests are ready to leave."

Instead of standing to go with him, Mom put a finger to her lips and nodded toward me. Max looked at me with curiosity, shrugged, and came into the room to eavesdrop with the others.

"How did she die?" I asked Rich.

"Who died?" Max demanded. Mom shushed him, but reached out, took the crumpled notepage from my hand and gave it to him.

"Hit by a car," Rich said. "Then run over, either by the impact vehicle or one that came along later. She was found by the bridge where Malibu Creek goes under PCH, on the parking lot of the Cross Creek Center. Coroner won't do the cut till sometime early in the week, so I won't have details about actual cause of death for a while, but it's pretty clear from the appearance of the body what happened. We're checking security cameras in the area to see if any of them caught something."

I realized I had been holding my breath while he spoke. In my mind's eye, I already saw the incident and its ugly aftermath unfold as if I were watching it happen on slow-motion film, the effect of many years behind a camera. When I spoke, my voice sounded reedy to my own ears.

"Last night, when I wanted her to go away and leave me alone, I never wished her harm," I said. "I never imagined something like this would happen to her."

"Of course not," Rich said. "But, Maggie, whatever her issues were, she won't ever bother you again."

—4—

"BEAUTIFUL MEAL, MOM."

We settled into the big leather chairs flanking the fireplace in the den, feet up on the ottoman between us. She tipped her glass toward me; we were drinking some very good Pinot Noir left over from dinner. Fire blazed in the grate.

The last of the dinner guests were gone, the kitchen was clean again, the rest of the house party was tucked in upstairs. Norah Jones's sweet, smoky voice—"Sunrise, sunset…"—played in the background. I sipped my wine and relaxed into the deep cushions of my chair, feeling content, happy to be home and in that room again, alone with my mother.

The den was small and dark, the walls lined with books, framed family photos on the shelves. When I was a kid, for about an hour before dinner every evening—whether we had guests or not—my dad would sit down in the chair where my mother now sat, fire in the fireplace if it was at all cool enough, and read. Usually, I would join him for at least part of that hour. When I was very little, I would climb into his lap, my body tucked in the crook of his arm, my head on his fortress of a chest—the safest place in the world, in my father's arms—and he would read to me. Didn't matter if he read to me from his own book or one I brought to him, snuggling on his lap was the important part. When I was too big to sit on his lap, I moved into the chair opposite his, where I now sat, and read my own books; Dad never minded interruptions for questions. Eventually, I grew tall enough to share the ottoman, a milestone of my youth.

It occurred to me belatedly that while Dad and I passed that lovely evening idyll, Mom was in the kitchen making dinner, often for guests my dad had invited at the last minute. Her world had been so different than mine became. I glanced at her, saw her gazing dreamily into the fire, lost to her thoughts.

"You must be exhausted, Mom," I said, breaking the silence.

"Not at all." She smiled softly, shifted her focus to me. She said her knees were bothering her just a little, which I multiplied by some factor of her pride plus denial to mean that she was in agony. "Good to have the house full of people again."

"Gracie Nussbaum looks fine," I said.

Mom nodded. "She still has some weakness on her left side from the stroke, but she compensates well, I think. And she's very consistent about going to therapy."

"Mmmm." I took a sip of wine, put my head back and watched the fire.

"Margot, dear?"

I turned toward her, found an odd look on her face.

"When you were a little girl, did you ever feel, well, left out of things? By the family, I mean."

"Funny question, but, sure, sometimes I did." In the flickering firelight, I couldn't read her expression. "Perfectly natural, considering that Mark and Emily were so much older than me. What were they, fourteen when I was born?"

She nodded. "Yes, fourteen."

"They were so smart, interesting, and lordy, they were tall. Mark was nearly six-five before he graduated high school, Emily almost six feet in the end. You and dad, both tall. I always felt like a pipsqueak around here; the tall genes skipped me."

"Both of your grandmothers were average height."

"Didn't help that I was the baby," I said. "No matter how hard I tried to keep up or catch up, well, I just couldn't. The fact that Mark and Em were twins—hell, they left everybody out to some degree. By the time I might have been in the least interesting to them, they were off into the world, Mark at war, Em in med school. So, yes, sometimes I felt left out."

"Did you ever feel Dad or I…?"

I shook my head; what had brought this on? "After Mark died in Vietnam, we all lost you for a while, Mom. I was a little kid, but I understood you were grieving. Dad always tried to compensate, gave me extra attention, had special treats for me. My God, I had a pony. Mark and Em never had a pony. Nobody I knew had a pony."

"Excuse me." Guido hovered at the door.

"Join us," I said, turning toward him. "Bring a glass."

"Tempting," he said. "But it's been a long day. I just wanted to say good night. Thank you, Betsy, thank you, Mag, for taking me in."

"You're always welcome, Guido," Mom said.

He had deep circles under his dark eyes. When he leaned over to kiss me, I put my palm against his stubbly cheek and looked into his face. "You okay, my friend?"

"Yes." He thought about it. "Maybe I'll do what you keep telling me to do, find a woman my own age." Then he smiled, firelight dancing in his big brown eyes. "But, damn," and I knew from our many conversations on the topic of his history with women that he was thinking about Shasta, the intern who dumped him, and her predecessors, beautiful, bright, supple, and young, every one. "With that, I wish you good night."

When he was gone, Mom asked, "Is his heart really broken?"

"Ego certainly hurts," I said. "He keeps bringing in these kids that have stars in their eyes about making movies. They latch onto Guido as their conduit to dream fulfillment. They decide they're in love with him, and he doesn't discourage their feelings; he's flattered by the adulation. After a while, they grow up a bit, dump him flat, move on to the next guru."

"I am only too familiar with the phenomenon. Remember, I was a faculty wife for nearly four decades," Mom said, a grim set to her mouth. "You know, Margot, there are very well-defined rules meant to protect students from inappropriate behavior by faculty. But there is nothing to protect the faculty from predatory students."

"Predatory students, Mom?"

"You know Guido's history. Guido leaves himself open, but who generally is the initiator? And who comes out feeling abused?"

"I see your point," I said. "But..."

"I know the 'but.'" She sipped her wine, eyed me over the rim of her glass. "The only thing old Henry Kissinger said that I ever half agreed with was that power is the ultimate aphrodisiac. And your 'but,' I'm guessing, was going to head off in the direction of the potential abuse of power by faculty authority figures over their vulnerable student minions."

"Something like that."

"But, Margot, I offer you the old faculty wife's corollary." She sat forward, wagging her index finger for emphasis. "For men of a certain age, the ultimate aphrodisiac, the ultimate power, is youth. To wit, your poor Guido's plight."

"That corollary applies only to men?"

"Well, not always." She smiled, gazed off again toward the fire, but

I knew her focus had trailed off somewhere I couldn't follow, probably into her memory.

"Spill it," I said.

She brought her eyes back to me, thought for moment, seemed to make a decision. With a girlish toss of her head, she said, "I had an affair."

"Mom?" As horrified as I was by that bald statement, I studied her face, softened by the years and the firelight, and remembered how pretty she had been once, was still. And because I absolutely knew the answer—the nose I inherited from my father had been edited by a plastic surgeon early in my television career, but I was still his spitting image—I dared to ask, as a tease, "You aren't going to tell me that Dad isn't my biological father, are you?"

She blushed. "No, dear. This was much later. Emily was somewhere in the east, already saving the world, you were in high school, off at that boarding school down in Carmel."

"Who was it?" I asked, appalled less than I was curious, running through the husbands of all of their friends, finding every one of them dull compared to my father.

"A young probationary professor. One of your father's protégés. A handsome boy, a lost soul whenever he stepped outside his lab."

"You robbed the cradle."

"I still had my figure." She sighted down her long nose at me. "And you might have the grace to ask, who seduced whom? The point is, I never loved your father more than when I was cheating on him."

"Mom?"

"I wanted my Alfred back as I once knew him, that brilliant young man who once depended on me. We were great partners in the beginning, your dad and I. I worked to put him through graduate school, he supported my concertizing until Mark and Emily came along. We worked together to establish his career, our life together. He became known far and wide. But somewhere along the way I became superfluous, the 'skirt' who from time to time accompanied a frankly pompous old physicist to university events, or played East to his West at bridge.

"I woke up one morning and suddenly I was over fifty. My husband's world was his students and his colleagues and his research; I knew they always had been. My children were finished with me. I felt left behind. My nest was empty."

"So you found a pretty new chickie."

"He was, you know." She laughed. "But the point is, the boy moved on and eventually your father and I found each other again."

"Did Dad know?"

She shook her head. From the expression on her face I wondered if she was disappointed that he didn't know.

I asked her, "What brought you and Dad back together?"

"Emily," she said, smiling softly as she remembered my sister. "After the shooting, when she was in a coma for so long, it took all the strength both Dad and I had to wait out the course of Emily's passing. We needed each other again, and the irony was that he needed me more than I needed him. Men always think they should be able to fix things. I knew I couldn't."

"A beautiful story," I said after a moment; I needed to let this bombshell sink in. "I'm shocked, I'll get over it. But why are telling me this? You think I should go out and find myself a younger man?"

"That, my dear, would be up to you." She reached into the pocket of her silk skirt and pulled out the slip of paper I had crumpled in the kitchen earlier. Slowly, she opened it up, smoothed it on the arm of her chair. She looked at the name I had written for what seemed like a very long time. She was working up her courage, choosing her words, and I began to find it difficult to breathe.

"Years ago, before you were born…" she said, pulling her eyes from the paper to look at me. "And you might remember hearing about this. Your father was invited by the French government to come over as an advisor to their new national nuclear power program."

"I remember hearing about it," I said. "You and Dad took Mark and Em to France for a year. A wonderful opportunity for everybody. I wasn't even around yet, and I'm envious."

"It was wonderful," she said, looking far away again. "For the most part."

I was beginning to get a bad feeling in the pit of my stomach, down where all that turkey and apple pie and sharp cheddar were churning around. "What was the not-wonderful part?"

"Isabelle Martin." Mom pronounced the name as the French would. She leaned forward, extending the slip of paper toward me. "Isabelle was a gifted young graduate student in nuclear physics, an intern on your father's French project."

I looked at the name I had written and then I looked at Mom. "Isabelle and Dad?"

She bit her lip and nodded.

There was a rustling behind me, stocking feet on the hardwood floor. I turned and saw Uncle Max. Clearly, he had been eavesdropping from outside the room. And because he seemed so calm, so serious, and because he came straight to me and took my hand as he settled onto the wide arm of my chair, I knew that what he had overheard was not news to him, and that he knew ahead of time that Mom was going to tell me about Isabelle.

"So, she was a crazy person," I said. "Had a fling with Dad and went off the rails?"

"Crazy?" Max chuckled softly as he draped his arm behind me, drawing me against his broad chest. "She was a brilliant young female physicist. And she was French. Who could tell from crazy?"

"You knew her?" I asked, leaning to the side so I could look up at his face.

"I met her," he said. "Went across the pond a few times to smooth out some of the legal details."

I weighed the two big questions on my mind, went for the bigger of them. I turned back to Mom. "When you found out, you stayed with Dad?"

She looked me in the eye and answered as if I had challenged her. "I chose to stay with the life we built together. Our children, our community, our home, our marriage vows."

"You're made of tougher stuff than I am." I was thinking of my own reaction when my first husband, Scott MacGowen, Casey's father, told me that he was having an affair with one of the young paralegals in his law office. "When I found out about Scottie and Linda, I showed Scottie the door and closed it behind him. End of story."

"Perhaps you had more options than I thought I had, Margot."

Mom sounded defensive, and I was sorry if I had made her feel bad. Her world was in fact very different from my own. Among other things, when I found out about Scottie's affair I was earning a good income and felt that I was tough enough to take care of my daughter and myself without being dependent on anyone. As it turned out, I needed Lyle, Guido, Max, Mom, Dad, and later, Mike. But I got by, as I knew I would.

I took a breath, caught Max watching me, expectant. I said, "Scottie and I had something very good for a while. Or I thought we did—until the day he walked out. Over the years, I have wondered if we could have worked things out over time. We never could have gotten back together, but it would have been better for Casey if we had become at least friends. Scottie said that's what he wanted. I regret the pain we caused her. But there was that one little detail...."

"The extracurricular baby?" Max said.

"That one," I said. "I give Scottie credit for making a commitment to take care of his baby with Linda, though the mere fact of that baby broke my heart, crushed a good part of what I thought I knew about *us*. But I didn't have what it took to make space in my life for another woman's child." No, I thought, feeling that tightness labeled guilt weigh on my chest again. I left Casey to juggle two households on her own.

Mom wouldn't look at me. Her chin quivered, a telling sign of the depth of her anguish, because my mother almost never cried. She asked, "Which would be the biggest issue for you, the baby, its mother who would inevitably come as an attachment, or the infidelity?"

"All of them," I said.

Max took my chin and turned my face toward his. He said, "I was shamelessly eavesdropping a little earlier. You asked Betsy a question in jest."

I had asked a lot of questions. In jest? The one I knew the answer to, "Was Dad not my biological father?" suddenly landed like a whirring Mixmaster to stir up that mass of turkey et cetera in my middle parts. I wondered if my legs would support me if I had to make a sudden run for the bathroom.

Looking at her hands folded in her lap, Mom said, "I hoped this day would never come."

Max went to her, knelt beside her chair, folded her in his arms. She let him hold her for a moment, her head resting on his shoulder, before she patted his cheek, reassured him with a game smile, and broke out of his embrace.

"Margot, my darling girl." She wiped her nose on the handkerchief Max handed her, and then looked directly at me. "Forty-three years ago, there was a beautiful young French scientist named Isabelle who had a baby, whom she named Marguerite. And then Isabelle gave her precious child to her lover's wife to rear. The wife named *her* little girl Margot."

— 5 —

ONCE UPON A TIME, forty-three years ago, there was a terrible storm in the night. My mother, Betsy Duchamps, all snug in her bed in Berkeley, wakened and knew it was time for me to be born. The weather was so fierce that my father was afraid it wouldn't be safe to drive Mom to the hospital. So he called his good friend Ben Nussbaum, the family doctor, and asked for advice. Dr. Nussbaum lived only a few blocks away. He came straight over with his wife, Gracie. But by the time they arrived all question of taking Mom to the hospital was moot because I was already on the way. And so, in the middle of a rainy, noisy, blustery night, I was born in my parents' bed, in the house in Berkeley, California, upstairs from the room where I now sat looking into the bottom of a wineglass, contemplating that story and other stories that were the foundations of who I had always thought I was.

Mom and Max had gone up to bed hours earlier. I promised Mom I would be up, that I just needed to think through some of what they had told me. I prowled around downstairs for a while, looking at familiar things in a new light, trying to remember all that had happened to me in that house, as if unsure I ever belonged.

A favorite old fairy tale, the story of my birth, had been taken away from me, and I was given a new one of equal or greater drama to replace it. I wasn't born upstairs. I wasn't even born in the United States. According to my mother—what else could I call her?—and Uncle Max, when my family left France to return home after their year abroad, Dad did not know that Isabelle was pregnant. For all the notions that people in the U.S. might have about the liberal sexual mores of the Europeans, forty-some years ago it was very much *not* all right with Isabelle's very traditional, middle-class French family or the university she attended that she found herself both pregnant and unmarried.

Isabelle appealed to my father for help, though neither Max nor Mom was at all clear to me about what sort of help Isabelle had in mind. According to them, I was born in the infirmary of a convent near Isabelle's family's ancestral home, a village in Normandy. My father was listed as the father on the original birth certificate. Because of that, among the little legal details Max went over to take care of, the American embassy in Paris was persuaded to add my name, which at that time was Marguerite Eugenie Louise-Marie Duchamps, to my father's passport. That done, the two men bundled me up and brought me home to Mom. To live happily ever after.

I should have known from the extravagance of names I was saddled with at birth that someone other than Mom had named me.

In a file in my house in Malibu Canyon I had a birth certificate bearing the official seal of Alameda County, California, that said I was born at home in Berkeley, and avowing that Dad and Mom were my true parents. Dear Dr. Nussbaum had agreed to sign the false birth certificate, attesting that he was the attending physician, and then he filed it with the appropriate government agency somewhat after my actual birth; delay of paperwork, he had said. Very tidy, if corrupt. The official seal did not change the fact that I was a bastard child who had unknowingly given false information her entire life to schools, government agencies, my employers, myself. My head spun, and not because of the wine I drank.

If, along the way, any of the people involved had said *no* to their part in the scheme, my life would have been entirely different. I would never have loved and been loved by Mike, would never have suffered through losing him. Casey simply would not be. That other life: better, worse, who knows? What I did know was that I cherished the life I'd had so far and the people in it. Most of all, the people in it.

There was one element that both versions of the story had in common about my first night in the house in Berkeley: a terrible storm full of thunder and lightning.

All of my life I have been terrified by electrical storms. Not pull-the-covers-over-my-head scared, but cold white panic and a screaming need to flee from the flashes of light and crashing, house-shaking booms of thunder that are inescapable.

Skittish colts have been known to run blindly to their deaths during electrical storms. Early Drummond, my neighbor, told me about a five-month-old roan on his grandparents' farm in Missouri who spooked during an electrical storm. In the colt's panic to get away, it ran itself into a barbed wire fence, got hung up there, thrashed violently, and somehow tore out an eye before it managed to break free. After that, it ran zig-zags across a meadow until it dropped dead out of exhaustion and pure animal fear.

When I was a little girl, if I were wakened in the night by an electrical storm, rare as they are in California, I generally did the little girl version of the colt in the meadow. I would run out of the house in a blind panic, thinking I was somehow safer outside from the rolling, approaching boulders of thunder. Summoned by my screams, my parents always ran out to fetch me, brought me inside, held me tight in their arms and told me, again, about the night I was born, until I was calm again. I was frightened, they always said, because the first sound I ever heard was thunder, the first light was lightning.

In the new version of that story there was a terrible storm on the night Dad first brought me to the house in Berkeley, but I was already terrified of thunder and lightning before that night. On that first night,

Mom and Dad took me into their bed and held me all night long. I only stopped screaming at dawn when the storm passed.

At some point in my life reason trumped panic and I was able to get through the worst of storms alone and without running away. But the fear was still there. Always.

I sat in my chair in front of the fire, looking at my father's empty seat—how I wished he were there to talk to—and thought about what Mom and Max had told me. There were big gaps in their story—my story—and I did not know anyone who could fill them. Isabelle, probably the best source, was gone before I even knew she existed.

At some point during the night, I hit some part of every one of the five stages of grief—denial, anger, bargaining, depression, acceptance—as I tried to shed parts of what I thought I knew about my life within a family and to believe a new reality, as sketchy as it was. By dawn, the most important fact that came out of all that cogitating was that the woman I always believed to be my mother had taken me to her heart and had loved me and cared for me, and would for the rest of her life. As if I were her own.

I felt very sad for her. Mom's two natural children, Emily and Mark, both died tragically while young. The only child left to her, in the end, was me, the paramour's daughter. I leaned my head back and closed my eyes, still trying to sort everything into neat answers that I knew didn't exist. Nothing worthwhile in life is ever entirely tidy.

I must have dozed off. When I finally dragged myself upstairs, stiff and headachy, a little hung over probably, it was full daylight. I stood outside Mom's bedroom door and listened until I heard her move around on the other side. Tentatively, I tapped on the door.

"Come in," she called.

She was standing in front of the mirror over her dresser, twisting her hair into its impossible bun. We looked at each other's reflections in the mirror, a small filter between the warm, flesh versions of ourselves. She seemed to be a little frightened. What next? was the unasked question on her face. Her eyes were swollen and red-rimmed. Even at my father's funeral my mother had not wept as she must have during the night while I was downstairs stewing.

I stood behind her, wrapped my arms around her, met her eyes in the mirror.

"Thank you, Mom," I said. "You are a remarkable woman. And I love you very much. I always will."

She smiled, reached back and patted my cheek with one hand while she held the hair she had coiled at the back of her neck with the other. "I was worried about you, Margot. So much to get used to."

"Don't worry," I said, releasing her so she could skewer her bun in place with its single long pin. "I'm fine."

"Questions?"

"Tons. First, who am I? When I've figured that out, the rest should be easy."

"Well." She laughed gently. "That little girl with two mothers and two names? She called herself Maggie. I'm confident that you have always known who you are."

"Then I suppose it doesn't matter what anyone calls me," I said. I peeled off the dress I had put on the previous afternoon before dinner and reached into my bag for my robe; I needed a shower. "Except, don't call me late for breakfast. I'm starving."

"As I recall," she said, laughing gaily as if a great load had been removed from her shoulders, "you drew breakfast duty."

"Damn. Slipped my mind." I wanted a nap, too. "Give me ten minutes to get cleaned up."

It took me twenty minutes, not ten, to pull myself together. When I opened the swinging door and stepped into the kitchen, I found Max making waffles, Guido putting a second pound of bacon into the microwave, Casey scrambling eggs, and Zia setting the kitchen table. Mom sat holding a mug of coffee and reading the morning newspaper.

"They got hungry and started without you, dear," Mom said, looking up, smiling, when I walked in.

"Hey, Ma," Casey greeted me. "You look like hell."

I reached for a mug and poured myself coffee. "Gran kept me up all night boozing."

"Uh-huh, sure." She loaded eggs into a serving bowl. "Anyone mind if Zia and I take BART into San Francisco after breakfast? We told some friends from school we'd try to meet them."

Mom said, "If you're bringing your friends home for dinner, give me fair warning so I'll know how much turkey to reheat. Lord knows there are enough leftovers to feed the masses."

"Mom?" Casey asked me.

"Sounds like fun." I yawned as I sat down. Good idea for the girls to look elsewhere for entertainment during the day. Guido and I had TV business to talk over with Max. But before that, I had some phone calls to make, first to Rich Longshore to give him more information about Isabelle, and second to Isabelle's family in France. Mom had given me their contact information before I got into the shower. I knew that would be an interesting conversation. And one I wasn't quite ready to share with Casey.

What would I say to those people? Hi, I met your mother/daughter/sister, now she's dead? You don't know me, but I'm your daughter/sister's bastard.... I had no idea what her family knew about me, or how they felt about me. And I was in no particular hurry to find out. I poured Mom a second cup of coffee and kissed her on the cheek.

After breakfast, after Casey and Zia left the house, Mom, Max and Guido—who was slowly getting the gist of the issues—stuck close to me to follow unfolding events. I called Rich Longshore.

I asked Rich, "Know anything more about what happened to Isabelle Martin?"

"Some," he said. "That little shopping center at that intersection of PCH and Cross Creek where the Martin woman was found? We got the surveillance tapes from a few of the businesses there—called their security providers—and by piecing them together we have a pretty good idea now of the sequence of events, and the events themselves."

"What can you see?" I asked. I am an investigative filmmaker. Asking questions is what I do for a living. Rich had plenty of experience being grilled by me, so he did not hesitate.

He began: "From the tape we got from the service station on the corner, we see Ms Martin walking along PCH, headed south, toward her hotel, I'd guess—hotel is just around the bend. Time stamp says ten-forty-five. The tape is black-and-white and not good quality and there aren't a lot of street lights along there, so all we really get is moving shadows. But whenever she walks directly under a light, we can see her clearly enough to identify her.

"The tape also captures a dark-colored, late-model Toyota Camry making a left turn onto PCH just after we first see Martin. The driver seems to be tailing her, driving slowly. She crosses the second driveway of the service station, then we lose her for a bit before she's picked up by the camera on the end shop.

"Next we see Martin step into the driveway that leads into the shopping center from PCH, and we see the Toyota accelerate into a sharp turn, cross lanes and head straight for her. After the impact, the car drives on into the lot out of range and we see Martin collapsed in a heap on the pavement. Can't tell if she's alive at that point. The Toyota circles around, then we see it enter the frame again at high speed. He takes a second shot at her that impacts hard enough to send Martin airborne.

She lands out of frame, but we got the tape from the bank on the opposite side of the driveway. From that one we can see a dark figure, sweatshirt with the hood up, no facial detail, drag something across the pavement and dump it in the dirt beside the bridge over Malibu Creek. That something turns out to be Martin's body."

I looked at all the faces at the table waiting for me to report what Rich was saying, and decided they didn't need all of the details.

"Did you get a license number?" I asked.

"We got enough of one to trace the owner. The car had been reported stolen the day before from a home in Encino, out in the Valley."

"So, this was a garden-variety mugging," I said.

"The vic wasn't carrying a purse. All she had on her was an electronic hotel room key and a few bucks in her pockets. The thing is, the guy didn't bother to find that out."

"Well, then, why on earth…?"

"Maggie, I could be wrong, but it looks to me like a hit. A professional hit."

My knees started to go out from under me. Guido grabbed me and slid a chair under me. I had dropped the receiver onto the tile counter. I'm not a fainter, but sometimes enough is enough.

"Maggie?" I heard Rich's voice somewhere off in the distance, lost in the buzzing in my ears. "You there?"

Guido picked up the receiver and handed it to me. I took a deep breath to clear my head. I said, "I'm here."

"Pretty tough stuff, sorry," Rich said. "But you always want all the details. Did I tell you too much?"

"No." I sat up straight. "Rich, it turns out that Isabelle Martin actually was my mother, just as she claimed." I glanced at Mom. "My biological mother; I never knew her."

I gave him the history in short form and the family contact information in France that Mom had given me, and told him we had no idea what that family might consist of anymore. He thought all this over for a while before he asked if I had any useful information at all, any ideas about anyone who might have wanted Isabelle out of the picture. I assured him that I did not, had not known Isabelle existed until she accosted me in the market parking lot Wednesday night, and had no clue about our relationship until my mother told me about her last night.

He said, "Maggie, I should have known when I got a memo with your name on it that this would not be a routine hit-and-run case. Anything more you can tell me about the woman?"

"Hold on." I put my hand over the mouthpiece and extended it toward Mom. "I think you should talk to Rich."

She hesitated, but she took the phone. After identifying herself and exchanging the usual greetings, she gave him the information she had about Isabelle, and me, but left out the part about my forged birth certificate, though she did courageously tell him that Dad and Isabelle had an affair. I doubt I could have been as sanguine as she seemed to be if I were in a similar circumstance.

It occurred to me that Mom might be relieved that this old secret was finally out. For a woman as honest and forthright as Mom, telling the same lie over and over for forty-some years must have been a nightmare. Dad was beyond protecting, and I was no kid anymore. What was the point now?

As Guido listened to Mom's end of the conversation lights came on in his face. He leaned over the table toward me and whispered, "Our next film project."

I agreed that it would be a doozy of a topic, but I wasn't sure I had the grit to make it. Not yet, anyway.

Mom extended the receiver back toward me. "Detective Longshore wants another word with you."

"Maggie, how sure are you that this woman is your biological mother?"

"I saw the original birth certificate last night. It has her name and my dad's name on it, and my original name. And my mom's word. Short of getting a DNA match, that's proof enough for me."

"So, that makes you the closest thing we have to next of kin, and from what you say there are people with you who actually knew the woman. We need a formal I.D., but she's a foreign national in the country alone." He paused, seemed to be mulling through something. I waited for him. "You have access to a computer where you are? Email?"

"Yes."

"If it's okay with you—and you can say no—I'd like to send you a couple of photos to make sure we're talking about the same woman you saw last night, and that the woman we found is Isabelle Martin."

"Coroner's photos?"

"A couple of those, but they don't look too bad; not the face, anyway. And the passport photo. Just a formality, but a necessary one."

I told him to send them. I heard him punch computer keys on his end, and he told me the photos were on their way. He stayed on the line while I carried the phone to my Dad's office, booted his computer, and accessed my email. I saw Rich's message line appear at the top of my New Mail file and opened the first attachment. Mom and Max, of course, looked over my shoulder, with Guido behind them craning his neck. The first attachment held the passport photo, clearly showing the woman I had spoken to.

"That's the woman." I turned to look up at my mom. "So?"

"That's Isabelle, definitely. Older, of course, than when I saw her last." She started to say something else, but her voice trailed off. Her eyes moved from the image on the computer screen to me and rested there.

I said, "What?"

"Definitely, that's Isabelle." She abruptly turned from me to look over at my uncle. "Max?"

Max agreed. "Definitely Isabelle."

"Hear that?" I asked Rich. "Unanimous on passport photo. She's my market lady and their Isabelle."

"Dear Lord," Mom gasped as the second photo appeared, obviously a coroner photo, showing Isabelle's face and naked shoulders. There was ugly, blue discoloration on the right side of her face, the side of primary impact, and bright rose contusions on her chin, forehead and points of her shoulders, but clearly, it was the same woman. The last photo was only further confirmation both of her identity and the damage.

"That's her," I told Rich, as I hit the Print icon and made copies of all three. "Is that all you need?"

"I'd appreciate it if you'd just hit Reply and send me a word or two in confirmation. When I get that, we're set to inform the family and the French consul general downtown." As an afterthought, he added, "Ask your mom to confirm the I.D., too, if she will, since she knew Martin. Just have her write a line after you type your name."

By the end of the phone call, it was agreed that Rich would contact the family in France, whoever they might be—parents, aunts, uncles, brothers, sisters?—to inform them officially. I would place a follow-up call to whomever he spoke with after he called me to report what he had learned from them, if anything. It was eight in the morning in California, so it would be five in the afternoon in France. Rich said he had a case status meeting he needed to attend. He probably wouldn't be free to call the family in France until nine, our time. That gave me a little over an hour to figure out what I should say to them.

Mom suggested that I take a nap. The house would be quiet because she, Max and Guido were walking into town for the Friday farmer's market. I decided, instead, to go for a quick run. To think.

It was a beautiful morning. I jogged at an easy pace to the end of our street, a gentle uphill slope at first, and then steep before the street ended at the Grizzly Peak fire road, which I ran along. It's a tough run, one I had made many times. At the top, I stopped for breath and a drink of water, and to look out at the view. Below, beyond the Berkeley Marina, San Francisco Bay shimmered in morning sunlight. To my left were Angel Island and the Oakland Bay Bridge, straight ahead the singular, spiky San Francisco skyline. Because it was a perfectly clear day, I could see the entire Golden Gate Bridge in the distance, and all the way across the bay to the top of Marin's Mount Tamalpais. A picture-postcard day.

I had lots of company, runners, walkers—with dogs and without—trail bikers, bird watchers, some photographers. It was a popular trail for the locals and every once in a while a tourist found his way up for the view. Because it was such a clear day, and it was a holiday, there were more people than usual. I certainly didn't feel alone, but I felt exposed somehow, vulnerable. I thought of Isabelle walking alone, late at night. Had she been afraid? Did she know she was in danger? In the end, why was she in LA at all?

Denial kicked in again. She couldn't have known she was in danger, or she wouldn't have gone out in the open late at night the way she did. Certainly she would have said something to me or the huge security guards if she felt endangered. But she hadn't. And hadn't I asked her if I could call 911 for her? She was a random victim, or a case of mistaken identity, I decided. Or, decided to believe.

Last night, after Mom went upstairs leaving me to my thoughts, I had Googled Isabelle Martin in case she left any footprints from her life on the Internet. And she had.

I learned that Isabelle was a nuclear physicist whose specialization was domestic uses of nuclear energy, my father's field as well. No surprise there, remembering how they met. According to an article in the *Journal of the World Nuclear Association*, Isabelle had retired a couple of years ago after nearly forty years with the French national power company, Électricité de France (EDF), as a high-level civil servant. The company directors had marked the occasion of her retirement with a gala. The article listed prominent guests, including Élodie Martin, Mr. and Mrs. Gérard Martin, and Mr. and Mrs. Frédéric Martin-Desmoulins.

I Googled each of them, as well. Gérard was a development executive with a large global company, and lived in London. Frédéric was a partner in a small, prestigious investment bank in Paris. About Élodie, nothing. Their relationships to Isabelle? No clue.

At the event there were speeches, lots of speeches, and presentations. The photographs accompanying the article were all group photos, making it difficult to see individual faces, though I thought I recognized Isabelle standing front and center wearing a long, dark gown. I printed the article.

The *Journal* included a brief summary of Isabelle's career. She had started working in the field of peaceful uses of nuclear power as a graduate student at the École polytechnique. When the first French-designed gas-cooled nuclear reactor, an electrical power plant, built in 1966, proved to be "unsatisfactory," Isabelle received a fellowship to work with American experts, who would have included my dad, to bring an American-built Pressurized Water Reactor purchased from Westinghouse into service to deliver domestic and industrial nuclear-generated electricity. The lingo in the article was familiar to me because it had been dinner conversation at my parents' house for many years.

As I read Isabelle's bio, I kept looking for situations that might have put Isabelle in the crosshairs of controversy, but I didn't find any. In the U.S. proposals to build nuclear power plants are frequently greeted with noisy, occasionally violent protest, perhaps because Americans associate anything nuclear with "the bomb" and the occurrence of three-headed toads. But in France the possibility of national energy independence was embraced very early on and, it appeared from what I read, continues into the present. Their motto is "no oil, no gas, no coal, no choice" when the alternatives are dependence on Mideast oil or knuckling under to the Soviets in the early years or Vladimir Putin's Russian thugs now for oil and gas pumped out of the Caucasus region.

I did find references to angry protests twenty years ago over the disposal of nuclear waste, but an acceptable solution was found. Twenty years ago.

There were several references on Google to papers she had published and addresses she had given, but there was nothing to be found about Isabelle's private life, not a single wild adventure or public disgrace worth noting. She had neither a personal Web site nor a Facebook page. No publicized whistle-blowing. So, who would hire a hit on a civil servant? A retired civil servant, to boot?

Big question number two, why had Isabelle, after forty-three years, decided to come looking for me?

I wheeled around when I heard a couple of men walking on the fire road behind me, speaking French. Two middle-aged men wearing perfect jeans and tweedy jackets, arms clasped behind their backs, heads close together in spirited debate, a thoroughly French posture, walked past me without glancing up and continued down the road. They certainly did not look like stalkers or assassins; probably were a couple of scholars visiting the university, or maybe tourists. Hearing them, associating them by their language with Isabelle, had, however, put me on the alert. I had not been alone since my encounter with Isabelle. I felt suddenly exposed and vulnerable, and decided it was time to get myself home.

When I set off on my run, I'd intended to circle down onto the campus of the University of California—Cal—and run along Strawberry Creek, then over to see the physics building where my Dad's office had been. Instead, I decided to take the short route back and came down off the fire road a couple of blocks from our house. Along the way, I ran into Gracie Nussbaum carrying a shopping bag, on her way home from the farmer's market.

"Smell this, dear." She held her bag open for me to sniff the contents. "Basil. So beautiful, I thought I'd make some pesto. Do you like pesto?"

"Love it," I said; I was too sweaty to hug her. "Why don't you join us for dinner tonight and bring some? How do turkey and pesto pizzas sound?"

"Wonderful!" She giggled with delight. I would confirm the invitation with Mom, but I knew that one more at table was always just fine. And I had questions for Gracie, a co-conspirator with my parents and uncle.

"Did you run into Mom at the market?" I asked her.

"Yes." She gave me a serious study. "She told you."

"You are aware that what you all did back then could land all of you in the federal slam for fraud or forgery or conspiracy or something?"

Gracie laughed, sort of a silvery trill. "No it won't. Your Uncle Max called us the day the statute of limitations ran out on our little crime. We are in the clear." She put her hand on my arm. "My conscience has always been clear about what we conspired to do, dear."

"Did Mom also tell you about Isabelle?"

She nodded. "Forgive me for saying this. I did not know Isabelle, but she has always been a dark cloud lurking on your horizon, whether you knew it or not. I am sorry that she is dead, and for the way she died, but I would be less than honest if I said that I was not also relieved that she is gone."

I tried to make a stern face, a cop's face. "Where were you between ten P.M. and two A.M. night before last?"

"At home." She pointed a finger at me. "But don't think I didn't consider certain possibilities more than once."

I walked her home, carrying her shopping bag for her. The rest of the way, she told me about the physical therapy program that was part of her stroke recovery regime. She said she had enjoyed her conversation with Casey the night before and encouraged her to consider medical school. Another doctor in the family, she said, and I knew she was including her husband, Ben, with my sister, Emily, as family.

Interesting, I thought after seeing Gracie safely inside her house. Mom had expressed no hostility toward Isabelle. Gracie had.

The phone was ringing when I walked in the back door. I made a dash for it, expecting Rich to be calling ahead of schedule—I had been gone just over forty minutes. I reached for the receiver with one hand and a water glass with the other.

Breathless from the dash, I managed, "Hello."

There was a pause before I heard a woman's voice. "Good morning, Madame. I am Élodie Martin, calling from Paris. I wish to speak with Madame Flint."

Almost no one called me by my married name. But as this call was coming from the Twilight Zone to begin with, why not?

"I am Maggie MacGowen Flint," I said.

"Ah, yes. I understand you call yourself Maggie." Such a pretty little accent, very similar to Isabelle Martin's. The voices were similar as well. "I am Grand-mère."

"Isabelle's mother?"

"She was your mother, *chérie*," she said, an edge to the tone in her voice, some reproof. I didn't hear tears. "I am *your* grandmother."

"Yes, of course. I'm very glad that you called. I'm afraid that I know very little about Isabelle, and nothing about her family. You understand that I only learned last night that she existed."

"We all have much to learn about each other."

"I am so sorry for your loss." What should I be saying here? "You spoke with Detective Longshore? He told you what happened?"

"I did," she said. "He told me what he wanted me to know. But, well, you know the police...."

"My late husband was a police detective," I said before she got any further. "Detective Longshore was a friend of his, is a friend of mine. He's a good man. You can trust him."

"Police? I heard your husband was," she paused, "*avocat*. Lawyer?"

"My first husband, Scott MacGowen, was a lawyer. Mike Flint was my second husband."

"I did not know. Of course, after a while we heard so little about you. When we learned you were called Maggie MacGowen and you were in television, we thought, *nom de guerre*, as it were."

"But you know my current married name?"

"Detective Longshore told me."

Move on, move on, I thought, keep jumping the potholes. "Madame Martin, I am sure that arrangements will be difficult for you to make from a distance. Please let me know if there is anything I can do on this end to help you."

"Of course, only normal you would wish to help. And please, call me Grand-mère, or I won't know to whom you are speaking." Apparently not a shrinking violet, my newly discovered grandmother. "We will get in touch with our consul general in Los Angeles to coordinate arrangements. I believe that, after the police release your mother, under the circumstances cremation is appropriate. I am certain that the consul's office will contact you when the event is scheduled so that you can attend. Afterward, we will arrange for transport to France."

"Please let me know how I can help," I said. "I don't know what legal details are involved for transporting remains abroad."

"The consul will take care of all details. Your Uncle Gérard knows his father well."

So, I had a French uncle, Gérard, the developer.

"You must forgive me, dear," she said, "but my English is quite rusty."

"Your English is very good, but my French is beyond rusty."

"So we shall both practice all week, shall we?"

"All week?"

"Yes, so that when you bring your mother home to Grand-mère next week we will be able to speak together without confusion."

I had flashes of what my life might have been if Dad hadn't lifted me out of Isabelle's arms. Trying to be noncommittal, I said, "I'll see."

"Of course. You will need to make arrangements. Your work, perhaps. Your family?"

"Work, yes. My daughter is away at university."

"You have a daughter?" Clearly, I heard delight in her voice; why had I brought up Casey? "*Comment s'appelle?*"

"Her name is Katherine Celeste, but we call her Casey."

"Casey? Oh, I see, *K* and *C*, her initials. Charming. Where is she studying?"

"UCLA."

"In Los Angeles? But you said she was 'away' at university. I understood you live in Los Angeles."

"She lives in a campus residence hall."

"Of course." Her tone softened when she asked, "Tell me, dear, how is the woman you know as your mother, Elizabeth, handling things?"

"With grace, as always." I did not want to talk about Mom with this woman. And I could not bring myself to call her Grand-mère. "I'll phone you when we know more."

"I look forward to that, my dear," she said. "In the meantime, the consulate will make arrangements. What number shall I give them for you?"

I thought about that before I decided to give her my number at the TV studio. The work phone was easier to manage, or avoid, than the home phone.

"*À bientôt,*" she said, a lilting farewell.

"Until later." After I hung up, I realized that, except for greeting me formally at the beginning of the call, she had not called me by name, as I had not called her Grand-mère. For both of us, the name thing was going to be awkward. I wanted to ask her what motivated Isabelle to come looking for me, but thought that was best left for another time.

I was still in the kitchen, thinking about the woman's assumption that I would take Isabelle's ashes to her in France, when Mom led Max and Guido in through the back door, all of them laden with bags of fresh flowers, bread, and produce.

"Waiting for Detective Longshore to call?" Mom asked, checking her watch.

"Yes." I glanced at the clock. "I just spoke with Madame Élodie Martin."

"Élodie?" Mom's eyebrows rose. "She must be a thousand years old by now. You called her?"

"She called me."

"And?"

"She expects me to take Isabelle's ashes to France."

"Will you?"

"Yes, I think I will, Mom. Unless you have some profound objection."

"I do, of course, have several," she said. "But it is your decision to make."

Max put an arm around her for comfort, and addressed me. "You know this whole situation is damn tough on your mother." He cleared his throat and amended that suddenly confusing last word, "On Betsy."

"I'm so sorry, Mom," I said. "I know all of this has to be painful."

"It is that," she said, very matter-of-fact. "But my concerns are for you, honey. No one would tell us what happened to you all those years ago, Margot, before you arrived here. But when you arrived you were one traumatized little girl. Whatever the event or situation, it was dire enough that a competent woman was willing to relinquish custody of her child. And may I add, a bright, beautiful, sweet-tempered child at that."

"I don't know about the sweet-tempered part," Max said, with a wink aimed at me. "How about mulish?"

"Certainly strong-willed," Mom said. She cupped my face in her hand and squeezed my cheeks giving me what we used to call the fish face when I was a kid, and meant she wanted my undivided attention. "And that's why I know you're going to fly over there to meet your other family. Where better than at a funeral?"

Guido said, "Can I come?"

I looked at him for a moment. "I'll have to think about that."

"It would be a great project, Mag," he said, unloading the contents of his bags onto the kitchen table. "Someone hires a hit on filmmaker's mother, a mother she never knew about, until…"

The telephone rang again. It was Rich.

"I've been trying to call, but the phone was busy and you have your mobile turned off."

"Mom believes call waiting is rude," I said. "Madame Élodie Martin called me for a chat."

"She didn't waste any time, did she? I hung up from talking to her and dialed you right away."

"Did you give her Mom's number?"

Max left the room in a hurry. Guido leaned his head near mine, hoping to overhear both parts of the conversation.

"No," Rich said. "She asked if I had spoken with you, and when I told her I had, she asked where you could be reached. I told her you were at your mother's house for Thanksgiving. Then I lied and said I didn't have the number, but I guess she found it. Or had it. I'm sorry about that."

"It's all right. I needed to speak with her." I asked, "How much detail about the death did you give her?"

"Very little. I told her automobile collision, the day, the time, the place. And I gave her the contact info for Public Affairs at the coroner's so she can get information about getting the body released."

I asked, "Why didn't you tell her more?"

"We're keeping a lid on things until we have a chance to investigate. No press releases for the time being. When something like this happens, we look first at family, friends, co-workers. But because as far as we know all those folks are in France, the job gets tough. Her mother said that other than you, Martin didn't know anyone in Southern California."

"She didn't know me, either."

"So I have no idea where to begin. Do you?"

"The car?"

"Car was abandoned. Someone ran it over a cliff near Piuma Creek Road. A hiker found it this morning."

"Piuma Creek isn't far from my house." I reconsidered the wisdom of what I had just said. I needed a long nap before I spoke with another person. "I was at home Wednesday night with my daughter and her roommate. And until last night, I had no idea Isabelle existed."

"Don't sweat it, Maggie. We already checked you out."

"Good to hear." I heard Max breathing on an extension phone somewhere in the house. I said, "My lawyer is listening in."

"Hey, Max, how's it hanging?" Rich asked.

"Fine, Detective, and you?"

"Guys," I said. "Now what?"

"Someone in France needs to look into things," Rich said. "Because I think that's where the answer will be."

"Maggie's taking the remains to France," Max said.

"Maggie, you go ahead and go to all their tea parties, or whatever it is they do over there, but promise me when you're over there you'll leave the investigation to the French police. We'll turn over copies of everything we have to them," Rich said. "Or to Interpol. I don't know how that will play. But Maggie, I'm telling you to watch six when you get over there, and butt out."

"Now I think about it," Max said, "I better go along."

"You two talk it over," I said, intending to do as Rich cautioned, to watch my back. "I'm hitting the shower."

⸺6⸺

I WALKED THROUGH the front door of the network studio early Monday morning ready to be back at work. The long weekend had left me feeling unsettled, oddly unsure of myself. I needed some time, and the distractions of a busy day, to let the various bits of my rewritten history settle in.

"Morning, Miss MacGowen." Omar, the uniformed guard on duty at the security desk, slid a sign-in sheet on a clipboard across his teak countertop toward me. "How was your holiday?"

"Interesting," I said, scrawling my name on the sheet. "And you?"

He traded me the sign-in sheet for a sheaf of pink message slips I had asked the switchboard to send over. "A long weekend with the family sure gives new meaning to being loved to death, doesn't it?"

I nodded, chuckling; if only he knew. I wished him a good day and headed for the elevator, looking through the messages: my producer wanted me to call her the minute I arrived, the French consul general had left his number, as had Élodie Martin, twice, that morning. It was afternoon in France when the sun came up in Los Angeles; I sensed impatience. The switchboard had captured the numbers of several callers who declined to leave messages—one of them had called three times already that Monday morning. Lots of people have *issues* they want to discuss with me, personally. I don't return anonymous calls, and the switchboard takes numbers but won't send those calls through. Too often *issues* became big trouble. Best to keep a distance.

Behind me, as I punched the Up button for the elevator, the big glass front doors opened and someone walked briskly across the marble floor of the lobby, exchanging greetings with Omar. I glanced over, saw a man in a FedEx uniform drop a padded envelope on the counter. Omar was a bit slow on the uptake—too much holiday?—and the delivery man had turned and walked back across the narrow lobby and out the door before Omar could hand him the delivery log to sign.

"Hey, buddy," Omar called after him, rising from his stool. "You need to sign...." But FedEx was gone. Omar picked up a phone and called the gate, asked for the courier to be stopped and I.D.'ed before he drove out.

"Damn holiday temps," Omar swore as he spun the envelope around to look at the address. "Don't know what they're doing."

The elevator dinged, the doors slid open. But before I stepped inside, Omar said, "Miss MacGowen, you expecting a delivery?"

I thought about it, hand holding the door open, said, "Not that I remember."

"Package is addressed to you." He picked up the telephone receiver again and punched some buttons.

I walked back toward his counter for a look. Into the receiver, Omar said, "Hand-addressed to Maggie MacGowen, no bar code, no packing slip, no tracking number. Guy didn't sign in. Miss MacGowen was here in the lobby when it arrived. Yes, she's still…"

Before Omar finished his sentence, Big Bill Carlisle, head of studio security, burst through his office door at the side of the lobby; I have brought him a few little situations over the years. He held up a hand to stop me from approaching the counter, but as I listened to Omar tell his boss about the package, I retreated back toward the wall, away from the desk. Ordinarily, I might have raced for first look, but remembering that I had biological kin waiting at the coroner for her turn in an autopsy suite, I stayed put as the elevator doors *whoosh*ed shut and the car ascended without me.

The desk phone rang; Omar said a few curt words in response to his caller before he looked up at Big Bill. "The guy didn't drive in through the gate. Didn't drive out, either."

"I'm ordering a studio lock-down," Big Bill said. "No one comes in, no one goes out until we find him."

Omar got busy with the phone.

"Sorry, Miss MacGowen," Big Bill said. "If you'll just wait right there." I waited.

Big Bill—he *was* big, an NFL linebacker before a career with Marine MPs—took a digital camera out of a pocket and photographed the envelope, a standard 8½ x 11 bubble mailer, from several angles, moving his body around instead of touching the surface.

Within minutes, I heard sirens, many of them. A film crew from our news department assembled outside the front doors, stopped from entering by Omar. The first uniformed Burbank PD officer through the doors led a pretty beagle on a leash. The beagle sniffed the air, immediately found what she was trained to find, walked straight to the security counter and, standing directly below the envelope, pointed with two sharp barks.

"We have explosives," the dog's handler announced into a shoulder mic. The officer looked at the three of us and barked, "Clear the vicinity. Now."

During the evacuation of the studio, the delivery man, minus the

FedEx uniform that he shed in a parking lot planter, managed to slip away. That afternoon, the Burbank PD bomb squad, observed by agents from Homeland Security and the FBI, detonated a homemade bomb—not a big one, but powerful enough to blow the hands and face off whoever opened the envelope—in a vacant field somewhere out near Sunland. The prints taken from the envelope didn't come up in the system.

Rich Longshore, alerted by Guido, came and fetched me from the studio.

"We aren't dealing with a ring of master criminals, Maggie," he said as we sat at my kitchen table that evening eating turkey sandwiches for dinner. "Strictly amateur hour. Any idiot with Internet access can make a mail bomb like that one. Same with the hit-and-run that took out the Martin woman. Sloppy work. Too much TV."

"But do you think this bomb came from the same people?" I asked.

"The stuff you get involved with, Maggie, who can say?"

I leaned closer to him. "You can. And you usually do. What do you think, Rich?"

"Me?" He grinned his crooked grin. "From what we have so far, I wouldn't be surprised if the Martin woman saw something—or some knucklehead thought she saw something, some local mischief—and eliminated her. Then he decided that you might have seen something, too. Sent you a present."

"If that's the case, then I'll be safer if I go to France than if I stay here, right?"

He laughed. "Doesn't matter what I say, I know you've already decided to go."

For the next few days, I worked from home. And on Thursday, in the afternoon, the French consul general assigned to Los Angeles showed up at my house in the canyon to escort me to LAX. His name was Jean-Paul Bernard and he was extraordinarily handsome, gracious, and solicitous. He may have been fifty—attractive little crow's-feet at the corners of his eyes, silver at his temples—but he was as slender and straight in his beautifully tailored suit as a man half that age. His driver, a young Hispanic, probably an LA local, followed him inside the house but stayed only long enough to fetch my bags, which he carried down the front steps and stowed in the trunk of a sleek black Mercedes parked on the drive.

"May I offer my most sincere condolences?" Bernard said, actually bending over my hand. I was a little disappointed that he didn't kiss my hand or click his heels, but hoped there might be a next time. "A terrible tragedy has occurred. My office is only too happy to be of assistance to you and your family at this very sad time."

I thanked him before I asked, "Have the local police told you, in detail, what happened to my mother?" After a week of helping Élodie Martin make arrangements I was getting used to using the word "mother" in reference to Isabelle, and "Grand-mère" to Élodie, because it eased getting the arrangements made.

"Yes," he said, showing a polite degree of sadness. "I have been in regular communication with the police; a Detective Longshore with the county sheriff is my contact. Indeed, at my request Sergeant Longshore forwarded copies of all reports to our National Police Judiciare and promised to continue sending information as he discovers it. As our National Police are the agency that represents France with Interpol, there will be a coordinated and rigorous investigation on both sides of the Atlantic."

He carried a very beautiful black leather bag. As he unzipped the top, he said, "I want you to see the contents so you will know what you carry to Madame Martin. I leave to your discretion how you wish to present them to your grandmother."

Inside the bag were Isabelle's ashes in a can that resembled a large tea tin, a certificate from the Los Angeles County Department of Health identifying the contents and attesting they were harmless to transport, and Isabelle's personal effects, packed into a plastic hotel laundry bag. There was an inventory list attached: gold stud earrings, a watch, a brown leather handbag with her wallet full of credit cards and her national I.D. cards, her passport, house and car keys, a few hundred dollars and a similar value of euros in cash. Her suitcase holding her clothing and toiletries, I was told, was in the trunk of the Mercedes and would be checked with my own bag, and should be retrieved when I landed in Paris for delivery to the family.

"The bag, of course," he said, zipping it closed, "is my small gift to you, Madame. A *memento mori*, if you will."

"Kind of you," I said. I had seen the label sewn inside the bag; someone had paid a great deal of money for this memento. Made me wonder, who?

On the way to LAX I sat in the back seat with Jean-Paul. Isabelle's remains were in front with the driver. Through Jean-Paul, I directed the driver onto Mulholland Highway, and from there to Malibu Canyon Road and over the mountains to the ocean.

"Have you visited the crime scene?" I asked Jean-Paul.

"No." He seemed surprised, indeed nonplussed that I asked. "I did not request it, but perhaps?" He shrugged as he thought things through. "Perhaps I should, if we are near. One never knows, yes?"

Instead of taking the shortcut down past Our Lady of Malibu Church—the Virgin of Malibu?—and the civic center, I directed the driver to continue on Malibu Canyon all the way to PCH, past Pepperdine University. As he turned left onto the highway, I pointed out the market where Isabelle had waited for me, the corner where I had last seen her, and then, a little further south, the driveway at Cross Creek Center where she was hit, and the bridge next to which her body was found. There was nothing left to show that a woman had lost her life there, only asphalt, dirt and weeds.

We crossed the bridge and continued south on PCH through the high-rent zones of Malibu, Pacific Palisades, and Santa Monica—average home price along that stretch, even after the real estate bubble burst, was two-point-one million dollars per oceanfront shanty—through the McClure Tunnel to the freeway to the airport.

I asked the consul, "Has anyone explained to you my relationship to Isabelle Martin?"

He shrugged, a very Gallic shrug. "She was your mother, yes?"

"Yes. But I had never met her before the night she was killed. At least, not since I was an infant."

He was genuinely surprised. "I did not know. Madame Martin, your grandmother, did not tell me."

"I am the product of a liaison between Isabelle Martin and a scientist she worked with, my father. He spirited me away to America when I was an infant. The woman I have known all of my life as my mother was his wife."

He canted his head to one side, a very worldly acceptance of certain realities apparent in the gesture. "I see."

"Don't you think it's odd that her death happened within hours of our first meeting?"

He nodded. "Yes. More than odd. What significance do you give this—" another shrug "—coincidence?"

"I'm not a big believer in coincidence."

"No, of course not. I am familiar with your work on television, Madame, and delighted to meet you, though I regret the circumstances. I have heard you say in your programs more than once that you don't believe in coincidence. And such a violent death. No, there was a plan at work. Someone with a grand design."

"Maybe you can help me here," I said. "Who was Isabelle? Who are her family? For all I know they could be mobsters or gun runners or fanatics of some sort. I would appreciate anything that you can tell me before I meet them."

He laughed, a good, full-throated laugh; the suggestion that the Martins were thugs of some sort was, to him, clearly absurd. He said, "No, I can assure you, none of those things. They are a family of civil servants, bankers and farmers. The family Martin have been in possession of an estate in Normandy since the time of the Vikings, and maybe before. Good, solid citizens."

"Not the sort who hire hit men, then."

"Ah." He paused. "Families can be very complex, no?"

"Indeed," I said. "But I can't imagine a family of bankers, civil servants and farmers would have the contacts necessary to hire an international hit, can you?"

"Well, such a thing can be quite easy to arrange," he said, matter-of-fact about it. "A Russian mobster will do the job for less than two thousand dollars, I understand, plus expenses if he comes in from Russia. Of course, your local prison gang, the Mexican Mafia, will perform the same service for half what the Russians ask, but they prefer heavy firepower, and that can be risky: noisy, untidy, perhaps traceable. And they brag. Part of *machismo*." Again, a shrug, just an elegant little lift of one shoulder. "I could go on, mention the Vietnamese and Cambodian youth gone astray, perhaps skinheads with certain proclivities."

He smiled, a world-weary submission to reality. "So, there are many possibilities if one wants someone removed."

"I wouldn't know where to look for a hit man," I said. "Does one run an ad, Help Wanted?"

"Perhaps not." He smiled again. "Searching for the contacts to make lethal arrangements, that is where the vulnerability lies for someone such as you."

"I'll keep that in mind," I said. "But the question remains, why was Isabelle killed the very night she found me?"

We were approaching the Century Boulevard exit for the airport. Jean-Paul gave scant notice to the row of strip clubs that greet airport visitors as they exit the freeway. He was lost in thought that seemed to have nothing to do with billboards promising TOTALLY NUDE LUNCH-TIME BUFFET. Was he deciding what it might be safe to tell me? How close were his ties to the family? Or was he sincerely considering my question?

He turned in his seat to look squarely at me. "*Ma chère* madame, have you thought at all about your expectations?"

"Are you asking whether I am expecting too much? Too little? The wrong things?"

"No, my dear lady, expectations for inheritance."

"Hadn't given that a thought." I had not. Had no reason to expect anything other than information about my own history.

"In France, all inheritance follows the blood of the deceased. And you, Madame, legitimate or not, are of the blood."

We pulled up in front of the Bradley international terminal. He said, "Perhaps you should consider them."

The car had diplomatic plates, so apparently we could park anywhere we wanted to. While the airport police aggressively kept traffic moving—curbside waiting is verboten at LAX—one of the officers opened my door for me and promised the driver he would keep an eye on the car. That was, by itself, worth remarking upon. But once we were inside the terminal we did not stand in a line. Instead, we were greeted by a young woman in an Air France uniform who escorted Jean-Paul, the driver carrying my bags, and me into a side office. My passport was scrutinized, but my carry-on and the bag with Isabelle's ashes were given only a quick peek. And then I was handed my boarding pass and assignment to a first-class seat, as well as a first-class ticket with an open return.

The check-in bags were tagged and whisked away, and so was I, with Jean-Paul at my side, again following a crisp Air France uniform. I don't know where the bags went, except that I hoped they went into the correct aircraft. Jean-Paul and I were shown to a VIP lounge where we were seated in big club chairs, each poured a glass of very good Côtes du Rhône. A tray with a selection of French cheeses, tiny gherkins, and slices of baguette was set on the low table between us.

Jean-Paul indicated a small, round cheese. "This one is very good. Very typical of Normandy. Camembert. Do you enjoy Camembert?"

"Very much." To be polite I spread some of the creamy white cheese on a slice of baguette and took a nibble.

"Fortunate for you." He was smiling at me as if he had a private joke. "When you are with Madame Martin, there will always be good Camembert on the table."

"Grand-mère likes Camembert?"

He nodded. "Some of the best is made on the Martin estate."

The cheese I tasted was very good. Very rich. Perfect with the wine.

But I wasn't really interested. I set the cheese and the wine aside and turned to look directly at the consul. "What happens when a crime is planned in one country but carried out in another? Assuming that the perpetrator is found, who prosecutes?"

"If arrangements were made in France, France could." A Gallic shrug that seemed to convey infinite possibilities. "If the crime occurred in Los Angeles, Los Angeles would. Or there could be prosecution for solicitation of murder in one country, extradition and prosecution for murder in the other." Jean-Paul straightened the perfect knot in his perfect tie. "The prosecution is not difficult in a situation like this. Finding the 'bad guy' usually is."

"You've been through a situation like this before, haven't you?"

"Not exactly like this, no. But from time to time my countrymen get themselves into difficulties within my region of responsibility, and, yes, I am then involved, as now." He picked up a gherkin—*cornichon* he would have called it, a baby pickle—and bit off half. After he swallowed, he said, "I had some dealings with your late husband, Detective Flint; Mike, wasn't it? Once, a situation of two young Frenchmen who wandered off into the wrong place—South Central Los Angeles—looking for the 'extreme' tourist experience."

"They found what they were looking for?"

"And more. Forgive me when I say this," he said, tapping the handle of the black bag, "but they also went home in little cans."

"Did you give them a send-off as lovely as this one?"

"No, madame." Sardonic grin. "They went home parcel post."

"Well, then, the Martin family must be very special for you to extend the courtesies you have shown me."

Jean-Paul took my hand in both of his and looked deep into my eyes. "Did Madame consider that any courtesy I may have shown was for her benefit, and her benefit alone?"

God, he was smooth. I would have bought that line simply because I wanted to, not because I believed it. Before anything could develop from it, a uniformed attendant interrupted our *tête-à-tête*.

"Madame may board at this time."

Jean-Paul and I were escorted to the departure gate and straight onto the waiting aircraft, bypassing the hoi polloi standing in line with not so much as a queenly wave to them. Diplomatic privilege extended beyond the departure gate, it appeared. Jean-Paul saw me to my seat in first class and stowed the black bag in an empty overhead compartment. After he closed the hatch, the compartment was not opened again until

I reached Paris, even though the flight was full and space was scarce. He bid me *au revoir* and actually kissed my hand before he deplaned.

Belted into my very comfortable seat, sipping my second glass of Côtes du Rhône while other passengers lumbered to their seats under the weight of their chattels, I wondered again, who travels this way, and who, indeed, were the Martins of France?

I wanted to share the experience I was having with someone who would appreciate the fuss, so I called Casey. She had just come in from a class and was on her way to volleyball practice when I caught her. During Thanksgiving weekend I had told Casey the true story, the new true story, of my origins, at least what I knew of it. It was her history as well as mine.

Casey was more intrigued than she was upset. When I told her I would be carrying Isabelle's ashes to her family in France, she asked—begged, actually—to come along. I reminded her that she had finals to prepare for, but meeting the "other" family seemed more important, certainly more interesting, than school at the moment. We'll go to France together, later, I had told her, without adding, after I've scoped out the issues.

"I can come over and meet you," she pleaded anew after I told her about Jean-Paul and my VIP treatment. "I'll talk to my profs, get class notes."

"Not a chance," I said, though I would have loved to have her company. "Do me a favor, though, and call Gran every day until I get back. I'm a little worried about her."

"Sure, but why?"

"This whole thing has been pretty tough on her. Imagine how she feels."

"I'll call her. But you know they have telephones in France," she said. "She'll expect to hear from you, too."

"Yes, of course. But as Gracie would say, it would be a *mitzvah* for you to reassure your grandmother that nothing has changed between the two of you."

"As if anything would," she said, matter-of-fact about her feelings for Mom. "Just promise that you'll think about letting me come over. Early Christmas present?"

"I'll think about it." That's where we left it.

The flight was uneventful, luxurious. I actually slept through much of the night. But it was a nine-hour flight, and plush seat or not, when I was wakened for breakfast I felt stiff and crusty from reclining fully clothed overnight. After I ate, I went into the lavatory to pull myself together before we landed in Paris. I washed my face and patted some foundation on the dark circles under my eyes. Before I had the cap screwed back on the plane hit some turbulence. A glob of makeup popped up out of its bottle and landed on my shoulder. You can't blot foundation out of navy blue wool with a stiff paper towel.

Mom had insisted that I take along two scarves from the atelier of Hermès, Paris—which means extremely expensive—that had been gifts to her during the family's year in France forty-four years ago. She had rarely worn them, but they were among her treasures. In France a woman needs a good scarf, she kept telling me. One could not go to France without a good scarf or two. So I brought hers home with me after Thanksgiving to appease her, and at the last minute tucked them into my carry-on, in case she was correct. At the very least, I thought, I would put one on, get someone to take my picture, and send it to her as proof that I had worn her Hermès.

Back at my seat, I pulled out one of the scarves, a huge silk square with a pattern that looked like Art Nouveau flowers—red, blue, gold— with sinuous green stems, as seen through a kaleidoscope. I folded it into a triangle, tied it loosely around my neck, and turned it so that the triangular ends of the scarf draped over the stain on my shoulder and the tails hung over the opposite shoulder. I felt like a Girl Scout.

The other piece of advice Mom gave me before I left: Don't smile a lot or the French will think you're a simpleton.

It does not take long to get spoiled by pampering. I admit that I felt a little peevish upon landing when I had to carry my own things—two carry-ons and a coat—down a long corridor into the customs area, and then wade through the mosh pit of sleep-deprived tourists from my flight who were waiting, like me, for their bags to appear on the luggage carousel so that they could then lug them through Customs and Document Control. I hoped I would recognize Isabelle's bag; every second bag seemed to be imprinted with the same designer logo as hers.

Élodie Martin, Grand-mère, told me there would be a driver waiting for me. She had been so efficient about making arrangements so far that I was sure someone would be waiting. But until I got through Document Control, it appeared, I was on my own. Damn.

I staked my claim to a small patch of floor space and waited for the baggage conveyor belt to start moving. From about four people over, a tall, imperious-looking woman took a bead on me with an intensity that reminded me of Isabelle that night in the parking lot. The woman ruthlessly shoved her way through a resistant mass to get at me as I clutched my carry-ons tightly and looked for an escape route or some beefy help. Before I had moved more than a few steps, trapped as I was between two very large ladies and their mounds of stuff, she was upon me. She gripped the end of my scarf, all but put her nose into it, and declared in a strident tone, full of British certitude, "Vintage Hermès. Wherever did you find it? Such good condition. No sign of wear. Must have been in a collection." She looked at me, accusatory. "Are you a collector?"

I gently retrieved the end of the scarf and smoothed it back over the stain on my shoulder. "Excuse me."

She put her face close to mine and whispered hoarsely, "You *do* know what it is worth?"

She reached for my scarf again, but was distracted when the alarm went off announcing that the baggage conveyor was moving—empty, but moving. As the crowd surged forward, I saw my salvation: a young man wearing a three-day beard—how do European men manage to have a three-day beard every day?—and a perfectly tailored dark suit, stood on the far side of the Document Control booths among a clutch of other dark-suited hire-car drivers, holding a card with my name MME MACGOWEN, printed on it. This would be the driver Grand-mère arranged for. I raised a finger, caught my man's eye, pointed at myself and toward the baggage conveyor. He nodded, he would wait.

Gripping the handles of my carry-ons as if they were nunchucks, I maneuvered into a spot where I could see the bags as they came out of the chute, and waited for mine to appear. Before they did, a uniformed airline employee waded into the crowd, stopped beside me and touched my arm.

"Madame Flint?" she asked.

"Yes," I said, surprised to hear my name. Margot MacGowen Flint was the name on my passport. I thought it odd that Grand-mère's driver had written MacGowen on his card because she never used that name, dismissed it, I thought, as an affectation for television. But then, I do have a confusion of names. I looked around for my driver, but did not see him.

"Please come with me," the woman said. "Your bags are in your car and your driver is waiting."

I wondered how this miracle had been achieved, but was delighted that it had. I walked away with my escort as if VIP treatment was what I expected. After all, I was the lady wearing vintage, if borrowed, Hermès. *Sic transit gloria.*

As we were ushered through Document Control with a wave, I asked, "May I please have my passport stamped? A souvenir?"

The airline staffer shrugged, exchanged a who-can-figure-tourists look with the Document Control officer. I got my entry stamp, and was whisked out of the terminal to a waiting car, another long, sleek Mercedes.

I still did not see my driver. Instead, a handsome young man, maybe a few years older than Casey, held the door. He wore skinny denim jeans and a form-fitting black T-shirt under a black leather jacket instead of livery. His dark hair was cropped military-short, and his cheeks were clean-shaven. Casual, but well-groomed.

The young man introduced himself as David Breton. He handed me a stiff, narrow calling card imprinted MADAME HENRI MARTIN followed by Grand-mère's by-now familiar telephone number. He said, "Madame Martin requests that you telephone her right away."

I felt a little uneasy as he handed me into the back seat and waited for me to buckle up. Who was that other man, the one in the good suit who needed a shave? Maybe there was another MacGowen among the passengers. Or, maybe the first man was a spotter or greeter of some sort who located the fare while the driver took care of bags and car. All things considered, I preferred being with the affable David Breton. The other man looked frankly arrogant.

I dialed Grand-mère's number. She answered on the second ring.

"You have arrived safely, my dear?"

"Yes. Thank you for making the arrangements."

"I must apologize for not being there to greet you personally, but I have a few little tasks to attend to this morning. And, if it is not too great an inconvenience, there is a little task that you might attend to, my dear. The administrator for one of your mother's accounts wanted very much to see you while you are in Paris; something about needing a signature. I hope it is all right that I arranged for you to meet Monsieur Hubert at his offices at eleven o'clock."

"Where are his offices?"

"In the Sixth Arrondissement. David knows where."

Someone was wasting no time about settling Isabelle's estate. I asked, "Will anyone else be there?"

"Anyone else?"

"Other members of the family?"

"No, no. Only you and Monsieur Hubert."

I told her, "Eleven o'clock is fine."

"Perfect. Then I will entrust you to our capable David until lunch. Anything you need, just tell him."

When I closed my phone, I looked at the time. It wasn't yet nine o'clock. What was I to do for two hours?

I had been to Paris as a tourist and on business several times, and always loved it. Paris is a fascinating place that somehow manages to hold on to its antiquities even as it embraces innovation: an Internet café installed in a twelfth-century building, the cockamamie glass pyramid I.M. Pei designed as the new entrance to the ancient Louvre Museum— first glance can be jarring, but it grows on you—the inside-out Pompidou Center with its plumbing running on the outside, ultra-modern in a neighborhood of stately old homes.

Every other time I visited Paris I felt the sort of eager, itchy anticipation that a kid feels before the sun comes up on Christmas morning: hurry up, let the delights begin. As we pulled away from the curb, I should have felt some of the old excitement. Instead, this time I felt wary.

David skillfully maneuvered the big car through the scramble of Charles de Gaulle Airport traffic and out onto a highway very much like a California freeway, with traffic every bit as heavy as the 405 is around LAX. Outside the car window I saw a frigid, gray day, typical, as Jean-Paul would have said, of Paris in the fall.

"David," I said, "where are we going now?"

"I should ask you that question," he said. "You have an appointment with Monsieur Hubert at eleven, and Madame Martin expects you for luncheon at noon, at her home in the city. She asked me to tell you that after luncheon we will drive to the family home near Lessay, in Normandy. The burial of Madame Isabelle will take place tomorrow, Saturday, in the afternoon." His English was as flawless as Jean-Paul's had been, textbook perfect, not infected by the argot of the street.

A slow-moving van suddenly pulled in ahead of us, sandwiching us between its rear end and a rapidly approaching car behind. I braced for impact, certain that we were about get up close and personal with the big purple rooster painted on the van's back door. David checked traffic in the next lane, found a narrow slot between two speeding cars on the left and slipped into it inches before he would have rear-ended the van and been in turn hit from the rear. Unruffled by the near-miss, David kept talking. I had to will myself to let go of the door handle; my knuckles were white. The van switched to the right lane. I turned and watched the purple rooster disappear down an exit ramp, wondering if the driver knew how close he had come to disaster.

"If there is anything you will need for the weekend," David said, "Madame believes it would be better for you to acquire it this morning in Paris because she thinks that where we are going you might find the shops to be quite provincial. She wanted me to tell you that she has arranged for you access to her accounts at various shops in Paris, and I will be happy to take you wherever you wish to go."

I thought for a moment before I asked him, "What do you think I might need other than the usual sorts of things one might pack?" Combat boots? Kevlar vest?

"She suggested you might want to select something especially smart to wear at the funeral."

"I brought a dress that I like well enough," I said. Was she expecting me to be a hayseed in need of cleaning up? Or was she trying to impress me, or endear herself, by letting me spend some of her money? Could be a test, though what the correct response was I had no clue. I said, "I'm not a big shopper. But thanks for the offer."

He looked at me through the rearview mirror. He had very nice, deep blue eyes that were full of mirth in lieu of an actual smile. "Perhaps Madame Martin has stayed too much in Paris, and a bit of city snobbism is the result. Believe me, there are very nice shops quite near the estate if you need something. Normandy is not a wilderness."

"I'm sure it isn't."

"So, then, as we are here, in Paris, and we have a little time to fill, I wondered if you might like to see some sights, stretch your legs, perhaps."

"I would, thank you." A happy idea, especially if I was going to be sitting in a car for much of the afternoon. I leaned back in my seat, elbow on the armrest, and watched the ugly industrial edges of the City of Light glide past my window. "What do you recommend?"

"You have been to Paris before?"

"A few times, yes."

"Then you have already seen for yourself that the *Mona Lisa* is quite small, and that the Eiffel Tower is quite tall, yes?"

I laughed. "Yes."

"Have you ever been to the basilica at Saint-Denis? Not exactly in Paris, but very close by. And on the way."

I told him I had not been there. He said he recommended Saint-Denis because, first, it was easy to find a parking place there; next, he knew an excellent café tabac across the square from the basilica where we could get a good coffee and a snack; and of course the basilica itself was very interesting because it was the royal necropolis, the burial church of French kings and their families dating back to the early Middle Ages. And last, there were some gardens next door and a quay along the Seine that were nice for walking.

After the noise and billboard litter of the elevated expressway, the narrow streets and ancient stone walls of Saint-Denis were a relief. From the car I could see the backside of Montmartre, the highest point in Paris, and the white dome of the basilica of Sacré Coeur at its top.

David told me that Saint-Denis had once been an outlying walled fortification on the Seine, built to keep out barbarian invaders. But as Paris expanded outward the town had become a close-in suburb.

There was a modern invasion of sorts currently underway, this time immigrants out of Eastern Europe and the old French colonies of North Africa, the Caribbean and Asia. A new "city wall" built largely to accommodate the newcomers rose a short distance outside the ancient one: solid ranks of cheaply built high-rise national housing towers—what we call projects in the U.S.—stretched outward from the perimeter of the ancient wall all the way to the Paris city limits. Poverty, high unemployment, disappointment, anger, youth and crime, a community always on the edge of open rioting, lay outside this historic bastion, I was told. The native French clamor about the immigrant problem and the demise of traditional culture and language, while the newcomers feel excluded, denied equal opportunity. I could have been in LA.

Inside the old city walls, people representing a rich cultural mix went about their ordinary daily business. We stopped at the café tabac David mentioned and found a table by a side window so that we could look across the ancient stone square toward the basilica. David ordered strong *cafés au lait* and *croques-monsieur*, open-face grilled ham-and-cheese sandwiches.

After the third "madame" in a row, I begged David to call me Maggie, at least privately. I asked him how long he had worked for Grandmère.

"I do not work for Madame Martin," he said, smiling graciously; had I offended? "My parents are residents on the estate, as were their parents. When Madame is at her home in Normandy, my mother does for her, you know, tends to her meals, does some housework. It is part of their arrangement."

"I assumed you were driving her car. I'm sorry."

He nodded. "It is her car. She knew I was between school terms and, of course, I am going to the funeral. So she asked me to drive her."

"And she threw in a trip to the airport and entertaining me?"

He laughed. "Maybe I should say Madame and I have an arrangement also. There are benefits for both of us."

I looked at his open, handsome face, and said, "Dare I ask?"

"I am studying at the École polytechnique near here. There are no fees of the sort Americans pay for public universities—no tuition—and I receive a state salary. But it is very expensive to live and the salary is very small. Let's say that Madame supplements my salary and in return, from time to time, she relies on me. It is a happy arrangement."

He paid for the coffees and held my coat for me. "A little walk?"

As we crossed the cobblestone square, I asked, "What are you studying?"

"Chemistry and genetics. The sciences of agronomy."

"Farming," I said.

He shrugged that Gallic shrug and frowned. "In the end, yes."

He told me he wanted to work on niche agriculture, localized specialty crops and farm products, so that small-holders could support themselves in the face of the globalization of commodities, and thereby hang on to their land, to the local culture, and to provide a wholesome food alternative to the over-engineered junk that comes plastic-wrapped in supermarkets. From the tone of his voice I heard disdain for the latter.

The Martin estate in Normandy, he told me, had several good examples of small-scale but profitable farming. His father was the cheese maker, my cousin Antoine made cider and Calvados—apple brandy— and others grew famous carrots in a soil amended with composted seaweed. He promised to show me around the estate.

We walked past a small formal garden with a stone statue of a headless man standing in its center. While France has some relatively modern history involving lost heads, the figure wore a medieval-era monk's robe and held his tonsured head in his hands as if carrying a gift to a party.

"Do you know Saint Denis?" David asked, patting the statue's cheek. He pronounced the name *San-day-knee.*

"We've never met," I said. "But I've seen him on cathedrals all over France. Who was he?"

"Early Christian martyr," he said. "He came to Paris when the Romans were still in power, third century I think. He tried to convert the people. That was, of course, a crime. So, the Romans arrested him and took him up to the top of Montmartre." David turned to indicate the rise of Montmartre in the distance to our right. "They cut off his head, and many other Christian heads as well, as an example to the people.

But Saint Denis did not die right away. Instead, he picked up his head and carried it all the way down this side of the mountain. When he got here, next to the River Seine, he sat down and God took him straight to heaven. The altar of the basilica is built directly over the spot where Saint Denis ascended. Or, that's the story."

"It's a good story," I said.

"Montmartre is named for Saint Denis and the other Christian martyrs, the martyr's mountain." The way he smiled, I didn't think he bought the story. "So this is a very holy place, and that's why the kings and their families are buried here."

We walked through the sanctuary and then descended into the catacombs below. The place was indeed full of tombs. The more recent monarchs built extravagant marble memorials, but the earlier tombs were more interesting, fairly simple sarcophagi with life-size stone effigies on top depicting ancient kings and their queens and children, and various family members, lying prone as if they were sleeping on low beds arranged in rows throughout the ancient church structure, in the sanctuary and the catacombs beneath as well, a sort of eternal royal dormitory.

"See this?" In the catacombs, David pointed out a dark stone box roughly half the size of a child's shoebox sitting on a shelf in a side niche among other, larger boxes. "In that little box is the desiccated heart of the last true Bourbon king, Louis Seventeen."

I said, "I thought there were only sixteen Louis."

He indicated a pair of simple effigies on tombs nearby. "There lie Sixteen and his wife, Marie Antoinette, and their heads, too, I believe, though the heads may be somewhere else. But here," indicating the box, "is all that is left of their son, the last legitimate Louis, the missing dauphin."

"Where's the rest of him?" I asked.

That one-shoulder shrug again. "No one knows. After his parents lost their heads, he stayed imprisoned in Paris. At some point he died of tuberculosis, but nobody now knows when. And nobody knows what happened to the body; into a mass grave in the Reign of Terror, perhaps."

"Except for the heart?"

"Yes. The royal doctor took it home for a souvenir."

"Gee, and I settled for a stamp in my passport." I took another look inside the niche and shuddered. "I'm afraid to ask, but what's inside the other boxes?"

"Royal infants." He gestured toward the stairway. "Shall we go outside and maybe walk in the gardens?"

As we walked up into the daylight, I said, "Thank you, David, for showing me your national family skeletons. Now, what can you tell me about my own family skeletons?"

He leaned his head close to mine and whispered, conspiratorially, "You can't wait until the family Martin gathers for dinner tonight?"

"Might be too late." I took a breath before I asked him, "Do you know my story?"

"Some of it." He tilted his head from side to side, a yes-and-no answer. "My grandmother Marie knows everything about everybody on the estate. It is a small world perhaps, but it has its big intrigues, and my grandmother doesn't mind talking. I have known about you all of my life. The mystery girl, stolen away to America."

"David, if you don't mind, before I meet my own grandmother, is there anything I should know?"

"A chart of the mine fields, perhaps?"

"Are there mine fields?" I asked.

"Of course," he said, matter of fact. "They are a family. And to make it worse, there is some money, and these are hard times. But the Martins are okay." He paused, thought for a moment, reconsidered. "Most of them are okay."

I didn't add, but one of them may be a murderer. The family in France still had not been told that Isabelle was probably the victim of a murder for hire. I was asked to stay silent while the police did some background investigation, not to alarm anyone. That worked for me, because I, a stranger, did not want to be the bearer of that particular piece of bad news. Carrying Isabelle's ashes home was all the drama I was prepared to deliver at the moment.

David gave me a quick sketch of the immediate family tree. Grandmère, a widow, had two children, my mother, Isabelle, and my uncle, Gérard. I had a half brother about three years younger named Frédéric Desmoulins, called Freddy, who had a wife and two teenaged sons.

Shortly after Isabelle's misadventure—that is, my birth—she had married a school teacher named Claude Desmoulins whom the family thought was as good a catch as she could hope for in the circumstances. A good match, perhaps, but a miserable marriage. Isabelle and Claude separated after only a few years, eventually divorced, and rarely had any contact with each other except through Freddy. Isabelle never took her husband's name, preferring to remain a Martin.

"One thing," David said when we returned to the car. "Some of them will try to make you believe otherwise, but everyone in the family speaks very fine English."

"Thanks for the warning," I said.

"And don't be offended when they correct your French. Think of it as the price you must pay to encourage them to speak in English."

For the second leg of our day's journey, I sat in the front seat next to David. As he drove out of the car park, he told me there was still some time before my appointment with M. Hubert. He asked if I would like to drive past Isabelle's apartment—it was in the same arrondissement as M. Hubert's office—just to see the neighborhood. He said we probably shouldn't knock on the door because Freddy, my half brother, was staying there at the moment, and dropping in on him might be awkward. David didn't know how Freddy had taken the news that I, the long-lost sister, was bringing his mother's ashes home.

I told him I would like very much to see where Isabelle lived. I knew so little about her, and the more I learned, the more curious I became. I asked, "What was she like?"

After a pause, he said, "She was very intelligent. She could be very kind, generous, but she often seemed distracted, her mind on some situation or problem or another. She was very successful in her work, and she was very passionate about the estate. She invested a lot of her time and her money to modernize the farm operations. Papa always said she was astute about the politics of agriculture, and I should listen to her."

For as long as he could remember, David said, Isabelle had spent nearly every weekend at the estate, usually bringing her mother with her during the winter. Grand-mère stayed on the estate almost full time from Easter until the fall harvest.

My brother Freddy, however, was more interested in his life in town. On weekends when he was young he would usually stay at his father's apartment in Chantilly, a Paris suburb.

About Freddy, David had little else to say, except that he worked in some area of finance, and seemed to be very successful. At least, he had a house in an expensive Paris neighborhood and always drove a nice car. His boys went to an excellent private school.

I refrained from asking him why Freddy was living in his mother's apartment if he had a house of his own in Paris, but there had to be a story there.

Isabelle's apartment was on the Left Bank of the Seine, near the Sorbonne, a very old district built long before cars, or electricity, or plumbing. Her home was inside a traditional high-walled compound that David explained would contain the homes of several families. The houses were built around a central courtyard, a commons area that now would include parking for residents' cars instead of stables for horses or workshops. From the street, all that was visible was the front wall and a gate wide enough to drive a car through. Inside, a very private world.

"Beautiful neighborhood," I said, as we slowly drove past.

"Very expensive neighborhood."

"Thank you for showing me," I said.

"I thought you would be curious," he said. He stole a few narrowed-eye glances at me. "Madame Martin discussed with you Madame Isabelle's estate?"

"No," I said. "And I certainly did not ask."

"No." He nodded. "Of course." He thought that over, seemed to find some significance in it. "It is time. I will take you to Monsieur Hubert now."

M. Hubert's office was above an umbrella shop in the neighborhood of the ancient and collapsing Church of Saint-Sulpice, on a side street off the very posh Boulevard Saint-Germain. The street was narrow and there was no parking, so David dropped me in front of the building and told me he would pick me up from the same spot after my meeting. I would have preferred to have him come with me, a little support, even though I had met him only a couple of hours earlier. I felt very much alone as I mounted the narrow stone stairway to the second floor, off into a vast unknown.

"Here you are." M. Hubert rose from his desk to offer his hand. His assistant, the efficient-looking young woman who ushered me in, relieved me of my coat, showed me to a red silk-upholstered chair facing his antique partner's desk, and retreated with orders to fetch coffee.

Hubert was a compact, narrow man, dressed all in gray, with white eyebrows sprouting behind dark horn-rimmed glasses. Wearing a cardigan under his suit coat, he looked like a kindly school teacher. Indeed, his English, like David's, was schoolroom-flawless and formal.

While I settled in my chair, Hubert studied me over the tips of his steepled fingers. "I knew this day would come, eventually. And, I confess, I have harbored some curiosity about how it would be when we finally met."

"You have me at a disadvantage," I said. "My grandmother told me you are the administrator of some account, but I know nothing about it."

"Well then, let me try to explain." He opened a large document box on his desk and pulled out a stack of files. "Are you at all familiar with a series of patents your father owned with your mother?"

My first thought was, of course, my parents held their assets jointly. California is a community property state. But we weren't in California, and Mom and Dad probably weren't exactly the parents he referred to.

Some of the files on his desk were yellow with age. As he thumbed through their tabs, looking for something, I asked, "Are my father's patents jointly owned by Isabelle Martin?"

"Yes, of course." A matter-of-fact statement, knowledge assumed. He found the file he was looking for, pushed his reading glasses up over his forehead, folded his hands atop the file and looked at me. "The patents resulted from work they conducted together. I believe their research was the basis for your mother's doctoral dissertation—but you must know that."

I didn't, of course. But it made sense that if Dad and Isabelle patented something together, that thing would have come from their work together all those years ago, when Isabelle was a graduate student.

Hubert took a breath. "The patents are registered internationally, but they are owned in France *en tontine*, under an arrangement made by your parents many years ago. All monies earned, the royalties, are deposited into the account of the *tontine* and distributed as they designated." He looked up at me. "Are you familiar with a *tontine?*"

"Vaguely," I said. "Something about rights of survivorship."

"Exactly. A *tontine* is like an exclusive club, owned equally by its members. Whenever a member dies, the club remains intact, and the remaining members continue to own the assets equally. Of course, when there is a death, each member's share grows larger. And, at the end, the last surviving member owns all of the assets."

"What is your role?"

"Very little. I receive, manage and disburse the money earned according to the instructions of the members." He slowly pushed the file across the desk toward me with two hands. I opened it and found royalty statements that went back over forty years. The money was divided equally between Dad and Isabelle and paid quarterly. The amounts ebbed and flowed over time, never a fortune, but there was always something. However much the patents earned, they certainly would be a nice boost to my professor father's state salary and, later, his pension.

I remember, when I still lived at home, Mom and Dad waiting for royalty checks to arrive, never knowing what the amount would be until they opened the envelope. They would speculate and plan: a big check could be a special family vacation, orthodontia for a kid; a small check could be a season subscription to the symphony or a new sofa. The checks paid for three kids to go to college and probably for my private high school tuition, and about once a decade bought a new car. Like the residuals I receive for reruns of my programs, the checks were a bonus, never primary income. But they came in handy, for instance when they covered unexpected expenses. Like home repairs.

I noticed two things in the recent record. First, the amounts paid began to surge about five years ago, until currently, they were indeed substantial. And, a little over a year ago, beginning the month after Dad died, the entire royalty was remitted to Isabelle. Thinking about Mom's leaky roof and why the repair costs were a problem for her, I asked M. Hubert why the change.

"It was the arrangement made those many years ago."

"And now that Isabelle has passed away, what happens?"

"From the beginning, the *tontine* had three members: your parents and you, their natural daughter. As last one standing, you are now the sole member, and all of the assets belong to you."

The assistant came in with a coffee tray, which she set on a side table, providing a welcome diversion—coffee, yes please, milk, yes, sugar, no, biscuit, no thank you—a moment for me to mull things through.

Before I took my first sip—the coffee was very strong, even with half milk—I knew that as soon as I could set things up, all earnings from the patents would go to Mom, as they should. Losing Dad was hard enough for her, but to have some portion of her financial security flow to Isabelle was just cruel. What had Dad been thinking when he agreed to those terms?

I asked question two. "The original patents go back over forty years, but recently they are earning more. Do you know why?"

He laughed softly, a self-deprecating chuckle as he hefted the files. "Don't expect me to understand the details of the devices your parents developed, except that they have something to do with conservation of energy; a valve system. The original devices pertained to nuclear power reactors, but over the years your father revised them, reconfigured them, and broadened their applications to the methods for recovery of petroleum from oil shale, and, more recently, solar-generated power. Indications are that as use of solar power increases, the income from the devices will increase as well."

"You said that over the years these widgets were revised and reconfigured by my father. But the original financial relationship with Isabelle continued?"

Hubert nodded. "Yes. Because the original device came from joint work and was legally the property of the *tontine*, any extrapolation of that work belonged to the *tontine* as well."

"Interesting," I said, checking my watch. Grand-mère expected me in less than half an hour. "What happens now?"

He pulled out a single piece of letterhead paper and squared it on the desk in front of him. With a small flourish, he took a pen from a holder and extended it toward me as he slid that single page in front of me. "For the time being, a signature, that is all."

Apparently, getting this signature was the reason he was in such a hurry to see me. The document, whatever it was, was written in French. I think I got the gist of it, or part of it. With my signature I would agree that M. Hubert would continue to manage the *tontine*. About the other parts, written in French legalese? Mysteries to me.

I slid the sheet into the royalty disbursal file. "Of course, I will need to have my attorney take a look before I sign anything."

He seemed taken aback, flummoxed. "If I can explain anything to you, madame..."

I smiled sweetly. "Regretfully, my familiarity of both French language and law are not adequate for me to understand the document or its implications. Even if it were in English, I would ask an attorney to go over it with me before I signed anything. You understand, I'm sure."

He stammered a bit before he managed, "Well, yes, of course I understand. You must be careful."

"Thank you," I said, and at the risk of being taken for a simpleton as Mom warned, I smiled. I gestured toward the document box beside him. "May I have a copy of the entire file, please?"

He furrowed his brow. "You must have copies of everything already, do you not?"

"Maybe, in my father's papers in California. But I'm here, and I don't have access. I want to go over the files with both a translator and my attorney."

That request made him no happier than my hesitation to sign his document had. Indeed, he seemed offended, as if he thought I didn't trust him.

He said, "I can assure that all of the accounts are in order, madame. Your mother sent someone she trusted very much to audit the records quarterly. Her initials are at the bottom of every page, as you can see."

He showed me, HGD, initialed in a tight little script.

"I'm sure that everything is in order, monsieur," I said, smiling again. "My father was a very careful man, and obviously he placed his trust in you for many years. However, this is all new to me. Before I make any decisions, I need to study the records."

He thought about it for a moment before he nodded. "A delay of a week will make little difference."

"Is there an issue with time?"

"Some, yes. There are some patent renewals that need signatures very soon. Before you return to America, I hope."

"I'll do what I can," I said.

He summoned his assistant and asked her to make copies. She told me that the accounting summary in my hands was a duplicate, and I was welcome to take it with me. All of the files, including the original patent diagrams, had been digitized. I could wait for paper copies to be made—there was a hefty stack of them, so it would take a couple of hours—or she could download the files to a memory stick that I could plug into any computer's USB port. Would that be all right?

Absolutely, it was. The download took less than a minute. I dropped the memory stick, smaller than a pack of gum, into my purse, thanked them both, and promised to call by the first of the week to set up an appointment. On my way back down the stairs, I sent a text message to my Uncle Max: GET FRENCH ATTY ASAP.

David was waiting for me at the curb, as promised.

"All is well?" he asked as he held the car door for me.

"I'm not sure," I said, tucking the royalties file with the unsigned document into my carry-on bag.

From the Left Bank, we crossed the Seine onto the Île de la Cité, passed behind the vast gray eminence of Cathédrale de Notre-Dame under the watchful eyes of its gargoyles, then crossed the Seine again and drove into the Marais District, named, David told me, for the marsh it used to be.

Grand-mère lived in a tall gray stone house on a wide street off the rue Vieille-du-Temple, mid-block among a row of other tall gray houses that looked to be maybe mid-nineteenth-century architecture. The house was imposing, as were its neighbors. I counted three stories plus an attic, and wondered if there was also a basement. And maybe a dungeon?

David maneuvered the big car down a narrow alley behind the house, and then through a wide door that opened automatically as we approached. We were in a roomy garage with massive wooden roof beams darkened by age. He told me this had once been the carriage house and stable. The house had passed to Élodie through her grandfather, a cheese broker.

"I hope you don't mind coming in through the back." He held my door for me. "Madame thought that because we will be leaving again quite soon, we should leave your bags in the car, unless there is something you need before we set out again."

The black satchel with Isabelle's ashes was on the floor next to my feet. Leaving it, as well as Isabelle's personal effects, locked inside the garage seemed like a very good idea.

We were halfway across a small back garden, winter barren except for bright chrysanthemum borders, when the back door was opened by a woman I guessed to be in her late forties or early fifties, dressed in a trim, dark brown skirt and matching cardigan buttoned up to the throat, lots of crisp white collar and cuffs showing, and wearing sensible low-heeled shoes. Her posture, the hands folded in front of her, said servant. She greeted me formally, *"Bonjour, madame,"* with a little bow of the head, no handshake. She backed toward the wall to make room for me to pass inside, into a real butler's pantry where a man—a butler?—who would be the pepper shaker to her salt shaker if they came as a set was assembling lunch plates.

Behind me, as I walked down a long corridor, the woman spoke to David in rapid French, every second or third word of which I caught. My school French was rusty, but it was slowly emerging out of my mental closet as I heard people speak. I was able to understand that Grandmère waited for me in the little salon, and that David would find his lunch in the kitchen with someone named Oscar, probably the man in the pantry. Did David think I needed to freshen up, or was I ready to beard the old lion in her den? Lion wasn't exactly the word she used, however.

Without waiting for translation, I said, in my best French, "I'm ready."

➤7➤

MY SISTER, EMILY, bore a strong resemblance to Mom. I looked a lot like Emily, but, as I've said, I was also the spitting image of my father. My brother, Mark was, an equal amalgam of both parents, or he just looked like himself. The one feature that all three of us siblings unarguably had in common was my father's prominent nose. We used to joke that his assertive nose genes had overwhelmed Mom's more delicate ones. The point is, when all of us stood together we looked like a family. I never thought that we did not, or that I looked less like a member of the family than the others did. But every tattered notion I still had about who I was and where I belonged, where I came from, vanished when a side door opened and Élodie Martin stepped into the hall.

Grand-mère stopped in the silvery shaft of light the open door cast on the dark, polished stone floor, and looked at me for a long moment before she approached. Watching her walk toward me through the pale light was like watching my own specter visiting from forty-some years into the future.

Unlike most people, because I see myself on the screen nearly every day, I know what I look like from all angles. Her gait, the set of her shoulders, the contours of her oval face, the color of her pale eyes, the shape of her hands and the way she held them, her skinny ankles, all were mine as well. As she reached her hands toward me I wondered for just an instant, if as I reached my own hands toward her, I would encounter the cold face of a mirror instead of warm flesh.

I remembered Isabelle begging me to look at her so that I would *know* her, and later the funny expression on Mom's face when she looked at Isabelle's passport photo and saw a face she had not seen for over forty years. Mom and Isabelle saw the resemblance that I had not. Or, had refused to see.

"Here you are." Grand-mère took both of my hands in hers and kissed me on both cheeks, *la bise*, the standard French greeting. Her eyes were misted with tears. "I would know you anywhere, my dear. Except…" She peered more closely at my face. "Except your nose. Where did you get that nose?"

I touched the sculpted bridge of my nose. "Dr. James Wells."

She furrowed her brow. "Pardon me?"

"Plastic surgeon," I said, letting her guide me into the room she had come from, a formal sitting room, and toward a small round table set for lunch that was placed in an oriel overlooking a small garden. "I had my nose altered for television."

She laughed lightly. "Did this Dr. Wells sell a particular nose for television?"

"He sold a nose that my bosses persuaded me was more acceptable to a midwestern-American audience than the 'ethnic' one I was born with." I sat in the chair she indicated. As an icebreaker, I thought, she stayed on the subject of my edited nose until the housekeeper I had seen earlier, whose name, I learned, was Clara, brought the soup course.

For my first television job, reading the news at a local station in To-peka, Kansas, Margot Duchamps publicly became the perkier-sounding Maggie MacGowen—my new married name at the time—and Dad's lovely, distinctive nose was amended to become perkier as well. I kept the name professionally even after divorce and remarriage, and was stuck with the nose as well, though I wouldn't mind having my original one back.

My initial qualms about meeting Grand-mère for the first time quickly gave way to a sense of familiarity as we talked. I found that she had a ready wit and was an excellent listener. During the meal, the con-versation skirted the real questions as we got to know each other, feeling around the edges before plunging blindly into delicate areas.

The food was wonderful. To start, a tall glass of very cold apple cider—from the estate, she told me—to accompany rich fish soup that was served with little pots of tomato mayonnaise and tiny croutons on the side. I followed her lead, dipping the end of my spoon into the red mayonnaise, topping that with a crouton before gliding the spoon into the soup. Crushing a handful of saltines into the soup bowl would give more or less the same effect, but involve none of the ceremony.

Clara cleared the soup and set a casserole of cold ham *pâté*, a bowl of *cornichons*, and a basket with thin slices of baguette on the table, along with a pitcher of red wine. *Vin ordinaire*, Grand-mère said. After drinking the cider, I hesitated to risk more alcohol, but tasted the wine and found that it was far from ordinary. Next came roasted chicken breast served with a rice timbale studded with sautéed shellfish, and, finally, a platter of cheeses and a glass of port. More food and certainly more alcohol than I would ordinarily consume midday, but according to my body clock it was still the middle of the night, so why not?

Through the entire meal, we talked: about Casey, my job, Mike, in a circumspect way about Isabelle and Freddy, the grandchildren, and about the estate in Normandy. The latter made her face light up.

Grand-mère told me it had been in her late husband's family for centuries. They had managed to hold on to it through the Hundred Years War, the French Revolution, and two world wars. Not a vast prop-erty, she said, but well-located and well-loved.

Through hard work and a willingness to adapt to the vagaries of the ages, until fairly recently the family had been able to support not only their needs but also the needs of a few resident families. Like David, she did not refer to those residents as tenants, and I wondered if her own family had once been among them.

For Grand-mère, "fairly recently" meant a hundred or more years ago. For a very long time, farm income was sufficient for the family to subsidize one scholar, priest, lawyer, or politician in every generation. But, since her father's time, most members of the family worked at professional careers in the city in order to subsidize one farmer per generation. No matter where they lived or worked, in their hearts everyone in the family felt that the estate would always be home.

Clara came in with a tray of coffee things and began to clear the table.

"During the last war," Grand-mère said, "when the Germans came, my husband and I joined the Resistance; we were very young." She wagged a finger, a caution against assumptions or skepticism. "Yes, it is now difficult to find a French person of a certain age who does not claim to have fought with the Resistance. However, in our case it was true."

She accepted a cup of coffee from Clara. "Certainly, we wanted to get those horrid intruders, those Germans, out of France altogether. But for us, my Henri and I, the true mission was to reclaim our home in Normandy for our children not yet born." Though she never raised her voice, there was a scary fierceness in her tone when she added, "We were prepared to die, as our ancestors were, to save our home; my brother-in-law was shot by the Germans when he resisted. We took extreme risks, and succeeded. We would do the same again, if necessary."

If there were ever a scrap, I decided right then and there, I'd want to be on her side. Safer that way.

Oscar entered the room. He bent his balding head toward her and spoke very softly. Apparently Freddy, my half brother, had arrived unexpectedly and was waiting in the foyer. I set my napkin on the table and, feeling nervous about meeting him, rose as Grand-mère rose. If Freddy was in Paris, I wondered, why hadn't he joined us for lunch?

Oscar was given instructions to tell Freddy to wait. As he left the room, Grand-mère turned her attention on me.

"Hermès, lovely. May I?" She reached up and untied my scarf, gave it a twist and tied it into an intricate knot that was interesting, elegant, but left the stain on my shoulder exposed. She saw it, said, "Oh, of course," and retied the scarf so that it was both elegant and covered the stain. The gesture was entirely affectionate, and it touched me. Again, it struck me that she did not feel like a stranger to me. Even the room felt somehow familiar, and I felt welcome there.

Perhaps, when I was an infant, I had been in this room with her. If I were, I would have been too young to remember. But is it possible that some emotional connection remains with us, the ghosts of comfort, fear, or love, long after actual memory dies?

Clara came in with a tray to clear away the coffee cups. Grand-mère instructed her to show me where I could freshen up, and then she stretched up and kissed my cheek, just one. "Please excuse me, my dear." She walked purposefully out of the room. Alone.

I was not to meet Freddy yet, it appeared. I wondered if anyone had told him that I was in the house. How big an issue was I for Freddy?

Clara showed me to a powder room down the hall and left when I assured her, in my imperfect French, that I did not need David to fetch my bag from the car.

The powder room was large and well-appointed without being ostentatious. From the slope of the high ceiling it was apparent that this room with modern plumbing had been fitted into an under-stair space some time after the house was built, when running water and flush toilets became available; always willing to adapt, Grand-mère had said.

I did what I could, washed my hands, combed my hair, powdered my nose using the powder and beribboned puff from a box on the mar-ble-topped vanity, fluffed the ends of my scarf. When I couldn't think of anything else that would make me fresher or more presentable for the drive to the estate, I opened the door and peered tentatively into the hall.

Raised voices came from the front of the house, a man and Grand-mère, something about equity or fairness and too many cars. And a baby? I knew from experience that a noisy discussion among French people did not necessarily mean discord, but the tone of the man's voice chilled me.

Quietly, I made my way back to the salon where we had eaten lunch, stood in the windows of the oriel overlooking the winter garden, turned on my mobile and checked messages while I waited for Grand-mère to return.

During my flight, Casey, Guido, Rich Longshore, Uncle Max, and my neighbor Early Drummond had called. All asked for a call back. It would be early evening in France, after we arrived at the estate in Nor-mandy, before I expected to have time and privacy to return calls. The time difference could be problematic.

Grand-mère and I settled comfortably in the back seat of the big Mercedes. David drove us out of Paris headed west on an autoroute, a toll highway, flouting the speed limit right along with everyone else on the road. Towns and countryside sped past the windows, a blur of bare, ghostly trees, villages and church spires, modern suburbs infected with stucco tract housing à la San Fernando Valley sprawl, harvested fields, tiny cottages too near the highway and huge châteaux in the distance.

"Beautiful," I said.

Grand-mère, looking out her side of the car, nodded. She had seemed distracted since her conversation with Freddy. Was her silence grief or fatigue, or family issues? She was eighty-something, and for all of her composure, I had to remember that she had just lost her daughter and had made very intricate plans to bring the remains home. And then, there was me and all the issues attached simply to my being, as well as my being *there*.

I ventured to ask, "How is Freddy taking my sudden appearance?"

She shrugged, this time the gesture connoting, who can fathom the mysteries at the depths of a man's heart? She turned her gaze toward me. "He knew his mother's purpose in going to California; she made no secret of it. It is a shock for him, certainly, that she is gone from us in this way, but that she found you is not." She added, "He will join us for dinner tonight."

"If you don't mind talking about Isabelle," I said, "may I ask, why did she come looking for me after so many years?"

"She did not tell you?"

I cringed. I hadn't told Grand-mère, of course, about the messiness of my encounter with Isabelle. I equivocated. "Our meeting was very brief."

"I see." Delicately, she dabbed the corners of her pale eyes with a lacy handkerchief, thereby taking a little time to compose her answer. "She wanted to speak with you because there was much to settle and she knew there was very little time."

I puzzled that over for a moment. Little time for what? The answer, when it came, shamed me beyond logic; how could I have known?

"Your mother was not well," Grand-mère said. "A progressive dysfunction of her bone marrow. She might have seemed well enough to look at, to speak with, but her health was very fragile. It was only a matter of time. But the accident happened first."

"Was it myelodysplasia syndrome?"

She showed her surprise at my question by a small lift of her eyebrows. "If she did not tell you, how do you know this?"

"A guess. A couple of my father's colleagues in nuclear research contracted MDS. There are no studies that prove a link, but Dad thought exposure to radiation was possibly a cause."

"That occurred to me, of course. Because of her work, I expected it would be cancer that would take her, as it took Marie Curie and so many who followed her. But Isabelle was so confident about her safety, she would not hear my concerns."

I hesitated before I asked, "Was she hoping I could give her a bone marrow transplant?"

"No, no. It was too late for that. My son, Gérard, went through the tests to be a donor, but her disease had already progressed to a leukemia-like stage by that time. There was no cure for her." She dropped her head, looked down at the tightly clasped hands on her lap. "I thought I was prepared for the day I would make this journey. But I find I am not."

"I am so sorry," I said putting a hand over hers. Her hands were like ice, the skin as smooth and dry as fine silk.

She slipped one hand free and placed it on top of mine, a stack of hands, and forced a game smile. "But now I have you, my granddaughter, come back to me. And, I have the comfort of knowing that your mother saw you again before the end."

Yes, but only literally saw me. I asked, "Why did she go all the way to California to speak with me? Why not write a letter? If she couldn't find where I live, information that is protected because of the work I do and that my husband Mike did, she knew where I work. She could have written or telephoned. You have my mother's number."

She shook her head. "There was an agreement made all those years ago. Isabelle was not to contact you, or your American family."

"But she decided that it was all right now?"

"You understand. Good."

No, I did not understand. When I was a minor, of course my family would have wanted to keep Isabelle from showing up. What a disruption her appearance, the mere fact of her, would have been to my life. But I haven't been a minor for a very long time. My child wasn't even a minor anymore.

Something wasn't adding up here. But the big question was: Why bother to murder a dying woman?

Grand-mère took her hand off mine and laid it against my cheek.

"You must be exhausted, my dear. I admit, I am a little tired, myself. If you don't mind, I will close my eyes and rest for a moment."

She fell immediately into a sepulchral sleep, head cradled against the plush leather headrest, face a mask, slender hands as still and stone-like as the effigies at St-Denis. In the cold, pale afternoon light I saw the grief that lined her face and felt a profound sympathy and compassion for her. The depth of my feelings for her surprised me.

I wanted to talk with David, but also did not want to disturb her. So, I leaned my head back and drifted off as well as we drove under the pale, dappled light filtered through the bare branches of trees lining the road.

Crazy dreams full of strangers supposedly speaking French, but a French that I could not understand at all except for someone yelling out in anger, *"Petite merdeuse,"* that, unaccountably, I knew meant "little shit," while wild drums beat and strobe lights flashed. Where in high school or college French had we covered the vocabulary of excoriating children?

In the dream, there were tables laden with food no one ate. Mom walked through with another version of my birth certificate and an official told me that my passport was invalid and that I had to give back the entry stamp. I was relieved when David's voice broke through the veil of sleep.

"Mesdames, we approach."

—8—

"WHAT'S IT LIKE THERE?" Casey asked, eager to hear about the estate. "Tell me that it's a magnificent château surrounded by vineyards, with cadres of loyal retainers to wait on you, and swans swimming in a moat."

"Drafty stone farmhouse, apple orchard, carrot fields, cows—I can smell them when the wind shifts—and lots of mud." I peered out the window of my upstairs bedroom in Grand-mère's Normandy house as I talked to Casey on my mobile. Various fields and farm attributes had been pointed out to me as we drove past them, but it was already dark by the time we arrived so I had seen very little beyond the low stone wall that surrounded the three houses in Grand-mère's compound, except outlines and amorphous shapes against the sky.

"No polo ponies in paddocks?"

"I'm told there are horses, but I haven't seen them," I said. "Percherons, huge plow horses. It's a working farm. Wish I'd brought rubber boots."

"Ah well, fantasy crushed." She laughed. "How's the weather?"

"Cold and gray today. Cold, gray and foggy forecast for tomorrow with a possibility of rain and ice."

"What did you wear on the plane?" Nineteen is still a teenager, but a wardrobe question? Not what I expected from Casey.

"Woolen slacks and a sweater," I said.

"Which slacks?"

"Navy pinstripes."

"Nice. I like those. Did you take your camel hair coat?"

"That's the one."

"What are you wearing to the funeral?"

"The gray dress you and Gran bought me to wear to Mike's funeral."

"Good choice."

I was reminded of the offer David extended from Grand-mère for me to shop for something especially smart to wear to the funeral. Should not funeral attire call no attention to the mourner? My gray dress was just fine. I had worn it to two funerals since Mike's, and it had been perfectly serviceable: good cut, good fabric, unadorned.

"What else did you pack?" Casey asked.

"Why do you ask?" Something was up, I could hear it in her voice.

"In case I ever get over there," she said.

"You can borrow my pinstripes."

"Mom." In this case the word conveyed disdain for a lame idea.

"From what I've seen," I said, "jeans are still the uniform for people your age. Make sure they fit; I've never seen a French girl with a muffin top bulging over her low-riders. Leather boots, leather jacket, skinny shirts, long wool scarves, throw in a skirt to wear for dinner, and you're set."

"Okay," she said. "Good to know."

"And something appropriate for a funeral?" I waited through a long moment of silence on the other end before I asked, "Casey, did you buy a plane ticket?"

"Élodie Martin bought me one. First class, Mom. It was supposed to be a surprise for you."

I worked through a tumble of emotions at once. At the forefront, remembering the raised voices I'd heard coming from Grand-mère's foyer that afternoon, I felt a buzz of concern for my daughter's well-being should she be suddenly tossed into this family pool, the depths and hazards of which I had yet to chart; still or stormy waters, who knew? Next I felt dismay at Grand-mère's presumption. She should have told me what she had done. Sneaky, manipulative—I would have to watch Grand-mère carefully. But in the end, I felt a selfish happiness that Casey would be with me during the weekend. Adrift, alone among strangers, I needed an ally I could trust. Maybe Grand-mère had sent for Casey as a gesture of support for me. Whatever her motives, she was a tricky one.

I asked, "When do you arrive?"

"Tomorrow morning. Tonight I'm taking the same overnight flight you took yesterday. Zia's driving me to the airport."

"Who's picking you up at de Gaulle?"

"Someone named Bébé Martin. I have his mobile number if you want it."

"I do." I wrote the number on a pad on the bedside table. I told her, "You won't be able to use your phone over here because it doesn't have international access, and it takes your carrier at least twenty-four hours to establish service. Not to mention, it's expensive if you send data, like texts. Get this Bébé person to stop at a telephone store so you can buy a cheap phone with a French SIM card and a local phone number. Load on a few prepaid hours. Maybe you can pick one up at the airport—look around. When you get the phone, call me first thing and give me the number."

"All right."

"Do you need pocket money?"

"No, I'm okay."

"I'll know that when I see your sweet face. Where's your passport?"

"Such a fuss, Mom," she said, laughing again.

"Casey," I said, "don't be dazzled by a first class plane ticket. These people are strangers to us. We don't know anything about their issues."

"Mom."

"This isn't a dance in an opera, Casey. It's the funeral of a murdered woman."

"You trying to scare me off?"

"How'm I doing?"

"I'll see you tomorrow," she said. "I have to run to class. I'll call you before I board. I love you."

I punched Bébé's number into my phone's directory before I returned any more calls, beginning with my neighbor, Early Drummond. Early worked for the same network I did, a technical director in the news division. He was looking after my house and the horses, and wouldn't have called unless there was an issue.

"Hey, Maggie," he said. "Glad you got back to me. Something I think you might want to know. That woman, the hit-and-run in Malibu, the one you had the thing with?"

"What about her?"

"Cops asked us to broadcast her picture during the evening news last night with an appeal for witnesses."

"Anyone call in?"

"I don't know about that, but, Maggie, I recognized her from the picture. She was up at the house last week, a couple of days before Thanksgiving."

"At my house?" I asked, in case I had misheard. "What was she doing?"

"Looking around," he said. "Took some pictures with her phone. When she started petting the horses I went down to see what she was up to."

"You talked to her?"

"I did. She said she was interested in the neighborhood. I assumed she was house hunting, or neighborhood shopping," he said. "She was a nice-looking, well-dressed lady. Didn't look like a burglar casing the place, so I talked to her for a minute."

"Did she ask about me?"

"Not specifically, just generally asked about people in the neighborhood, you know, what sort of people live around there. Were there movie and television stars? She didn't mention you, neither did I. Wanted to know about the horses. She asked about riding trails, so I pointed out the Bulldog trailhead across the way. She said she'd like to take a look at the trail, said good-bye and walked away."

"Do you have Rich Longshore's number?" I asked.

"I already called Rich and told him. Hope that's okay."

"It's very okay. Did he say anything?"

"You know Rich. He said uh-huh a few times, asked me to write down everything I remember about the conversation and email it to him. Then we talked about football. He did say that if I talked to you I should remind you about what he told you, but he didn't say what that was."

"He told me to watch my back and to let the local police do the investigating."

"Good advice," Early said. "Good advice."

I was scrolling down through the contacts entered in my phone's directory for Rich's number when there was a knock on the door. I slipped the phone into my skirt pocket and went to answer.

Julie, David Breton's mother, handed me the sweater I had worn on the plane; Grand-mère had asked her to sponge out the stain on the shoulder. Julie was a comfortably round woman in her mid-forties— my age—apron tied over her sweater and jeans. David told me that his mother had an arrangement to "do for" Grand-mère when she was in Normandy, but their relationship seemed to be very casual, friendly, chatty even, unlike the formality I had seen between Grand-mère and her Paris couple, Clara and Oscar. If Julie seemed formal with me it was probably because she didn't understand much of anything I said any better than I understood her. The Norman accent was very different from the Parisian. And, she did not know me.

Julie acknowledged my *Merci, madame* with a little shrug and a curt *De rien, madame*, meaning don't give it a thought. I was learning that it was as important to be able to decipher the significances of the many-nuanced little shrugs, nods, hand gestures, and frowns as it was to understand the words spoken.

After Julie left, I put the sweater in the wardrobe with the clothes she had carefully unpacked for me. The beautiful black satchel with Isabelle's ashes and personal effects was on the wardrobe floor. Her suitcase was beside it. I had offered nothing to Grand-mère yet, because I intended to look through Isabelle's things before I gave them up. I needed to know what she had been up to.

The small effects Isabelle left in her hotel room had been piled into a plastic laundry bag imprinted with the logo of the hotel where she stayed in Malibu, and the bag had been placed in the black satchel. I loosened the drawstring at the top, looked inside, saw her telephone, and took it out, tied the bag back up and closed the closet. There was only about a third of a battery charge left. I turned on the phone and opened the media file, where I found the photos Early had mentioned.

A series of images appeared on the tiny screen as I scrolled through the file, all of them taken of the environs of Maggie MacGowen in Malibu Canyon: my house, the horses, the mountains, my roses, the rustic chairs and table up on our front deck that Mike had built out of twisted eucalyptus tree prunings. Mike and I would sit on the deck at night in those chairs with a bottle of wine, hold hands and star gaze. The pictures were an intrusion into a very private place, my place—our place. I wondered, if Early hadn't intercepted Isabelle when he did, how far would she have ventured into that private place?

The last two pictures were taken from an overlook about a quarter of a mile up Bulldog Trail. Shot from above, looking down through the dense canopy of trees, the pictures showed the wicked curve of the road just below my house, a glimpse of the front of my yard, some rails of the corral we shared with Early, my horse's handsome flanks, the roof and chimney, the naked mountainside behind the house that we keep stripped bare of vegetation as a firebreak. Isabelle had been up to something far more involved than simply setting up a meeting with me.

Isabelle had forwarded the photos to someone. I wrote down that phone number and then sent the entire photo file to Rich with a brief text message: PIX FROM IM'S PHONE. I also gave him the date they were sent—two days before Thanksgiving—and the number Isabelle sent them to.

My own phone rang, a Los Angeles area code, a number I didn't recognize. I hadn't finished with Isabelle's phone, so I opened the wardrobe and slipped it into the toe of a shoe, feeling like a kid who didn't want Mom to discover a between-meals candy bar when she put away my laundry. The phone wasn't mine to hide, or to nose through, but I intended to keep it until I'd had a chance to go through Isabelle's call record.

I closed the wardrobe and flipped my telephone on. As I always do when I don't know who is calling, I waited for the caller to speak first.

"Hello, hello? Are you there, Maggie?" The cultured tones of Jean-Paul Bernard.

I was so surprised to hear his voice that I felt oddly about the same way I did as a teenager when the first boy called to ask me to the movies: tongue-tied, dry-mouthed, heart pounding in my ears. I had a sudden flash of tanned wrist showing at the end of a crisp white shirt cuff as we rode together in the back seat of his Mercedes on the way to the airport, and felt that flutter I hadn't let myself feel since Mike died.

During the eight months that I had been a widow, the only sexual thoughts I could handle related to my too-brief time with my husband, Mike Flint. Mike had been sick—surgery, chemo, surgery, chemo—for a full year before he made the decision to sing a solo version of "Auld Lang Syne" accompanied by his service automatic.

Vividly, I remembered how it felt to be in his arms, remembered the last time we held each other—on his last morning. But I could not remember exactly how long it had been since I had felt any interest in sex, or had felt that urges of a particular sort would be anything but a betrayal to Mike, living or dead. I know what he would have said to me: What a waste. Get on with your life. He would have cheered the stirrings.

All I could think to say was, "Jean-Paul."

"You are there in Normandy and settled in?"

"Yes. Thank you for all of your help. How did I ever get myself on an airplane before you came along?"

He laughed politely. "If I have been of any service to you, I am delighted."

I dabbed the sweat off my upper lip, feeling like a silly ass for having such a girly reaction. This very gracious man was doing no more than making a courtesy call to the daughter of a constituent.

"You have been wonderful," I managed to utter. "I am beholden."

"Wonderful, am I?" Again he laughed. "And you're beholden? Does that mean I am in the position to ask for a little favor?"

"Of course." I must have cringed, thinking here it comes, time to pay up, fool. I also thought I needed to be careful if I could feel so vulnerable to the charms of a stranger so quickly. But it had been a while....

"Do you know how long you will be in France?"

"Not yet," I said. "The funeral is tomorrow, and then there are some details to take care of. I'll probably be here through the first of the week."

"As it turns out, I am needed in Paris on business next week," he said. "I thought I would come over a few days early. There is an auction of saddle horses on Monday morning at the Haras in Saint-Lô, the national stud, not so far from where you are. I would like very much to see what's on offer. So, as we will be practically neighbors for a short time, if it is not too much of a burden and your family can spare you, I would very much enjoy your company for dinner Sunday evening."

"Dinner?" Be still my heart. And be careful, old girl. "How could dinner with you be a burden, Jean-Paul? Yes, of course. With the caveat that some family situation might present itself. If it does, will I call you at this number?"

"Yes. This number will always reach me. Shall we say seven o'clock, unless I hear from you?"

"Seven is fine."

I still had a silly grin on my face when another knock on the door startled me out of my reverie. I opened the bedroom door.

"Ah, you exist." The man standing in the hall outside my room was about my age, had my eyes. He smiled, took my hand and gave it one firm downward shake as he leaned forward to kiss me on both cheeks, *la bise* again. "I am Antoine, your cousin, son of Gérard, your uncle. Welcome."

"Happy to meet you," I said, glancing down when I caught myself staring. Among other things, I checked out what he was wearing: loose-fitting medium brown cords and a black cable-knit sweater, dark leather shoes. Grand-mère told me that the family did not dress for dinner, but I had no clue about where, on a scale that began at sweats and ended at black tie, their notion of appropriate family dinner attire would fall. So I went for the middle ground. After a shower, I had put on knee-high flat-heeled boots, a mid-calf–length brown suede skirt, and topped it with a cream-colored turtleneck for warmth. Grand-mère's house was an ancient pile of rock that had been retrofitted with central heating at some point, but the old place still managed to be drafty and had pockets of cold lurking in corners and at intersections of hallways.

"Pardon my intrusion," Antoine said. "You have a visitor."

"Who is it?" I shut my door and walked down the hall beside him. Surely he wouldn't refer to a member of the family as a visitor.

"Les cognes," he said, irony indicated by the lift of one eyebrow as he jammed his hands into his pockets and slouched gracefully along beside me. "The police. Promise me you aren't a notorious criminal trying to hide out on our humble estate."

"Sorry, no." I laughed, albeit nervously. I felt a powerful sense of déjà vu; we looked like blood kin. "It's probably something about Isabelle."

"Of course." He shrugged. "So sad, so unexpected."

Before I could think of the appropriate response, he asked, "Do you speak French?"

"Like a tourist," I said. "I studied French in school, but that was a long time ago. I can understand ordinary conversation fairly well, and I can manage to ask directions to a train station or order a meal, but beyond that…"

"Even if you were fluent, you might not understand the locals; the Norman accent is very strong. Shall I sit in with you?"

"Please," I said, grateful for the offer.

The salon at Grand-mère's house, typical of French homes, served as living room, dining room, family room, and general domestic cross-roads, and took up much of the ground floor. When we walked through, Julie was setting plates on a large refectory table that was placed in the center of the room in front of an immense fireplace. There was an arrangement of sofas and chairs at one end of the room, at the other a tall sideboard set with cider, wine, apéritifs and glasses. It all looked very cozy, very comfortable. But I saw no one except Julie.

I looked up at Antoine. "Where—?"

He interrupted my question by touching one index finger to his lips and pointing upstairs with the other. Obviously he did not want

Grand-mère to know that the police had come visiting. He told Julie he was taking me next door to meet his family, and promised to have me back in time for dinner.

We walked outside without stopping for coats. This would be normal for me to do, habit, because there are so few occasions in Southern California where a coat is actually needed. The day before, I left Los Angeles during a Santa Ana wind–driven heat wave, and had nearly forgotten to bring a coat at all. But we were not in Southern California now, and the night air was frigid. I wrapped my arms around my chest and shivered. Antoine seemed unaffected.

"We are just there." He indicated a house about a dozen yards from Grand-mère's, an obviously new confection built in the style of the grand châteaux of the Loire Valley, but on a much smaller scale. It looked ridiculously opulent tucked into the same compound as Grand-mère's ancient, unadorned rectangular block of stone and the house opposite, a modern, austere version of Grand-mère's, with steel where hers had wood, sharp corners where hers were worn round by age and weather.

Antoine followed my line of vision, and, indicating that starkly modern house, said, "That is your mother's house. Your brother and his family will be staying there this weekend."

Mention of Freddy reminded me of my conversation with Casey and the overheard conversation after lunch, something about a baby, or, in French, *bébé*. I asked Antoine, "Who is Bébé Martin?"

He turned toward me, smiling broadly; apparently this was a happy topic. "He is my brother, Charles. When we were little, I called him my *bébé* and to this day he will not be called by any other name. Not even in school. How do you know of Bébé?"

"He's picking up my daughter at the airport tomorrow and bringing her here."

"Don't worry then, she is in very good hands. She will love Bébé, she must, everyone loves Bébé." Then he glanced at his house and his smile took on a wry cast. "Almost everyone loves Bébé."

As we approached his front door, I asked, "Did you build this house?"

He bent his head closer to mine and whispered, "My father built it. I won't ask you what you think of it."

He opened the front door, and what I saw stopped me in my tracks. I forgot to feel cold as I found myself looking into the deep, warm brown eyes of a beautiful woman.

A portrait, nearly life-size, hung on the foyer wall facing the front door, centered so that it could not be missed by anyone who entered the house through that door. The woman in the portrait was more than stunning, painted in the reverential *fin de siècle* style of John Singer Sargent. The pale skin of her face, her bare arms, and her décolletage was luminescent, as if lit from within. Fathomless brown eyes, amazing eyes, had a fire of their own. Her dark and gleaming hair was parted in the center and pulled back into a classic chignon. A long green-black gown was a dull shimmer of silk that skimmed the curves of a slender, graceful body. A woman in her prime, her beauty timeless.

Awed, I asked Antoine who she was.

"My mother, the angel of this house. Bébé painted her from memory." He kissed the fingertips of one hand and touched them to the frame. "She keeps the devil from our door."

"She is beautiful."

"Yes. She was." A shadow crossed his face. He turned from her, indicated the passage to the right of her wall, her shrine. "Inspector Dauvin awaits."

We walked into a large salon. I was surprised to find that, within those opulent walls, the furnishings were very simple and functional. I was also surprised to see David Breton there. He sat at a round table at the far end of the room, facing two teenaged boys whose backs were to us. Spread out on the table in front of the boys were textbooks, notebooks, and a pair of laptop computers. We had, obviously, interrupted a tutoring session.

There was a man with them, fortyish, dressed very much like Antoine in casual slacks and a sweater. I quickly decided that he was the father of the smaller of the two boys because of their obvious familiarity with each other, the man leaning over the boy's shoulder and interacting with him as the youth puzzled through a problem. They all turned toward us when David waved a greeting. The adult nudged the boys to rise to their feet: A lady had entered the room.

I saw no policeman, and began to wonder if there actually was one.

"You know David," Antoine said. "We are taking advantage of his visit. Usually he tutors Chris and Gus online, so this is a treat for them. The boys are preparing for their *baccalauréat* exams in June. If they work very hard and score exceptionally well, as David did, they will qualify to prepare for the *grandes écoles*. If not…" He turned and, with a teasing scowl, jabbed his finger at the boys. "If not, they will milk cows for the rest of their miserable lives."

The boys scoffed.

"Chris." Antoine presented his son to me. "Greet your cousin. Cousin, here is Christophe."

Chris obliged with the handshake and *la bise*, and the formal "Delighted." Then, with an impish grin, he said, "My parents are wondering, but are too timid to ask, how shall we address you?"

"Please call me Maggie," I said as Antoine feigned boxing the boy's ears for his sauciness. "Among all the available choices, I prefer Maggie."

Chris looked at his father, shrugged both shoulders, held both palms up, frowned, a wiseass series that said, how difficult could it be to just ask? He glanced at David who gave him an I-told-you-so single-shoulder shrug; I had told David the same thing earlier in the day.

Chris pressed the second boy forward. "This is my friend, Gus Dauvin."

From Gus I received only the handshake and a shy smile.

"Maggie," Antoine said, eyes sliding toward his son as he pronounced my name, "may I present Gus's father, Inspector Pierre Dauvin of the regional office of the Police Judiciare."

"You're friends?" I hesitated as I reached for Dauvin's extended hand.

"Of course. We were in school together," Antoine said. "As our boys are now. We played football together, like these two. Only better."

He suggested that the boys get back to work—it was nearly dinner time—and that the adults retire to the arrangement of sofa and chairs in front of the fireplace at the far end of the room.

Dauvin and I made our way toward the chairs. Antoine went to a sideboard and, as he filled three glasses with cider from a stoneware pitcher, he spoke with David, in French. "I told your mother that I will get the croissants in the morning and pick up Grand-mère Marie; she is making the soup. Are you able to get the bread for lunch? Take my car."

"I'll go, Papa," Chris chimed in. "Just give me your car keys."

David flipped a pencil at him. "The world trembles at the prospect of you behind the wheel, Chris. Yes, Antoine, I will get the bread."

"Nice kids," I said to Dauvin as we sat down, proud that I had understood their exchange. Maybe my French was coming back; I had learned French easily, and had as easily lost it. Dauvin nodded and smiled, but obviously he did not comprehend what I said. I tried again, dredging up my fragmented vocabulary. He smiled again, but I doubt that I made myself understood. I was relieved when Antoine joined us.

First there was the ritual of sampling the cider—it was made on the estate, by Antoine—and compliments delivered, before he took the chair facing us.

It was clear to Dauvin that my French was not adequate to understand the message he carried—he never faulted his lack of English fluency—so he agreed that Antoine should stay and translate. But first he swore his old friend to secrecy: The reason he wanted to speak with me here instead of at Grand-mère's house was that no one else was to know until after the funeral tomorrow that there were questions about the manner of Madame Isabelle's death.

Antoine seemed sincerely shocked—I watched for his reaction—when it was explained to him that Isabelle's death had not been an accident caused by some wild California driver, but something more sinister. Dauvin assured us that the police—the LA County Sheriff, Interpol, and the Police Judiciare—were actively investigating, had been through all of last week, but discreetly for the moment. The case was complicated, of course, had presented some unusual difficulties, he said, but several avenues were being pursued, and there had been some success. He would not give us any of the specifics, but he did tell me that I must be cautious, and gave Antoine the obligation to be not only my protector but the protector of the entire Martin family. My cousin's shoulders went back and his hand reached out and covered mine. Of course, he said, no need to worry.

Dauvin looked into Antoine's face, the concerned expression of an old friend. I understood enough of what he said next to figure out that Isabelle's death reminded Dauvin of the event that took away Antoine's mother, the angel of the house, three years ago. Except that Isabelle had not been driving a car, and no one had dared to suggest suicide. I also understood that Dauvin was worried. When he realized that I understood the gist of what he said, he blushed.

There was a ruckus at the front door, a confusion of female voices speaking at once, shoes hitting the floor, the sound of a ball bouncing. A teenage girl a few years younger than Chris and Gus, all coltish legs and energy, entered the room dribbling a soccer ball between her stocking feet. She lifted the ball with a toe and bounced it off her head. Antoine reached out and scooped the ball from the air before she could catch it.

"Lulu, Lulu, think of your poor mother. Football stays outside."

"*Allô, allô.*" Lulu kissed both her father and Dauvin, and stopped in front of me, eyes wide, eager face still rosy from the outdoors.

"Say hello to your cousin," Antoine said.

"Call me Maggie." I rose to exchange cheek kisses.

"Hello." She turned to give her brother a quick wiseacre glance; the big question had been answered. "Maggie." Then she looked back at me. "Do you have children?"

"Yes. My daughter Casey will be here tomorrow."

"How old is she?"

"Nineteen."

I saw her disappointment. "How old are you?"

"Fourteen." She shook her head. "I am the baby of the family."

A woman, speaking in rapid French, came in carrying a pair of muddy soccer cleats and an armful of jackets. Obviously, this was Antoine's wife, the mother of Chris and Lulu. She was a surprise to me: thick, curly dark red hair blown wild by the wind, flashing green eyes, wearing jeans and a hooded sweatshirt. When she spotted me, she stopped in mid-sentence.

As she came toward me, I met her halfway. I offered her my hand and my cheeks, and said, in my best French, "Hello, I'm Maggie Mac-Gowen."

"I know," she said in perfectly unaccented, very rapid American English. "Good to meet you, at last. My folks—they grow peaches outside Fresno—record all of your TV programs and send them over to us. When Tony and I were in college he told me all about you, the mystery child. Such a great story. We talked about looking you up and dropping in on you. We didn't know where you were going to school—I think we're the same age, forty-three?—but we knew where your family lived and it wasn't that far away."

I looked from her to Antoine. "Far away from where?"

"From campus," she said, offering a dazzling smile that gave evidence of expensive American orthodontia. "Tony and I met at Davis—University of California at Davis, Ag School."

Again I turned toward Antoine. "I had no idea."

He shrugged, smiled. "I always had a weakness for California girls."

"And California fruit-tree propagation." She put her hand on my arm. "I'm Kelly, by the way. And just so you know, I'm not the only foreign bride in this tribe, if you were wondering why they deign to speak English from time to time." She leaned toward me and lowered her voice. "Wait till you meet the other one. As they say over here, *oh-la-la*."

"Aaahhh." At the suggestion of that other one, Lulu gripped her throat and performed a death spiral, dropping onto her father's lap and burying her face in his neck. She pleaded, "Promise me, not her. They aren't coming are they?"

"Of course they are," he said, smoothing her tousled auburn hair. "And you will be a gracious hostess, or I will scalp you."

"I won't share my room with Jemima."

"Of course you will," Kelly said, ignoring the dramatics. "Upstairs to the shower, Lulu. Dinner is in half an hour. David, maybe you should wrap it up. Those two studmuffins can absorb only so much calculus at a sitting."

Dauvin stood to exchange *bises* with Kelly, after which she bent down to kiss her husband. "Freddy drove in right after me, Tony. You should take Maggie over and introduce her."

Antoine nodded, pried himself from his daughter's arms and out of his chair.

Ready or not, I thought, time to meet Freddy.

Antoine and I walked Dauvin to his car to receive his last words of caution, condolences, and good-byes. Dauvin handed me his card, a stiff piece of cardboard printed with raised police insignia, and told me that tomorrow he would be at the funeral and at Grand-mère's house afterward for tea. But if I wished to speak with him, I should not hesitate to call at any hour. He assured me that he was sincere when he said, call at any hour. Then he aimed a questioning finger at Antoine. He nodded; of course, his translation services would be available at any time, as well.

As Dauvin drove across the compound and out through the gate in the stone wall, I looked up at the turreted entrance to Antoine's house and asked, "What was here before this?"

"Until recently, a simple house; I grew up there. My parents took down the burned-out ruins of an old stone barn that once held the cider press and the Calvados distillery and built a home on its foundation."

He put his hands in his pockets and resumed his elegant slouch, a posture that said he was thoroughly comfortable with himself and with his place in the world. And, maybe, with me.

He said, "Shall I tell you the story about what happened to the barn?"

"Yes, please."

"It isn't a pretty story, but it might explain some things to you about our family and about this place."

"I would like to hear it."

He took a breath and began. "During the war, the last one, my grandfather, Henri, was in the French army, as his father had been during the Great War of 1914, and his grandfather had been when the Germans invaded in 1871. Three generations, three German invasions."

We began to walk slowly across the compound toward Isabelle's house to meet Freddy. "So, in the early months of the last war, the Germans captured my grandfather and put him into forced labor, but he managed to escape. For a while, some members of the Resistance hid him in the crawl space under a house in Belgium. They helped him with fake papers and he eventually made his way home. But, when he arrived here, he discovered that this region was under German occupation, and to make the situation worse, there were German soldiers living in his house." Antoine pointed his chin toward Grand-mère's house. "Local girls were impressed to cook and clean for the soldiers, and…"

He hesitated, uncomfortable, obviously searching for the right words. I said, "They took the girls to bed?"

"That's a delicate way to explain a very ugly situation, but yes, that will do." He canted his head back to indicate his house behind us. "In the old barn, cider and Calvados were stored in barrels on the ground floor, and upstairs there was a dormitory for the workers. The girls stayed there. My other grandmother, Grand-mère Marie, was among them."

He smiled gently. "I believe you met her grandaughter, my cousin Julie."

"David's mother?"

"Yes," he said. "So, Grand-mère Marie was very young during the war, not much older than my Lulu is now.

"At night, the Germans, drunk on the cider and Calvados they had with their dinner, would come out to the barn looking for more to drink, and for the girls who lived upstairs."

He took a deep breath. "My grandfather was furious that the village tolerated the situation. He went storming into the village to gather the men together to attack the Germans, but the only men left were either very old or very sick. So, he went looking for Grand-mère Élodie. They were already betrothed, and she was already working with the Resistance. He found her hidden in a convent in Lessay, protected by the nuns.

"Grand-mère and Grand-père came up with a plan. First, they collected knives from the farms around, sharp little pruning knives and the ones used to castrate bulls and horses. Grand-mère sneaked into the barn and instructed the girls how to use the knives to rip a man's jugular out of his neck—and whatever else they chose to rip out. She told the girls to give the soldiers plenty to drink with dinner that night, and to invite them out to the barn afterward for a village celebration of the bottling of the new season's Calvados—a local tradition, they were to say.

"That night, when the Germans came to the barn for the celebration hoping for more drink and village girls, they did not leave again.

"It is said that some of the soldiers were only dead drunk but still breathing when Grand-père marinated them in Calvados—fifty-proof stuff—and set the barn on fire. All that alcohol made a magnificent fire, so big and so bright that it became a bit of a legend around here. Grand-père destroyed his own barn to reclaim his estate and save its people."

Antoine looked at me, smiling wickedly. "People still say a lot of good booze was lost for a noble cause that night. But the truth is, it wasn't good booze. During the war, with no fertilizer, no chemicals to treat leaf mold and root rot, no oak for new brandy barrels, the Calvados made better fuel for a funeral pyre than it did a good drink."

"Quite a story," I said. "I'll remember to go to bed tonight sober and to lock my door."

He laughed. "Don't worry. You aren't German. Around here, Americans are the heroes who kicked out the Huns for good, remember?"

"But does anyone think of me as the invader?"

He shrugged. "We'll see, yes?"

Feeling uneasy about his answer, I moved on to another topic. "Does Isabelle's house have a story?"

"Not a very interesting one," he said. "She took down an old storage shed and built a model of energy efficiency long before that became a fad—you could say it has a zero-carbon footprint. At the time she built it, she was working at the nuclear power plant nearby at Flamanville, so it was convenient for her and Freddy to live here for a few years. Later, it was a weekend house for her.

"On the outside, the house looks a bit sterile, but it is really very nice. Very comfortable and efficient, cheap to maintain. And there's a greenhouse in back."

"What was she like, Antoine?"

"Your mother?" Both shoulders came up: what can be said? We were no longer walking, but standing in the middle of the compound, facing Isabelle's house. "She was very brilliant, and maybe because of that she could be impatient with people who weren't as smart as she was. And, of course, none of us was smart enough to keep up with her in some things, except maybe David and Grand-père; she was very close to both of them. But she was never cruel intentionally, but sometimes—" He thought for a moment, his eyes on the house but his mind some distance away. "Sometimes, she could be erratic. My wife described her as a space cadet. Do you understand the expression?"

"My father was something of a space cadet, too." From Antoine's description of Isabelle, I could see where Dad might be added to her short list of acceptable people. My dad was the smartest person I ever knew, but he could lose his way between the campus and our house, a distance of a few blocks.

"Also, I think that both your mother and my father inherited from their parents a very strong will." Antoine looked down, making arcs in the gravel with the toe of his shoe. "For example, when Grand-père and Grand-mère wanted their property back, nothing could stop them. In that case, it was called heroism. But, in another situation, that force of will could be called, simply, stubbornness."

His description, sympathetic but not sentimental, was helpful to me. My very brief meeting with Isabelle showed me how determined, how willful, she could be when she wanted something. Or felt she was entitled to something? I would have to work on that.

Antoine, eyes still downcast, sighed deeply. "Your mother criticized my father for building what she thought was, in her words, an unsustainable, inefficient throwback of a house that was neither historically representative nor esthetically pleasing," he said. "On that, my mother agreed."

"Your mother wasn't happy here?"

"On the estate, yes, of course. She grew up here. Her parents grew up here."

"Here, on this estate?"

"No, the property adjoining," he said with a wide sweep of his hand toward somewhere in the dark. "But she thought Papa's house plans were horrible."

"And he was stubborn about them," I ventured.

"Exactly," Antoine said. "Before the house was completed, my parents separated."

"Because of the house?"

His head came up. "More because there was another woman. You will meet Gillian later tonight, I think. They're coming over from London."

We were still a few yards from Isabelle's front door. I was freezing, but tried not to show it because I wanted Antoine to keep talking. I sensed that there were things he needed me to know, for his benefit as well as for mine. I rolled my nearly numb hands into the bottom of my sweater, using it as a makeshift muff.

"What does your father, Gérard, do?" I asked.

"He's a developer, always working on a big scheme, he and Gillian together. He develops properties and arranges financing. She is an estate agent—she markets the properties." He pursed his lips, shrugged, frowned, meaning he did not think much of his father's schemes, and probably not much of Gillian, either. "Usually, they work on big commercial projects. But their latest one is very personal."

I thought of the ugly house: one house didn't make a big project. I asked, "What is he working on?"

"He wants to take out half of the farm operations to build a large subdivision here. He can't sell the land, of course, because it belongs to the family, to all of us. But he can offer leaseholds, if we agree." He looked at me, wanted my reaction. When I winced, he nodded, and continued.

"Over the last decade, many thousands of British retired people have migrated to France—to many parts of Europe, actually. For years their pound was so valuable against the euro that they could live like princes over here on their pensions, almost twice as well as they could live in England."

"So your father wants to develop a community for English retirees?"

"Yes. Complete with a golf course." Antoine scowled. "He calls the development Le Vieux Château, the old château. On the prospectus there is a drawing of the house—hardly old, is it?—and some bragging about the Calvados and Camembert we make here. But of course, they would no longer be produced by us if he gets his way."

I was appalled by my vision of ranks of identical stucco houses with faux turrets tacked on the fronts, all built around a frozen golf course. "Grand-mère agreed to this?"

"No. Never. But Papa still thinks she will come around. Or, forgive me for saying this, she will die first; Grand-mère is almost ninety."

"You said he wants to develop half the estate. Why half?"

"When we lose our Grand-mère, a sad but certain eventuality, Papa will inherit an undivided half of the land here." He was still studying me. "And Aunt Isabelle would have inherited the other half. But…"

"Good Lord." I saw flashes of possibility. "What happens now?"

"You and Freddy inherit Isabelle's half interest, equally."

"Me?" I felt the ground open up: You know that fantasy we've all had, maybe during a dark hour when you didn't know how you were going to pay the rent, and you thought how perfect it would be if someone you never knew died and left you an inheritance? I've had that fantasy, except that never did I pencil in a murder, a possible suicide, some really ugly infidelity, and myself as a linchpin in an ongoing family drama. Under the circumstances, all I could think to say was, "Holy crap."

"Exactly."

"What does Freddy think of your father's plans?"

"You'll have to ask Freddy," he said. "But the issue may resolve itself. When the big economic crash happened in 2009, the pound collapsed with it. And Papa's plan? *Merde*, shit. No one is buying houses. With good luck, the economy will stay shitty long enough for the whole plan to evaporate."

"I understand what you're saying," I said. "But for all our sakes, let's hope for a recovery."

"Of course," he said without enthusiasm. "Papa is still optimistic that things will turn around, but it will need to happen very soon or all is lost for him. You understand that a development on such a large scale requires enormous forward planning, and the start-up expenses are huge. To get launched, he borrowed short-term money at high interest, expecting advance sales to generate income to service the note and attract investors. But, of course, the bottom has fallen out. There are no sales, no investors, and the note came due."

"So it's finished?"

He shook his head. "To buy himself more time Papa took on new loans secured by liens against his expected inheritance."

"That's dicey," I said. "Not to mention a bit premature."

"It's not uncommon to encumber one's expectations." Antoine shrugged. "Grand-père did it after the war to get money to replace the trees in the apple orchard with healthy stock. The difference is that Grand-père managed to pay off the loans, and my father has not. He has missed enough payments that he is in default and the lien holders are preparing to assume his right to title."

I shuddered. "Strangers will claim Gérard's share of the estate when Grand-mère dies? Tell me that can't happen."

"I'm happy to know you feel that way, cousin." He pulled his right hand out of its pocket and offered it to me. I took it and kept it because it was warm. He said, "Cousin Maggie, meet Lien Holder A, *moi*. Bébé is Lien Holder B. And you and Freddy are now Lien Holders C, as co-heirs of your mother."

"You all lent Gérard money so he could continue with his scheme?"

"A bailout so he could service his debt without involving strangers, not to pay off his debt. In the end, it wasn't much of a gamble, and not a huge investment. We did due diligence; thank Freddy for investigating.

Papa is so far underwater and his prospects for finding new money are so small that unless he finds a very large cash miracle very soon, we have prevented him from continuing with his scheme. And we got it cheap."

I didn't add, And prevented your father from destroying your livelihood. I knew the lengths our grandparents had gone to save their property. How far would Antoine go?

—9—

THE FRONT DOOR of Isabelle's house opened, and a shaft of light shot across the compound. A man I assumed to be my half brother Freddy stood silhouetted in the doorway. He was taller than Antoine, broader in the shoulders. Even before I saw his face, I saw something about him that was eerily familiar.

"Hey, farm boy," Freddy called out. "It's fucking cold out there. Don't you know enough to bring the poor woman inside where it's warm? What, were you raised by cows?"

I did not know how to interpret that conversational stream. I got the idea earlier, after overhearing angry voices in Paris, that Freddy wasn't happy about something that just might have to do with my sudden appearance. And now, here I was, standing nearly on his doorstep.

I looked at Antoine to see how he reacted for cues about what I might need to be prepared for, and saw him smiling, relaxed.

"Soft city boy, goddamn hothouse-raised flower," Antoine called back, gently impelling me forward by the hand. "It's perfectly balmy out here. We were just discussing going for an ocean swim before dinner. You tough enough to join us?"

There followed some prolonged hugging, back slapping, multiples of *les bises*. In the process, Freddy's grief broke through his façade of bonhomie. He held Antoine in a desperate embrace and wept into his cousin's shoulder. Antoine expressed his own grief, professed his love for Isabelle, and for Freddy. When they broke apart, Freddy pulled out a handkerchief and blew his nose. He turned to me, started to say something, gave it up, wrapped me in his arms, pressed me tightly against his chest and sobbed some more. I patted his back while I waited for him to regain his composure.

Antoine put an arm around Freddy and, with Freddy supported between us, we walked this family clutch further inside. Antoine guided us to a sofa in the salon, poured garnet-colored wine into three stemmed glasses, and brought it to us.

As Antoine ministered to Freddy, getting him to take a drink, I, a stranger, felt embarrassed to be in the middle of a very private situation. I turned away, looked around, looked for anything that might reveal Isabelle to me.

Antoine had been correct; Isabelle's house, though austere on the outside, was very comfortable inside. Radiant heat rose up from the ceramic tile floor, warmed my feet, found its way under my skirt to warm my legs. The furnishings were obviously selected for comfort and practicality, an eclectic mix of very old and fairly new chests and tables, a variety of lamps and upholstered pieces that all seemed to get along together; the velvet cushions under me were stuffed with down. Two walls were covered with shelves crammed with books. But oddly, I thought, there were no framed photos, nothing sentimental, on those shelves.

Freddy blew his nose again, gasped a few times, got his breath, sipped the wine, sat back and took a good look at me.

"I'm Maggie," I said.

"Of course. You look just like pictures of Grand-mère when she was younger." He gripped my hand and stared into my face. Tears spilled down his cheeks. There was a hitch in his voice when he said, "At last, we meet."

Again, I had that sense of familiarity, only it was stronger with Freddy than it had been with the others. I caught myself staring, comparing our similarities—same eyes, same hair and hairline, male and female versions of the same hands, similar overall carriage. If I had been born a boy, I would look very like Freddy. The realization was disconcerting.

Antoine was perched on the arm of a chair facing us, as watchful as a chaperone while Freddy and I shyly studied each other. He thrust his chin toward the dark stairwell and asked Freddy, "Where's your family?"

"Lena and I had a big row this morning. She threatened to stay away from Maman's funeral."

"Bloody stinking," Antoine said.

Freddy acknowledged that it was, but he added, "Any disrespect was intended only for me, and not for Maman. Lena was speaking out of her frustration with me, our present situation. I am sure she regrets what she said."

"Of course." Antoine's tone was rife with sarcasm.

"Believe me," Freddy softly begged. "Lena is taking Maman's passing very hard. Very hard. For two full days after she heard, my dear wife was distraught. Missed work. Kept to our room, paralyzed by her grief."

Antoine looked up from under his brows, dramatics notwithstanding, not buying the part about paralyzed by grief. "Did she rank the probabilities for you—will come, won't come?"

Freddy tossed him a sad smile before he turned to me. "Lena is an actuary at an insurance company. She can tell you the probability of just about anything happening that you can imagine."

"Important stuff," Antoine said, "like the age you are most likely to suffer a coronary if you prefer opera, say, to Mah-Jongg. She's like the bookmaker for the insurance company: when you buy a policy you bet against her odds."

"Handy to have around," I said.

"She is very good with numbers," Freddy said.

"So?" Antoine raised his palms in front of Freddy and juggled the possibilities: Will come, won't come?

"She'll be here, odds on," Freddy said with a marked lack of conviction. "I told her I was glad she wasn't coming. If she believes that, she'll be here by lunchtime. If she doesn't believe me, she'll let me stew for as long as possible and show up at the last minute."

"Where are the kids? She can't keep them away."

"Papa is bringing them in the morning. Lena wouldn't let me take them from school early today." He sighed heavily, drank more wine. "I stopped by Grand-mère's house this afternoon and asked her to excuse Lena and the kids from dinner tonight. She wasn't happy, but what can I do?"

"Get a lawyer."

"I can't afford divorce," Freddy said, smiling ruefully. "Not with the market as it is. I am *fauché*." He raised a fist and twisted it as if snapping off something. "Broke. Doomed, trapped in my Lena's tender clutches."

Freddy turned to me. "Sorry, terrible way to welcome you. I am indeed happy that you're here, sister of mine. I apologize for letting this frankly beastly situation get the better of me."

"All things considered," I said, "I think you're doing very well."

"I'll drink to that." And he did.

He looked over the rim of his glass at Antoine. "Speaking of men who need a divorce lawyer, when is your father arriving?"

"He said he and Gillian would be here for dinner." Antoine checked his watch. "Grand-mère expects us at seven, and it's quarter to now, so there's hope the Chunnel is blocked and they can't get through."

"Where are they staying?"

"We get them. Papa and Gillian have the guestroom, Jemima goes in with Lulu. Chris is giving his room to Grand-mère Marie for the weekend and sleeping in the little office. So that leaves Bébé on the sofa. Can you take him in?"

"Love to, please, yes, give me Bébé," Freddy said, relief or delight bringing color to his cheeks. "But if Gillian still won't walk past the portrait, don't get the idea that they, too, can come here."

"Ah," I said, reacting when I realized exactly who the devil was that the portrait of the mother angel protected against: Gillian, the step-mother.

"I need to get home." Antoine rose from his perch and took his empty glass back to the sideboard. "Kelly won't be happy if Papa and company arrive and she's left alone with them."

Freddy rose, stretched, exchanged *la bise* with his cousin. Our cousin.

Antoine asked me, "Shall I walk you back or do you think you'll be safe enough with this urban wimp?"

I looked at Freddy, made sure he was smiling about this character-ization of him—he was. I exchanged cheek kisses with Antoine. "Thank you for everything, especially for the story. I'll make sure Freddy gets to dinner on time."

As Antoine turned to leave, Freddy called after him. "Don't forget to close the door behind you, farmer. This isn't a barn, you know."

Antoine, his back to us as he walked away, chuckling, flipped us a backhand wave. "Sissy."

There was an awkward moment when Freddy and I were alone. I broke the silence.

"You and Antoine, you're very close," I said.

"We are as much brothers as we are cousins, Bébé as well," he said. "Only four days separate me and Bébé. Now might not be the time to say this, but their mother was sometimes more mother to me than…"

"Than Isabelle?"

He tilted his head, yes, and rose to replenish his glass.

"Tell me about her."

Freddy grew thoughtful, watched the wine flow into his glass as he poured, took a sip before he answered my question.

"She gave me all that she had to offer. But…" He walked back across the room and sat in a chair opposite me, put his feet up on the table between us, studied the inside of his glass a moment before he shifted his attention to me.

"Let me tell you this: Whenever I was out alone with Maman, I was always terrified that she would forget about me and leave me some-where. She wasn't negligent—please don't think that—but she would start thinking about something and simply forget I was there. When I was older I would follow behind her and pick up the things she left behind, her handbag, her shopping."

"Did that ever happen? Did she ever leave you somewhere?"

He nodded. His face showed only fondness, maybe nostalgia at that point. "I could always call Grand-mère or Papa or Aunt Louise to come and rescue me, depending where I was when she forgot me."

"Louise?" Hearing his aunt's name, I choked up. Didn't expect that reaction to happen, and didn't know why it did, except maybe that it caught me unawares. My name is Margot Eugenie Louise-Marie, and I had no clue where any of that came from, until that moment. I asked, "Who is Louise?"

"Antoine and Bébé's mother. Our aunt." He cocked his head and studied me again before he said, "You can't remember, of course, but Aunt Louise was your godmother. She always remembered your birth-days with candles at the church."

"Do you have any idea who Marie and Eugenie are?"

"Marie Foullard, of course, Aunt Louise's mother."

Antoine had referred to Grand-mère Marie. "David's grandmother?"

"Great-grandmother," he said. "She is your other godmother. You'll meet her tonight. Eugenie? I don't know. Some saint?"

I tried my first shrug, hoped it conveyed, *who knows?* When he smiled wistfully I decided I had performed the gesture well enough.

"Maman and Aunt Louise were the closest of friends," he said. "They grew up together; the Foullard estate adjoins ours. I think that she was the only one who ever fully understood Maman, accepted her eccentricities. When Maman would feel sad about losing you, she would comfort her."

"I didn't know," I said. "I'm sorry."

I rose, crossed to the sideboard and set my glass next to Antoine's. So strange to learn that all of my life there were people, total strangers, praying for me, lighting candles for me, weeping for me, wondering about me, following my career—watching me on television, Kelly told me—claiming me. It was as if I existed in two parallel universes at once: one was the world I knew, the other a shadow world inhabited only by the specter of a lost child. I felt disoriented—okay, and jet-lagged—and longed to put my arms around Casey, that solid artifact of my known and familiar world. It was going to be a long night.

I was so lost in thought that I didn't hear Freddy walk up beside me. As he set his glass with the others, he said, "I was prepared to hate you, Maggie. All of my life I was jealous of you. I used to wish that you were here so I could beat you up. But now that I meet you, I don't feel that way. It's not fair to blame you for something you knew nothing about."

"Thank you." I touched his arm. "I admit that I feel a bit lost right now. You all know who I am, but I don't know any of you."

"Don't worry. You'll be fine," he said, smiling into my face. "Everyone will be really kind to you. Until they get to know you, of course. When they stop being so kind, that's when you'll realize you're accepted as a member of the family."

"Good to know." I glanced at my watch. "We should get ourselves to Grand-mère's. But before we go…" I took a deep breath. "Freddy, I have…" I started to say Isabelle's, but said, "I have our mother's ashes. I don't know whom to give them to."

"The curate will come to the house tonight to settle details about the funeral tomorrow and take the prayers of anyone who wishes him to hear. We will give the ashes to him then."

I liked the way "we" sounded.

"One more piece of business," he said. "Maman's solicitor—here we say *notaire*—wants to discuss her will. I made an appointment with her Monday morning in Lessay. I would like you to be there if you can."

"All right. Tell me where and when." I met his eyes. "Are you ready for dinner?"

"Still too sober for a family evening, but yes." He took a leather jacket off a hook beside the front door and slipped it on.

On our way out, I said, "Antoine speaks English with a California accent, and you speak English with a British accent."

"London School of Economics for graduate school." He shrugged. "I met my wife there. She studied statistics."

"What do you do?"

"Investment banking. Though, the way things are right now, maybe I will have to move in here and learn how to make cheese."

"Would that be so awful?"

"Not for me," he said. "But for my wife? Disaster."

As we walked across the compound, gravel crunching underfoot, I asked another of my many questions. But, as I've said, I ask questions for a living. "What happened to Aunt Louise?"

"Very sad." He wove his hand through the crook of my elbow and leaned his head close to mine to deliver a confidence, even though no one was near enough to overhear. "Three years ago, her car went over a cliff near Barfleur and straight into the sea."

"What happened?"

"No one saw."

"Did your wife assess the probabilities?"

"Endlessly."

"Was it suicide?"

"I never thought so," he said. "But everyone knew she was distraught, perhaps desperate."

"Because of Gérard's affair?"

He nodded. "She discovered that Uncle Gérard not only had a mistress, but also there is a child."

"Jemima?"

"Yes. Antoine's half sister Jemima is almost exactly the same age as his son Chris."

"How cruel," I said, having gone through something similar with my first husband, except that my uncle had managed to keep both his affair and child secret for a decade and a half, while I knew on the day a certain dip stick turned pink that my life, and Casey's, was about to change.

Gérard's affair outlived his marriage. I wondered about the woman, Gillian, who had waited in the wings all that time. There must have been moments—months, years—when she expected her lover to dump the legal wife and make her, and their child, legit. What level of delusion, or cussed determination would that take?

Oh, hell, we all live in some state of delusion or another, or so my film partner Guido always says. How else can we get through the realities of our lives? For the lover whose paramour had known that one day their child would receive a share in a French estate, legal marriage might only have been a conventional nicety, not a requirement: Gillian's daughter, like me, had as equitable a claim on family assets as the children born within a sanctioned union. In France, legally there is no such thing as an illegitimate child. I wondered what satisfaction that fact might have given Gillian over the years.

"What Gérard did to Louise was cruel, of course, yes, but there was more," Freddy said, drawing me back to whatever he had been saying. "A local notary came to Aunt Louise for her signature. Gérard assumed his wife's permission to encumber land she inherited from her family, to include it in his development. Louise of course would not sign, and instead she began an investigation. That's when she learned that while

Gérard was trying to screw her out of her birthright, he was screwing another woman, his long-time business associate in London, a woman she detested."

"And so Louise divorced Gérard?"

Freddy shivered though he wore a leather jacket, so I didn't think he was cold. "Louise died first. Shortly after our aunt was buried, Gérard married Gillian and gave his name to their child." He tilted his head toward Antoine's house. "And he built that abomination."

"Where Antoine now lives. Where he and Bébé hung a portrait of their mother that Gillian won't walk past."

He laughed. "You catch on fast."

"But if it's Gérard's house…"

He swept his arm in a broad, all-encompassing arc. "For as long as she breathes, everything here belongs to Grand-mère. Our grandfather left her *usufruit*, lifetime use of the estate. She decided that Antoine and Kelly should live there, in that house, close to her. It's practical because Antoine manages all of the farm operations. Besides, Gillian hates us and hates this place, so they rarely come near us. They haven't visited since Easter."

"Poor Uncle Gérard, commuting between women," I said. "Was it Louise in Normandy Friday through Sunday and Gillian in London Monday through Thursday?"

He shook his head. "When Gérard received a promotion to head the London office of his company—a big promotion—Aunt Louise wouldn't go with him."

"She wanted to raise her sons in France?"

Again Freddy shook his head. "They were already grown. Antoine and Kelly were married by then, still living in America. Bébé was working in Paris."

So, then, Gérard and Louise separated a long time ago. She stayed in Normandy near her mother while he took comfort in the arms of a mistress in London. Then Gérard upset the status quo by futzing with property that wasn't his to futz with; I wondered how bright my uncle was. Or did he just feel entitled?

I shivered and Freddy wrapped an arm around me, drew me close to him. It felt very nice. The brother I knew, Mark, used to cuddle me in his long arms, read to me, talk me through thunderstorms, explain some of the realities of life my parents were reticent about broaching. I worshipped Mark. I still mourned him. Freddy could hardly give me the same feeling of sanctuary I used to feel when engulfed within the web of my lanky big brother's embrace, but there was welcome comfort in his presence.

I admit that I fought some resentment—how dare Freddy presume to be my brother?—but caught myself up short, reminding myself that Freddy had just lost his mother, and I, a stranger, was the closest blood relation he had in the world, and he was mine. Weird, for both of us.

"One more question," I said, freezing, anxious to be inside the spotty warmth of Grand-mère's house. "If you can stand it."

"Of course."

"Will you tell me about Claude?"

"My father?" Freddy shrugged, a quick one, a short story to tell. "He is a school teacher in Chantilly, outside Paris. Very intelligent, but not up to Maman's standards; he went to a lesser university. They separated when I was very young, and eventually they divorced. I think that the best and worst I can say about my father is that he works hard and is constant, without much imagination. When you meet him, you will be able to decide about him yourself."

Freddy reached for Grand-mère's door latch, but paused before he lifted it. "Tomorrow, I hope we will be able to talk further. Alone. We have much to decide, sister."

—10—

FREDDY AND I walked into the middle of a meltdown in progress. I saw Julie Breton peer in from the kitchen, quickly assess the scene unfolding in Grand-mère's salon, and retreat immediately.

A sulky teenage girl, as implausibly blond as she was impossibly thin, had removed herself to a far corner where, arms crossed, posture rigid, she scowled at the man and woman nastily tiffing nearby. This gloomy triptych had to be my Uncle Gérard, his wife Gillian, and their extracurricular daughter, Jemima.

"You saw it perfectly well, Gerry," the woman seethed, but he only shrugged, dismissing the importance of her issues. They were obviously so wrapped up in their argument that they were oblivious to our arrival or the various sets of eyes that checked on the course of their argument through a crack in the kitchen door.

Gillian was not at all what I expected. She was not merely well groomed. She had been polished, buffed, waxed, sanded, painted, coiffed, and then pinched into a hand-tailored spring-weight silk pantsuit until she looked absolutely untouchable.

My notion of a mistress was a woman who would drop her clothes at the wink of an eye to engage in whatever level of sweaty, messy sex her lover desired, and to comfort him whenever his spirits felt ruffled. I could not imagine this woman, my aunt-by-marriage, ever agreeing to participate in any activity that involved sweating, mussing, or comforting. Alabastrine is the only word I can conjure that might describe her: carved of cold, white stone.

Gérard, a full half foot shorter than his wife—a difference she exaggerated by wearing ridiculously high heels—and at least twenty-five years older, wore a sweater under a beautiful tweed jacket. He looked every bit the country squire, albeit one with a massive domestic problem.

"They painted 'Scullery Entrance' over the back door," Gillian said, urging her husband's ire to rise on her behalf. "You know as well as I do they intended that for me."

"If their sense of humor bothers you," Gérard snapped, "then enter through the front door."

"I will not. Not with *her* hanging there. They did it intentionally, Gerry. To hurt me. What are you going to do about it?"

The stick figure in the corner chimed in, "Yes, Daddy, what are you going to do about it? I refuse to share a room with that horrible child."

Gérard looked up finally when Freddy cleared his throat. When he saw us, he blushed furiously, humiliated.

"Please." Gérard grabbed Gillian by the elbow and squeezed until her eyes popped wide, a signal she seemed to understand meant to shut up, because she did. He hissed to her, "Remember where we are, and why we are here."

"Uncle Gérard, this is…" Freddy began to introduce me, but Gérard had already turned his back on Gillian and came rushing toward us, arms outstretched toward me, cooing a greeting.

"Here you are, our little Marguerite. I would know you anywhere." He kissed my cheeks wetly, held my hands and gazed into my face. Gillian shook herself, squared her shoulders and tottered along behind as Jemima dropped into a chair, arms still crossed over her chest, and turned her face to the wall, snubbing Freddy and me.

"You have turned this sad occasion into a reason to rejoice," Gérard gushed before making a pseudo-mournful face. "How your poor mother longed to see this day, her little girl back with her family. What a shame that this is what brings you home to us."

I did not know how to respond to that. Was Gérard sincere? Or was he loading on guilt, trying to shame me for my many years of absence?

Reminding me I was an outsider? Recruiting me? Ditching the argument with the wife? Perhaps because both Freddy and Antoine had described him as a schemer, I was wary of Gérard and his intentions before I ever met him. Maybe that wasn't fair.

He leaned in very close to me and whispered, "We must have a quiet chat later, you and me. Alone."

Gillian dutifully exchanged *la bise* with Freddy, though no surfaces were actually touched in the exchange. When Gérard released me, she took my hand in a straight-armed English handshake; no perfumed kisses whizzed past my ear.

She offered some well-worn platitudes about how lovely Isabelle had been, what a terrible shock and loss, shame I never knew her, and so on. I sensed a lack of sincerity, the *faux* interest that might be a prelude to a sales pitch. Again, maybe that assessment wasn't fair. However, Gillian's immediate economic future just might rest on decisions made by Lien Holders C, me and Freddy. I had certainly found myself in an interesting position.

Gérard ordered Jemima to come and meet her cousin. Reluctantly, the girl rose. Poor kid, I thought, like me the inconvenient and breathing evidence of a husband's infidelity. I wondered if the family had accepted her, an unknown dropped into their circle. Beastly situation for a kid, I thought. As awkward as I felt in that place, at least I had the advantage of being an adult and having a return ticket in my bag. Did Jemima have a ticket of her own?

The clank of the front door latch followed by a gust of cold air announced Kelly's arrival. She carried a covered dish wrapped in a big linen kitchen towel, trailing the aroma of something delicious. Lulu reluctantly, but dutifully, followed her mother.

"Gérard, here you are," Kelly said, almost scolding. Perfunctory kisses were exchanged. "We saw your car and wondered where you'd gotten to. Tony and Chris have taken your bags out of the trunk and put them in your rooms. Jemima, Lulu is delighted to have you as her guest."

"Delighted," Lulu managed, and even managed a stiff offering of *la bise* to her teenaged aunt, who as stiffly reciprocated.

"Maggie, good, you've met everybody." Kelly offered her cheeks to Freddy. Before she left the room to take her covered dish to the kitchen she instructed Lulu to go tell her father that Gérard had been found. Lulu sped from the room, obviously happy to comply.

"Do you ride?"

It took me a moment to realize that Gillian was speaking to me. I followed her glance down to my feet. I was wearing flat-heeled boots that looked something like riding boots, but certainly cost nothing near what the real thing would.

I said, "I ride for fun."

"Do you keep a stables?"

"That sounds grander than the corral we share with a neighbor," I said. "We have a few trail horses."

She frowned, sort of; her forehead refused to wrinkle. "What breed is that?"

I shrugged—it was becoming a habit. The three horses we kept were quite a mix. I said, "They're family pets, all shelter rescues."

"I see," she said, two words heavy with smug superiority, as if the answer were what she might have expected from a mongrel like me. "Gerry rides. Polo, you know."

"I hate horses," Jemima offered. "They smell. Worse than cows."

During the lull that followed that pronouncement I could hear activity in the kitchen, several women speaking rapidly in French, and all at once it seemed, as Kelly joined them. I was tempted to excuse myself and join them myself. But before I could, the kitchen door burst open and a very old woman wearing a severe black dress burst through, with Grand-mère following in her wake. The woman made a beeline for me, walking surprisingly fast though she needed a cane for support.

"Moggy, *ma chère petite* Moggy," she said, tears running down her face as she reached for me, letting her cane clatter to the stone floor.

Just at the moment when she wrapped her arms around me and smooched my face I realized that if I said Maggie with a French accent, it would sound like Moggy. So, *I* was her dear little Moggy. But who was she? And what was she saying? I could only catch random machine-gunned words. With a glance, I appealed to Freddy for help.

He touched her hand and said, "Grand-mère Marie, have I become invisible?"

She turned to him, beaming affection, tapped his face for his impudence before she kissed him. What she said to him I understood: You were always jealous.

He smiled, he shrugged, as in, what can I say? So, here was my godmother, Marie Foullard, who had helped Grand-mère and Grand-père slit the throats of German soldiers. Such a tiny, sweet-faced woman, who would think it possible?

Grand-mère—my Grand-mère Élodie—was making the rounds,

welcoming her son Gérard and his family. Antoine arrived with Chris and Lulu, David with them. I saw David's mother, Julie Breton, watching from the kitchen with Kelly, her cousin by marriage, at her side as greetings were exchanged with the newcomers, and as the sound level rose. Gérard saw Julie, broke away from the family huddle and crossed the room headed toward the kitchen door.

"There you are, Julie," he said, hands extended toward her. "How have you been?"

"Excuse me," she said, saying something about a pot of soup—that much I understood—before she turned away and disappeared into the kitchen, door closing behind her.

Stopped halfway, Gérard seemed chagrined, unsure where to turn. Apparently he hadn't expected a cold shoulder from Julie, who was his dead wife's niece. Possible hard feelings? Let me count the ways: first a mistress, then a shady attempt to wrest away her inheritance. I wondered if Julie might have inherited something from the Foullard estate, as Louise had, and how might Gérard's plans have affected that property? In a way, I had to admire Gérard for even daring to show his face. Or, did he fear what might happen behind his back if he didn't show?

Grand-mère Marie looped her arm through mine, and leaning on me as much as on her retrieved cane, she walked—hobbled—me over to the sideboard and poured us each a glass of deep ruby-colored port. She talked to me nonstop. I asked her to forgive my pathetic French and to please speak more slowly, which she remembered to do as she told me a long story. The parts I understood were, she helped to bring me into the world, she gave me my first bath and changed my first diaper, and I was so-o-o-o tiny, pink as a little rosebud. As she talked, she would reach up and pat my cheek and make cooing noises, as if I were still a little baby; I had to be six inches taller than she was. She pulled a silver locket out of the bosom of her dress, opened it, and showed me the little face captured inside: me.

I recognized the photograph that the little face had been cut from. My parents had a framed copy of the full snapshot in their den, taken when I was a toddler, perched on my father's shoulder, picking an apple from a tree. Obviously, there had been some communication between the two families after I left France as a baby. Unless…

Until Mom told me that I had named myself Maggie, I assumed that my nickname came from my brother and sister, who called me Maggot. So, if I named myself, how old was I? And where was I when I did that? For no good reason I had assumed that my father removed me from Isabelle's arms when I was still an infant, but no one had actually told me that. Maybe, because the new story about my origins replaced a made-up story about my birth, the image I still held in my mind was of an infant arriving during a terrible storm. And maybe that was incorrect. The estate had several orchards. Where was the apple tree in the photograph?

Grand-mère joined us, beaming. Her old friend Marie cupped both our faces in her hands and told us we could be twins. Grand-mère thanked her, but said Marie should apologize for comparing me to an old hag. They both laughed.

I asked Grand-mère, "How old was I when I left here?"

She looked me directly in the eyes, smiling fondly, her dry hand stroking my cheek. "Two years, four months, and eight days."

Gillian interrupted by wedging herself between me and Grand-mère, cutting me out as neatly as a cowboy cuts a calf from a herd. She placed a solicitous hand on Grand-mère's arm. "My dear, Gerry and I are quite concerned about you being alone in the house. We thought it best that we should stay here with you tonight, to be close."

"Very kind of you, my dear, to think of me." Grand-mère patted Gillian's hand where it rested on her arm. "But don't you think Gérard should be with his family? His grandchildren haven't seen him since Easter."

"But—" Gillian ventured.

"And I won't be alone. Marguerite is here with me." Grand-mère excused herself and went to speak with Julie about the table.

Nice try, Gillian, I thought. But Grand-mère saw through you.

Gillian aimed her attention at me. Looking down from her perch atop her stilettos, she said, "I am confused, as are the others. What is your surname?"

"My late husband was Mike Flint."

"And MacGowen?"

"My first husband."

David touched my elbow, presented me to his father, Jacques Breton. Jacques was an older version of his son, and as handsome. His skin was weathered from working outdoors, as Antoine's was. And, like Antoine, he wore enviably comfortable slacks and a beautiful handmade sweater. There was about him, as well, an air of confidence, a man at home in his world.

Jacques was the estate's cheese maker, and he was very proud of his product. With David to bridge the language gaps, Jacques invited me to the kitchen to sample some of his Camembert. His wife, Julie, scolded him for being in the way and for feeding me cheese before the meal and not waiting until after. He silenced her with a noisy kiss on the lips. She chastised him for that as well, but the brightening in her face belied the protest; she liked the kiss just fine, and he knew it.

Jacques was rightfully proud of his cheese. I am not an expert, but the fully ripened Camembert he gave me on a crust of bread was better than any I had ever had: hints of butter, salted nuts, fresh cream, just an edge of the bitterness the French believe enhances other flavors. He glowed when I described what I tasted in the cheese, asked if I found any hint of apricots. I tasted again, said no, but that I did have an aftertaste of pepper. He nodded and invited me to drop by his cheese plant—the *fromagerie*—for a tour. With an affectionate wink he told me he would teach me the proper way to milk a cow. I caught the innuendo. So did Julie, who punched his shoulder in reproach.

When I returned to the salon, I found the family settled into a few conversational clusters, most of them holding glasses of something: wine, cider, scotch. For a moment, I stood on the outside and watched. An attractive group of people, I thought. And not one among them looked like a murderer. But after all, what does a murderer look like?

All families have issues among their members, certainly. But for the time being, and perhaps because of the occasion and out of respect for Grand-mère and Isabelle, this clan had set those issues aside. Even Jemima was engaged, talking with Chris, Lulu and David in an apparently civil manner, from time to time even laughing.

Jacques came from the kitchen carrying a huge, steaming porcelain soup tureen, with Julie behind him giving orders: Don't spill it, set it in front of Gérard's chair, there isn't enough bread. When the tureen was safely landed, she announced, *"À table,"* and a general movement toward the table began.

Grand-mère, standing at the head, asked me to sit on her right and put Freddy on her left. As Gérard seated his mother, Freddy held my chair for me, and patted my shoulder for reassurance when I was settled.

Conversations continued, three or four of them at a time, volume rising and falling, some laughter, some intense debates. It all felt very familiar, not unlike the atmosphere around the table at my parents' house in Berkeley when there were guests for dinner.

Tears suddenly stung my eyes. I took my napkin from beside my plate, and looked down as I laid it across my lap, hoping no one had seen the emotion that spilled over.

All day, there was a profound question percolating at the forefront of everything I had learned, and that I had not dared to ask about. These were decent, responsible, educated, relatively well-to-do people who seemed to love their children. How could they have let a little rosebud of an apple-picking girl who was only two years, four months, and eight days old get away from them? Forever.

— II —

WHEN I AWOKE, there was only the barest hint of morning light coming through my window. I had no idea how long I had slept, or what time it was. And, for a moment, I wasn't certain where I was. My body clock was no help.

I reached for my telephone on the night table, turned it over to see the time. It was after seven in the morning, but where was the dawn? The day before, I had been surprised when the sun began to fade before four. Now, where was the dawn? The short, late fall days of the northern latitudes were something I was not accustomed to, and didn't much want to be.

The house was quiet. No smell of coffee came up the stairs. I pulled on long johns, and over them sweatpants and a hooded sweatshirt, then thick socks and running shoes. I slipped my telephone into the pouch of my shirt, and went outside.

To say the gray morning was brisk would be a gross understatement. With every step my shoes cracked through an icy crust on the ground. I was tempted to go back inside and crawl under the lovely, warm down-filled duvet on my bed, but my body felt stiff, and stressed, and I was curious to see what I could of the estate, unfiltered by my many hosts.

So, I took a deep breath, steeled myself against the cold, and set out at a fast walk, moved into a jog when the kinks from a long flight, followed by a day spent going from car to parlor to car to parlor, began to work loose. It felt good to be out in the open and alone with my thoughts. By the time I passed through the compound's gate I was running at a steady pace, not thinking any more about kinks or footfalls, letting the fragmented bits of information I had acquired over the past week sort themselves into coherent streams. Or not. There were still plenty of unattached bubbles of fact and supposition floating around.

The previous night, after dinner, I called Rich Longshore and asked him how the investigation was going. He told me they had a witness who saw a man steal the car that ran down Isabelle. The witness thought he could identify the thief if he saw him again, but his description fit half the county's male population between the ages of eighteen and thirty: medium height, thin, dark hair. One bright spot of hope was that the thief had been talking to someone on a cell phone as he approached the car, and the witness thought he sounded "foreign," though he couldn't pinpoint the accent.

Records from the closest telephone cell towers were being searched and there was a good possibility the police would be able to narrow down both the sender's number and the receiver's. But it would take time. Other than that? Nada.

Rich again warned me to be careful.

When my Uncle Max didn't answer at his home, his office, or his mobile, I called Guido.

"Max has worked out a tentative agreement for us with the studio," Guido told me. "Staff cuts will happen, but it looks like the series will not only be picked up for another season but you and I will get a raise."

"How did Max pull *that* off?" I asked.

"He told the suits that we're already working on the first project for next fall, and if the network didn't lock us in right away, Max was going to shop our series to another network. Or maybe take it to HBO or Showtime."

Good old Max, I thought. "Anybody ask him what the topic of this project might be?"

"He laid it out going in," Guido said, hesitating before he continued. "He told them that Maggie MacGowen was in Normandy at that very moment investigating the murder of the mother she never knew existed until the woman was murdered. Your story has been all over the news since last night, connecting you to the 'mystery woman' the police were trying to identify last week. I suspect Max planted the story for the benefit of the suits."

"He wasn't supposed to spill that she was murdered," I said.

"Well, he did."

"Some idiot took pictures that night of me and Isabelle playing tug-of-war with a shopping cart," I said, remembering a camera flash twice. "I suppose they've gone viral."

"What idiot took pictures?"

"I assumed he was a lurking paparazzo, hoping for a celebrity sighting."

"No photos have shown up," Guido said. "Yet."

I was more surprised than I was relieved. Those opportunistic photogs earn their living selling their wares to news outlets, the skuzzier the better. They mine news reports hoping they have something saleable in their files, and they waste no time getting their shots delivered. Even a small story, such as this one, would earn the guy who took the pictures outside the market a paycheck because of the news tie-in. I did not want those shots to be aired, but I found it odd that they weren't.

I fulminated with Guido for a few minutes about using my story as a project topic. I didn't want to exploit Isabelle's murder or possibly hurt people I cared very much about, specifically Mom. Maybe later we'd do something, I told Guido, and only some parts of the story, and my mom would have to agree before we did anything.

Guido suggested that it was only fair for us to do a full-on examination. Over the years, he reminded me, we had snooped into very personal corners of various people's lives and broadcast their secrets on national television. Now it was my turn for the exposure. I told him I would think that over. And, I told him, if he were concerned about playing fair he had better come up with a story of his own that was worth telling. He laughed, said that if that was the case he'd have to either invent something or commit something.

After talking with Guido last night, I called Mom, but got only her machine. I was worried about her. This morning, I was still worried about her, wanted very much to hear her counsel. But I would have to wait until evening to try her again. By then, the funeral would be over. We had a lot to talk about.

In the meantime, I was determined to get a look at the estate. The sun was finally up, though "up" was maybe an exaggeration. There was no dramatic instant of transition from night to day of the sort I saw every morning in Malibu Canyon. Instead, the dark Norman sky gradually became a lighter shade of gray. Rain was forecast for the entire weekend, maybe turning to ice. Now, I thought, before the weather broke, might be my best opportunity to get out and explore.

I ran down the center of the estate's narrow perimeter road, a typical sunken road of the region, the sort that bedeviled American tanks when they were put ashore on D-Day in 1944; the landing beaches were about thirty miles to the east. The sides of the road were thigh-high to me and were outlined on top by a continuous ridge of *bocage*, hedgerows of straggly cedar and thorny hawthorn. The hedgerows grew out of a root mass that was maybe three feet high and made a wall around the fields above the road.

On one side of the road there were carrot fields, the black soil plowed and resting until spring. On the other side there was an apple orchard, the branches of its bare, pruned trees as pale as smoke against the heavy sky. To my left, I could see the long white buildings of the cheese plant, the *fromagerie*.

I breathed in a rich mix of scents: Wasn't it Proust who said that smell is the memory sense? What I smelled, instead of Proust's madeleines at his aunt's house, was the rich damp soil of the carrot fields, the woodchip-carpeted orchard, a little bit of cow, and wood smoke from a distant fireplace. I knew I had smelled that particular earthy perfume before. I knew I had been in that place before. I just did not know when.

The snapshot of me picking an apple, was it taken near here? I tried to recognize a landmark, but the photo had been taken when the trees were in full leaf and heavy with fruit. My dad was in a light shirt, and I wore a little summer dress and sandals. The orchard now, at the approach of winter, looked nothing like the orchard in the picture.

I ran at an easy pace down the farm road, lost in a sort of reverie, mind wandering as I looked around, getting some idea about the place. Mike would call that dithering along as a nudge for me to pick up the speed. But Mike wasn't there and I could run at my own pace. It felt wonderful to be out, alone.

Without the background hum of a city or freeway, every sound I heard was crisp and bright in the cold air. When a gate closed or a hammer struck a nail, a tractor drove out into a field or a bird cawed overhead, the sound rang out over a long distance, and seemed much closer to me, accustomed to the white noise of the city, than in reality the sources of the sound were. Now and then I heard cars passing on the village road on the far side of the carrot field: a long approach, a sharp moment as it passed, a long retreat.

Before I could see it, I heard a vehicle coming up behind me. I turned left into a side lane, headed toward the *fromagerie*, and looked across the angle of the field. There he was, a white service van, probably a deliveryman, driving the rutted road as if he were competing at Le Mans. I waved, didn't know if he saw me, stepped to the side of the road in case he made the turn, and jogged along next to the soil wall. He had plenty of room to pass.

When the van didn't slow as it approached the T-intersection, a sharp right-angle turn, I expected it to stay on the straight-of-way. So I moved back to the middle of the road.

A sudden squeal of brakes made me turn, run backwards to look.

I saw a great spray of mud and gravel shoot out behind the van, knew that the driver was going to try to make the turn late, traveling too fast, and knew he was an idiot.

He fish-tailed coming out of the curve. I stopped to watch, expecting him to spin out and hit the berm on one side or the other. I gripped my cell phone trying to remember: was Paramedics 15 and Police 17, or the opposite?—so easy to get everyone in the U.S. by hitting 911.

Somehow—brute strength and dumb luck—the driver managed to regain control and straighten out. But during that maneuver, I caught a glimpse of the back of the van and knew I needed to get the hell away.

Painted on the rear doors—a flash-by that took a nanosecond to recognize—was a purple rooster, exactly like the white service van that nearly forced David into a collision yesterday as we left Charles de Gaulle.

I didn't wait to see who the driver was or what he wanted. I scrambled up the muddy road wall, snagged my sleeve on hawthorn going through the hedge, ripped it loose and started running across the newly plowed field as fast as I could, headed for the *fromagerie*; there were four or five vehicles parked there. It was tough going on the soft ground. I kept hearing Mike's voice in my head—put it in gear, baby, put it in gear—and got mad enough to find more speed.

Behind me, I heard the van come to an abrupt stop; a door slid open, someone swore, and then heavy footsteps and grunting followed me. I risked a look back, saw a man with the hood of his sweatshirt drawn tight around over his face, covering all but his eyes and nose, saw him struggle over the mud in heavy boots. I turned back and kept running.

The *fromagerie* was a short distance ahead. I aimed for it, hoping it was a haven. Suddenly, I heard a second vehicle coming from the direction I was headed. I saw a tiny green truck, not much bigger than a golf cart, with huge tires, careen around the side of the *fromagerie* at a crazy speed. The little truck drove straight across a gravel yard and onto a narrow tractor path that bisected the carrot field, and straight at me. This didn't feel good, a setup of some kind, I thought. I kept thinking about Isabelle walking in the night, the car following, lying in wait. The man behind me swore louder.

I veered off toward the orchard, not knowing where to go to escape what looked like a pincer maneuver to me—two men, me in the middle. I pulled my phone out of my pocket, gave up on the emergency number and punched Antoine's number instead, got a no-service-available beep, swore at AT&T, and picked up my pace.

The man behind me let loose with a great stream of profanities in English, fell back, and ran the other way, back toward his van. Ahead, the tiny green truck changed course and kept coming straight at me—the take-over man, I thought. The truck was small, but it mustered plenty of speed, its fat tires shooting out sprays of mud as it covered the ground.

I reached the edge of the field, scrambled through the hedgerow, dropped into the road, crossed, scrambled up the other side, dropped into the orchard. The truck couldn't follow.

In the distance I heard both vehicles, couldn't see either, didn't know where they were. Cold air burned my lungs, breathing was hard work: I ran. I vowed that if I got away intact, I would be more consistent about running. I looked at the vast orchard all around, bare trees and open sight lines, and fought despair; where could I go to get away?

"Maggie, Maggie!"

I risked a look, saw Jacques Breton coming through the hedgerow at the edge of the orchard, his clothes covered by a starched white smock, a white toque that looked like an inverted ramekin pulled low over his brows, black rubber boots on his feet. The green truck idled in the roadway behind him.

"Please, *chérie*. Stop. It is me." He held his arms out to me, imploring me as he jumped down from the root berm. He held a telephone in one hand. "I am so very sorry, my dear, I did not intend to scare you. I saw what was happening and came out to help you."

I stopped, doubled over and tried to gulp in air. Jacques looked like a starched Pillsbury Doughboy, but underneath all that white I knew he was in pretty good shape. Still, if I could ever manage to breathe again, if he were not the innocent he appeared, I could take him on, put up a decent fight at least.

"I have called Seventeen, emergency," he said walking toward me. "The police are coming. Who was that man chasing you?"

I managed to gasp out, "I don't know, but yesterday, leaving the airport, he cut in front of David, almost caused a collision."

"You saw him, in Paris?" Jacques seemed horrified. "Yesterday?"

"Yes." I managed to stand upright again and I could almost breathe, but my hands shook and my heart pounded, and not because of the run.

Jacques reached out and put a hand on my arm, pulled me gently toward him, searched my face. "He didn't…" The question was difficult for him to get out. "Did he touch you?"

"No. When I recognized the van I just started to run. And then, you came." I smiled at him. "Like the cavalry in a cowboy movie."

He tossed his head to one side, a little smile behind his pouty, self-effacing expression. "But I frightened you. I'm sorry."

"All I saw was a second truck coming at me. I didn't know it was you." I looked at the top of his truck—which was about all I could see of it—and back to him. "Jacques, how did you know I was in trouble?"

"I didn't." His palms came up. "But I was watching for you. Kelly called and asked me to keep an eye out. She saw you run out of the compound and thought you might be headed this way. When I heard a motor, I thought I should get in the truck and go take a look around for you. Then I heard swearing, saw you running from a man, and..." He leaned his head closer to mine. "My dear, considering what happened to your mother, is it wise for you to be out alone?"

Note to self: Antoine wasn't very good about keeping secrets. Even when asked to by Inspector Dauvin.

"I needed to stretch my legs," I said.

"Of course." Jacques took my elbow and walked me back toward the road, to his truck. He had to make several attempts at his invitation before I understood what he was saying. The police were coming, should be there very soon, and would want to talk to me about what happened. After they were finished, I could stretch my legs by accompanying him on a tour of the *fromagerie*. Neither his workmen nor his cows were good company in the morning, so I would be doing him a favor. Afterward, he would drive me home.

"D'accord?" he asked. Agreed?

"D'accord," I said, getting into his truck.

Mom seemed to be whispering in my ear something about not taking rides with strangers. If she were there, I might have replied that it's usually friends, not strangers, who are dangerous to us, but in the current circumstance that wouldn't be a good argument. Jacques was no stranger, and I felt thoroughly comfortable with him. Was that fool-hardy? Who knew?

During the short drive back to the *fromagerie*, he told me about the plant, his cows, and the two shifts of workers who came in every day of the week. Clearly, he loved what he did, the people he worked with, and this place. If Gérard managed to pull off his development, he would uproot far more than a few cows.

I was covered with mud. Jacques showed me to the workmen's scrub room—the plant was as clean as a surgical suite—and gave me a spare pair of his jeans, a pullover sweater, a stiff white smock to wear over them and a matching toque to cover my hair—required, he said—and black rubber boots like his own. The jeans were too long and a little snug in the hips, but were a great improvement over sodden sweats that were black to the knees, cold, and heavy with damp.

I was instructed to leave my dirty clothes in the hamper for the laundryman to take care of. Jacques had taken my muddy shoes from me when we walked inside, wrapped them in the morning newspaper, and set them beside the door to be cleaned by someone named Jochan.

Inspector Dauvin picked up David on his way to serve as translator. When I came out of the scrub room, I found the three men waiting for me in Jacques's office, all seated around a table drinking coffee. Dauvin looked me over.

"You look a proper cheese maker," he said, through David.

Jacques handed me a mug of strong coffee lightened with warm milk and pulled out the chair next to him. The two witnesses, he and I, faced the inquisitor and his translator across the table.

The inspector asked me to tell him what happened. I started with the van: it was white, full-size, not a make I recognized, not American. There was no registration plate on the back, something I had noticed the day before as well. I did my best to sketch the purple rooster for him; not an exact likeness, but a fair representation, I thought.

David remembered the incident on the freeway, and the van. He thought the rooster emblem belonged to a poultry company he had seen around, but he didn't know the name. The van was a Volvo, he said. He gave the model and year, both verified by Jacques. But, the day before, even though he had taken in those details, David had been more focused on the dimensions of the space between a BMW and a Honda that he needed to slip into to avoid a collision.

The car behind us, the one that would have hit our rear if David hadn't gotten us out of the way, was an older model Renault with primer paint on the hood, an old beater of a car. At the time, he'd wondered if the drivers of the van and the Renault weren't gypsies trying to set up a wreck so they could claim damages, an increasingly common ploy on the highways, and one he always looked out for.

Neither of us noticed the van's driver in Paris. It was my impression that the man who came after me was young, fairly tall, and not French; he swore in English. That last made Jacques and David exchange satisfied nods—not a local, a good thing. He wore dark pants, a dark hooded sweatshirt, and heavy boots like Doc Martens six-holers, not good for running through soft soil. He had a foul mouth, an attribute Jacques verified.

After he saw Jacques coming, the man doubled back, got into the van and sped away as maniacally as he drove in, chewing up the unpaved road quite a bit. Jacques had called 17, the French equivalent of 911, and gave a description of the van. Dauvin said an alert went out. Chances were good it would be found.

When we had nothing more to tell him, Dauvin closed his notebook. And then he scolded me for being out alone. Hadn't he warned me? It was very possible I was a witness to something on the night Isabelle was killed, even if I weren't aware of it. He leaned forward and, looking directly into my eyes, he said, "I am told by your Sergeant Longshore that a certain envelope was delivered to your work place, yes?"

I nodded. As soon as I recognized the white van, I thought about the explosive-sniffing beagle that walked in the network studio door and went straight to the FedEx mailer that was addressed to me. I said, "The man who delivered the envelope was not the man who chased me this morning. Different build; the other man was older."

That nugget of information seemed to interest Dauvin. Once again, he cautioned us all to stay quiet. They were developing information and didn't want to alert anyone prematurely, screw things up. After the funeral was soon enough, he said. But let him make the announcement of the murder. To myself, I counted off the people who already knew. When Dauvin got around to the big moment, it wouldn't be much of a surprise.

Dauvin told us he had a good man coming out to make tire and footprint impressions. Our tracks were certainly easy to find. Now, what to do about me?

Jacques claimed me. He had promised me a tour and a lesson on cheese-making, he said. He and his workmen would make sure I was well watched over. I thought it was a good idea, better than sitting around stewing. Dauvin thought not.

We all looked toward the door when we heard a car drive up, a car door slam.

"Jacques?" I heard Antoine call out. *"Où toi te trouve?"* Where are you?

"Ah," Jacques said with a happy lift to his brow as he rose from the table. "Croissants."

Sounded like a good idea to me; I was famished.

"Bonjour." Antoine came in from outside carrying a muslin bag, shed his shoes beside the door before he looked up.

"Ah, Maggie," he said, obviously surprised when he realized it was me draped in white dairy garb. "Have you taken up milking?"

"I'm thinking about it."

"Pierre, David, Jacques," he said, brows furrowing with concern as he looked from one face to another. "What's happening?"

Dauvin shrugged. "Madame wanted a tour of the *fromagerie*." Then he reminded Antoine that the croissants were getting cold.

With a shrug, Antoine pulled a basket out of a cupboard and dumped the contents of his bag into it, croissants still warm from the bakery—I could smell them from halfway across the room. He set the basket and a stack of *serviettes*—paper napkins—on the table in front of us, and poured himself a cup of coffee.

I followed David's lead and took a croissant, cradled it in a napkin, and ate it as it was. Nowhere in the world outside France can you find a croissant that comes close to the wonders of the real thing. Buttery, flaky outside, creamy and tender as air inside. And when they are still warm…

Jacques pushed a button on a speaker mounted on the wall and announced into it, *"Croissants, mes amis."*

Almost immediately I heard men stamping their boots outside the door. Out of a small refrigerator, Jacques took dishes of butter and jam, a pitcher of milk, and a plate of sliced ham, and set them among the mugs and small plates on the counter, next to a beautiful round of Camembert.

"I need to get home." Antoine rolled up his empty muslin bag. "More deliveries to make. Maggie, David, anyone need a ride?"

I exchanged a glance with Dauvin. He dipped his head in approval of the offer; his mouth was full of croissant.

I said, "Thanks, Antoine, I would appreciate a ride." I handed Jacques back his toque and smock.

David said he would like to hang out with his father for a bit, but Jacques reminded him that he had promised to help Grand-mère Marie with her soup pot; it was too heavy for her. David needed to go with us.

No one mentioned the morning's adventure to Antoine. I met Jacques's eyes. He raised his shoulders, a moue on his face—pouty lips. I read, Our little secret, or Yikes, what he doesn't know…

Antoine's red Mini station wagon was filled with the aroma of warm bread. On the back seat there were three more bags of croissants, one for each of the houses in the compound. He had left the engine running and the heater on while he made his delivery to the *fromagerie*, to keep them warm.

David moved the bags aside and climbed into the back. As we pulled out, I could see Jacques's tire tracks heading into the carrot field, and on the far side, two sets of footprints churned into the mud. Visually, I retraced my path, saw where I veered to go into the orchard, and where my pursuer doubled back. Antoine followed my gaze.

"That field was just plowed," he said. "Wonder what happened, cow get loose? I have to get out the tractor anyway. Looks like there was a mishap on the road in. Someone made a mess we'll need to grade before it rains."

The police had just arrived and were setting up a barrier around the tire and boot tracks with plastic stanchions and blue caution tape. We were waved around the site and ordered not to stop.

Antoine was ready to argue with the policeman: this was his family's place, his area of responsibility, no one had told him there was a problem that would bring out the police, he had a right to know. He rolled down his window, obviously to argue.

David said, "Drive on, Antoine. I'll tell you what happened."

Antoine turned around. I said, "Please."

I saw confusion, and anger, sweep across his face, but he caved to us. He closed the crack he had opened in his window and drove away, headed for the compound. I told him about that morning; David told him about Paris. Antoine grew visibly more upset as the story unfolded.

As he turned into the compound gate, I said, "Maybe it would be best for all if I get a room in the village."

Antoine put his hand over mine. "Absolutely not. Dear God, Maggie, if we can barely keep you safe with all of us around, what will happen if you are alone among strangers? No. Absolutely not."

He stopped his car inside the gate, got out, and with some effort, pulled the gate closed and latched it. From the racket the hinges set up, I wondered how long it been since it was last closed. Right after World War II?

"Not very practical," I said, "considering all the people who will come through that gate today."

Finally, he laughed at himself. "Wish we had a tower we could secure you in. But, in the meantime, I'm sticking to you like paste."

"Like glue," David corrected. "Sticking like glue."

"Whatever."

Antoine parked between his house and Grand-mére's. He took the three bags of croissants from the backseat and handed me Grand-mère's, gave Freddy's to David. To me he said, "I hope we can find a time to talk about some things, cousin. Some important things that will affect us all. Maybe later tonight?"

"Of course. You know where to find me."

Grand-mère was in the kitchen, setting butter and a plate of ham and cheese on the table when I walked in.

"You're up early," she said, offering her cheeks to kiss as I handed her the croissants. "Did you go to the bakery with Kelly?"

"No. Kelly is helping Grand-mère Marie with the soup, so Antoine went. He picked me up at the *fromagerie*; Jacques promised me a tour."

"Oh?" She poured us each a coffee with hot milk, and gestured to the chair I should take. "And what do you think of our *fromagerie*?"

"Very impressive," I said, neglecting to mention the drama that preceded the tour, or that the tour consisted of a brief peek. "A thoroughly mechanized operation, making cheese in a very traditional way. It's interesting, the old with the new."

My answer seemed to please Grand-mère very much. Inordinately so, I thought, though all she said was, "Jacques is a craftsman. He was taught by his father and his grandfather. We are very proud of our cheese."

I had already consumed one rich croissant that morning, but when Grand-mère offered me another, I accepted. French croissants aren't nearly as big and bready as the greasy dough-logs we call croissants in the U.S., but they are every bit as rich.

"Try the raspberry preserves," she said, passing me a small, lidded pot. "I made it last summer. I am also proud of my preserves."

She had reason to be proud; the preserves were tart and delicious. I wondered how these people ate the way they did and still managed to stay so thin. It wasn't yet nine o'clock and already I had eaten about a six-mile-run's worth of calories. I needed to find a way to get out for a run again, or else I'd need to shop for new clothes.

While we ate, Grand-mère told me what to expect during the rest of the day.

First, the family would come to her house for lunch. Afterward, there would be a simple religious service at the chapel of the Convent of the Sacred Flower, even though Isabelle professed to be an atheist. Following the service, Isabelle's ashes would be placed inside a niche in the crypt below the nave of the convent chapel. During the afternoon, guests from the funeral would come by the house for tea and cake. It was the local tradition, she said, seeming resigned to an all-day ordeal.

I would have taken her in my arms, but Grand-mère was so fragile that morning, maintaining her composure only by dint of great effort, that such a gesture would not have been a kindness. She was enough like Mom that I knew it was important for her to present a game face, to seem intact even when she felt otherwise. So, I served as her sounding board, and listened while she went over the details of meals and accommodations, responded when appropriate, all the time helping her to stay ten degrees north of reality, which was: she was preparing to inter her only daughter.

Every time there was a lull in our conversation, tears filled her pale eyes. As profound as her sadness was, I knew from my own recent experience, losing Mike, that the hard grieving would come once all her guests had gone away, the daily routines had resumed, and she was alone with only memories of Isabelle to fill a void where her daughter had been. My heart broke for her.

After we ate and tidied the kitchen, Grand-mère walked me around outside to show me her gardens, a way of filling time before lunch. There were still red cabbages, turnips, leeks, and late carrots growing, but she told me I had missed the garden at the height of its wonders. She pointed out the bare frames for peas, green beans and squash, and the raised beds for lettuces and asparagus. When she pointed out the trellises for her raspberries she asked me to imagine them heavy with bright red fruit. I had missed the flowers, as well, she said, sighing with regret.

"But that is the way of the year." With a wistful smile she pinched a shriveled pea pod from a limp remnant of a vine. "Now, while the orchards and the fields are at rest, Antoine is busy distilling Calvados from the cider he pressed in September. About the time he is finished, it will be spring again and the trees will begin to waken. And then—how can I describe it? Magic happens." She turned toward the bare orchard, raising her palms as if she were pushing up a window or bringing up house lights in a theater. "The trees blossom all at once. So magnificent that I cannot describe it." She gripped my arm and looked deep into my eyes. "But, of course, you will see for yourself."

Telling me about the estate made her happy, kept her distracted. As she talked about the seasons of the various enterprises on the estate, I got the impression that she assumed I would be around to see the full farm cycle, forever. I, however, had assumed that I would only be there for a long weekend and would maybe visit later if the weekend went well.

While I admit that the portrait she drew of life on the estate was seductive—never mind that the outdoor cattle enclosures on the far edge of the estate did stink and that all of the estate's enterprises required a great deal of back-breaking work—and I could imagine myself spending an earthy idyll in Normandy, I knew I was never going to be more than a visitor there. I had a life, and a job, and a family on the far edge of a different continent altogether. And, at least for the time being, that's where I intended to remain.

By the time we made our way to Isabelle's greenhouse I was feeling deceitful by simply being attentive. Grand-mère seemed to interpret any interest I showed, and it was all interesting, as my acceptance of my place there.

"I apologize for the state of things in your mother's greenhouse," she said as she ushered me inside.

The greenhouse was warm—stored solar-generated heat, she told me—and humid from the automatic irrigation system and plant respiration. There were still a few things growing, mostly herbs and lettuces, but everything looked to be in need of a good weeding and trim. Grand-mère asked me to imagine the greenhouse full of the colors of ripe vegetables, even in the dead of winter. She said, "All that is needed is more attention."

She told me that, several years ago, when her illness was diagnosed, Isabelle's doctors had told her to avoid direct contact with the soil because her illness left her vulnerable to bacterial infections; her white cell count was very low and her immune system was suppressed. But Isabelle disregarded their advice, as she disregarded any advice that didn't suit her, until last summer when a potentially deadly infection sent her to the hospital for a few weeks.

After she recovered Isabelle stayed away from the estate. There were some important affairs she needed to take care of, she told her mother. But once those affairs were settled, she would be back, the greenhouse would flourish again. She promised there would be lilies and iris in time for Easter.

"Isabelle should have known that could not be." Grand-mère sighed as she looked around at the sorry state of her daughter's greenhouse. "A garden is like a child. It cannot be neglected for a moment."

─12─

CASEY CALLED when I was on my way upstairs to shower. I was relieved to hear her voice and her assurance that all was well. Her flight over had been uneventful. Bébé was waiting for her at the airport in Paris when she came through Document Control as he told her he would be. He had taken her to buy a phone, and now I had the number captured in my directory. They were on the "freeway," driving as fast as a NASCAR racer, and would arrive at the estate right on schedule. Or before.

"So, Mom," she said. "You'll never guess who was on my flight."

"Elvis?"

"No, someone you know."

"I know it wasn't Guido," I said, a likely prospect. I had talked to him at home, in his house behind the Hollywood Bowl, hours after Casey's plane had taken off last night. "So, who?"

"Uncle Max," she said. "We sat together."

I wasn't surprised, indeed should have known when he didn't answer any of his phone lines that he was up to something. Bless his heart, watching over Casey and me, as always. He must have paid a fortune for a last-minute first-class ticket. I was very happy that he had come, because I had plenty of questions for him to answer. And I needed a lawyer right now.

I asked, "Is Uncle Max driving with you?"

"No. Bébé offered, but Max said he had a car reserved. Anyway, Bébé's car is so tiny I don't know where we would have put him. Max said to tell you he'll see you at the church this afternoon."

After her call, when I was in my room with the door shut, I called Max's mobile phone.

"Hi, sweetheart," he said as greeting. "I was expecting to hear from you."

"So, how's the weather in lovely Southern California?"

"Yesterday it was damn hot for November," he said. "I know that by now you've had a conversation with a little birdie named Casey, so you know damn well I'm speeding in your direction. And I do mean speeding. These Frenchies drive like maniacs, come right up on your bumper traveling nearly a hundred MPH. Scares the shit out of me."

"So, Max, another little birdie tells me someone leaked a story to the press about me and Isabelle."

"Guido also tell you I got you more money?"

"What if I don't want to make a film about my own sordid history?"

"You know you do," he said, "because it's a story worth telling."

He was probably right, but I wasn't anywhere near as certain about it as he and Guido seemed to be. Not yet, anyway.

"How's it going there, Maggie?"

"Curiouser and curiouser," I said, leaving out the morning's occurrence. "I'm being well treated. Awfully well. Haven't seen this many people so very happy to meet me since I went through sorority rush my freshman year of college. Something is up, Max. Everyone wants to get me off alone to talk about important stuff. Grand-mère already took her shot; she expects me to move in. I don't know who to trust, if anyone. I'll be very glad to see you and Casey. Are you staying at the house with us?"

"No, honey. We'll talk about why not when I see you. I'll be with an old friend over in the village of Créances, just a couple of miles from you. But I'll be at the church to watch your back this afternoon, unless one of these guys runs me off the road before I get there."

"Do you know a good French lawyer?"

"You betcha. The old friend I'm staying with. Why?"

I told him about my meeting with M. Hubert, and the document he wanted me to sign.

"You didn't sign, did you?"

"Of course not."

"Good girl. Anything else?"

"One little thing." I told him about being chased across a carrot field by a man who tried to run me off the road the day before. I listened to him spout off until his battery ran low, acknowledged the wisdom of his warnings, and told him to calm down and drive safely. He was of far more use to me, I told him, if he remained intact.

After we said good-bye, I found myself hurrying to shower and dress, magical thinking, I suppose, as if by getting ready sooner I would speed Casey to me. After the event that morning, I transferred fear for myself to fear for my daughter, and wanted her with me, under my wing, and not driving across France at what I knew would be insane speeds in a tiny car with a stranger, albeit one with a DNA link. It didn't work. The minute hand on my watch seemed frozen, the hour hand petrified.

When I was assembled, dress on, hair brushed, I checked myself in the mirror. The suitcase wrinkles had fallen nicely out of the gray funeral dress. An extra croissant and all that cheese hadn't yet changed the way it fit, but give them time. For warmth, underneath I wore a silk thermal vest, opaque tights the same gray shade as the dress, with thermal knee-length pants over them. Thinking about trekking across damp gravel, my boots would have been more practical, but low-heeled black pumps were more appropriate to the occasion. I opted for the pumps.

Again I looked at my watch. It seemed that time had hardly advanced.

Inspector Dauvin asked us not to discuss the cause of Isabelle's death until after the funeral, the suggestion being that he would make an announcement soon after, and from then on his investigation would become more open. At some point very soon, I would need to take Isabelle's things from my wardrobe and hand them over. I realized that the only opportunity I might still have to look at them was now, before we left for the funeral.

I took the black bag out of the wardrobe and pulled out the plastic hotel laundry bag into which Isabelle's personal effects had been packed—by whom I did not know. I spilled the bag's contents onto my bed and checked them against the typed inventory list stapled to the top: gold stud earrings, a Cartier watch, a brown leather handbag with her wallet, credit cards and her national I.D. cards, her passport, house and car keys, including keys for the Hertz rental car she picked up at LAX when she arrived. There were a few hundred dollars worth of euros and U.S. dollars and an open-ended return ticket voucher.

There was an LA-area map on which she, or someone, had circled the Malibu Colony and drawn arrows to locate her hotel and the market where she waited for me. She had also circled my studio in Burbank and the street where I lived. I needed to know how she found my address, because I am well sheltered from inquiring minds. It had taken Isabelle some genuine effort, perhaps some professional help, to get so close to me.

She was taking three prescription drugs, and one of them had been filled at the pharmacy next to the supermarket in the Malibu Colony. I wrote down the names of the drugs printed on the labels.

In Isabelle's wallet I found a clear-plastic sleeve that held two photographs back to back. One was a studio portrait of Freddy with an attractive woman and two handsome boys, doubtless his wife and children. The other held yet another copy of the snapshot of me sitting atop my father's shoulder in an orchard, the same shot that Grand-mère Marie kept in her locket and Dad had in his den. What had been the occasion?

Isabelle's copy had faded over time; the edges were frayed from handling. Where she folded it to fit into the plastic sleeve, it was cracked, torn. I thought it was sad that she kept a picture of her lost daughter in her wallet. And pathetic that the photo she had chosen also captured her former lover, my dad. Surely, during the two years I spent with her other pictures were taken of me but without Dad. Made me wonder.

In her change compartment, Isabelle had a little address book. I thumbed through it and found, written inside the front cover, two numbers with Los Angeles area codes, no names listed. One number was for the central information line at my studio. I dialed the other number and reached a recording for a private investigator that gave an address on Grand Avenue, downtown LA, near the federal and county courthouses.

It was only eleven A.M. in France, both too late and too early to expect anyone to be picking up a business line. I would try the investigator again later.

Isabelle's phone was still in the toe of a shoe in the closet. I retrieved it, accessed her directory and logs of incoming and outgoing calls, and compared those numbers to the numbers in the little book. She had called Grand-mère a couple of times. There was a call or two each made to Freddy, Gérard, and Antoine, and three to her doctor in Paris, possibly about the prescription she had filled at the pharmacy in the Malibu Colony. She called both LA numbers, the second one, the P.I., several times. And, she called two numbers in France that weren't in either her little book or in her phone's directory. I wrote down those numbers on the pad beside the bed, tore off the top page and stuffed it into my dress pocket, along with the address book.

I returned everything else to the plastic bag, including the phone. Being careful not to disturb the inventory tag, I pulled the drawstrings at the top and tied them into a bow.

I also went through Isabelle's suitcase. Good quality, well-maintained clothes, a cosmetic bag with the usual things, from shampoo to toothpaste. I admired the efficiency of her packing, a few well-chosen, coordinating pieces, and no inessentials; an experienced traveler.

Having learned very little, but with a few more questions to ask, I latched the suitcase and set it on the floor next to my bed, balanced the tied plastic bag on top of it. All of it was ready to be handed away.

Again, I checked my watch. Basing my estimate for Casey's arrival on the length of time it had taken Grand-mère and me to make the same trip yesterday, Casey should be at the house very soon. The call made me somewhat more anxious to see her face, safely in front of me.

From the wardrobe, I took my camel coat and the silk-and-cashmere Pashmina scarf Mike had bought me during a trip we took to Italy, draped them over my arm, and went downstairs to wait.

In the salon, Grand-mère's Paris couple, Clara and Oscar, were setting the table for lunch. After I hung my coat and scarf on a peg by the front door, I ventured into the kitchen following voices and found my grandmother, Grand-mère Marie, Julie, and Kelly. All of them were dressed for the funeral, with big white aprons protecting their clothes.

"Can I help with anything?" I asked.

"Oh, my dear, what a smart costume," Grand-mère said, giving me a top-to-bottom inspection. "The dress suits you well."

She wore a trim charcoal gray suit with black leather buttons, and no jewelry. Grand-mère Marie, in black, held a long wooden spoon over a soup pot, steadying herself with her cane, looked me over and nodded approval. Kelly and Julie exchanged glances, sly little smiles. I suspected that they, Kelly in a simple forest green dress and Julie in navy blue, had also passed inspection.

After first-of-the-day greetings were exchanged all around, Kelly stayed close beside me. Very close. Obviously, Antoine had told her about the morning's kerfuffle.

"I think we're all set. Just waiting for everyone to get here so Grand-mère can strike the gong," Kelly said. "Lunch is Grand-mère Marie's famous potato leek soup, followed by braised beef—not horse or goat, don't worry—and, of course, fruit and cheese after. Clara and Oscar will serve. They'll stay behind to clear away after lunch and set up tea and cakes after the service."

Kelly gave me a spoonful of the soup to sample, but didn't pause for comments. "There could be as many as two hundred people dropping by. This is a small village, and everyone is related to everyone else to some degree, so they will all make an appearance. Isabelle's work friends may come; don't know how many. We have plenty of cakes, and Jacques has brought cheese for the masses.

"The issue is teacups," Kelly added. "Several women have brought theirs over, as is the custom. With theirs and ours we have a good start. But we still need to be vigilant. When an empty cup is set down, we need to scoop it up, bring it here to Clara and Oscar for washing and reuse."

"The logistics need a general," I said.

Kelly hugged Grand-mère. "We have one."

Grand-mère patted Kelly's hand. "*Bien sûr*. But the true general is tradition. We merely do what is always done."

My telephone vibrated in my pocket. I took it out, recognized Casey's new number on the readout.

"My daughter," I said, and started to leave the room to take the call. "Excuse me."

"No, no." Grand-mère reached for my arm. "No need to go." She nodded at the phone in my hand, expectation on her face. She wanted me to answer it right there, where she could overhear.

I opened the phone. "Casey, what progress?"

"We're here," she said, jubilant. "We just turned into the drive. I can see the compound wall and the houses."

"I'll be outside waiting for you." I closed the phone and looked at the four faces watching me. "Casey and Bébé are just driving up."

All of the women in the kitchen followed me outside, everyone grabbing coats and sweaters from the pegs by the front door on the way. The day had grown colder, the sky heavier, portending rain, soon. Perfect funeral weather, I thought.

We stood together and watched as a small convoy of cars approached. In the lead was Antoine's red Mini station wagon, followed by a tiny, bright yellow and black Smart Car. A sleek green Jaguar sedan brought up the rear.

David, driving Antoine's Mini, pulled up beside Grand-mère's door and got out, opened the back hatch and took out a tall, thin wicker bread basket, a panier, with a dozen or so yard-long baguettes sticking out of the top. I remembered Antoine asking David to pick up the bread for lunch.

"Such a nice greeting committee," he said, grinning, as he came toward us.

"It's good to see you," I said. "My daughter and Bébé are right behind you."

"I wondered who that was with Bébé." David turned to watch the arrivals with the rest of us, arms wrapped around his long panier. The warm bread it held smelled wonderful. How could I be hungry again?

With much stirring of gravel, the Smart Car came to a quick stop next to the Mini. The passenger door opened and two incredibly long, thin, denim-clad legs emerged. Boot-shod feet found the ground, and then all six feet of my Casey unwound from the tiny car.

David was transfixed as he watched her rise to her full height and stretch. Kelly caught the panier as his grip around it faltered.

"Careful, son," she said, setting the basket on the stoop next to her. "Close your mouth, you'll catch flies."

The two grandmothers tittered with delight as they watched his reaction to my daughter. I wondered if they were scheming about great-great-grandchildren in their future. I wouldn't put it past them.

Casey scanned the assembled faces, smiled back at them, slung her duffel over her shoulder, and said, "Hey, Ma, meet Bébé."

Bébé, a compact, more hip version of Antoine—tight jeans, close-cropped dark hair, the ubiquitous three-day beard—joined the group. I thanked him for taking care of Casey, and he assured me that picking her up and having her company for the drive had been his pleasure. When Grand-mère Marie teased him about fitting all of Casey's length into his ridiculous little car, it was Casey who responded to her, in very nice French.

"The car actually has plenty of room inside." Casey hefted her duffel higher on her shoulder. "But it's a good thing I didn't pack a trunk."

"No problem." Bébé shrugged, with a pixie-ish smile. "I would simply have strapped either the trunk or the girl to the roof of the car."

Antoine told me that everyone loved Bébé. Almost everyone, anyway. Certainly, he had charm. And dimples.

Grand-mère moved forward and claimed Casey right away. Gripping both of Casey's hands, she said the same thing to Casey she had said to me when we first met: "I would have known you anywhere." Indeed, there was a marked family resemblance.

Grand-mère made general introductions, initiating a full round of *les bises*. David blushed furiously when Grand-mère formally presented him to Casey. As the two young people offered each other their cheeks, I caught Casey giving David a quick, but full, appraisal that ended with a smile of approval aimed my way.

During this noisy, kissy exchange, no one paid much attention to the green Jaguar that pulled up in front of Isabelle's house. All four car doors opened simultaneously. I recognized the three passengers as the woman and two boys with Freddy in the picture Isabelle kept in her wallet: Freddy's wife and sons. The driver was an older man, maybe in his late sixties, early seventies; feathery remnants of gray hair on an otherwise bald head, stooped posture as if carrying too much of the world's weight on his narrow shoulders. He gave us the barest of glances before he began taking luggage out of the trunk.

Freddy came out his front door, kissed them all, rough-housed with the boys a bit. He waved to us, took a leather bag from his wife's shoulder, and gathered his family to come and join our clutch. The older man picked up luggage and went into the house without another glance our way.

I leaned my head close to Grand-mère and asked, though I thought I knew the answer, "Who is that man?"

"Claude Desmoulins, your stepfather."

We were introduced to Freddy's wife Lena—pronounced *Lay*-na—and his two boys, Philippe and Robert. Freddy was very gracious when he introduced himself to Casey as her long-lost uncle. She had the oddest expression on her face, puzzlement, as she leaned toward him for the exchange of *la bise*. I thought she might have recognized the family resemblance she and I shared with Freddy. I still found my resemblance to this group of strangers to be more than a little bit disconcerting.

Robert, the younger of Freddy's sons—I had been told he was sixteen—after a foot-to-crown visual measurement of Casey, asked her if she played basketball.

"No," she told him. "Volleyball."

"Super," Robert exclaimed, eyes alight. It was Philippe, the eighteen-year-old, who asked her to show them the game sometime. They had watched beach volleyball on TV—the names of gold medalists Misty May-Treanor and Kerri Walsh came up—and apparently thought the sport was indeed *très* cool. I wondered which was more interesting to them, the game or the statuesque bikini-clad Olympic champions?

David jumped at the idea of a game. He said there was a nice sandy beach nearby at Anneville-sur-Mer. Maybe tomorrow they could set up a net of some kind, borrow one from a fisherman. A soccer ball would have to serve as a volleyball, but they would make do. Anyone who was interested could join the game. He feigned a jab at Bébé's flat midsection and added, "Those who are fit enough, of course."

Lena stayed a little to one side, aloof, shy maybe, hands primly folded in front of her, mouth drawn tight. Was it grief? Freddy said that Lena had been distraught over Isabelle's death. Or did I see disapproval of me and Casey in her posture, distaste for the mere fact of our existence on that exquisite face? Displeasure, perhaps, at being somewhere she simply did not want to be?

Lena was beautiful. But even if she were plain, she would seem beautiful merely by the grace with which she carried herself. I don't know how French women manage to look so perfectly pulled together, and chic, with what appear to be the simplest of elements. Lena's were: classically tailored woolen slacks and jacket, fine-knit sweater, cordovan leather boots and matching handbag, a silk scarf tied just so at her neck. Doubtless, the ensemble cost the equivalent of the GNP of a small country. Whatever the cost, everything she wore, including her chin-length brown hair, was understated, perfectly cut, perfectly fitted, perfectly natural. Perfectly perfect.

Poor Gillian, for all of her overwrought efforts, came nowhere close to Lena's apparently effortless elegance, no matter how much she invested or the hours she spent in the attempt.

Lena was reserved in her manner, a bit queenly. She studied me as if I were an oddity that might bite. As she exchanged greetings with the

others, I saw a shadow under her politesse, something more than re-
serve. If she were, as Freddy said, distraught about Isabelle, might Lena
consider the friendly banter of the group, banter she pointedly stayed
aloof from, to be inappropriate to the occasion?

Mourning, of course, travels a different path with every person. But
what I read in her demeanor was wife-in-exit mode. One of the first
signs I picked up that my marriage to Scottie was in trouble was his sudden aloofness around my parents, with whom he had always been very
close. If Lena, like Scottie, had made the decision to go, shows of affection for people she was leaving behind might not be worth the bother.

At one point, Freddy put an arm around his wife's shoulders. She
did not shrink away from him, but she certainly did nothing to encourage his affectionate gesture, or let him linger in the embrace. Almost immediately, in a tone that could freeze the tits off the devil himself, Lena
said, "Boys, we need to get ready for lunch."

She took her bag off Freddy's shoulder—I recognized the maker,
had a pretty good idea what she had invested in it—rounded up her sons
and walked away toward Isabelle's house. Their departure left a moment
of silence in its wake.

Freddy, chagrined, spoke first. "Bébé, do you need help with your
things? Antoine has a full house, so you're staying with us."

Grand-mère frowned. "Is Claude staying over tonight, Freddy?"

"Yes." He looked uncomfortable affirming this tidbit. "He's driving
Lena and the boys back to Paris tomorrow night."

"Then where will you put our Bébé?" Before Freddy could answer,
she hooked her hands around Bébé's and Casey's elbows and turned
with them toward the door, her entire focus turned on them. "You two
come with me. I'll show you to your rooms."

David followed them inside carrying his panier of bread, with Julie,
Grand-mère Marie and Kelly behind him. Freddy touched my arm, a
request to stay behind.

"Everything all right?" I asked him.

He shrugged, he wasn't sure. "I want you to know that Lena, my
dear wife, is a wonderful woman. But the last year has been very difficult
for her. She was accustomed to a certain life. But then financial nose-
dive. *Catastrophe*. The adjustment has not been easy for her."

I said, "These are challenging times for a lot of people."

He nodded, an understatement. "You were told that my family is
living in Maman's Paris apartment?"

"Yes."

"And you know she was sick?"

"Yes."

"When we moved in with her, everyone believed I was the devoted son, making sacrifices to care for his mother."

"I'm glad she had you."

He looked down, shook his head slowly. "We were a great inconvenience, I'm afraid. Maman cherished her solitude, an impossibility with two teenagers underfoot. But…"

When he didn't finish the thought, I said, "I'm sure it meant a lot to her to have her grandsons with her. Your boys are wonderful."

"Thanks to Lena." He shifted his gaze to the black-ribbon-wrapped wreath that had been placed on the front door that morning. Stress lines bracketed his mouth, making him look older.

"Will you move back to your own home now?" I asked.

He shook his head. "The truth is, we lived with Maman out of necessity. Maman's apartment, or here, those are the choices at the moment. And my wife…" His shrug was poignant. He had already told me that life in rural Normandy was an adjustment Lena was not interested in making. "She has a good position at her firm. In Paris."

"You'll figure things out, Freddy."

"Hah!" A quick reaction that reeked of doubt. He moved a small step toward me and met my eyes. "Now is not the time, sister, but don't forget that later you and I must talk. There are very large decisions to be made. And the outcome is very important."

"And I'm the unknown quantity, yes?"

"Yes." He shifted his focus toward Isabelle's house, and the door closing behind his family. "I hope we can agree on the best course."

I had no idea what the best course would be, only that there were several family factions. Out of respect for Isabelle, and guilt about the way I had treated her, until I understood what the issues were, I needed to stay unaligned.

All I could think to say was to repeat a lame cliché, "Things will work out."

"Of course. We'll find a better time to talk. Right now, please excuse me. I should see to Lena and the boys." He kissed my cheeks, turned and walked briskly back to Isabelle's house. I was tempted for a moment to call after him, to reassure him, to tell him that I would not be a problem for him, but I honestly could not make such a promise, yet.

Inside, as I hung up my coat, I spotted Casey, in stocking feet, creeping down the stairs.

"Sweetheart?" I said.

"Good, there you are." She came to meet me. "I was hoping to find some of that bread David brought in."

"We're going to eat in about half an hour," I said. "And you need to change."

"Bébé offered to stop and get something to eat on the way, but I was in such a hurry to get here that I told him I wasn't hungry. But, Mom, I'm starving. Do you have a cookie or something squirreled away?"

I looked around the salon. The table was set for lunch, but other than butter and some condiments there was no food set out yet. I told her we could probably talk whoever was in the kitchen out of something. But as I passed the sideboard, thinking *cookie*, I had a flash, and not knowing why, bent and opened a lower drawer, slowly, knowing it would squeak and give me away. It did. And, as also expected, inside the drawer there was a small cookie tin with a familiar picture of Mont St-Michel on the top. I took out the tin and opened it, knowing that inside there would be, or should be, little shortbread cookies, each with a dab of raspberry preserves filling a thumbprint in the center. The cookies were there.

As I offered the open tin to Casey, I glanced toward the kitchen door and saw that Grand-mère and Grand-mère Marie, probably alerted by the squeaky drawer, were watching us. They both had tears in their eyes.

Grand-mère Marie spoke first. "I told you, Élodie, she remembers."

I said, "Growing girl needed a snack."

"Delicious," Casey said around her first bite.

"They are your mother's favorite," Grand-mère Marie told her. "I baked them yesterday and put them in her secret place for her to find."

My grandmother raised the skirt of her apron to her face and wept into it. I went to her, put my arm around her and led her to a chair. She gripped my hand as she looked up at me.

"You do remember," she sobbed. "My poor little Marguerite, what else do you remember?"

⟶13⟶

"HERE YOU ARE."

Uncle Gérard's voice echoed along the gray stone corridors of the Convent of the Sacred Flower. While some members of the family were receiving communion from the local parish priest before the funeral service, Gérard had guided Gillian, Jemima and me into the bowels of the convent in search of a rest room. He remembered one near the refectory, the community's dining room, from earlier visits.

I was glad for the guide. The convent's interior passages were a windowless labyrinth full of sudden turnings and dead ends, and I doubt I could have made my way back to the chapel alone unless I'd left a trail of bread crumbs.

The company was surprisingly agreeable, as well. Gillian was flinty to be sure, but I began to see the real toughness underneath her fustian that, in a man, would probably be admired as dogged determination. She had clearly come up from some place she had no intention of returning to, or of ever seeing her daughter descend into.

And Jemima? I could hardly blame her for being unhappy about the forced show-up *chez la famille Martin*. Everyone was polite to her, overly polite. She understood the resentment that the mere fact of her existence generated among Gérard's other children, but understanding didn't make it any easier to live with.

While we were washing our hands and waiting for her mother to get all of her complex parts reassembled, Jemima quietly asked me whether, if the tables were turned and we were not gathered for my mother's funeral but her father's, people would behave as warmly toward her as they were toward me. There was such profound sadness in her question that I wanted to take her in my arms. My situation was strange. Hers was bloody awful.

The answer I wanted to give her, but didn't, was that her acceptance into the bosom of this family might depend upon how much of their future comfort rested with her. Instead, I said, "Give them time. When they get to know you better, things will be different."

She turned toward the door, the way back to the others, and shuddered. "And if not?"

"Then to hell with them."

Gérard must have checked his watch four times after Jemima and I rejoined him before Gillian finally emerged from the rest room. He never prodded or groused, though. And when she came out, he told her how lovely she was. It sounded sincere.

"My dearest and my dearest," he said to his wife and daughter. "If you think you can find your way back, I have been asked to take Maggie to meet the abbess. Will you excuse us?"

He got them started back in the right direction, gave instructions for the rest of the trip, kissed them both. We waited to see that they made the first turn, and then he put his arm through mine and led me away.

The ancient stone building was cold. Not merely drafty like Grand-mère's old house. There was a pervasive, solid, permanent cold in the walls and floors that came up through the soles of my shoes and seeped through the fabric of my heavy coat, made our breath visible in the air.

"Quite a maze," I said, looking into a dark side corridor as we passed. "I understand why Grand-mère hid out here during the war. Who could find her?"

He dropped his head near mine to share a confidence. "Rumor has it there is a network of underground tunnels that extend all the way to the beach, in case you need to escape, or to sneak in someone under cover."

"Is it true?" I asked, intrigued.

"I only know the stories." He whispered, "Remember, this is a convent. I have never been invited to explore its mysteries."

"I was told that I was born in the infirmary here. Do the nuns take in unwed mothers?" I asked. "Maybe sneak them in and out through the tunnels?"

"The nuns offer sanctuary and hospitality to anyone who asks, but unwed mothers specifically, no. As for sneaking, well…" He studied me, seemed to be considering something before he said, "Your mother did not need to hide herself. No, that is not the reason she came here."

"No?" I asked, hoping he would keep talking. When he didn't, I said, "A modern woman, a scientist like Isabelle, would surely prefer a hospital to a convent when it came time to give birth to her first child."

"Perhaps." Gérard checked his watch, a device to avoid answering. "The abbess knows more about it than I do."

We came to an intersection of corridors as a phalanx of black-habited nuns marched past, walking in pairs, an indistinguishable mass except for the faces, framed by stiffly starched white wimples, looking out from under their veils. No one acknowledged that Gérard and I were there. No one spoke at all. The only sounds were the reverberations of hard-soled shoes on the stone floor, the rhythmic *click-clack* of rosary beads swinging from their waists, and the fluttering of heavy black fabric swaying in cadence with the movement of unseen legs.

The wave of nuns was familiar to me. As a teenager I had been sent to a convent school for reasons that were never clear to me. The teachers, all in black habits, would sweep through the halls in a similar formation on their way to and from chapel every morning, hands buried inside their sleeves, rosary beads swinging. But the teaching nuns kept their eyes up and watchful, and they were never silent during their progress, nor would they have hesitated to speak to us: your skirt is too short, miss; see me after class, young lady; get rid of the chewing gum; do I smell tobacco? Seeing the nuns approach, I felt a familiar shimmer of general guilt for yet-to-be-enumerated infractions.

"Did you notice," Gérard said when they had passed by, "that all of the younger nuns come from the old colonial regions? They are African and Asian and Pacific Islander. What you will rarely see any longer is a European girl in a habit. It is possible that the future of the Mother Church lies beyond Europe. Interesting, is it not?"

"It is," I said, pondering the role of a time-worn institution such as this one in a modern, post-industrial state. Did it still have a function?

I kicked myself for not having a camera in hand to capture that black-shrouded procession, even from the back, and made a mental note to call Guido to begin talking about arrangements to bring our little film crew over. Damn, I hated Guido when he was right. How could I not make a film here?

Gérard cleared his throat. "I thought what Lena had to say at lunch was quite interesting, didn't you?"

"Interesting, yes," I said. "But I'm not sure it was the most appropriate topic to bring up at the time."

He thought that over. "No, probably not."

Lena, an insurance company actuary—an odds-maker of sorts—announced that if Isabelle were going to die in Los Angeles, considering all the factors—age, income, interests, neighborhood—the most likely cause of death other than natural causes would be a car accident. She admitted that the probability was very low, though Isabelle raised the odds when she went walking alone after dark.

No one mentioned the little factor that screwed up the odds: someone hired an assassin. I could not look at Grand-mère during Lena's discourse, and was relieved when Freddy pointedly changed the subject.

"Just along this way," Gérard said, guiding me through an archway and into a narrower side passageway.

"Gérard…" I said. There were a few things I wanted to know about my Sunday night dinner companion, and this might be my best opportunity. "Grand-mère told me you're a friend of Jean-Paul Bernard."

"Yes, we ride for the same polo club. Wonderful seat on a horse," he said. "Why? Do you know him?"

"I met him. He helped Grand-mère make arrangements for me to bring Isabelle home."

"You cannot call her Mother, yet?"

"Not yet," I said. "Is his family from this area?"

"Here? No, no. Versailles I think, or near there."

"Wife, six children?"

He made the most wonderfully dramatic sad face, *tsk*'d a couple of times while he wagged his head from side to side. "So tragic. His wife: one morning at breakfast, she looked at him with a funny expression on her face, she said, 'Oh dear,' and just like that, she was gone."

"Dead?" I was appalled.

"Brain aneurysm."

"Recently?"

"Maybe two years ago. Her passing was the reason he accepted the appointment to Los Angeles. A fresh start, you know? He has his son with him; nice boy, about the same age as Jemima."

We made another turn. About halfway down the passage an open door spilled light as well as the sound of voices into the corridor. Casey and Kelly, and someone I did not recognize, were having an animated conversation. I looked up at Gérard, but he answered my question before I asked it.

"Looks as if our daughters have already come to visit Ma Mère, the abbess." With a formal bow and sweep of the hand, he ushered me to the door. "Shall we join them?"

Ma Mère was a tiny woman about the same age as Grand-mère. She sat with her hands folded atop a large desk in a perfectly ordinary-looking office furnished with metal filing cabinets, copier and fax machine, with a computer and printer on a side table. A collection of small space heaters took the edge off the building's chill, but only just barely.

The abbess turned from Casey and Kelly when we entered, and smiled up at us. Her dark eyes had an unmistakable twinkle.

"Mom, thank God." Casey rose from her chair in front of the desk to hug me. "We've been waiting. It took you so long I was afraid you got lost."

"I was in good hands," I said, not mentioning how long Gillian kept us waiting while she patched and repainted.

"Ma Mère was worried." And so, I understood from the tone of her voice, was Casey.

The abbess, smiling sweetly, made eye contact with Gérard and gave him a little nod, an indication that she was waiting for him to do something. He understood.

"Ma Mère," he said, "may I present my niece, Maggie MacGowen?"

"Maggie MacGowen?" One of her index fingers broke free of the clasped hands on the desk and waggled at me, those brown eyes full of mischief. "I was present the day Father Victor christened a little child named Marguerite Eugénie Louise-Marie Duchamps, right here in our chapel. So who can this Maggie MacGowen be?"

"It's complicated," I said. She did not offer me either her hand or her cheek.

"Indeed." When she raised her thick eyebrows, they disappeared under her wimple. She looked pointedly from Kelly to Casey to Gérard in turn. "Would you all please excuse us? I would like to have a word with this child who bears such a complexity of names."

"Certainly," Kelly said, rising.

Casey stood her ground. "I won't leave you here alone, Mom. I promised Uncle Max."

I grasped her hand as I turned to the abbess. "Ma Mère, may my daughter stay?"

There was an instant of hesitation before the abbess nodded her consent.

Gérard leaned over and gave me *la bise*. "I will tell Maman you are safe."

I thanked him for being my guide, said good-bye to Kelly, and settled into the chair she had vacated. When they were gone, I turned to Ma Mère and, still holding Casey by the hand, told the abbess, "I know that you might feel some delicacy about discussing certain matters in front of my daughter. But she is an adult. She knows just about as much as I do about Isabelle Martin. I value her counsel."

"Yes?" The abbess offered a small smile, but I had no clue what she might be thinking. Nuns are like cops. They don't reveal anything in their faces that they don't want you to know. "And what is it you think I might be able to tell you, delicate or otherwise?"

"Maybe you can give me some pieces to the puzzle that is Isabelle." I looked at Casey. She gave me a reassuring smile and kept a grip on my hand. I loved that she was there with me, my wise child. I told the abbess, "Until ten days ago, I did not know Isabelle existed. Until ten days ago, I thought the woman who raised me was my natural mother."

"So, is it the puzzle of Isabelle or the puzzle of Marguerite you wish to solve?"

"Both," I said.

She reached over and tapped a button on the corner of her desk two times. It buzzed in the next room—I could hear it through the door.

"I thought maybe some tea," she said, hands clasped again. "There is time before the service. Élodie will excuse you from accepting condolences if she knows you are with me. Now, it seems you have questions?"

"To begin," I said, "I have learned two things about Isabelle. First, she was an avowed atheist. Second, she was a scientist. So, why did she come here to give birth instead of going to a modern hospital?"

Ma Mère considered the question. "Did you consider that she might have come to us for sanctuary?"

"Sanctuary?" I thought about various connotations of the word. "For safety? For protection?"

"That, yes." She gave the slightest nod. "But we also offer sanctuary for people in need of quiet contemplation. A young woman who found herself in Isabelle's situation might be of an unquiet mind, do you agree?"

"Of course."

"Isabelle came to us twice before you were born," she said. "The first visit was in the winter, shortly after she discovered her…" she glanced at Casey while she chose her words "…her situation. There was much for her to consider, and she wanted both peace, as you said, and protection."

Unquiet mind I understood, but danger? I asked the abbess, "Protection from what?"

"The influence of others." Ma Mère took a long breath and studied her folded hands for a moment. When she looked up again, she addressed Casey.

"Katherine?"

Casey was taken aback when she heard Ma Mère use her given name. "Everyone calls me Casey."

"I understand you were christened Katherine Celeste. Is that correct?"

"Yes," Casey said.

Ma Mère gave her a curt nod; question asked and answered. "Katherine, it might surprise you to know that even before your mother arrived on this earth, in some parts of Europe it was already legally possible for a young woman who found herself expectant to…" again a hesitation "…to terminate."

I asked, "Did Isabelle contemplate that option?"

"Option?" Ma Mère did not like that word. "If Isabelle considered taking such an action, she wisely rejected it very early on. However, she felt pressured to act."

I thought through the possibilities of people who might want her to get an abortion. There were several. But the obvious one made my stomach hurt just to think about: the father. I fought back an unwelcome welling of tears. It was a visceral reaction, not a logical one.

As she watched me struggle, a horrified pall washed over Casey. Her voice broke when she said, "Don't even think what you're thinking, Mom. Grandpa would never have wanted that. Grandpa loved you, Mom. He came over here and saved you."

When I had enough breath, I said, "After the fact, yes. But when he first learned… Poor guy sure got himself into a pickle, didn't he?"

"A pickle?" Ma Mère frowned; she didn't understand the use of the word.

"Une situation difficile," Casey said.

"A pickle." The abbess made a note of it on a small pad of Post-its.

The door at the back of the office opened and a young nun came in bearing a tea tray. Ma Mère spoke to her in Chinese. The young woman responded with a few words, set the tray on the desk next to her abbess, and, with head bowed, backed out of the room.

Casey turned to me. "Ma Mère is fluent in six languages."

"In this world, it is necessary. How easy it must have been when all Christian children were educated in Latin." The abbess picked up the teapot and began to pour. She held up a flowered china cup on a matching saucer and asked me, "Milk?"

"Plain, please," I answered, and she handed me the cup.

The hot tea felt as good to hold as it did to drink. Even in the abbess's office with all of its little space heaters, we needed our coats. I wondered how many layers of long johns Ma Mère wore under her heavy habit.

"You said Isabelle came to you a second time," I said.

"Before you were born, yes." Ma Mère poured milk into Casey's tea, unasked, as she would for a child, and extended the cup toward her.

"After the summer, near the end of her time, Isabelle came back to us. The pregnancy was a healthy one, but she had worked long hours for months on a project of some sort, a part of her doctoral work, and she was exhausted. Also, I believe there were a great many people offering her advice that she neither asked for nor wanted. So she came again for rest and quiet. When her hour arrived, she asked permission to give birth here."

"Privately?" I asked. "Or in secret?"

"Yes, there is a difference, isn't there?" After a moment, she said,

"Quietly. We called a doctor from the village to attend. Isabelle's mother, my sister and my niece helped her through her ordeal."

"And Marie Foullard," I said. "Grand-mère Marie told me she was there."

She smiled as she nodded. "As I said, my sister, Marie Foullard, and my niece, her daughter Louise."

Casey chimed in with, "Should have guessed. I knew you had an inside source about what's happening at the estate, Ma Mère."

I cocked my head, maybe to see the abbess from another angle. Nuns, I knew from experience, are not all sweetness and light. They plunge into the most benighted, infested parts of the world to be of service. Issues of faith aside, has there ever been a gutsier band of women?

I remembered what Deputy Ray Valdez had said about my sister Emily going into the most crime-ridden projects of LA, unarmed, alone, tracking disease to protect the poorest and most defenseless people among us. In another age, Emily would have been a dandy nun. Issues of faith aside.

Ma Mère watched me study her for a moment before she asked, "Do you have another question for me, Marguerite?"

"Many," I said. "But one in particular. Ma Mère, if you don't mind, where were you during the war?"

Appearing completely calm, hands again folded on the desk, she looked me directly in the eye. "I was a housekeeper at the Martin estate during the German occupation."

I looked at her sweet face with new appreciation. She met my eyes and nodded slightly. Along with Grand-mère Marie and other women from the area, this pristine woman was a survivor of an unspeakable wartime ordeal. And her tormentors? Baptised in Calvados and consigned in flames to meet their maker.

Church bells began to peal somewhere above us.

"We are summoned." Ma Mère rose and gestured toward the door. "There's a shortcut to the chapel through here. Shall we?"

"One more question, if you don't mind," I said, getting to my feet.

"Yes, my child."

"That complexity of names," I said. "I have figured out who Louise and Marie are, but who are Marguerite and Eugenie?"

"Marguerite, of course, is for your grandfather's mother." She opened a cupboard beside her desk and pulled out a large plastic box with prayer cards and saints' medals organized in slots. She selected a card and a medal and handed them to me: Sainte-Eugénie's face was on both. Odd, I thought, Ste-Eugénie's feast day is 25 December, Christmas Day, not my birthday in September.

"That is perhaps one of the missing pieces to your puzzle, Marguerite." Her hands disappeared into her sleeves. "Study it carefully. We'll chat again."

—14—

"AND HOW'S JEMIMA Puddleduck?" Bébé slipped into the line between Casey and Jemima, positioning himself immediately behind his half sister as she began to ascend the stairs leading up out of the crypt after the interment of Isabelle's ashes, trapping her between himself and a solid block of a man from the village.

The stairway was so narrow that we had to walk in single file, a long, bad trip for the claustrophobic. With a dozen people in front of her, and twice as many behind, there was no way for Jemima to escape her half brother. Except for a perfunctory greeting when the family gathered for lunch, all afternoon she had made a point of putting distance between herself and Bébé.

While Inspector Dauvin was keeping the investigation into Isabelle's murder quiet until after the funeral, the family also, it seemed to me, had put a lid on whatever issues or feuds they might have among them until the main event was over. All morning I had felt a building dread for this moment when, with Isabelle safely tucked inside her niche, people would drop their company manners and get down to issues. We weren't even out of the crypt yet, and Bébé, it seemed, had fired the first volley.

Jemima turned her head and demanded, "Don't call me Puddleduck, Bébé."

"What?" He pretended surprise. "But Jemima Puddleduck is an English literary figure beloved of millions of sticky little children the world over. You should be flattered."

"I'm warning you, Bébé."

"Very well, Puddleduck." He looked over his shoulder at Casey and at me behind her, and winked, expecting us, I thought, to go along with him. "Tell you what, in honor of our newfound American cousins and your exalted status vis-à-vis Chris and Lulu, that you are their auntie, from now on I shall call you after a great American woman. Forthwith, you shall be Aunt Jemima."

When Casey made a choking sound Jemima turned, saw Casey

nudge Bébé's shoulder in reproach. Eyes narrowed, Jemima stopped short, holding up the progress of the entire group behind her, and peered around him to challenge Casey. "Does that mean something to you?"

Casey shook her head, refrained from explaining who, actually what, Aunt Jemima was in the United States—an unfortunate stereotype adopted as a commercial logo that bore no resemblance to the too-thin, intentionally nearly albino teen who shared the name. Freddy had told me everybody loved Bébé, almost. Certainly Bébé wasted none of his charm on his half sister.

Jemima glared at Bébé. "You'll be sorry. My boyfriend will be here later. Have you any idea who he is?"

"Aunt Jemima's boyfriend? Uncle Ben, of course."

"Sergei Ludanov, Junior, you prat," she said, adding a threat: "You'll see."

"I'm quaking in my boots."

"You should be."

"Bébé, you're awful." It was Casey who came to Jemima's defense. "If Sergei doesn't beat you up, I might have to."

"So sorry." Bébé, obviously chagrined, turned and wrapped his arms around Casey, kissed her cheek. "I've gone too far, haven't I?"

"It isn't me you need to apologize to," Casey said, pushing him away and turning him toward Jemima.

Bébé bowed slightly before his half sister. "I'm a fool."

She accepted his gesture of contrition with a little bow of her own. "Just so we're clear."

She turned her back and marched up the stairs. Bébé gave her a little space before following.

To me, the truly chilling aspect of this exchange was that it was Casey, and none of the adults, who came to Jemima's defense. Not even I.

A drizzle fell outside, but no one seemed to pay much attention to it as they walked back up into daylight, such as it was. People sorted themselves into small groups, greeted each other, had a word or two, then split off to greet others. David, resplendent in his dark blue university dress uniform, a short knife in a scabbard buckled around his tunic, a very military-looking costume, had been watching for Casey, and came forward as she emerged from the church with me. At lunch he had explained to her—Grand-mère had seated the two together, again—that the *Grandes écoles* of France were in some ways similar to the American service academies, West Point and Annapolis.

Casey certainly seemed interested in what he had to say. She had asked me earlier if she and David were related. I told her probably, but distantly, and that pleased her; he was very handsome, and very bright.

Freddy came out of the chapel directly behind me and Casey. He walked beside us as we joined David, making small talk. But when Claude Desmoulins and Lena emerged, Freddy made his excuses and went to them; Claude hadn't been at lunch. I spotted Uncle Max standing alone at the edge of the crowd. Leaving Casey and David to their conversation, I made straight for him.

Uncle Gérard and Gillian stepped forward and intercepted me.

"So, Maggie," Gérard said, much chummier since our trip to the loo, Gillian as well. "How did the meeting go with Ma Mère? Did she answer your questions?"

"Several," I said. He had seemed affectionate when we were alone, and I trusted him then. But somehow, outside, with Gillian on his arm, towering over him, I felt my protective barriers come up again. I may have felt some grudging admiration for her, but I also knew she could be a steamroller, and I might be a boulder in her path. That collision could get ugly.

She said, "You've had some opportunity to look around a bit. What do you think of the place? Must seem rather drab and primitive around here compared to 'Los Anguhleeze.'"

"Not at all. It's lovely," I said, partly to twit her. Knowing about Gérard's scheme to obliterate the landscape to build mass housing, I added, "So peaceful, so genuine. I understand why the family cherishes the land and the people, and is so fierce about protecting this wonderful place. I hope the area remains this unspoiled forever. Now, if you'll excuse me, I haven't said hello to my uncle yet—he's just arrived from America."

"Is that Max Duchamps?" Gérard asked, following my sightline. "I haven't seen him for, well, a very long time. Wonderful stroke on the links. I'll just say hello."

"I'll give him your best wishes," I said. "But if you don't mind, I have some business to discuss with him. TV business. Please excuse me."

He acceded with a nod, but he seemed disappointed.

Max held out his arms to me. As I entered his embrace, I removed the contents of my dress pocket and transferred them to his overcoat.

Holding me close, he whispered, "What did you give me?"

"Isabelle's address book and some phone numbers she called when she was in LA; she contacted a private investigator. There's a computer memory stick from Monsieur Hubert that has Dad's patent files. Let's make sure his records match ours."

"What is it you want me to do with this collection?"

"Call those people you call and get them snooping into the phone contacts," I said.

"Find out anything else, Sherlock?"

"This and that." I stepped back to look up into his earnest face. "Where is the document Hubert wanted you to sign?"

"In my bag. I'll show you later." I squeezed his hand, happy he was there. "You and I need to talk, alone."

"Tell me when and where."

"Right now would suit me, but my dance card seems to be full at the moment. I've been put on notice that several of these people want a private minute with me."

"They all have bridges to sell you?"

"I suspect they do," I said. "Grand-mère has asked you to come back to the house for tea. Maybe I can get off teacup patrol for a few minutes so we can sneak away."

Grand-mère's invitation didn't seem to thrill him, but he nodded. He would come. "How is the old girl?"

"All things considered, she's all right," I said. "You need to give her your condolences."

"I need to check on my girls first. How's Casey doing with this mob?"

"So far, fine." We both turned to see where she was.

Casey was still with David, near a small fountain. We saw her abruptly shift her focus away from David to glare at Claude Desmoulins, who stood nearby with Freddy and Lena. Something Claude said obviously upset Casey. Whatever he said upset Freddy as well, or, maybe he was upset that Casey overheard. She dipped her head close to David and asked him a question. His answer made her no happier. I knew the expression on her face: righteous anger. I was relieved when, instead of rebuking Claude, she looked for me, found me, and strode my way.

I heard Claude laugh as he watched her walk purposefully toward me. Something about that laugh made my chest tighten. I expected him to say, *Petite merdeuse*—little shit—and leaned into Max, looking for a shield, feeling as if I needed one.

"What is it, honey?"

"That voice," I said. "That laugh."

There was a sudden flash of lightning and I immediately felt the old panic, cold hands squeezing my chest, keeping air out, filling my head with noise. Desperate to get to a safe place, I started to run. Max caught me before I had taken a second step and pulled me tight against him. Thunder and lightning scare the shit out of me, always have. But I hadn't run away from the flash and noise of a storm for many years, even when I desperately wanted to.

"Count, honey," Max whispered, his face in front of mine, eyes locked to mine. "One-thousand, two-…"

"…thousand," I began, trying to concentrate—what came next?— as we measured how far away the lightning was by the length of the interval until the clap of thunder, just as we had done when I was a frightened little girl. At the count of ten and still no thunder I knew this was a distant storm, nothing to be afraid of. I began to uncoil inside.

"I thought you grew out of all that, Maggie." Max pressed me against his chest.

I shook my head, feeling the soft cashmere of his overcoat against my cheek. "I just learned how to cover better."

Casey came up behind me, wrapped her long arms around my shoulders, leaned over me to press her cheek against mine. "I can't leave you alone for a minute, can I, you old scaredy-cat?"

I took a breath and nodded. She was so tall she could almost rest her chin on the top of my head. We broke the clutch and separated, getting a little daylight between us all. Casey studied me, as she had been doing ever since Mike died, looking for evidence of rips in the seams that held me together. I wondered, when had our roles changed? Wasn't I supposed to be her rock, her comfort giver?

"Just a little lightning," I said, forcing a smile. "Nothing for you two big kids to be afraid of."

Max laughed, a single nervous bark that drew glances from the people nearest us.

"Mom," Casey said, "do you know that man talking to Freddy?"

"He's my stepfather," I said. "Claude Desmoulins."

"The bastard," Max muttered under his breath.

I saw a very worried expression on my daughter's lovely face. I asked, "What happened, Casey?"

"I heard him tell Freddy that he should have drowned you like a stray puppy when he had the opportunity. What did he mean?"

I turned to Max. "What did he mean, Max? What happened to me here?"

"Later," he said, glancing up and seeing, as I did, that Grand-mère and Grand-mère Marie were headed our way. "Ride in the car with me to the house, we'll talk."

The two grandmothers were gracious as they greeted Max, and he was to them as he offered formal condolences for their loss, though I sensed some wariness between Grand-mère and Max. Marie seemed genuinely delighted to see him. I was surprised that they knew each other so well. Clearly, Max had done more than file some legal documents for my dad all those years ago. Indeed, there was a reference in their conversation to a particularly memorable picnic at the beach. I was also surprised by Max's fluency with French.

I didn't ask, but I wanted to know, had Mom been at that picnic? Were Emily and Mark there? Were Dad and Isabelle already involved then? When did her family know about the affair? When did Max? Or, did the picnic happen later, and I was there? How many people conspired to deceive Mom? My heart hurt for her.

My father had always been my hero, but lately his shining armor was looking more than a little tarnished. But no more than tarnished. So he jumped off the rails for a while, but he went back to his family, and he took me with him, didn't he? That peccadillo, though a doozy, didn't define him.

Dad had always been wonderful to me, and to Mark and Emily. His relationship with Mom always seemed fond. He certainly treated her with consideration and respect—we'll skip over that part about the paramour for the moment—and he encouraged her various fads and projects. How things were between them when they were alone behind their bedroom door, like most children, I didn't want to think about. Outwardly, there never seemed to be big issues between them. They were both well informed, and they were both willing to hold their own in sometimes noisy discussions about issues, but those issues related to the world beyond our front door, not within. It never occurred to me that they were other than totally committed to each other and to their children. True partners.

Had I missed signs of discord? Trying to dredge memories out of a void made my head hurt. I was relieved when Inspector Dauvin, standing near the chapel with Antoine, caught my eye and quietly gestured for me to join them.

I excused myself from Max and Casey and walked over.

Dauvin had a few small questions to ask me, Antoine said, and had asked him to again serve as translator. Did I mind?

A few small questions? Of course I did not mind.

Dauvin asked me how well I had known Isabelle before she died. I told him about our encounter at the market, and that the messy interlude was the entirety of our acquaintance. He wore the closed face of a cop, registering no reaction. But as Antoine heard about the night Isabelle and I met—I had told no one in the family any details about that meeting—he grew visibly upset. He began peppering me with questions of his own, some of them full of challenge about my behavior that night. Dauvin clapped a hand on his friend's shoulder and asked him if he was able to continue translating for us, a strong suggestion that Antoine needed to get a grip.

"I live in a small village," Antoine said to me by way of apology. "I feel no need to lock my doors at night. If an older woman, a stranger, ever approached me, I hope I would at least listen to her. But I know the situation is different for people who live in a big city, especially in America where so many people carry firearms. I realize that a public figure like you would need to be very cautious."

His glance moved from the chapel to the crowd milling about. "But, especially at this moment, I am thinking about my Aunt Isabelle and feeling very sad. I believe your rejection would have been very difficult for her to bear. But how could you know that? She was a stranger to you."

When Dauvin reminded him that Isabelle could be quite eccentric, Antoine smiled ruefully and agreed.

"Forgive me," he said, addressing both of us. "I promise to behave. Shall we continue?"

Dauvin went back to his first question, and asked whether, in fact, I had been in contact with Isabelle consistently during the week before she died. He said he had been in touch with Detective Longshore of the LA County Sheriffs, so he knew that Isabelle had been to my home on at least one occasion, and had taken photographs there. She had also been captured on the security cameras at my place of work at times when I was there. Also, if I had not spoken with her, how would she know where I bought groceries?

Before I said anything, I looked for Max. He was watching my back, as I knew he would be. When I caught his eye, he turned an imaginary key on his lips, meaning don't say anything.

But I told Dauvin, "I know nothing of Isabelle's activities at any time before the night she died, and nothing after I saw her standing on Pacific Coast Highway a little after ten o'clock on the night she died."

He had a last question, the one I suspected he most wanted answered. "Before Isabelle Martin died, did you know you stood to inherit half of her sizable estate?"

I shook my head. "I did not know she existed."

It was Grand-mère who rescued me this time. I was so nonplussed by the inference Dauvin's questions conveyed, and was trying so hard not to show that I was upset, that I was not aware she had walked over until she put herself between me and Dauvin. Pointing a finger up at his face, she scolded him in rapid French.

"You come into my home as a friend, and yet, on the day I bury my only daughter you behave as an uncaring stranger to my family, right here, in this holy place. Your blessed mother, may she rest in peace, deserves better."

She turned and gave Antoine a withering, narrow-eyed glare. "And you." *Et tu* in French, the same accusatory words the mortally wound-ed Julius Caesar aimed at Brutus in Shakespeare's play. Poor Antoine, from the look of him I suspect that a sound whipping would have been easier for him to take than those two little words delivered by his grand-mother.

Saying nothing more to the two men, Grand-mère took me by the arm and walked me away.

"Pierre Dauvin," she muttered under her breath. "What a fool."

"You heard what he asked?"

"Yes. He should have the courage to ask me those same questions. I know the answers better than you."

"I'm sure he will get around to asking you, when he recovers," I said. "Grand-mère, you would have made a great headmistress."

She smiled at the idea. "You know, my dear, all mothers are when it comes to their children, are they not?"

Drizzle turned to downpour. The crowd quickly moved toward their cars for the short drive to Grand-mère's house. When Casey and I asked Grand-mère for leave to ride with Uncle Max, she agreed, saying we probably had many things to talk over. And, of course, we did.

As Max pulled his rented Toyota into the long queue of cars headed for the estate, I repeated the questions Dauvin asked me, and my re-sponses.

"Routine stuff," he said, flipping on the windshield wipers. "We have to be careful, though. In a small town like this where half the popu-lation are cousins, we can get home-towned."

"What does that mean?" Casey asked.

"The comfortable way out of something as serious as a murder is to pin it on an outsider," he said, glancing over his shoulder to look at her.

"Tag, I'm it?" I said.

"We won't let that happen." He patted my knee. "You said you had some questions for me."

"More than some." I turned in my seat to look at him. "Did you know that when Dad died Isabelle began receiving all of the money Dad's patents earned?"

He frowned. "That's wrong. That's not the way we set things up—I did all the original paperwork with the lawyer friend in Créances I'm staying with. The royalties were to be split equally between Isabelle's account and your folks' joint Berkeley bank account during their lifetimes. Now that Isabelle is gone, her half will—or should—come to you, Maggie. The other half should continue to be deposited in the Berkeley bank for the remainder of Betsy's life. When we lose her, honey, everything will be yours."

"Unless?" I asked.

"No unless," he said. Then he added, "Unless you formally relinquish your rights in the tontine. In which case, at this juncture, as your legal heir under French law Casey would assume your ownership; you can relinquish your inheritance but you can't relinquish her expectations."

"So somebody screwed up," Casey said.

"Why didn't Betsy say something to me when the deposits ceased?" Max looked anguished.

"Pride, maybe. Or grief," I said. "After Dad died, Mom had a lot to deal with. Add Mike's illness to the pile. Maybe any issue that came Isabelle-attached was one issue too many."

"What do you want me to do?" he asked.

"Make things right again. If the whole shebang belongs to me, I want you to arrange for Mom to start getting her share of royalty payments again. As in, now."

"Okay, I'll get on it." He frowned. "Is there an issue?"

"Her leaky roof," I said. "A five-figure repair bill."

"Ah," he said, lights of comprehension coming on. He must have noticed the water damage. "Good for you, honey. We'll put things straight again. Now where is the document Hubert gave you to sign?"

I pulled the document out of my bag and handed it to Casey to read aloud because her French was better than mine. Some of the unfamiliar words she had to spell. When she got to the bottom, I asked Max, "What is it?"

"When Isabelle died, Hubert's fiduciary relationship to her died. He wants you to keep him on, to let him continue managing the money, to collect his commission. We won't agree to that, of course. Not now. First thing Monday, you'll thank him for his services and we'll redirect royalties from Monsieur Hubert to a stateside account. And we'll get an auditor."

"Isabelle had someone audit her account. Don't know who; the initials are HGD," I said, "I have an appointment with Isabelle's *notaire* Monday to read her will. Will you come with me, Max?"

"Of course. First we'll talk with Monsieur Hubert." He glanced at me. "Question next?"

"There's a snapshot that everyone seems to have of Dad and me in an apple orchard. Dad framed a copy and had it in the den. I look like I'm about two."

"Exactly two," he said, nodding. "That picture was taken on your second birthday."

"Here, in Normandy," I said. "I was two, and Dad was here."

He nodded again.

"Were you?"

"No. Not that time."

"You and Mom told me that it was after the family's year in France, after the affair with Isabelle was over, that Dad learned I existed. And then you and Dad came over and retrieved me."

"That's the short version."

"I need the long version, Max," I said. "First, Isabelle told Dad she was pregnant as soon as she knew."

"Says who?"

"That's what the abbess suggested," Casey answered.

"Hmmm." His eyes narrowed. "Hardly non-partisan; the woman is part of the clan."

"So she told us," I said. "The thing is, there's a two-year gap in the story you told me. And I know Isabelle didn't just hand me over. Something happened."

"Several things happened." He turned briefly to look at Casey, a status check. "First of all, the affair lasted, off and on, for some part of three years, beginning the year your folks were over here working, and lasting until about two years after. Your dad was deeply in love with Isabelle, enthralled with her actually. And he was in love with you. When he finally came to his senses and broke it off with Isabelle, he made it clear to Betsy that he would not abandon you."

"Max, he asked Isabelle to abort me."

"Not to abort *you*, Maggie," Max said with some heat. "*It*. I don't want to get into a biological or metaphysical or theological discussion about when life begins, but when your dad asked Isabelle to consider terminating the product of their illicit behavior and failed birth control, *you* didn't exist yet to him."

"Product of failed birth control?"

"If she actually used any," Max said, looking out the windshield and pointedly away from me. "Anyway, first she told your dad she was on the pill. Later she told him she terminated the pregnancy."

"Obviously, she lied," I said, remembering my conversation with Mom about predatory students. "Whatever Isabelle did, it still usually takes two to make a baby."

"Don't be too hard on your dad, honey. You have to give him credit—he never abandoned you."

"He abandoned Isabelle," I said. "Now let's talk about what he did to Mom."

"It's easy to judge, Maggie." He gave me a hard glance. "Have you never screwed up?"

I laughed, though nothing was funny. "You're my lawyer, Max. You know the answer better than anyone."

"There you go. In the end, your dad did what he hoped was best for all of you," he went on. "When he first learned that Isabelle had not terminated the pregnancy—he didn't learn that until after you were born, by the way—he tried to work out a legal joint custody arrangement with her so that he could visit you without any hassle. He never managed to get anything formal in place, but she was very agreeable to visits. For a while, anyway. Periodically he'd make the trip over, usually during university breaks, so he hit most of the holidays."

"And my birthday," I said.

He nodded. "He was here for your second birthday party. Isabelle took that snapshot of you and your dad in the orchard."

"So, of course, whenever he came to see me, he would see Isabelle, too," I said. "Mom must have been furious."

"When she found out she was."

"When was that?"

Max risked a glance at me before launching his bomb: "The night Isabelle called and told him to come and get you."

I needed clarification, as if maybe I misheard that. "He travelled back and forth to see me for two years before Mom even knew about me?"

The pitch of my voice was about as high as a distressed dolphin's. I had to take a breath, try to calm down. When I panicked over lightning earlier, if I had just kept on running I wouldn't be hearing this. And I might have been happier.

Casey patted my shoulder. "Mom, you okay?"

"Yeah, sorry." I rolled down the window a crack, letting in an icy stream of air. "So, where does Claude come into the picture?"

"You were maybe a year old. Isabelle caved to family pressures—or maybe she wanted to hurt your dad; she could be like that—and she married Claude Desmoulins."

"I'm guessing that Claude wasn't happy about Dad's visits."

"Unhappy is one way to put it. I know she tried to keep the visits from Claude. Sometimes she succeeded, and sometimes she disastrously failed. Claude was one very angry man last time I saw him."

"Do you blame him?"

"No."

He had something more to say, but he wasn't saying it. I touched his cheek. "What are you thinking?"

"Just remembering the fallout from Isabelle's call. It wasn't pretty, Maggie."

"Tell me," I said.

Casey muttered, "Poor Gran."

Max glanced at her, nodded.

"Tell us," she prodded.

"About a month before the call, your dad came over to see you, Maggie. Right after Christmas, I think it was. He'd made the decision to make a final break with Isabelle and to tell all to Betsy. But first he wanted to formalize a legal shared custody arrangement so he could continue to see you. But Isabelle didn't agree. Once she knew that visit was to be your dad's big kiss-off of her, things got very ugly."

A passing car sprayed the windshield with mud. Max fumbled with levers until he found the window washer. I urged him to continue. "What happened?"

"Isabelle accused him of trying to steal you, and abandoning her, and yada, yada." He shrugged. "End-of-the-affair entrails, you know? Nasty stuff. Isabelle wasn't big on sharing."

"Sharing me or my dad?"

"Both."

"Poor Claude," I said. "Merry Christmas to him, huh?"

"Yeah, poor bastard."

We drove through the compound gate at that point. I wanted Max to back out and drive around some more, to finish the story, but the crush of cars pouring in through the gate made that impossible.

Max parked next to Antoine's Mini. He gave my hand a squeeze. "Honestly, honey, I don't know exactly what happened. But when we took you home to Betsy, you had a black eye and a plaster cast on your little arm."

"Jesus Christ," a horrified reaction from the backseat.

Before either Casey or I could grill Max further, Antoine opened my door and held out a hand to me. The rain had abated for the moment, but the sky promised more.

As we walked toward Grand-mère's house, Max sticking close beside me, Antoine asked, "Have you forgiven me, cousin?"

"Don't give it another thought," I said. "Dauvin was just doing his job, and you were being honest."

Grand-mère's Mercedes, with David driving, pulled in beside Max's Toyota. Freddy made a beeline across the compound toward us. He took Casey gently by the arm and asked if he could have just a little word with her. I didn't intervene, but I watched them closely. He seemed to be apologizing to her, probably for what she overheard Claude say; so many apologies, so many worries. How big were the stakes?

Interesting, I thought as I watched Casey and Freddy, standing side by side alone for the first time, how very much alike they were—a closer resemblance to each other than to any other of the blood kin there. Much closer. Why hadn't I noticed before?

Both Casey and Freddy had Élodie's patrician nose, they were both tall, broad in the shoulders, narrow in the hips. His wide, clear brow was very much like Casey's, which I found interesting because it was in the shape of her face and in her build that Casey looked most like my sister Emily. I couldn't see anything of the angular Claude in Freddy, but I did see something of Emily, who, as far as I knew, had absolutely no genetic relationship to Freddy. Interesting, I thought. Very interesting. I began to make a few computations.

The conversation between Freddy and Casey seemed to end on a friendly note, and they were smiling and chatting happily when they started for the house, David now tagging along with them. Max, ever protective, excused himself from me and Antoine and joined that trio, just to make sure all was well with his grand-niece.

Antoine went ahead to give Grand-mère Marie a hand as she slowly walked toward the house, leaning heavily on her cane. I caught up with Grand-mère and Bébé. After the usual remarks were exchanged about the service, it was fine, and about the crowd, it was large, I looked across Grand-mère at Bébé, who walked on her other side.

"Antoine tells me you and Freddy are almost twins," I said.

Grand-mère answered for him. "They are only four days apart."

"Who's older?" I asked.

"Freddy is," Bébé said. "And I never let him forget it. So what if we both turned forty? He's still older, and always will be."

"When was the big birthday?" I asked.

"In June."

He had just told me exactly what I wanted to know. Everything after that was just conversational shuffle. I asked "Was there a party?"

"A small celebration." He shrugged; times are tough. "Grand-mère took us for dinner and there was cake and champagne after. Very lovely, and very generous."

She reached up and patted his cheek. "If my Bébé is forty, how old am I?"

He captured her hand and kissed it. Looking deep into her face he said, "Not nearly old enough, my dearest dear. Not nearly old enough."

She leaned her head against his shoulder and we continued into the house.

The crowd inside was quite subdued. I greeted people, met people, was kissed and patted and offered condolences as they came, paid their respects, had some tea, moved on. Whenever I saw a dirty teacup, I dutifully picked it up and delivered it to Oscar in the kitchen.

At the first opportunity I had for a break, I found Max and took him outside on the pretext of showing him the garden. We stopped under a pergola for shelter from the weather.

When I was certain that no one could overhear us, I said, "Isabelle carried Dad's picture in her wallet until the day she died."

"Yeah?" He thought that over. "Interesting."

"After you and Dad took me to the U.S., did Dad ever see or hear from Isabelle again?"

"From time to time. They held those patents together so there was some ongoing communication about renewals and revisions, legal docs back and forth. But Hubert was usually the middle man."

"Nothing more?"

"Your dad kept all contact to a minimum, but he did respond to her. He was afraid to ignore her."

"Why afraid?"

"For you. He always expected that Isabelle would change her mind and come and fetch you back, especially after she divorced Claude. He didn't want to trigger something: She could pull some pretty weird stuff. For the same reason, there were no legal actions taken to get her to legally relinquish custody rights once you were in the States."

"Dad thought she wouldn't sign me away?"

"He knew she wouldn't."

"Did you know that Isabelle was pregnant when you and Dad came and got me?"

He frowned, deep V's forming between his thick brows. "Says who?"

"Do the math. I was two in September, and Dad was here, with Isabelle. Freddy was born the following June."

The frown deepened. I wondered if the fingers on the hands thrust deep into his coat pockets were counting backward. Finally he said, "So what? She was married to Claude at the time."

"So what? Look at Casey and Freddy together, then you tell me," I said.

"Goddamn it." He sank into a dark reverie, working things through.

"Why was my arm in a cast?"

He roused himself, shook his head. "We were never given a good answer. Isabelle and Claude were living in Paris at the time. Late one night some neighbors found you outside in the middle of the street during a thunderstorm, nearly naked, obviously hurt and screaming your head off. The police were called, a social services file was opened. We were ready to use the file against Isabelle if she ever changed her mind and came after you."

"She must have offered you some explanation."

Max shook his head. "Claude said the storm scared you and you hurt yourself when you ran outside."

"That's plausible," I said.

"Except you had a spiral break. Someone twisted your arm until it broke. Ben Nussbaum made a careful X-ray record in case we ever needed to go to court."

"Mom!" Casey, coatless, shivering—it had begun to sprinkle again—came around the side of the house. "Here you are. I've been looking all over."

"I'm not lost. I'm with Max."

"You've got to come inside."

I had guessed right that once the funeral was over pretense and politesse would quickly slip away: fatigue, alcohol, grief, history, who knows what the catalyst was that afternoon? Certainly Bébé's needling of Jemima before we left the chapel was a harbinger of animosities to be revealed.

The ugliness, it seemed, began while I was in the garden with Max. In my absence, Claude had taken some cheap shots at me, questioning my intentions in coming to France. As soon as I walked back into the salon he confronted me directly. Obviously, he had been drinking.

"How do we know, except on your word," Claude demanded of me, "that we just interred Isabelle Martin?"

Freddy, profoundly chagrined, tried to quiet his father, but his efforts only seemed to anger Claude more. Claude brushed his son aside.

Pierre Dauvin stepped in. "We have certification from the Los Angeles coroner that proper identification was made."

"Based on what?" Claude wanted to know. Pointing at me, dismissing me by his tone of voice, he said, "*Her* word? She doesn't remember her mother. How could she identify Isabelle?"

Grand-mère clapped her hands like an angry school teacher. "That is enough, Claude."

"No it is not," he shouted. The rest of the room fell into an embarrassed silence. "How do we know this woman is not an imposter?"

Uncle Max stepped forward. "I knew Isabelle. I verified her identity with the coroner. And I can assure you that my niece is who she says she is."

"Max Duchamps," Claude spat. "You are the last man I trust to tell the truth here."

Then he wheeled and pointed at Casey. "That one says she saw police photographs of Isabelle, but she refuses to produce them. And who is she, anyway?"

Casey held her shoulders back and her head high during this verbal assault, and I was proud of her. I wanted to put my arms around her, but instead I used them to restrain Max. I was afraid he would deck Claude and break all those borrowed china teacups. It was David who went to Casey's side and put a supportive arm around her.

I turned to Antoine and said, quietly, "Tell Dauvin that I do have some of the coroner's photographs of Isabelle. If it is all right with Grand-mère, I will show them to Claude."

Antoine asked both Dauvin and Grand-mère for approval. Then he turned to me and, gesturing toward the next room, said, "Please."

Dauvin, Freddy, Max and Claude went with me into the small library off the salon where some of the young people had retreated to play video games. I asked Chris, Antoine's son, to lend me his laptop.

While Freddy asked the kids to go outside for a few minutes, I accessed my email via the Internet and pulled up the message Rich sent with photos attached. When the first one, Isabelle's passport photo, was on the screen, I turned the monitor to show the others.

"Is this Isabelle Martin?" I asked.

They all three agreed that it was.

As Claude began to protest that the passport photo proved nothing, I pulled up the first of the coroner's postmortem shots. It wasn't gruesome, but it was apparent that the subject had been terribly injured. There were obvious contusions, her skin had a blue tinge and she looked dead, not asleep. LA County Coroner, the date and time, were stamped in a bottom corner.

When he saw the image, Freddy gasped and crossed himself. Dauvin's face was set in grim lines; he had seen them, but showing them to the family seemed to distress him.

Freddy opened the third of the attached photos, saw the more graphic of the coroner's pictures Rich had sent, and announced, "Papa, enough. Go home. Now."

As Claude stormed out, I told Freddy and Dauvin that I had Isabelle's effects in my room. Through Freddy, Dauvin informed me that her things had been removed from my room during the funeral and were currently at the local police station. I was disappointed, because going upstairs, and taking Casey with me, to retrieve the bags would have given me a plausible excuse to disappear for a few minutes, to cool off, to talk through the situation with my daughter.

I was unnerved by the intensity of Claude's animosity toward me, and furious that he had turned on Casey. I was grateful when he was gone, though shimmers of his pent-up rage still filled the house after the front door slammed behind him. Forty years was a long time to harbor such very bad feelings, especially toward a little kid. I wondered if, along the way, Claude had done some of the same math that I had concerning his son's birthday.

Max was huddled with Casey when I went back into the salon. I saw her shake her head firmly as he spoke to her; she did not agree with whatever he was asking of her. My guess was that he wanted to spirit the two of us out of there. I went to my daughter.

"That was brutal," I said. "Are you all right?"

"My God, Mom, what is the guy's problem?"

"He's a variation on the fairy-tale cliché, the wicked stepfather," I said.

"Wicked is right. You stay away from him, Mom," she ordered, gray eyes narrowed. "Promise me."

"I will do my very best." I turned to Max. Again, his face was set in a series of downward-pointing V's—thinning hairline, furrow between the brows, frown, brackets around his mouth—the way it looks when he's worried.

I asked, "Spiral fracture, huh? What else?"

"The question, my dear, is not what, but who?"

"You're right," I said, looking around the room at groupings of heads bent together, the susurrus of many quiet conversations rising and falling like wind in trees. People were beginning to leave, embarrassed maybe to have seen such a raw family contretemps at a time of mourning. Soon, only the family would be left, their issues unbuffered by the presence of guests. Thinking about that moment, I felt dread rise up from the pit of my stomach and settle in the back of my throat, like a burr I could not dislodge.

Freddy was headed for the door. I assumed his intention was escape from the barely veiled scrutiny of the others. His face still glowed from humiliation. I felt deeply sorry for him, caught in the middle between his father and me, and certainly now the object of pity. Before the situation deteriorated further, he and I needed to talk.

I leaned into Max and whispered, "Stick close to Casey. I'll be back."

"Maggie." He snagged my arm. "Where…?"

"Trust me." I kissed him on the cheek and took my arm from him as I turned to my daughter. "Casey, stay with Max. I have my phone."

On my way out the front door I stopped for my coat and an umbrella. Freddy was already halfway across the compound, bareheaded—it was drizzling again—bypassing Isabelle's house where, I assumed, his father had been exiled in disgrace. Where was he going?

"Freddy!" I called, opening the umbrella as I dashed toward him. He saw me, hesitated, doubled back and met me. I held the umbrella over us both. "Where can we talk?"

He glanced at Isabelle's house, shuddered—shivered?—took my elbow and nodded toward the compound gate. "Walk with me? I want to show you something."

Before we got to the gate, a bright yellow Lamborghini muscled its way into the compound. The low-slung car churned mud and gravel before it rumbled to a stop so close to us and so suddenly that we had to jump back to avoid being splashed. The driver, a young man with obviously dyed blue-black hair, wearing wraparound sunglasses in a rainstorm, rolled down his tinted window a few inches and asked, arrogantly, in English, "Where's the party?"

"The memorial reception is there," Freddy said, reproach rife in his tone as he pointed toward Grand-mère's house.

Without another word, the window went up and the car rumbled on.

I had seen the lower edge of a bruise below the shades on the young man's left cheekbone. Someone had landed a punch to his handsome face. There was something about the kid that was familiar, the cast of his head, maybe. Familiar from where, though? TV? Supermarket tabloids? Did he have a tiff with paparazzi?

"Who is that?" I asked, intrigued.

"Jemima's boyfriend." Freddy pulled a scarf out of his coat pocket and wrapped it around his neck.

"Sergei Ludanov, Junior?" Jemima had invoked the boyfriend's name as a warning to Bébé.

"That is what I'm told."

Ludanov, Junior, parked his six-figure, six-hundred-plus horse-power ego-boost so close to the front door that anyone going in or out would have to walk around it. He, however, would not get wet going between car and house.

"He's a punk," I said, turning away, walking on.

"Antoine says he's a Russian mafia prince." Freddy took the umbrella and held it over us; I put my hands in my pockets. "His father is quite notorious, owns casinos, clubs, a resort or two on an island he owns off the coast of Cambodia. He's suspected of having a hand in various criminal activities, currently big-scale money laundering. But he's never been brought to trial. Something always seems to happen to the witnesses against him. They shut up, or they disappear."

"Gérard allows Jemima to see this guy?"

"She's eighteen. What can he do? Assuming he wants to do anything. The guy's family is very rich, and Gérard has some pressing needs at the moment."

As we turned onto the village road a companionable silence settled over us. I was running through various hypotheticals that could involve Junior and maybe his father, and their money. Freddy was lost in his own thoughts. He looked so miserable that I reached over and patted his shoulder.

"Maggie," he said, capturing my hand and folding it into the crook of his elbow. "How can I apologize for my father's behavior?"

"Don't even try," I said. I had forgotten about Claude for the moment. "I gather that he is not happy that I popped up."

He shook his head, agreeing with me.

"I have a feeling that some of the others are unhappy, too," I said.

"It's what you said earlier." Freddy gave my hand, where it rested on his arm, a squeeze. "You're an unknown quantity. It's natural that some people are worried."

"Are you?"

He cocked his head, not yes, not no.

I asked, "If it were up to you, what would you do with our mother's assets?"

He took a moment to organize his thoughts as we walked. He asked, "You've heard about Uncle Gérard's subdivision scheme?"

"Antoine told me about it."

"Just so you know, I believe his scheme is ridiculous. I see the influence of Gillian in it, typical English slash-and-burn approach to the land." His tone expressed profound disdain for all of the above. "First, the proposed scale of the development is too large for the region and for the market, both. Next, by ripping out the orchards, the fields, and the *fromagerie* and replacing them with endless ranks of cheap, oversized modern houses—you call them McMansions?—he would destroy exactly those qualities that would attract his target market, retired people on fixed incomes."

"Antoine told me that Gérard is already so far underwater with his scheme that it's a dead issue, right?"

"Perhaps. There is always the possibility he will find a miracle with deep pockets. But the miracle will need to appear very soon."

Gérard must be fairly desperate by now, I thought. I wondered if he was desperate enough to appeal to Sergei Ludanov, Senior or Junior, for a bailout. That notion was scary enough by itself, but coupled with what Jean-Paul Bernard had told me about how easy it is to arrange for a hitman—mentioning Russian mobsters, among others—if one has the contacts, I felt my chest constrict.

Last question: Was Gérard desperate enough for money to pimp his own daughter to Junior? Was Gillian?

I checked six, as Rich would say: I turned around to make sure we weren't being followed. No white van, but Dauvin was there, creeping along the road in his plain blue car.

We turned down a gravel side road and suddenly I saw the ocean, surprised how close it was to the estate.

The long tide of the English Channel was rising, its approach refloating small fishing boats that had motored in during the morning's high tide and been tied to posts driven higgledy-piggledy into the ground. When the tide receded, the boats were left mired in the mud until the tide returned.

The scene was beautiful: brightly painted boats lying at odd angles; green, red, yellow, blue, contrasting with black mud, dull pewter water, dark gray skies. I took out my phone and snapped a few pictures, regretting not having a better camera.

When we eventually made a film here, it would be gorgeous. I began to see images filling a screen as the structure of that theoretical film as well as its topic began to emerge and become insistent, a story that needed to be told, a place that should be captured and shared.

Damn Guido, I thought again. We have been making films together for a very long time. He knew this moment would happen to me, the film asserting itself, becoming an imperative.

The road came to a dead end above the tide line and we paused there before venturing onto the sand. A look of contentment washed the deep stress lines from Freddy's face as he watched the sea slowly march toward us.

"What do you think, sister?"

"Could be heaven," I said. "Is there a swimming beach around here?"

"Yes." He gestured toward the south. "There are several nearby."

"It's beautiful."

"Imagine living in a house built right here, just above the high tide line."

"The view would be fantastic, but you'd need to wear waders whenever you left the house."

"The marsh can be filled," he said. "Much of the farmland beyond here is fill. Right here, along the seaboard, salt infiltration ruins the soil for farming. However, building in this place is another issue, and one that is fairly easily fixed."

I puzzled that over. I looked around us, saw carrot fields behind us, the Martin orchards beyond them, knew where the *fromagerie* was, and Grand-mère's compound. I turned to Freddy, "Who owns this land?"

"We do," he said. "This is verge land that accretes—builds up—out of the sea. We have a very old charter that deeds to us access to the sea at this place, even as the shape of the land changes over time."

"What are you thinking?"

"I have to give Uncle Gérard credit for one thing," he said. "His idea about building housing to accommodate retired people is a good one, but his plan is too big, and all wrong. However, even in this rotten economy there are still plenty of people with good pensions who are selling their large family homes and looking for a retirement place. The right place."

"Please," I said, "don't tell me you want to build a wall of high-rise condos on this beautiful shore."

"Not at all. Leave that to the Côte d'Azur." He smiled. "Tell me, what is it that people want when they retire?"

I thought about that for a moment before I offered, "Financial security, comfort, safety, an interesting way to pass the time, medical care nearby."

"Exactly."

I must have looked skeptical, though. All of my life I have watched subdivisions multiply and sprawl across the California landscape, both in the San Francisco Bay Area where I grew up and in Southern California where I moved to be with Mike. I never found any charm in the endless canyons of stucco boxes cleaved by asphalt rivers. It would be a crime to sully Normandy with an infestation of that sort.

A blast of icy wind that was full of the perfume of the sea hit me full in the face. Cold as it was, it felt wonderful to be outdoors. I covered my head and ears with my Pashmina, tucked it in over my chest, and buttoned up my coat as I walked over to join Freddy, who had walked over to a marsh grass–covered knoll to look out at the sea.

Dauvin watched us from his car. I waved, he raised a hand in return.

"Is that Pierre?" Freddy asked, turning. "What does he want?"

"He's just being cautious," I said. I didn't add, after this morning he stays close. Thinking about the questions Dauvin asked me at the church, I wasn't sure if he was keeping an eye on a possible suspect or protecting a possible target. But I was glad he was there.

I looked up at Freddy and asked, "What would you do here?"

"Imagine," Freddy said, spreading out his arms, embracing the scene. His embrace encompassed the village about a quarter mile further down, the tower of its abbey visible above the naked trees. The convent where we interred Isabelle that afternoon was directly behind the abbey. "Along here, low-profile seaside cottages built on lanes that run into the village. Each will have a small private garden and all will be single-story—think of Grand-mère Marie and her sore hips."

I nodded my understanding. "My mother has arthritic knees; stairs are a problem."

"Maman?" he said, a furrow between his brows as he questioned me. "I didn't know."

"I meant the woman who raised me."

"Of course." He thought that over. "How is she, your other mother?"

"She seems to be taking everything with grace, but I know that the reappearance of Isabelle in our lives has stirred up some old pain."

"One day, maybe we'll meet."

I looked at his gray eyes, so like mine, so like my father's, and hoped that never happened. I said, "You were saying?"

"There are currently two demographic trends, a growing population of retired people struggling on fixed incomes as prices rise, and a declining rural population," he said. "Farming is not as attractive to young people as it might have been for their parents."

"Like your family. Only Antoine is still here."

"Exactly," he said. "So, as the local population declines, consumption of course declines, and so does employment. Local producers and tradesmen suffer.

"But, if we bring in retired people with their pension incomes we can reverse that trend. It is far cheaper for them to live here than in the city. People of a certain age can enjoy the village life that perhaps they left when they were young to find work in the city. Or perhaps the village life they always imagined, where there is a genuine community and all the support that way of life offers."

"Jobs created, jobs preserved," I said. "An elevated standard of living. A win-win scenario?"

He looked across the landscape as if he could already see the newcomers heading into town to shop and nodded.

"I like your plan much better than Gérard's," I said. "How would you capitalize it?"

"It shouldn't be too onerous," he said. "First, the infrastructure is already here, and all of the necessary conveniences: the village has an exceptional baker, a fine butcher, a general store, a library, two pharmacies, several cafés, a state-of-the-art clinic, a community recreation facility, a small inn for visitors, and on Saturdays a market.

"We have a good chance for regional development assistance from the government, and the tradesmen's associations will be enthusiastic. But for seed money, we put up Maman's Paris apartment and other assets as collateral; there is a fair amount of value there. If we need more, then of course we issue an investment offering."

He turned to me, an expectant look on his face. "What do you think?"

"You've done your homework."

"Homework?"

"Studied the various possibilities."

He smiled almost shyly. "Remember, I am an investment banker. I have studied a great number of project proposals over the years. I hope I am able to sort the good from the doomed."

"Can you be objective about your own proposal?"

"Hah!" A quick outburst followed by a chuckle and a shake of his head. "Of course not. This would be an affair of the heart."

I asked, "What does the rest of the family say?"

"Grand-mère is supportive. She worries that after she dies the estate will break up and disappear. If Uncle Gérard has his way that is exactly what will happen. But if we succeed, there will be Calvados and Camembert made here for a long time into the future, local people will not be displaced, and our home place remains for us to enjoy."

"What about Antoine and Bébé?"

"Antoine calculated the additional gallons of cider and pounds of cheese he could sell, and he seems favorable. Bébé, who visits only occasionally, wants the estate to remain as it is, forever. He will not hear that sometimes we have to make changes in order to preserve what we have."

"That's why he joined with Isabelle and Antoine to bail out Uncle Gérard?" I said. "To preserve the estate?"

"In part. It was a good investment for many reasons." Freddy brought up his palms with a shrug. "Also, Bébé would do anything to embarrass his father and Gillian. He is very bitter about what they did to his mother."

"Will he come around?"

"If we can get backing, probably. The best revenge for him would be to share in a great success that excludes his father." Freddy leaned over and plucked a pebble from the sand. Rubbing it clean between his palms, he said, "For Bébé there is one hitch. If Gérard defaults on the loan we made to him, he is obligated to relinquish his right to inherit the estate—an irrevocable relinquishment. His rights will fall to his children."

"Including Jemima?"

"Exactly." He tossed the pebble in a long arc toward the incoming tide. "For Bébé, that's the rub."

"What will Gillian get?"

"Here? Nothing."

"What does Lena say about your idea?"

"Lena?" He seemed to fold in upon himself at the mention of his wife, as if the balloon of his optimism had been punctured. "As usual, my beloved wife thinks I am a fucking idiot."

I heard a distant clap of thunder and looked up, searched the clouds for lightning, tried to breathe normally, fists clenched into hard balls stuffed into my pockets. I felt the sting of sleet on my face.

Freddy took me by the elbow. "We should get back. It's nearly dark."

As we approached Dauvin's car, he got out, opened the passenger side doors. He said, "The weather is turning. Get in." More an order than an invitation.

Freddy climbed in back, I took the front, shotgun to Dauvin; we were grateful for the car's heater.

The road was already slick with ice by the time we turned off the beach access lane. Icicle flags built up on the car's antenna as we drove. A confetti of sleet and raindrops danced in the headlights.

Night fell. Everything beyond the black ribbon of asphalt unreeling in front of the headlights was lost in the dark. But in my head, the synapses were firing brightly. If Isabelle had never contacted me, if I never met Grand-mère and the others, never saw the estate, and then one day a letter came from a lawyer informing me that a stranger had bequeathed to me property that was six thousand miles and a continent away, what would I have done?

I'd like to think that I would have investigated. But, times are tough. If the letter arrived on a bad day, say, the day the studio bosses announced cuts to my production unit, I might have simply accepted a cash offer and been grateful. Question next: cash offered by whom?

I turned in my seat to ask Freddy, "You knew Isabelle was coming to see me, right?"

"I knew she was going over," he said. "I didn't know she decided to speak with you."

"Did she tell you what she hoped to accomplish?"

He shrugged, eyes out the side window, watching the treacherous road fly past. It took him a moment to decide on a response. What he said was a surprise.

"When you were a little girl, did you have a horse?"

"Hardly a horse," I said. "I had a pony, a little cob."

"And did you have to beg your parents endlessly before they gave you that pony?"

I shook my head. "I never occurred to me to even ask for such a thing. No one around us had horses."

"But?"

"But one day a truck with a horse trailer pulled up to the house and delivered a pony." I smiled, remembering the excitement of that day. All of the kids in the neighborhood, and many of their parents, converged at our house when word got out that there was a pony. My mother was so furious with my father that I assumed the pony was his idea and that she had not been consulted about it.

Not long before that singular day, my brother Mark was killed in Vietnam. The entire family was still walking around under a shroud of grief and disbelief when the pony showed up. I thought she was my consolation prize after losing my much-loved big brother.

"One day a truck pulled up," he echoed. "Just like that?"

"Just like that. I was a little girl. Kids believe in miracles."

Hell, I was so happy to have a pony that I wasn't going to ask questions. I remember thinking that it must be a mistake and that the rightful owner would appear and take her away as suddenly as she arrived. But Dad put up a fence at the back of the yard to keep her out of Mom's flower beds and we kept her there, in violation of several local zoning laws, and with the complicity of the neighbors, until I went away to high school.

"What did you call her?"

"Amy," I said.

"Why?"

I shrugged. "I don't know. I took one look at her and knew that should be her name. My Amy."

"Maggie, I should tell you something about Maman." We turned into the drive and approached the compound. Lights showed from the windows of all three houses. Most of the visitors' cars were gone, including Max's little rental. "No, better that I show you something."

⟶ 15 ⟶

"WHERE IS YOUR FATHER?" I asked when Freddy led me to Isabelle's front door.

"Sulking, probably," Freddy said. "Don't worry about him."

Before we went inside I took out my mobile and called Max to tell him where I was. He and Casey were at his friend's house in Créances having a long talk, he told me. He insisted that he was coming to fetch me as well, but I put him off by promising to call again within the hour, and to keep my phone turned on and within reach.

Inside, we shed our wet shoes. Freddy slid a pair of soft, Sherpalined mules toward me. Obviously they were Isabelle's. I hesitated before I put them on, but my shoes were wet and my feet were cold. The slippers fit perfectly. Truly, it was an odd feeling to walk in Isabelle's shoes. Forget the Native American exhortation about walking a mile in another man's moccasins before you judge him. What was remarkable to me was that another person's well-worn shoes conformed to my feet. How rare is that?

Claude was in the salon, slouched down on a sofa with a drink in his hands, watching the evening news on television. When he saw me walk in with his son his eyes grew wide, his cheeks freshened, and he started to rise. But Freddy told him, in a very firm tone, to stay put. And then Freddy took me upstairs.

"This was Maman's room," he said, opening a door and ushering me inside. "Later, you and I will have a conversation about what should be done with her personal things. There is a little jewelry, a few small treasures."

I looked around, thoroughly curious, wondering what this room would reveal about Isabelle, but also feeling like an intruder in a stranger's very private place. I saw a very standard room, a double bed covered by a puffy duvet, an easy chair, a wardrobe, a dresser. On top of the dresser, in front of a round mirror, were a single bottle of perfume, Lancôme's Trésor on a small silver tray, and a wooden jewel chest that looked very old. The room was immaculate, could have belonged to anyone, except for towers of precariously stacked books and papers that entirely covered an upholstered window seat.

I said, "She read."

He nodded, an understatement, as he crossed to the wardrobe. Obviously he knew exactly what he was looking for and where to find it, because he reached right in and brought out a large yellow, silk-covered candy box, the fancy sort of thing that is found in expensive European chocolate shops and are perfect for keepsakes when the candy is finished. Freddy set the box on Isabelle's flowered duvet, climbed onto the bed beside it, folded his legs under him, and removed the candy box lid.

"Sit," he said, reaching across the box and patting the bed. I perched on the edge, tentatively, as he began to remove letters and photos from the box. There were cards and notes from Freddy, some handmade obviously when he was very young, the sorts of things only a mother would keep. He put them aside, and set a bundle of letters tied together with a blue velvet ribbon next to them.

I recognized the handwriting on the top envelope of the bundle— my dad's—and felt a little sick. It wasn't a thick bundle, not many more than half a dozen letters in all. I picked them up and fanned through them, confirming that all of the letters had been sent by Dad. The return address was his faculty office at the university, not our house. I checked the postmarks. The most recent letter was nearly twenty-five years old.

"Have you read these?" I asked.

"Those old letters?" He glanced up from the photographs he was sorting. "No."

"My father wrote them," I said.

His head snapped up, an expression of surprise. *"Vraiment?"* Truly? "May I have them?"

He thought for a moment, shrugged, before he said, "Why not? You have a right to them."

I tucked the bundle next to my leg as Freddy handed me a snapshot. What I saw knocked me right off my axis. There I was, again about age two, sitting atop Amy with Isabelle in the saddle behind me, holding me around the middle; the *fromagerie* was visible in the distance. Handwritten on the back was *Marguerite sur sa Amie*. Amy, *amie*: friend. We had been friends, the pony and I, before either of us was transported to Berkeley.

At some level I must have recognized her, and she me, I thought, remembering how she had come straight to me out of the horse trailer she arrived in and nuzzled me, stayed close to me. The big revelation here, however, was that it was Isabelle, and not Dad, who had given me the pony. I wondered if he was as surprised to see Amy as the rest of us were. And no wonder Mom was so furious.

As I studied that snapshot, Freddy spread others across the duvet. They were all taken of me after I left France: at about age eight, playing tetherball at recess at my neighborhood school; at nine or ten riding Amy on the Grizzly Peak fire road in tandem with my best friend, Sandy Bell; in a wet swimsuit at about fourteen, a high school swim meet, arms hugging my chest, obviously cold, probably shivering, as I hurried along the deck toward the team bench where my towel would have been. There were others, all taken when I was out in the open, vulnerable to the prying eye of the camera lens, and all taken with me unaware of the camera's presence.

"Who took these?" I asked.

"Maman, I assume. She would get a big idea from time to time and go over to check on you. She would bring back photos to show the grandmothers and Aunt Louise."

"I didn't know she was there," I said, looking at each of the pictures. I wouldn't want to be Isabelle if Mom ever found out she was lurking around me. And my dad? No clue how he would react; I felt that I didn't know him any longer. Maybe later, when I was alone with Dad's letters, I would find some of the answers I wanted.

I heard Freddy sigh as he placed yet another photo of me on the duvet with the others.

"How did you feel about those visits, Freddy?"

"Oh." He shrugged, thought over his answer. "I was jealous, of course. But not so jealous as my father, even after they were divorced. To compensate, to make us both feel better, he would always arrange a little trip for the two of us while she was gone." The smallest smile crossed his face; bittersweet memories. "We went on manly adventures, like camping in the Black Forest or fishing in the Mediterranean. How do you say it? Guy stuff."

"Sounds like fun," I said.

"Yes." A child's handmade pencil drawing of a deer in the woods fell out of a store-bought birthday card. The card was addressed to MAMAN, and signed FREDDY. Carefully, he put the drawing back inside the card. "I hope you don't judge my father by what you saw of him this after-noon, Maggie. He is the best father a son could hope for, constant, lov-ing. Wise. I try to be all of that for my boys."

"I'm sure you are," I said. "Your boys are wonderful."

"Lena deserves the credit. Their welfare is probably the only reason Lena still tolerates me." He held up his palms: What's to say? "Divorce, never. But murder?"

I cleared my throat, hesitated before I spoke. "You said your father was jealous. Jealous of me?"

He wagged his head from side to side, a sort of yes-and-no response. "You, your father, Maman's success, the Martin family's comfort and influence, and more, I think. Papa always felt he was an old brown shoe and the rest of Maman's life was a shiny Gucci loafer; they never made a pair. He worried that in my eyes he did not measure up."

"Am I a buckle on the Gucci loafer?"

He nodded. "And I think your father was another buckle, a very shiny one."

"Did Isabelle talk to you about my father?"

"Not openly, no. But he was—what do you call it?—a *leitmotif*, a recurring theme. And for me, a very mysterious one." Freddy studied me through narrowed eyes as he said, "I met your father once."

"When?"

"I was about twelve years old. Maman had a professional meeting, a bunch of scientists, in New York, and she took me with her. We went to a musical on Broadway, saw the usual sights. And we went to dinner with your father." He gathered the snapshots together and held them out to me. "I didn't know he was your father at the time, but I have put it together since. He was Dr. Duchamps, an old acquaintance of Maman, that was all I knew; at home, your father was only referred to as 'Alfred.' "

"Just a friendly dinner?" I tucked the photos in with Dad's letters.

"Dinner was friendly, yes," he said. "But afterward, at the hotel, there was a big row, and that's why I remember the meeting so clearly. I don't know what they argued about—they sent me to my room, and anyway, my English couldn't keep up with them—but I know that both Maman and your father were furious. When your father left, he looked as if she had beaten him with a stick."

"Wonder what it was about," I said, though I had some suspicions. The more I saw of Freddy, the more he did not look like Claude. And the more he looked like Dad. "Do you remember anything they said?"

There was a pause, during which Freddy was very still. He seemed to be trying to dredge up some elusive nugget. In the end, he shook his head. "What was singular about that argument, other than seeing Maman argue so heatedly with a stranger, was that in the end he refused her. And she accepted his refusal. Maman never gave up easily. After that, her trips to America ended. Until, of course, week before last."

"And, week before last, for the first time, she approached me," I said. "Wish I knew what she expected from me."

"Maggie." He leaned forward, put his eyes level with mine. "Don't you understand? The purpose was…" He searched for the word. "It was an interview, an audition, if you will. She wanted to know what sort of person you became, what decisions you might make about your inheritance when she was gone."

Made sense, I thought. I said, "We'll never know how I did in the audition, will we?"

He cocked his head and looked at me, a crooked little smile lifting a corner of his mouth. "You have heard of the telephone, sister?"

"Oh, right, she called you."

"Yes, and Grand-mère, and Uncle Gérard, and her solicitor. She sent photos of your home, your horses...."

"And the studio where I work," I said. "And what did she say about it?"

"You did well," he said. "She was excited that you still have horses, and that you choose to live in the country. She was optimistic about you. And now, as you see, you have the job."

There was a tap on the door.

"Entrez," Freddy called out as he piled Isabelle's mementoes back into the yellow candy box.

Kelly peered around the edge of the door. "Well, here you two are. We wondered what happened to you."

"A little walk," Freddy said as he rose and put the box back on its wardrobe shelf. "A little talk."

"We're having a light supper at our house." Kelly spoke very rapidly; a habit from speaking French, or nerves? Too much family togetherness? "Clara made soup and there are salad and cold meat. Maggie, your uncle called. He and Casey are dining with a friend in Créances, though I should tell you that Grand-mère Élodie is not very happy about that. Both of the grandmothers are a bit frothy right now, wondering where you two got to. If I were you I'd get a move on, go over and kiss some old lady cheeks."

Freddy snapped to attention, clicked his heels together—they would have clicked if he weren't wearing velvet house shoes—and saluted. *"Jawohl, meine dame."*

"Shut up, Freddy." But she was laughing. "What a day, huh kids? Maggie, is your daughter all right? Claude really did a number on you two, didn't he? Shame on him."

"We're okay," I said, looking away from Freddy as color rose in his cheeks, chagrined all over again. "But I'm glad Casey is with Uncle Max right now. This situation is very strange for us. She needs some time to process what's happening."

"It's strange for us, too," she said, matter-of-fact, as she headed out the door. She stopped and pointed at Freddy; damned American directness. "I asked your dad to join us, but he declined."

"Probably for the best," he said.

"Got that right," she muttered. "We'll send a plate over."

We followed Kelly down the stairs. Freddy tilted his head and looked at me. "Maybe tomorrow we'll find some time to go through Maman's things."

I held up the letters and pictures. "Freddy, I have everything of Isabelle's that I want. But if you need a friend to be with you when you go through her things, I'll be glad to help you."

He shook his head. "You think she was a stranger to you. But she wasn't. She wanted very much for you to be here."

"Do you?"

"Me?" He laced his hand around my arm. There was no smile when he said, "Depends."

— 16 —

"LOVELY OF YOU to meet me at the airport."

"Pardon me?" Sergei Ludanov, Junior, raised his chin to take a bead on me down his hawk's beak of a nose.

"I saw you at Charles de Gaulle yesterday," I said. "Holding up a sign with my name on it."

He scowled, turned abruptly from me as if to dismiss me as a lunatic. But I stuck close, the two of us off to the side of the salon in the house Gérard built, facing out a window overlooking a dark garden and seeing only the white streaks of falling ice refracting light emitted from our side of the glass.

When Freddy, Kelly and I walked inside, the house was abuzz with the usual pre-dinner activity. A collection of wives, Lena, Julie, and Gillian moved back and forth between the kitchen and the salon with Uncle Gérard, looking rudderless, drifting in their wakes and generally getting in the way. Bébé had gone with Antoine and Jacques to check on the progress of the day's Camembert.

Both grandmothers were napping, Grand-mère Marie, snoring softly, on a sofa in front of the fireplace and Grand-mère Élodie at her own house, quiet now that all the guests were gone. I did wonder, when we learned this, why Kelly had told us they were, as she said, frothy about our absence. Seemed to me that it was Kelly who wanted to keep tabs on us. Freddy went to check on Grand-mère.

The voices of the young people and the beeps of the various electronic gizmos that generally accompanied them filtered down from upstairs. But it was Sergei, standing alone, separate from all the activity, who caught my attention right off.

Earlier that afternoon, when I glimpsed Sergei through the window of his Lamborghini, he had seemed vaguely familiar, though I couldn't place him. From TV or the tabloids, maybe, I thought then. When I walked into the room and saw him standing at a distance, wearing his beautifully tailored charcoal suit, holding a glass of wine, I recognized him.

The dyed hair, the bruise—he had recently taken quite a blow on the point of his cheekbone—and the Lamborghini threw me off, but his posture gave him away. Unquestionably, he was the same young man I had seen at the airport when I first arrived in Paris, holding a sign that read MME MACGOWEN in the same way he now held his wine glass. He was the hire-car driver who disappeared when an airline staffer came and fetched me out of Customs and took me to David.

"Look, lady," he said now, trying to dismiss me, but speaking quietly as if he didn't want the others to hear.

"Maggie MacGowen," I said, offering my hand. "But you know that."

"I'm sorry," he said, keeping both hands wrapped around his glass. "I don't know what you're talking about."

"So, thank you for coming for me," I said to him, ignoring his denials. "There must have been some confusion about arrangements. Grand-mère sent her car for me. Who sent you?"

"You're a crazy woman," he said, and walked away. He got as far as the staircase, but paused for a moment with one foot resting on the bottom step, looking up into the open space above; he checked his watch. I wondered about the hesitation, and wondered why Jemima wasn't with him. I had heard her laughter, so I knew she was upstairs with the others.

I went into a small study off the salon, took out my phone and dialed Dauvin, but the call went straight to voicemail; he had driven away after he dropped off me and Freddy. Speaking slowly in my best French, I left a message saying that I needed to talk to him, and to please return my call as soon as he could. I hoped Sergei stayed around until Dauvin called back.

After the second van incident, I began to think again about the disappearing airport driver: was he a spotter, getting a visual I.D. on me and the car I got into so that we could be tailed? Now that I recognized Sergei as the man who performed that vanishing act, idle wondering took on new weight. I was worried about Jemima, and glad Casey wasn't in the house.

Waiting for Dauvin's call, feeling on edge, I went into the kitchen looking for company.

The kitchen was a hive of female activity, very much like Mom's house at Thanksgiving. I asked if there was something I could do to help. Julie pulled a long wooden spoon out of the soup pot and said I could bring her a glass of cider, please. Her face glowed hot from leaning over the stove.

On my way to fetch it, Lena, with an imperious little smile, handed me a platter of canapés, little toasts with chopped egg, caviar and onion, to take with me, and gave me the assignment usually relegated to kids at my house: "You can set the table."

"Happy to," I said, an excuse to get out of the kitchen where I felt like such an outsider. Whenever I walked into a room, conversation stopped dead, or suddenly changed course.

Kelly followed me out through the swinging door. "If you could set the table, that would be a big help. Julie is at meltdown stage and I want to stay close to her; she can't stand to be in the same room with Gillian. Remember, Louise was her aunt, too."

"Tell me what to do," I said, grateful to have my hands busy. I poured cider into a tall glass and handed it to Kelly to take back into the kitchen to Julie.

"Let me see." Kelly scanned the table quickly. "Oh!" She glanced down and noticed that I was wearing Isabelle's Sherpa-lined mules. "Good for you."

"Freddy insisted," I said. "My shoes are wet."

She dipped her head close to me as if we were sharing a confidence: "Someone should have told you to bring waders." Then it was back to the business of setting the table. "Just a dinner plate at each place. Stack the bowls at the foot of the table by the trivet for the tureen. Cheese plates can stay on the sideboard." She pointed out the cutlery and glasses to use, patted my shoulder and went back into the kitchen to whatever tasks I had interrupted.

I picked up a stack of dinner plates, sturdy country crockery, and began setting one in front of each chair. Some of the chairs had been carried over from Isabelle's house.

The bustling around, everyone pitching in, felt so normal, so familiar. Not familiar because of that déjà vu thing that kept happening to me, but because gatherings at my parents' house had the same sort of atmosphere, the swapping back and forth of chairs and serving pieces.

The difference between their parties and this one was that, with my parents, the community was friends of their choosing. Here, everyone was related by blood or marriage.

Until I arrived in France, my family was Mom, Casey, Uncle Max, and two cousins on the East Coast that I barely knew. Now, suddenly, in Normandy, I had a big family. And as suddenly I wasn't at all certain where, or if, I fit in anywhere.

"May I help?" Uncle Gérard took the stack of plates from my hands and held them for me to place, following me as I made my trip around the long table.

"Handsome boy, isn't he?" Gérard said as I took a plate from the stack.

"Sergei?" I watched the young man's back as he checked his phone and, finally, began to slowly, maybe reluctantly, mount the stairs. What was he waiting for? "I can't say much for his manners."

"Ah, well." A very Gallic gesture of dismissal, a shrug, an exaggerated frown. "What can I say? He is Russian."

"I say, 'Handsome is as handsome does.'"

Gérard seemed to be at a loss for only a moment before he recouped and launched into another topic, the one I suspect he intended to broach at the outset. "Dear niece, you promised your old uncle a few moments of your time. Now is as good as later, yes?"

"I suppose." I dreaded this moment. But if it had to happen, better that it happen in a room with others around.

Gérard had refrained from bringing *it* up—the big scheme—until after the funeral. He'd had an opportunity that morning when we were alone at the convent, but, graciously, had not. So I would listen to his pitch now, but I would not be pressed for a firm answer to what I feared he might propose. I wondered whether, in the end, should he and I not close a deal to his liking, he would continue to be so genteel toward me.

Plates finished, he helped me place water and wineglasses on a tray. He held the tray for me as he had held the dinner plates while I set the full variety of glassware above each plate.

As we made our second tour around the table, he opened his appeal. "My dear, may I say first that your mother would have been delighted if she could walk through that door and see you here among your family. It was always her greatest wish to be reunited with you."

"I'm beginning to understand that," I said. He had said exactly the same thing the day before when we first met. Did he have a script?

"Because of her profound affection for you, Maggie." The name came out Marg-gy, as if he had started to say Marguerite but changed his mind, shifted mid-tongue to Maggie. "She has left you in a position to influence decisions that will affect the future of the entire family."

"In what way?" I asked, as if I didn't know. Just about everyone had already said some version of the same thing. I saw a flutter in one heavy eyebrow that revealed his skepticism about my innocence, and maybe my sincerity.

"You are a well-informed woman," he said, the old buttering up. "I don't need to explain to you the devastation the recent economic downturn has had on people all over. Myself, for one, a developer, trying his best to salvage a very worthy project, to raise a community out of pending collapse, if you will."

"Antoine told me about your plan," I said. "It's very ambitious."

"You say ambitious," he said, smiling broadly. "I say optimistic. Maggie, think of the benefits such a development would bring to the region."

"For example?"

"Jobs," he effused as if dropping a magic word. "Have you considered how many jobs we will create just in the building phase alone?"

"Jobs?" Glasses in place, I went back to the sideboard for cutlery: soup spoons, coffee spoons, meat forks, salad forks, dessert forks, dinner knives, butter knives, cheese knives. I kept my eyes on the cutlery drawer as I counted enough of each, and did not look directly at my uncle as I said, "I think there is a big difference between a 'job' and temporary 'work' like construction. But jobs, well, those are more permanent sources of employment. If your development goes forward as described in your prospectus, when it's complete and the construction workers go off in search of their next gig, how many jobs in this region will have been permanently lost?"

He shrugged. "An insignificant number, I am certain."

I looked up at him briefly to check his expression, pausing as I laid a row of forks beside a plate. "Not insignificant to the people who lose them."

"My dear..."

"I visited the *fromagerie*," I said. Kelly came in from the kitchen and hovered for a moment, being nosy, before she went back. "I know that the cheese operation supports two shifts of workers every day, not counting Antoine and his family and Jacques Breton and his. How many families depend on the cider production? How many the carrots? The horses? I can't think the loss of their jobs would be insignificant to any of those people."

He set the tray on the edge of the table to free his hands so that he could make a broad backhand sweep that seemed intended to dismiss my questions. "Apples, carrots, cheese: do you not see that these are remnants of a primitive era? They barely cover operating expenses and will always be dependent on some level of outside support to survive. But you must see the potential here for something magnificent. It is time for progress in this region."

"Maybe we don't define progress in the same way," I said, holding a bouquet of knives gripped in my hand, feeling dismayed. "I grew up in California. I have seen what your notion of progress does to the land. It would be a crime for you to ruin this beautiful place; once it's gone, you can't ever get it back."

"Marguerite," he began. I could see he was surprised by my reaction and was trying to bring down the emotional level. He seemed so heedless about the catastrophe his success would be for those he claimed as his near and dear. In the end, what mattered to Gérard? "Let us discuss this at another time. We have all had a very trying day, yes?"

"Yes."

"Forgive me." He gave me *la bise* by way of apology. "I have behaved badly, and I am heartened by your obvious affection for our estate. I was a bull to introduce so delicate a topic so badly. We will talk later, and we will do what is best."

"I hope we will know what that is," I said. I noticed that both Lena and Kelly were now hovering in the salon, eavesdropping, and that Gillian was standing in the kitchen door looking very apprehensive.

The clang of the front door latch distracted us all. I heard my daughter's voice out in the entry hall—she was supposed to be with Uncle Max in Créances—as she came in with David. There was a moment of silence, and then she said, with awe, "She is so beautiful! Who is she?"

"Aunt Louise." David's voice in reply; Casey had seen the portrait of Louise. "She was my great-aunt, Antoine and Bébé's mother. Bébé painted the portrait."

"Bébé told me he was a graphic artist, but I had no idea he was so-o-o-o talented." Casey continued this enthusiastic conversational stream—uncomfortable for some to hear, to be sure. I saw both Gillian and Gérard blanch at the mention of the late Louise, the angel of the house. Kelly grinned like a happy cat.

As the young pair walked into the salon, each the entire focus of the other, Casey naïvely asked David, "What happened to Louise?"

David glanced up, caught Uncle Gérard's eye. Looking straight at

Gérard, David said, "A mystery. Her car went over the cliff and into the sea at Barfleur one fine, sunny day."

"Casey." I walked over to my daughter before she got both feet firmly planted in family quagmire. "I thought you were having dinner with Uncle Max."

"That was the plan," she said, giving me a quick hug. "But Grand-mère sent David to ask me to come back here instead. I thought that if it was that important to her…"

"Since you're here," I said, "would you help me with the table?"

"Sure." She unwound a long woolen scarf from around her neck and draped it over the back of an easy chair. Both she and David were in stocking feet, having shed wet shoes in the entry. She noticed Isabelle's mules on my feet. "Those are cool. Where did you get them?"

"Actually, they're warm," I said and she gave me a good-humored you-are-so-lame eye roll in response. "They were Isabelle's."

Kelly came forward. "You know what they say about too many cooks, Casey. Why don't you and David go upstairs where the rest of the hooligans are hanging out until we call you for dinner?"

Casey looked at me for approval, I nodded, and she and David, talking all the way, went up to join the other young people.

As I turned back to my job, I caught Lena, standing next to Kelly at the far end of the table, staring at my daughter's back with a chilling malevolence. Why would she care enough about Casey to have such obviously strong feelings?

Without shifting her focus from Casey's retreating back, Lena tilted her head toward Kelly and muttered in French, "So appropriate, the bastard's daughter together with the peasant's son."

Kelly must have seen that I overheard, and understood. She flushed a furious red and buried her face in her hands, and muttered, "Hélène, jeez."

Lena glanced at me, quickly realized her faux pas—her lovely face transformed into a fright mask—and retreated into the kitchen. A great clattering of pans, a tantrum expressed via cookware, immediately followed.

From the salon, we could hear Gillian's sharp rebuke to Lena. "That will do. Stop it. Now."

There was a last clatter, then rapid, sharp footfalls on the stone kitchen door, followed by the slamming of the kitchen door.

Kelly walked over and removed a plate from the table. She said, "One less for dinner, I think."

"Surely she'll be back when she cools off," I said.

"Lena?" Kelly shook her head. "Lena doesn't cool off."

Freddy came in through the front with Grand-mère, looking frail, on his arm. "Was that my wife I just saw flash out the back, or is the kitchen on fire?"

"Is there a difference?" Kelly asked.

"Perhaps I should…"

"Leave her," Kelly said firmly as she wrapped an arm around Grand-mère. Gently, she escorted the older woman toward the easy chairs in front of the fire. She looked over her shoulder. "Freddy, will you give the *fromagerie* a buzz and tell Antoine, Jacques, and Bébé that it's time to come in for dinner?"

Grand-mère touched my arm as they walked past. "Sit with me, my dear."

I took charge of Grand-mère from Kelly and settled her into a cushy chair facing Grand-mère Marie's napping spot. With some effort, Grand-mère put her feet up on an ottoman. I spread a hand-knitted afghan over her lap.

"Thank you, my dearest Maggie." That was the first time she did not call me Marguerite. While I was still bent over her, tucking in the afghan, she reached up and caressed my cheek. "Please, stay here beside me."

The big chair next to hers felt warm and lovely; I hadn't realized how tired I was. Jet lag, certainly, but so much more. If I was tired, Grand-mère, more than twice my age, had to be exhausted.

I asked her, "How are you?"

"Feeling every one of my years." She smiled in a sweet but self-deprecatory way. "And how are you?"

I thought about the question for a moment before I answered. "I'm confused. I think I understand what Isabelle wanted me to do, but I can't be sure what the correct thing is."

She nodded as she took my hand in hers. "I have confidence in you."

"That makes one of us."

Grand-mère glanced at her old friend, made certain that Grand-mère Marie was still asleep. And then gripping my wrist as if I were a flight risk, she asked, "Will you tell me the truth if I ask you a difficult question?"

"I won't lie to you," I said. "But whether I answer depends on the question."

"Fair enough." The chair seemed to engulf her, made her seem very small, indeed. Her eyes filmed with tears. "I keep thinking about the questions that fool Dauvin asked you at the church. There was no need for them, unless... My dear, was my Isabelle murdered?"

"Yes." No reason to equivocate. Dauvin's investigation was about to descend on these people.

"Do you know by whom?"

I shook my head. "Detective Longshore—you spoke to him—believes it was a hired assassin. But who hired him and why? I'm still a stranger here. I can only guess."

Her calm acceptance surprised me. "Do you know that we watch your television reports?"

"Kelly told me her parents send them over."

"From what I have seen of your work, I know that you have probably formed a fair guess based on the information you have already learned. Am I wrong?"

"I have a few ideas about why, none at all about whom. But are those ideas worth anything?" I shook my head. "I promised Detective Longshore that I would leave everything to the police."

A sharp cry from upstairs, a male voice, stopped all conversation in the salon as all eyes went toward the broad staircase. Sergei, a streak of good suiting as he flew down the stairs, crossed the salon without another word and fled out the front door, slamming it shut behind him as if he needed to make a last comment.

"Gérard!" Grand-mère called to her son. "See to the boy, please."

But before Gérard could get his shoes on and raise the front door latch, there was a roar of massive Italian car engine coming to life, and then the churning of mud, ice and gravel as it sped past the house, headed toward the road.

Gérard came back into the salon, looked at his mother and shrugged with both palms up, as in, He's gone.

Several of the youngsters wandered down the stairs in the steamy wake of the Russian prince, curious, aroused by the drama. Kelly spotted her daughter. "Lulu, tell the others to come to the table. Now, please."

Casey wandered down in the middle of the pack. When I caught her eye, she came to me, sat on the arm of my chair.

"What happened?" I asked her quietly.

"I don't know," she said. "We heard someone shouting, but it came from down the hall someplace."

Jemima was getting a similar questioning from her father, and seemed to give a similar negative.

I asked Casey, "Were Sergei and Jemima arguing?"

"God, no. She was with me and David. She says she hates Sergei."

"But she told Bébé he was her boyfriend," I said.

"She only said that to get Bébé off her back," Casey said. "He's always teasing her. She wanted him to stop."

"Dear God," Grand-mère said. "I will have a word with Bébé."

"Not necessary, Grand-mère," Casey said, laying her cheek against her grandmother's. The affectionate gesture brought new tears to Élodie's eyes. "Jemima can take care of herself. That black eye Sergei has?"

"What about it?" I asked.

"Jemima gave it to him."

—17—

GÉRARD WAS JUST serving the soup when Inspector Dauvin knocked on the door. I thought he might have chosen that post-funeral family gathering as the time and place to formally drop his bombshell about Isabelle's manner of death, though that piece of news had already leaked from Dauvin to Antoine to Kelly and Jacques, and from me to Grand-mère. Probably better that they knew and had time to prepare themselves before he said anything officially.

Dauvin had a bombshell to drop all right, just not the one I expected.

"Yes, I know who drove the yellow Lamborghini that was here earlier," Antoine told Dauvin in answer to his question. "A young man named Sergei Ludanov."

"Sergei Ludanov?" Dauvin scowled, skeptical of the answer. "Surely not. Ludanov is a middle-aged man."

"Junior," Bébé chimed in, glancing sidelong at Jemima. "Sergei Ludanov, Junior. What's the young pup done now?"

"He's wrapped that yellow car around a tree, not a mile from here."

"Dear God." Uncle Gérard rose to his feet as if pulled upward by a string attached to the top of his head. "He isn't…?"

Dauvin shook his head. "Not yet, anyway. He was taken to the clinic in Lessay by ambulance. Surgeons are working on him. I don't know the extent of his injuries. But the car is finished."

I glanced at Jemima, curious to see her reaction. No dramatics, no great surprise there either. A sort of quiet disgust crossed her face as if she were thinking, The dumb shit, what now?

Dauvin flipped open a pocket notebook. "The car is registered to Zed Entertainment, Limited. Is the boy an employee of the company?"

"Fat chance of that," Jemima muttered as she folded her napkin and tucked it delicately under the edge of her plate. "Employee? Sergei work for a living? As if."

The interpretation of that statement took Antoine a couple of tries before Dauvin understood: Sergei was not employed. Through Antoine, the inspector asked Jemima, "Did Ludanov say where he got the car?"

"He didn't tell me, and I didn't ask," she said. "It's not as if we're together."

"But Jemima," Gillian began, apparently surprised to hear that bit of news.

Bébé's face registered both confusion and some disdain as he asked his half sister, "Then why was he here? He's hardly an old family friend."

"That's what *I* asked him," Jemima said, glaring at Bébé. "He only met Isabelle once. At Easter."

I said, "Jemima, maybe you would prefer having a private conversation with Inspector Dauvin."

"Thanks," she said, giving me an appreciative nod. "But it's not necessary. There's no big secret or anything. Look, Sergei came by our flat day before yesterday. I wasn't expecting him. We broke up a week ago— he started behaving like an unbearable braggart, so I cut him loose. Then he suddenly showed up and wanted me to come over with him, but I said no. He drives like a maniac." She dropped her eyes when she realized the awful truth of her last remark.

"But that doesn't answer my question," Bébé said. "If he wasn't here as your boyfriend, why was he here?"

"He told me he had some sort of business deal in Normandy to finish—he didn't say what it was—and because he would be in the area, he would drop by to pay his respects. I told him not to bother, but he came anyway, didn't he?"

Jemima met Casey's eyes, a question in her expression, an appeal for support. Casey said, "You might as well tell them, Jem."

Jemima looked at her father, Gérard. He gave a small shake of his head, a caution, but she continued, anyway.

"When I told Sergei that I wouldn't come with him, he got very angry, vile actually. He wouldn't tell me why it was so important for him to be here. He just said that it was, that's all. At one point he grabbed me, tried to force me into his car." Again she glanced at Casey, who nodded encouragement. "So I hit him in the face."

There was a moment of quiet. Gillian was the first to speak. "You should have—"

"Should have what, Mummy?" Jemima challenged heatedly.

Dauvin broke in: Did Jemima have a number to contact Sergei's family?

"I only have Sergei's mobile," she said.

"Just a moment. His father..." Uncle Gérard shuffled through a stack of business cards he pulled from his wallet and selected one, which he handed to Dauvin. When various members of his family seemed puzzled or concerned that he had the personal card of Sergei's notorious father, he said, "Sergei's father and I sit together on the Greater London Youth Football Council."

I doubt many bought his explanation; Gérard was not very popular with this crowd.

Dauvin took the card, put his notebook away and apologized for interrupting the meal. As he turned to leave, Grand-mère asked him, "Who is with the boy now?"

"Clinic staff," Dauvin said with a shrug. "And a district gendarme, in case he is able to make a statement."

"Then he is alone among strangers," Grand-mère said, looking from one face to another, making a circuit of the table, challenging us all. "The boy was a guest in this house."

"Yes, of course." Antoine kissed Kelly on the cheek as he rose from his seat. "I'll call you when I know anything."

Dauvin turned to me. "You left a message. What is it you wish to discuss?"

"Young Sergei," I said.

He gestured over his shoulder with a thumb, as in, You come, too. As I rose, I leaned close to David, who sat on my right, and asked him to make sure that Casey got safely back to Grand-mère's house after dinner. Then I asked Grand-mère to excuse me, and hurried to catch up with Antoine and Dauvin. On my way out I borrowed my daughter's boots from the rank of shoes in the entry. They were too big for me, but they were dry and warm.

In the car, through Antoine, I told Dauvin about seeing Sergei at the airport the day before, and that, when I confronted him, Sergei had denied being there. I wondered if he had anything to do with the two van incidents and the delivery of an explosive envelope, and whatever that *thing* was, did it in any way explain why he insisted on being with the family today?

Dauvin said he would look into it. I also told him that Sergei had argued with someone, though I had no idea who it was—maybe by telephone—immediately before he left the house in a great rush.

"Stupid kid," Dauvin said. "That car was more machine than he could control. He put his foot on the gas, hit a patch of ice, and…" He didn't need to say more.

The village road was a long straight stretch of pavement. As soon as we turned out of the compound drive we could see the flashing blue and white lights of emergency vehicles in the distance. Summoned by a nearby householder who heard the collision, help had come quickly, and in force.

France is famous for bloody, deadly car accidents because people drive so fast. Even on country roads, like those around the village, crazy speed is the norm. So when a collision happens, as the French say, *catastrophe*. The local first responders are well practiced.

At the crash site, Dauvin pulled over to the side of the road next to a tow truck and we all got out.

The night was frigid. A steady icy drizzle fell. Icicles dangled from the branches of naked trees and sparkled in the flashing lights, turning the wreckage scene into a macabre fairyland.

We read the skid marks on the road: Sergei, speeding, hit ice, spun out of control and smacked a tree broadside with enough force to shake loose its icicles. Shards of ice glittered on the black ground around the rear half of the cleaved Lamborghini. The front end came to a stop a hundred yards away, out in a freshly plowed carrot field. Oddly, the driver's seat and the fragment of chassis it was attached to had broken free during impact. When the rear end of the car came to an abrupt stop, the seat was spit out like a cherry pit and continued traveling, cartwheeling along the pavement. It landed upright, intact, in the middle of the road, the path it traveled in its crazy trajectory painted in blood.

Mix a six-hundred-grand speed bomb with naïveté and bad weather, add anger, and you get a yellow Lamborghini sliced in two as cleanly as a knife would halve a ripe banana. And you get its driver *in extremis*.

I felt heartsick, imagining what happened to Sergei, strapped in that car seat. The ambulance crew, long gone now, left a litter of bloody dressings in the roadway. Sergei's beautifully tailored jacket was reduced to shreds and discarded among the medical waste.

I picked up the jacket, smoothed it over my arm and turned to Dauvin. "You said he is alive?"

The inspector held up a finger, made a call, asked that question of whoever answered, and then said, "He is alive. In surgery still. Prospects?" He glanced heavenward. "In the hands of the angels."

Dauvin took the jacket from my arm and went through the pockets: mobile phone, slender leather wallet, small comb, packet of breath mints. He checked the phone's call log. Something he saw there interested him enough that there actually was a little twitch at the corner of his mouth. He closed the phone, rummaged in the inner pockets of his overcoat, found a plastic evidence bag and slipped Sergei's effects into it.

"Was he drinking before he left the house?" Dauvin asked as he wrote the date, the time, and his name on the bag after he sealed it.

"Sergei was holding a glass of wine when I came in," I said. Dauvin stuffed the plastic bag and its contents into a pocket and took out his notebook. He made notes from Antoine's translation of what I said. "I have no idea how much he drank before I arrived. You'll have to ask the others. Maybe ten or fifteen minutes after I arrived, Sergei went upstairs. Not long after, we heard him shout, he sounded angry, then he ran out and drove off. My daughter told me that Sergei did not join the other young people upstairs, so I don't know who or what he shouted at."

"Did you know him well?" Dauvin asked Antoine. Antoine did not always translate for me the questions that Dauvin addressed to him. I had to struggle to make sense of what he was asked, and what he answered.

"No, we did not know him well," Antoine told Dauvin. "He came with Jemima at Easter, but that is the only time I met him."

"Was there any argument at Easter?"

Antoine shook his head. "The usual, you know. A meal, a visit to the cemetery. The apple trees were in bloom, we took boughs to my grandfather's grave."

"Young Ludanov went with you?"

"Yes."

Dauvin elevated a palm: a question, a prod for any other information.

"I remember," Antoine said, "at lunch he told the women he could get designer leather goods for them, cheap. My wife warned him he would get into trouble if he sold bootleg knock-offs. But he said they weren't knock-offs. When he offered my daughter a little handbag he took from the trunk of his car, my wife made her give it back." Antoine ran his fingers through damp hair. "The only discord I remember that day was between my wife and my daughter about returning the handbag—Lulu loved it, pink Louis Vuitton."

"Did anyone accept bags from him?" Dauvin asked.

"Not openly," Antoine said. "Not with Kelly there. My wife is…" He appealed to me. "How do you say it in America?"

"A regular Girl Scout?" I offered.

"Exactly. She complained later that she knew the bags were either counterfeit or stolen, and she worried about Jemima hanging out with him. I didn't see anyone go away with Sergei's bags, but he did hand out his card, so anyone could have contacted him later."

"Who, for example?"

"The family. All of us except I think Bébé. Some project in Paris he couldn't get away from."

Dauvin raised his eyebrows at Antoine as a challenge and Antoine amended his statement. "Bébé came by the morning before Easter Sunday and stayed only long enough to hang the portrait of Maman in the entry so that Papa would see it first thing when he arrived. And then he left again. We did not tell Grand-mère he was there at all."

Dauvin nodded. The new version apparently meshed with his recollection. The men were friends, their boys hung out together. Surely he knew the story of the portrait.

The inspector gazed away toward the wreckage, apparently oblivious to the nasty weather as he watched the accident investigators go about their jobs taking pictures, measuring skid marks, studying the remains of the car. I ventured to ask, "Could we get out of the rain?"

Jerked back to focus on his companions, Dauvin was effusive in his apologies. "Of course. So inconsiderate of me, yes."

In the car, he turned the heater and defroster on high, and drove away from the scene as soon as the fog had cleared from the windows. I was just beginning to thaw out when we arrived at the clinic, a small modern hospital.

Sergei was still in surgery when we arrived. A woman police officer stationed outside the surgery suite rose and stood at attention when she saw Dauvin. She reported: internal bleeding, the spleen had been removed, every extremity suffered compound fractures from his tumble along the pavement strapped into the bucket seat. There was some conversation among the surgeons about possible amputations.

But there was some good news, or, more correctly, some not-so-damned-awful news, good and bad often being relative terms. First, near-freezing temperatures had slowed his blood loss so he survived until the rescue crew arrived. Second, the seat back was high enough to protect his head and neck from significant trauma. Whatever the extent of his injuries, if—a big if—the boy survived, he faced a long and ex-cruciating recovery. But he was talking when he arrived at the hospital.

"What did he say?" Dauvin asked.

"His father was going to kill him. And he kept saying something in English about a deer. A goddamn deer. It was difficult to understand him."

"He swerved to avoid a deer?" Dauvin asked.

After the officer said "goddamn," I heard her say a word that An-toine translated as deer, but that I expected him to translate as some-thing else. I asked, "Are you sure she said 'deer'?"

"A female deer, a doe," Antoine said, looking around for help. He asked for the officer's pad, found the word she had written and showed me: *biche.*

I said, "I think he was saying, 'goddamn bitch.'"

The officer overheard and pointed at me. *"Exactement."*

"He was mad at a woman."

"Of course." Antoine smacked his forehead. "I've been back here too long. I'm losing my English."

"Maybe just the rude parts," I said.

Dauvin and Antoine had a discussion about who should call Ser-gei's family in London. Because Antoine spoke English, it was decided that he should be the one. The two of them went off to a small waiting room where mobile phone use was permitted, and placed the call.

I followed them, went to a far corner of the room, found a perch in a window niche where the phone signal was strong, and called Uncle Max. Casey had already given him the essentials, up to the point where we left the house. I gave him an update, and told him about seeing Sergei at de Gaulle.

"I don't like it," Max said. "I don't want you two around there for another minute."

"You're a sweet old fusspot," I said to him. "But we're all right. I'm in a public place with two *flics* within arm's reach. There's a nice young man staying close to Casey. Don't worry about us. This accident was just that, an accident. It has nothing to do with us."

He groused a bit. I changed the subject, talked to him for a few minutes about making a film in Normandy. "Wish I'd brought at least a little palmcorder to make some rough shots."

"I'll see what I can do," he said. "Do you want Guido to come and give you a hand?"

"Not yet," I said. "When I left LA we had just begun working on the film for January sweeps. Guido needs to stay with it. I'll be back by the middle of next week."

He agreed that we should focus on keeping our current film on schedule. We were midway into the current season's contract. The Normandy film, my family film, would open the fall season next year, and had to wait.

I asked Max if he had spoken to Mom, because I had not been able to reach her. He said he had tried a couple of times, but had missed her, and blamed the time difference. He reminded me that she kept her days full. I promised to phone him if I learned anything, and he promised not to hover. Not to hover too obviously, that is.

Next, I tried Mom at home again; she won't carry a mobile phone. When there was no answer, I called her friend Gracie Nussbaum. If anyone knew where Mom was, it would be Gracie. They had been close friends since long before I was born.

"Betsy has been staying with me," Gracie told me when I asked if she knew where Mom was. "This Isabelle thing has been hard for her. She seemed terribly sad so I invited her to come here for a few days."

"You're a good friend," I said.

"I hope that's so," she said. "Betsy isn't here right now, though. It's Saturday. She's accompanying a tap dance class at the Senior Center. You might try her again in about an hour."

"I will," I said. "But, Gracie, while I have you, I want to ask you about something you said to me the day after Thanksgiving."

"Something *I* said?"

"When I met you coming home from the farmer's market, you told me that Isabelle was always a dark shadow hanging over me. I thought you were being metaphorical. But I found out that from time to time Isabelle actually did shadow me, taking pictures. Did you know?"

"Of course I did. So did your parents." She sounded very matter-of-fact. "Remember this place where you grew up, honey? Do you think that if one of the mothers in this town saw someone, a stranger, taking photographs of one of our little hatchlings that she wouldn't be on the phone to the mother ASAP? I, myself, saw Isabelle hanging around near your school one day—you were maybe in the third grade. I figured out who she was—something about the way Frenchwomen wear their clothes—and told her to keep the hell away from you."

"Gracie," I said, visualizing the reaming out that Isabelle must have received from Gracie Nussbaum. "Your language shocks me."

"Bullshit," she countered, laughing. "Maggie, dear, why do you think your parents parked you in that convent school down in Carmel when you were a teenager?"

"Because I was an obnoxious teenager and they wanted peace in their house?"

"Of course you were, and maybe they did. Obnoxious is the teenager's job," she said. "But you were no more so than your sister or brother were. Or my kids, for that matter. No, Maggie, they hid you away down there."

"From Isabelle?"

"Yes. Isabelle was spotted at one of your swim meets when you were about fourteen, maybe fifteen. Betsy was afraid that Isabelle would decide that you were old enough to hear the truth—Isabelle's version of the truth—and approach you."

"Maybe I would have understood."

"Do you believe that for a second?"

"No," I said, remembering how Isabelle had frightened me when she got around to delivering her message to me, and the way I reacted to her when she popped out at me at the market, and I'm far from being a kid. There was no finesse, no gentle, measured approach. Just, Hello, I'm your mother. If she had accosted me the same way when I was a teenager, I would have screamed for someone to call the police.

I asked, "I've heard Isabelle described as eccentric a few times now. Absentminded and doggedly determined. Anything you want to add to the characterization?"

Gracie thought for a moment before she said, "My darling husband, Ben, was certain that she had some sort of personality disorder."

"Some sort?" I could see Dr. Nussbaum making a pronouncement, loudly and with finality, probably waving a fat, ingredient-shedding sandwich while he pontificated. "Nothing more specific?"

"He never met her, dear. But look up mental disorders in the *DSM-IV*. You just may find Isabelle's face in a citation."

I love Gracie, forthright to a fault. This time, a morsel or two learned, another few confirmed, and my spirits were buoyed enough knowing Mom was in good hands that I was ready to soldier on.

Out in the hall, the young woman officer attending the surgery suite's door had begun to pace; boring duty. When I caught her eye, she raised her palms and shook her head: no further news on Sergei's condition.

There was an agitated conversation underway across the room. I looked over and saw both Antoine and Dauvin with telephones to their ears. Antoine looked a bit ill. Whatever he was hearing was not good news. Dauvin, as usual, gave nothing away.

I dialed Rich Longshore. On the third ring, the desk at the LA County Sheriff's Homicide Bureau picked up for him.

"Detective Hartunian." Someone I knew, another friend of Mike.

"Hey, Kevin," I said. "It's Maggie MacGowen. I'm looking for Rich Longshore."

"That's probably why you called his line," he said, ever affable, acknowledging the silliness of his remark. "You still over in France?"

"I am."

"Any Frenchmen surrender to you yet?"

"Good one, Kevin," I said. "You managed to get both sexual innuendo and a shopworn cultural slur into one sentence. Takes skill of a singular variety."

He chuckled. "Yeah, well, Rich said he was expecting your call so I had time to hone it."

"How are Judy and the kids?" I asked.

"What kids? Our baby made me a grandpa last month."

"Congratulations." After hearing the details, sex, weight, degree of cute, I congratulated him again and asked, "Is Rich around?"

"He's involved in a three-way, Maggie."

Both Antoine and Dauvin still had their mobile phones to their ears. Dauvin would speak in French, Antoine would speak in English, then they would both listen. So, Dauvin was on the phone with Rich, and Antoine was translating through a conference hookup.

"I can see that."

"Where are you?"

"Across the room from the two invited to Rich's party. Tell Rich to call me, please. And say hello to Judy for me."

Not thirty seconds after I hung up, both Dauvin and Antoine turned and looked at me at the same time. I waved. Obviously the message that I called Rich had been relayed to them.

I rifled my bag for something to write on and came across the card that Jean-Paul had given me. He hadn't told me when he was leaving Los Angeles. He might already be in France. Just the thought of that made my heart do a loop-the-loop. I repeated a caveat to self, Tread with care.

I was very attracted to Jean-Paul, but he was an acquaintance of Gérard, a polo buddy, Gillian said. Gérard knew Sergei's family. Sergei was hawking designer-label leather goods of questionable provenance. Jean-Paul had made a gift of a very fine bag to me; I assumed from the label it was very fine, but… Hard to imagine that the French consul would be party to anything as sleazy as handing out fake French designer leather goods, but any Jean-Paul–Gérard–Sergei connection needed to be exorcised before I got any further with the man.

Antoine and Dauvin closed their mobile phones at the same time. Almost immediately, mine rang. Without looking at the caller I.D., I said, "Hello, Rich."

"You called?"

"I did. I have a favor to ask of you."

"Okay."

"I understand that there are ways to verify whether a designer knock-off is genuine or not, a pattern in the stitching or something about the lining that would be too expensive for a counterfeiter to replicate." When he asked if I was doing a little back alley shopping, I explained about Sergei's out-of-the-trunk enterprise, that I had a bag whose *bona fides* I wanted to verify, and asked how I could find the information to do that.

"Easiest way would be to take the bag to a store that sells the brand," he said. "They would recognize a fake."

"The thing is, the bag in my possession has a serial number engraved on a little brass tag sewn inside, like a Rolex does. If it's genuine, my questions could get back to the person who gave it to me."

"Who was that?"

"The French consul general in LA."

"Bernard?" His laugh was derisive. "You don't expect a class act like Jean-Paul Bernard to be involved with a bottom-rung hood like this Ludanov kid, do you?"

"Not directly, no. But I can come up with several scenarios that might put knock-offs of expensive French-label items in his hands to distribute as, say, gifts, without making him dirty."

"I get you," he said. "I know a guy in Customs who specializes in counterfeits. He gave me a Web site that lists the information you're looking for. Hold on a sec. I'll get it for you."

I heard a drawer open and a folder snap open—Rich is extremely meticulous about filing information—and then he was back. During the pause I dug out a pen.

"Thanks," I said as I wrote down the URL he gave me on the back of Jean-Paul's card. "Rich, *is* Sergei a bottom-rung hood?"

"Looks like he's trying to make his bones. Interpol has a watch on him."

"Watching him for what?"

"Nothing major, so far. Look, you okay there at the hospital with Dauvin and that guy—what is he, your cousin?"

"Yes. And I'm okay. I don't have wheels or I'd go home and finish dinner."

"Would you do me a favor and stay put there for a little while longer?"

"Why?"

"To humor me."

"You going to throw me another bone or two of information, Rich? Might make it easier to sit on these rock-hard chairs for a while. Almost as bad as the chairs at the DMV."

"When you put it that way." He laughed. Antoine and Dauvin had gone to speak with the policewoman. Dauvin glanced at me, and the woman officer's gaze followed his, so I knew they were talking about me.

"So?" I said.

"Phone company sent over the incoming and outgoing calls recorded on the cell towers in the area where the car was stolen, the one that hit your mother. Lots of calls to track down. From the single eye-witness account, we were able to narrow our timeframe significantly, and from his description of the thief, we were able to narrow down the pool of callers to a hundred or so."

"Some are more likely culprits than others?" I asked.

"Oh yeah. We tracked one number to a gangbanger from Reseda, kid with a juvenile record that includes car theft and joy-riding. Name's Chuy Cepeda," Rich said. "He placed a call from that neighborhood during our time window to a guy who runs a so-called auto repair shop in Pacoima. A Russian guy, Something-something-ovich—no vowels, so don't ask me to pronounce it."

"Is it a chop shop?" I asked.

"Looks like it, yeah. Something-ovich gets an online order for a particular model car—color, accessories, year, wheels, whatever the buyer wants—and then he contracts with gangbangers like this Cepeda kid to go shop the streets until the exact car is found. The kid gets a finder's fee when he brings it in. 'Ovich switches out the VIN plates and jiggers up new registration papers and delivers the cars to the buyer. All the money is handled through an offshore account. The arrangement's what you call half-smart: Worked fine until we caught him. Whole thing unraveled in a hurry."

"Very enterprising," I said. "But what can any of that possibly have to do with Isabelle Martin?"

"I don't know yet," he said. "But your Inspector Dauvin just gave me another piece to worry about. We got 'Ovich's phone records—personal, home, shop, all we could find. He made and received a lot of calls, but one number stood out because of the frequency of the calls clustered around the time of the Martin event, and because the number went to a blind, an unregistered phone. Probably a disposable with a counterfeit or stolen SIM card."

Rich paused, maybe to let all that sink in. He is a gifted storyteller when he puts his mind to it, likes to draw out the suspense. So far, his was the tale of a group of small-time crooks who figured out how to profit by pilfering off a buffet of other people's property.

"And the missing piece Inspector Dauvin gave you?" I said, prodding him to continue.

"That blind phone?" Another infuriating pause. "Dauvin found it in the pocket of Sergei Ludanov, Junior, at the scene of his accident."

"Merde," I said, French for holy shit, among other things. I had handed the jacket with the phone to Dauvin.

Dauvin and Antoine heard me swear, were watching me, their expressions full of expectation: how would I react to this discovery? Now they knew. Antoine came over and took a chair beside my window perch, solicitous, looking worried as he sat down. Overly worried, I thought.

"Have you spoken with Chuy?" I asked Rich.

"We went by his house yesterday afternoon—he was living with his mother. But we missed him."

"So, you're still looking for him."

"Oh no, we found him all right," Rich said. "Last night we caught a drive-by shooting call over in El Sereno. Chuy Cepeda took one in the chest and one to the noggin."

"And because Homicide Bureau caught the call," I said, "I'm guessing Chuy was already singing with the angels, instead of singing to you."

"I doubt there are angels in the choir where Chuy went, but yeah."

"Damn." Dauvin was still watching me. "Do you think Chuy did it? Killed Isabelle, I mean."

"Starting to look that way," Rich said. "But he was only the trigger man, so to speak."

"For Sergei, via Whosit'ovich?"

"That's my guess. But the big question still is, what did Sergei hope to gain?"

Given a little time to think through various implications of what he had just learned, Antoine was about to come unglued. His breath came in ragged shudders, there was no color in his face. I reached over and took his hand, gave it a squeeze. He then gripped mine in both of his; his hands trembled.

"Maggie," Rich said after a pause. "You told Guido that a paparazzo snapped pictures of your encounter with Isabelle that night. You asked him if the shots made the news or the tabs."

"Did they?"

"No, and that puzzled me, because you've been all over the news for the last couple of days, first because of your relationship to a murdered woman, and next because the network hitch-hiked on the buzz that story generated to announce your new contract and the film you're making about the case. I won't tell you the adjectives they're using because it would only piss you off. Except I heard 'emotional personal journey,' 'straight from the heart,' and 'terrifying.'"

"I can only imagine," I said. "Maybe those photos were unusable."

"No, they're pretty good. Your face and her face, looking right at the camera. A paparazzo could have gotten fair coin for them." That damn pause again before he said, "We found them on Chuy Cepeda's mobile phone."

"How did he get them?" I asked.

"The Russian mechanic snapped them and sent them directly to Chuy's phone."

"The Russian took them?" I felt horrified. The photographer had been no more than eight feet away from me when he snapped the pictures. "Then I saw him."

"Would you recognize him again?"

"Probably not. It happened really fast. And he was behind the flash."

"The thing is, Maggie," Rich said. "There are two women in the picture. You were moving around when the pics were taken, and the car was moving. So, the thing is, in one picture you're on the left and in the other you're on the right."

"Makes sense, changing perspective on a moving subject."

"Wrong picture sent, language barrier, stupidity, who knows what happened? But we think the hitman made a mistake. After that guy in the van went after you this morning, we don't think Isabelle Martin was the intended target. We think it was you."

━18━

"YOU'RE COUSINS?" I asked.

"No, she is my niece." Jacques Breton beamed proudly at the young policewoman standing watch, Jacqueline Cartier, his sister's daughter, his namesake and goddaughter. Why was I not surprised?

Jacques was sent to the hospital in his little green four-wheel-drive truck to bring Antoine and me a basket of food and drink. Hardship of all hardships, we had not gotten past the soup course at dinner before we left the house with Dauvin, and therefore must be in need. He brought a meal for his niece, as well, because her mother was worried that she hadn't eaten, and for Dauvin, because that's how things were done. Jacques didn't add, because it would have been redundant, that his sister—the entire family—expected him to come back with a full report about what was going on. Clearly, this mission of mercy was also a fact-finding junket.

Inspector Dauvin offered to take over guard duty to give young Officer Cartier a break, and suggested that she, Antoine and I go relax in the staff lounge. Antoine was looking very ragged. I asked if we could go home instead. The answer was "Soon." We left Dauvin chatting with Jacques outside the surgery suite.

The staff lounge was like staff lounges everywhere, a threadbare affair with a small round dining table and plastic chairs, a sagging sofa, a collection of antique magazines, a microwave, a small refrigerator, and a sink that needed a good scrub. Antoine set the basket on the counter next to the sink and found tumblers and mugs for drinks in a cupboard.

Julie had packed the basket with a feast: sandwiches made from lengths of thin baguette sliced open, spread with butter and young Camembert, garnished with a few leaves of fresh basil and filled with the *charcuterie*—cold cuts—we missed at dinner. There were also an insulated carafe of hot chocolate and a bottle of red wine. I poured myself a cup of chocolate because it was hot, but didn't feel like eating.

Jacqueline ate with the appetite of the healthy young. She quaffed a tumbler of wine, took a second sandwich from the basket and refilled her glass from the bottle—refreshment for Inspector Dauvin, she said— and excused herself to go back on duty.

Antoine got up from the table, refilled his tumbler with wine and took a long drink. We stood side by side with our backs resting against the sink counter.

"Are you all right?" I asked him. He had been very quiet since the conversation with Rich.

He patted his chest with his free hand to simulate a wildly thumping heart. "I am distraught, in need of stiffer drink than this. But you? You seem so calm. How can you be so sanguine?"

"Trust me, I'm not." I cradled the warm mug of chocolate between cold hands. "Today, all at once, I find out that three different people have wanted to get rid of me at various times. I suppose I'm lucky just to have lived as long as I have."

He narrowed his eyes and cocked his head as if he couldn't have heard correctly. "Pardon?"

I gave him my best imitation of the Gallic shrug, intending to convey, who can figure? "The abbess suggested to me that my father asked Isabelle to abort me. Claude suggested he should have 'drowned me like a stray puppy' when he had the opportunity. And now this, a cut-rate assassin misses his target, me. I'm lucky that three times isn't always the charm. Maybe the next guy will get it right."

"Surely this detective in Los Angeles is incorrect."

"Rich Longshore is a damned fine detective," I said. "My husband, Mike, thought the world of his abilities. I listen to what he has to say."

"But what he said is still only speculation, Maggie."

"Think about it," I said, turning to face him. "What he said makes sense. Isabelle was sick. She wasn't going to live much longer. Why take the risk of hiring some idiot to speed things along?"

"But why would anyone want you dead?" Antoine said. "That certainly does not make sense."

"What are the usual motives for murder?" I asked him.

Palms up, mouth turned down—which could have meant I'm thinking, or, Who knows?—he offered, "Assuming sanity? Greed, lust, rage, jealousy, fear, revenge, expedience—shall I go on?"

"That's a fair start." I said. "Now, just for argument's sake, assume I was the intended target, and not Isabelle. I think you can take lust off your list of motives—who here knows me well enough to lust after these old bones?—but any of the other motives you listed could apply."

"Again, but why?"

"It doesn't take a lot of imagination, Antoine," I said. "After I arrived in Paris yesterday, before I met Grand-mère, I was shuffled off to a conference about my inheritance. Even before I got on the plane to come over I was asked about my 'expectations.' Removing me from the pool of heirs would make a big difference."

"For whom?"

"In some ways, for all of you."

Arms tightly crossed over his chest, my cousin shook his head, refusing to accept what I said.

I went on. "Assuming that the motive involves the estate, then logically the person who hired the assassin is a stakeholder."

"One of the family?"

"Or a person dependent on someone in the family coming across financially."

He liked that answer better. He gave me a curt nod, arms still folded as a barrier against what I was saying.

We both looked up as the *whop-whop-whop* racket of a helicopter beat the sky above the clinic. It hovered briefly before it landed on the parking lot.

I said, "Medevac for Sergei?"

Antoine shrugged, turned his attention back to me. "Go on with what you were saying."

"For just a moment, let's assume that someone in the family had a hand in hiring the hitman," I said. "Wouldn't it be easier for that person to arrange to remove me, a stranger, an abstraction, the mystery daughter on some far shore, than a loved one, as I believe Isabelle was?" I didn't add what Uncle Max said earlier: it wasn't *me* Dad wanted to get rid of, but an *it*.

"You are wrong." Antoine surprised me when he took the mug from my hands, set it aside and folded me into his arms. Holding me against his chest, shaking with emotion, he kissed the top of my head and patted my back. "You are not a stranger to me, Maggie."

I pulled back to look up into his face.

He smiled down at me with such a sweet fondness that I had to catch my breath; my brother Mark used to look at me that way. He said, "I am a few years older than you—the old man of the children. I remember you very well, even if you do not remember me."

"You do?" News to me.

"Yes. You were a funny little thing, a sort of wild creature until Maman took you in hand and taught you the meaning of yes and no. Isabelle was somewhat inconsistent, and she left you with us very frequently," he said. "You and I would ride together on your pony—*Amie* you called her—or we'd build castles out of mud. I taught you how to kick a soccer ball. We slept in the same room because you were afraid to sleep alone. And when there was a storm you crawled into my bed. I was very sad when you were gone. I missed you very much."

"I'm sorry, I don't remember."

"Of course not. I was six when you were two. I don't remember very much from then. But I do remember you. Believe me, you were not ever an abstraction to me." I leaned my head against his shoulder and listened as he continued talking. "Maman, Papa, Grand-mère, Grand-père, Grand-mère Marie—we loved you very much. Even though Freddy and Bébé never met you, you were always very real to them, a part of their family."

"Antoine?" I backed out of his embrace so that I could look directly into his face. "Both Freddy and your dad have told me their ideas about the future of the estate. Freddy said that you agreed with him. Do you?"

"Pshh, Freddy's plan." He made a broad gesture of disdain, as if wiping the plan off the table. "Pie in the sky. Is that the expression? Who knows? Maybe he can make it work. Can't be as wrong-headed as the Canadian oil shale project Lena talked him into backing. That one turned to shit in a hurry."

"Lena talked him into backing?"

"She's a force of nature, that one; Hélène, the face that launched a thousand ships—that sank. Yes, Lena was so sure about it."

Lena, short for Hélène. A common enough name, but where else had I heard it recently? Probably didn't matter where, I thought. But it bothered me. Where?

I asked Antoine, "What *do* you want?"

"Me?" He poured himself more wine, the last of the bottle, and took a couple of sips as he composed an answer to the question. When he was ready, he turned to look at me directly.

"Kelly and I want to go back to California," he said. "I have tenure in the Ag department at the state university in San Luis Obispo. I've hung on to my position by teaching and directing their semester-abroad program in Normandy and monitoring several graduate students in residence here working in the area of niche agriculture."

His face lit up when he said, "In the summer our humble estate is overrun by California aggies."

He cocked his head. "Kelly is a gifted winemaker, and did very well with the Central Coast wineries in California. Here she is adrift in cider country. Besides, she wants to be near her parents. They're getting older, they miss their grandchildren. We're all tired of the gray winters here."

I nudged him. "All those years you were in San Luis Obispo, you were so close by and you never even called me."

Finally he smiled. "Don't think we weren't tempted."

"So, why did you come back to Normandy?"

"Several things," he said. "Our grandfather died and the estate was falling into ruin. The *fromagerie* and the distillery needed modernization. My father and mother had separated and were in a legal battle over property rights. Maman wanted some help. Isabelle was off on some project. Grand-mère was in over her head. And she missed her grandchildren."

He paused to sip his wine.

"So, you came over," I encouraged, wanting him to continue.

"Yes, but we didn't intend to stay so long," he said. "Kelly and I want the children to be truly bi-cultural. We wanted them to have the experience of living in France. A couple of years we thought, then back to California, to spend our summers here. But…" He shrugged shoulders that seemed to bear an enormous weight.

"What?"

"It's time to go back," he said. "We've done what we needed to do here. We brought the operations of the estate into the twenty-first century, got the profit stream flowing, and now we are finished. Jacques manages the *fromagerie* brilliantly. I have a very good man at the distillery, ready to take over production. Carrots? That land we can lease to a local farmer to work. And the Percherons haven't been more than an expensive hobby since my grandfather bought his first motorized tractor."

"What's keeping you here?"

"Concern for Grand-mère, of course. But other than that?" He raised his open palms—there was nothing on them. "Chris will take his *baccalauréat* exams in June. We'll wait for the results. If he scores in the top two percent he will get into one of the *grandes écoles* like David. He's bright, but the odds are against him. If he doesn't make it, well, for students anywhere except in the elite academies the French university system is very complex, very chaotic, and a student can take years getting through the classes necessary to finish a degree. In that case, Chris would be better off at an American university. As a fall-back, he applied to three American schools. We'll hear from them in the spring.

"And my Lulu—what can I say? She is a far better soccer player than she is a scholar. Kelly and I both believe that she would thrive in an American high school and later in a public university."

"What about your expectations here, Antoine?"

He shook his head. "I have very few. My father is a gambler and a fool, on the edge of financial ruin because of that. It was expensive for me, Bébé, and Aunt Isabelle, but we managed to stop him from wreaking havoc on the estate, this time or any time, with his schemes. When Papa sold his inheritance rights to us, what are my brother and I left with? Peace of mind and not much else."

"I wouldn't sneeze at peace of mind," I said.

One corner of his mouth lifted in a wicked smile. "Be prepared. Farming can be an expensive hobby."

"Psst." Jacques leaned into the room. "Help, please. There is a very unpleasant man demanding someone who speaks English."

"Promise me he isn't an American," I said in my best imperfect French.

"*Russe,*" Jacques answered.

Indeed, the angry newcomer was Russian, Sergei's father, accompanied by two blond monoliths encased in expensive black velour warm-up suits and sneakers as big as redwood stumps. The helicopter we heard earlier flew them across the Channel from England.

Sergei, Senior was a pipsqueak of a man, his lack of stature exaggerated by proximity to his huge companions. The excess fabric in the thirty-inch waist of his buttonfront Levi 501s was gathered under a belt. Looked more like clown pants on him than the western stovepipes they were intended to be. Besides blue jeans, he wore a white dress shirt open to show a graying chest pelt, a blue blazer, and black boots with heel lifts. He added something to his height by teasing the rug atop his head into a sort of controlled version of a Don King frizz. However, the size of his personality compensated for the shortcomings of his physical stature.

Ludanov, the dad, nailed me with an accusatory finger. "You, you speak English?"

"When it suits me," I said.

"I don't need a wiseass right now, honey," he hissed in heavily accented English. "My kid's been in an accident and no one here seems to be able to tell me what happened."

"He wrapped a Lamborghini around a tree," I said.

"What shit-for-brains gave a dickwad kid like Sergei the keys to a rocket like that?" From hiss to shout in under five seconds, impressive.

"Car's registered to Zed Entertainment," I said, keeping my voice calm and quiet, making him listen closely if he wanted to hear me, a tactic I learned when I had a toddler going through the tantrum phase.

"Aw shit." He dropped into the closest chair. "Aw damn, fuck and shit."

Dauvin was getting a simultaneous translation from Antoine, who rendered that stream as *"merde, merde, merde."* Such a universal, multipurpose word, *merde.* English needs a word like that.

Antoine asked Ludanov, on behalf of Dauvin, "Do you know this Zed Entertainment?"

"Yeah. They owe me money. I'm holding some of their assets as collateral."

"The auto?" Dauvin said, trying his English.

"Could be," Ludanov said. "I don't bother with the details."

He seemed to lose his starch all at once when he realized that there was no one present he could blame, except maybe himself and his employees. And his kid. Maybe just for the practice he shot an accusatory eye at his two men, who were positioned to block both of the access routes into the anteroom of the surgery suite.

Ludanov, voice back in normal registers, asked me, "How is my boy? You know?"

"Touch and go," I said, and gave him the information I had about broken bones and internal injuries.

"And who are you?"

"My name is Maggie MacGowen."

He thought that over before he asked, "You're American?"

"I am."

"I've seen you on TV, haven't I?"

"Could be."

"What's your interest in my son?"

"None," I said. "He showed up at a family gathering after my mother's funeral this afternoon."

"Where was that?"

"Here. At my grandmother's house."

"With a name like MacGowen, you can't be a frog. What is it, your husband's name?"

"Yes."

He was coarse, rude, and really ugly. But his son lay near death a few feet away, and as soon as Antoine contacted him, he had flown over out of concern. We owed him a modicum of patience; people react differently in emergencies. He had lost control of one area, his son's survival, so maybe he just needed to exert control over another. I decided to give him an opportunity.

Rich had spelled out the name of the man, Something'ovich, who ran the chop shop in Pacoima, the man who apparently was in cahoots with Chuy Cepeda, the kid who ran down Isabelle. I had written out 'Ovich's full name on the back of a business card I dug out of my bag. I showed the name to Ludanov.

"Do you know this man?" I asked.

He pronounced the name. Then he paused too long before he said, "Never heard of the bastard. I don't know nobody in America."

Nothing on the card indicated that the man was in the U.S. One of his velour-clad monoliths caught the gaffe and lost the beginning of a guffaw. Antoine caught it also, and translated for Dauvin, who laughed out loud.

When Ludanov saw the general reaction, he thought over what he said, heard his own internal replay and turned a furious red.

"So, who is he?" I asked.

"A nobody." Dismissed the guy with the wave of his hand. "He borrowed some money from me once, that's all."

"So maybe he owed you a favor?"

"No, no. Like I said, he owed me money. That's all."

"Your son seems to know quite a bit about your business," I said.

"Sure, of course," he said. "Family business, you know? Sergei works for me."

"Doing debt collection?"

"What?" He looked horrified. "You crazy? He's in executive training, of course. I own some clubs. He advises about attracting the young crowd."

I could only imagine. I asked him, "Why did a guy who runs a chop shop in Los Angeles come to you for a loan?"

"I know his father, from the old country. We come from the same village." (He pronounced it "willitch.") "He comes to me and says his boy is a good mechanic, wants to open an auto repair business, can I give him a hand getting started? So, I make a loan. Strictly business."

"Does Sergei know this mechanic?"

"Sure. Maybe. I don't know." He pointed his chin toward the door of the surgery suite. "Ask him yourself. Why do you want to know?"

So far, Dauvin had let me ask my questions, probably because Ludanov was more likely to talk to an American TV person than a French cop, a frog in his parlance. But before I went any further, I glanced at the inspector. He barely moved his head from one side to the other, but I read *No* perfectly well. I would leave it to the police to tell Ludanov about his son's connection to a murder.

Two emergency workers, still wearing the vivid blue jackets festooned with reflector tape that we had seen on the crash site crew earlier, negotiated their way in past Ludanov's men. Dauvin, with a little toss of his head, had them follow him off to the side where the three of them had a quiet conversation.

One of the men held up a Ziploc bag with a dark, slender shaft about eight inches long inside. Dauvin pulled up the bottom corner, bent down for a closer look. Piece of the wreckage? Evidence of something? I could ask about it later. But I might only have one shot at Ludanov. I turned my attention away from the investigators, curious as I was about the meaning of their rather complex hand gestures, and focused again on Ludanov.

I said, "I understand you know my uncle, Gérard Martin," pronouncing the name as the French did.

Ludanov frowned as he shook his head. "No, I don't think."

"Jemima's father?"

With that prompt, apparently he did think. "You mean Gerry Martin?" He pronounced the last name with the accent on the first syllable as it would be in English, instead of with the accent on the second, as I had. Gillian, I remembered, called Gérard Gerry.

I said, "Yes, Gerry Martin."

"Oh yeah, sure. From the kids' football board. Gerry's a good guy. Big supporter. His kid could turn pro. She looks like a toothpick, but don't let that fool you. She's quick, you know? And aggressive. Whoo, shoulda been a boy."

Jemima, a football star? Of course. In Europe *soccer* is football. It hadn't occurred to me, as I imagined oversized boys in massive shoulder pads and helmets when Gérard said he was on a youth football board, that he was supporting his daughter, the soccer player. My mistake.

"Have you ever done business with Gerry?" I asked.

"No, why would I?"

"Or with his wife?"

"Hah!" Sounded like a squeaky door. "No way. Never. I don't much care for that lady. That one has to take the stick out of her ass before she can even sit down."

I dropped my face to hide my smile—couldn't have described Gillian better myself. But he saw it, and gave my back a hard thump. When I looked at him, he smiled, tapped the end of his nose with his index finger as he said, "Uh-huh, you know what I mean, yes?"

A little much-needed levity. I didn't trust what Ludanov had to say, but I trusted his reactions—I don't think he was much of an actor. Certainly he was too upset about Sergei to be thinking clearly, so he was vulnerable, as his gaffe earlier showed. I asked him one more question.

"Mr. Ludanov, why did Sergei come here today?"

"This funeral, Jemima was there?"

"Yes."

"My boy went around with her for a while. They were friends, you know? He's a well-brought-up boy. He just came to pay his respects to her family, you know?"

A doctor, a middle-aged woman still wearing blood-stained scrubs, pushed through the surgery suite doors. Her face was drawn with fatigue. She pulled the surgical bonnet off her head and twisted it in her hands as she looked at the expectant faces focused on her.

"La famille?" The family?

Antoine introduced her to Ludanov and stayed to translate.

Sergei was failing, the doctor told Ludanov. His liver was perforated and they worked for over an hour to stop the hemorrhage. Still touch and go. They removed his spleen. When Sergei's right femur shattered it shredded his femoral artery. Blood loss was severe; thank God it had been a cold night or they would have lost him before the ambulance arrived. The surgeons could not repair the damage to the artery, so the leg was amputated below the hip. Kidneys were shutting down, heart was failing…. He needed a miracle. If there were last words, now was the time. Should she call a priest?

Ludanov was white with shock and grief. When the surgeon asked if he wanted to come in and see his son, it clearly was an invitation to say good-bye. The little man's breathing hitched as he tried to hold back sobs. When he couldn't contain his despair any longer, he looked around the room, decided on me, and offered himself into my arms. He wept, engulfed in the horrible reality every parent fears most, the loss of a child. Tears streamed down the faces of his giant attendants, also. Everyone in the room fought back tears.

After a few moments, one of the big companions took him around the shoulders and half carried him through the big doors to see his son.

But Sergei was gone before his father reached his bedside.

—19—

EXHAUSTED, I HUNKERED down under the duvet on my bed, propped up on pillows, a glass of red wine—*vin ordinaire*—from the half carafe on my nightstand in hand, a plate of Grand-mère Marie's little shortbreads on the bed within reach, the bundle of Dad's letters Freddy had given me tucked in beside me. I was prepared to read about some of the mysteries surrounding my early life, but I couldn't settle down enough to focus on the words. I kept seeing the crash site, everything glittery in the flashing lights of the emergency vehicles, and the father, bereft, who was as much a part of the wreckage as the young man and his car were.

Casey, tired to the point of stupor when she came upstairs, was sound asleep in her room next door with her iPod earbuds in her ears and music playing, a strategy she learned from living in a college dorm. Before I got into bed I listened at her door until I heard a little snore, just to reassure myself that all was well. Feeling unsettled, I left my door open so that I could see anyone who came down the hall from the direction of the stairway; I was shamelessly hovering over my kid.

Bébé was in his room across the hall, sitting in an easy chair beside a lamp, reading. His door was open enough that I could see the shadows of his hands move along his rug whenever he turned a page. He told me he planned to stay up for a while in case Grand-mère needed anything, but I thought he intended to keep vigil over everyone in the house that night.

News of Sergei's death had sent the entire household into a tailspin. A family already stretched emotionally by Isabelle's death and funeral, and the awful news about how she died, not to forget the stresses of spending a couple of days together in lockstep, seemed ready to snap.

When Antoine and I returned from the hospital, we delivered the emotional coup de grâce: Just moments before the doctors called Sergei's time of death, two crash site investigators arrived to show Dauvin a discovery they made in the wreckage of Sergei's borrowed Lamborghini.

At some point before Sergei roared out of the family compound, someone shoved the narrow blade of a boning knife laterally into his right front tire and snapped it off below the handle. As the kid drove, the weight and motion of the Lamborghini forced the blade deeper, torqued it, exacerbating the damage caused by the initial thrust.

Driving conditions were bad to begin with that night. Add too much speed, too little experience, and a shredding tire and what you get is a trifecta for disaster on an icy road. You also get a case for premeditated murder.

Interestingly, it was Bébé who stepped forward to take charge of the family. He declared the day over and ordered everyone to their rooms. He then helped Clara and Oscar deliver bedtime snacks to everyone. I thought when he set off on that errand that he was also making a bed check of all three houses, making sure all were safely in and accounted for.

Across the hall, Bébé coughed a couple of times. I got up and went to his door, looked around the edge.

"Can't sleep?" he asked, looking up. He put a marker in his book and set it aside.

I shook my head. "Quite a day."

He chuckled softly; an understatement.

"How are you?" I asked.

"Me?" He lifted a shoulder. "I'm safe and warm. Can I hope for more?"

"At the moment, maybe not."

"Anything I can get to help you sleep, Maggie? Read you a bedtime story, maybe?"

"Thank you, but wine and cookies should be enough." I offered a shrug—I was getting more practiced, had a growing vocabulary of gestures and their nuances. I added a moue for emphasis.

His focus had slipped off to a spot over my left shoulder, his train of thought drifting onto its own track. From that faraway place, he said, "Can I ask you something?"

"Sure." I leaned against the door frame, arms folded, ankles crossed, feet warm in Isabelle's slippers, wrapped in my flannel robe. "What's on your mind?"

"My mother." His eyes came back to me. "You know how she died?"

"In her car."

A small, sad nod. "On a clear day, alone, on a straight piece of road."

"What do you think happened?"

"Until tonight, I wasn't sure," he said. "I was a little afraid to know."

"And now?"

"Now I am very much afraid." He shook his head. "When it happened, I asked Lena what were the odds that it was an accident. She said that every time we get into a car we reset our odds. What happens on any car trip is always a function of multiple intersecting variables— that's how she talks. Health, state of mind, condition of car, condition of road, random events like birds flying at the windscreen. She said only Maman could answer what happened in the moment before she left the road. But, of course..."

But of course his mother, my aunt Louise, was beyond answering.

I came further into the room and sat on the ottoman next to his chair, propped my elbows on the arm. "Was she recovered?"

"A navy rescue team immediately came around the point from Cherbourg. But they were too late." He shuddered, remembering. "It was horrible, Maggie. Maman was very alive when the car went into the water. She fought like hell to get out before she drowned."

It is fairly common for suicidal people to change their minds after it is too late. Or to panic out of instinct when they can't breathe. I was sure I didn't need to tell him that.

"She wasn't drunk." Bébé began to count off on his fingers, beginning with his thumb. "No drugs, sound heart, no injuries. No bird through the windscreen. No dead creatures on the road. No skid marks."

"What about the car?"

"More or less intact," he said, pausing for me to appreciate the significance. "No sign of collision or malfunction. When the car was brought out, once it dried out a bit, it started right up. From all indications, Maman just went straight off the road, over the side and into the water."

I know I frowned as I imagined the scene. "No car damage?"

"There was some to the undercarriage and to a tire. She crossed two meters of rough ground after she left the road."

He closed his eyes as if visualizing the scene. "At the place where she went over the edge, there are still some remnants of old German blockhouses from the Occupation. Mostly they are chunks of concrete with rebar sticking out," he said. "The assumption was, the rebar damaged a front tire and nicked the muffler as Maman went over."

"But now you aren't so sure," I said.

He finally looked directly at me. "I never was sure. I am not sure now."

"Where is the car?"

Both shoulders rose. "Junkyard. Sold for spare parts. Who knows?"

"There must be photographs," I said. "Can you ask someone to take another look at them?"

"No." He picked up my hand and pressed it momentarily against his dry lips. "The immediate assumption was suicide, so there was no care given to preserve anything that might affirm that assumption. There are no photographs."

"Surely the insurance company…"

"No insurance claim was filed, so they merely signed off. If there were a claim, the underwriters would have investigated more thoroughly, of course, and Papa did not want that to happen."

Papa or Gillian? I wanted to ask. Instead, I said, "The police, then?"

He looked straight into my eyes, the way an adult does when he's trying to explain something difficult—worldly—to a child. The posture said, You are about to lose your sweet innocence.

Bébé said, "You have to understand, Maggie. Normandy is quite provincial. Quite traditional. And we are an old family here. Everyone was afraid that a thorough investigation would confirm what they assumed from the beginning."

"That your mother intended to end it all?"

Slowly, he nodded. "The official police determination, signed by Pierre Dauvin, our cousin by marriage, was 'undetermined cause.' The insurance company signed it off as 'traffic misadventure' in deference to the finer feelings of your sister-in-law, Lena, who is an executive with the company."

"Incredible," I said.

"No," he gently protested, reaffirming the hard truth to the innocent, sanding the hand he still held against his scratchy cheek. "Entirely believable. You see, if anyone wrote 'suicide' on an official document the local priest would have issues about burying Maman in the church. What was done, or not done, was seen as a kindness for all concerned. Do you understand?"

"Yes. But?"

"But, I drove from Paris to watch the recovery of Maman's car," he said. "I watched it hang in the air from the arm of a crane. And what I cannot tonight get out of my mind, after what you and Antoine told us about Sergei's misadventure, is the condition of that one tire."

"Yes?"

"Shredded. A nearly new Michelin steel-belted radial tire. Shredded."

I rose and paced across the room, looked out the window, saw rain and sleet cover the garden behind the house with a silvery glaze. A miserable night out there. I pulled the heavy velvet drapes across the window to block the cold emanating off the glass, leaving the room in a warmer glow from the lamp on the table next to Bébé.

"Not a single photograph?" I, the filmmaker, asked, unconvinced.

He shook his head.

"Then draw it, Bébé," I said. "Show what that tire looked like. Make it as real as the portrait you painted of your mother from memory."

He laughed or he coughed; the sudden sound was the same. "By God," he said. "By God. Yes, of course."

I stretched forward and kissed the top of his head. "Good night. Try to get some sleep."

He stopped me as I crossed the threshold of his room. "Maggie?"

I turned back to look at him.

"Tomorrow, the kids want to play volleyball. Do you think, under the circumstances, it would be appropriate?"

"Yes," I said. "Under these circumstances, I think burning off some energy would be a very, very good plan."

"Good," he said. "I traded a fisherman a drawing of his boat for an old net. So, the game is on. I will see you on the beach at Anneville-sur-Mer, after croissants in the morning, weather be damned."

— — —

I set my empty wineglass on the night table and took Dad's first letter out of its envelope. He had typed it on plain white paper without a single typo or strike-over using the old Smith-Corona electric that sat on his office desk—I recognized the typeface. The paper had yellowed with age, its edges feathered from much handling. How many times had Isabelle read it over the years? And, as I read it, I wondered how many drafts Dad had written before he managed to say exactly what he wanted to say. The language was familiar, a bit formal, and the various messages he needed to convey were very clear:

6 October, 1967
Ma Belle,

You ask if I am surprised. There isn't a word powerful enough to express what I feel about your amazing news, but, yes surprised, and certainly, as you suggest, a bit angry. How could a man be with a woman as I was with you for all those months and not know that she still carried his child? Why did you not tell me the truth before we left France in May?

Be assured that I am delighted to hear that we have a daughter, and that you are both safe. You called her Marguerite for your grandmother? A lovely name. As my grandmothers were Hyacinth and Myrtle, better you chose to name her after your own.

I will find a time to come and meet my little girl as soon as I can arrange it. There is a conference scheduled in Bonn toward the end of the month. I will make a pretext of attending, and come to you instead. Details re arrival, etc., to follow.

In the meantime, I would appreciate a photograph if you have one to spare. Who does she look like? Please, have passed to her your nose and not mine.

On to practical matters: Of course, I will assume financial responsibility for Marguerite. How and from which pocket may prove problematic, but I will figure that out. In the meantime, do you need anything? Please let me know right away if you do.

More practical matters: as I informed you in my August

letter, I have gone forward with the design of the energy recovery system. With Max's assistance I filed for patent protection. Because the system came from our shared work, you will, of course, be co-owner, as we agreed right along. Let us hope the system generates revenue for us both. For us all. Max will forward paperwork to you for signature probably by December, if not sooner.

News here? Mark and Emily started high school mid-September, happy to be back in familiar surroundings, but also missing their French friends. They both shot up like weeds over the summer. You would hardly recognize them since you saw them last.

Mark's voice has continued to change. Over the summer he went from alto to tenor, and seems headed for basso profundo if this keeps up. Emily has grudgingly accepted wearing the hated brassieres that Betsy put in her bureau drawer in case. Some damn boy made a comment about her "jiggling." My God, kids can be cruel.

Sorry for the digression, but you can imagine what I am up against. The next may not be words you wish to read at this time, but I will remind you that from the beginning, my affection for you notwithstanding, I was very clear in my commitment to Betsy and our children. I remain steadfast to that commitment even in the face of this extraordinary event. Certainly, the path ahead will not be an easy one, and there is no way to avoid hurt feelings all around. I will do everything I am able to smooth the way.

I know you are consumed with the little bundle in your arms right now. But please do take some time to consider the best way to proceed. By that, I mean the best for all involved.

Ma Belle, I remain your besotted, befuddled old dear.

The signature at the end of the letter was my father's familiar scrawl.

Quite a juggling act he had going. He both reassured Isabelle that he wouldn't abandon her, or me, and let her know, firmly, that he would not abandon Mom, either. And that the essential connection between them still was their work.

I read the line again, "I will remind you that from the beginning, my affection for you notwithstanding, I was very clear in my commitment to Betsy and our children," and thought about the various assessments of Isabelle I had heard: determined, stubborn, willful, absentminded. I would now add my own: manipulative.

Dad must have been besotted. I'd expect that after his paramour's pregnancy was safely resolved—or so he thought—he'd hightail it back to Mom, scared straight, as it were. But he didn't. They carried on until Dad left the country; she would have been about five months along, and at least beginning to show.

I folded the letter into its envelope and took out the second one, sent a month to the day after he sent the first one. When he wrote it, Dad had already been to see me, and was back in Berkeley. Any communication sent between the dates on the letters, "Details re arrival, etc.," apparently hadn't been kept.

Odd, I thought as I read, that there was no shift in his tone between personal and business matters. Not much of a love-letter writer, my dad.

6 November, 1967
Belle,

I have been back only a few days, but I miss that leaky little creature terribly. How quickly she took possession of my heart. I cannot put into words how difficult it was to leave knowing it will be nearly two months before I can hold her again. How much she will have changed, and how much I will have missed. I envy you your every day together.

Max has arranged for monthly deposits to be made into your Paris bank account. Please don't hesitate to call Max if you need anything.

I will meet you in Edinburgh 27 Dec. for the IANS meeting, as agreed. You must bring Marguerite with you! We are scheduled to present the research underlying our joint project 28 Dec. That presentation plus publication of your dissertation should complete the last requirements for your doctorate.

To answer your question, no, I have said nothing yet to Betsy. Until several of the issues you and I have discussed have been resolved, I want to maintain the status quo, that is, my pain, her ignorance. Be patient, please, Belle.

Thank you for the photos. I cherish them.

Dad signed his name, forgetting to be the besotted old dear. As I folded the second letter and put it back into its envelope, it was clear to me that Dad had not once said to Isabelle, I love you, though he was clearly crazy about me. Had she saved the letters as evidence that he acknowledged paternity? Was she reading something between the lines that I was not seeing?

I heard a faint rumble of thunder, took a deep breath, poured the last bit of the wine from my bedside carafe and finished it in a gulp; after the sweetness of the shortbreads, it tasted sour.

I leafed through the letters and found one dated in December two years later, after my second birthday and just weeks before Isabelle called and told Dad to come and get me.

> 19 December, 1969
> Isabelle,
>
> I am the greatest fool that ever lived, or so your note persuades me.
>
> The child you say you carry can be mine neither legally nor morally. It is assumed that, as you and Claude are married, you share a marriage bed. Therefore any child born to you is then also the child of your husband. For that reason I will not give you the blood sample you ask for. Nor will I consider your suggestion that we disregard the feelings of everyone else and move away together with two babies.
>
> I understand from Louise and Élodie that M has been with them at the estate since her birthday, while you have been in residence in Paris with your husband, and that you have not been to see her once. In my mind, you have abandoned custody. I intend to come as soon as I am able to claim my daughter. I have redirected my support payments from your account to Élodie for Marguerite's care.
>
> I will arrive in Paris 27 December with Max to discuss our situation. I suggest you find a legal advisor as well. Any further communication should be directed to Max.
>
> Respectfully yours,
> Alfred Duchamps

When my father, working around the house, whacked his thumb with a hammer or impaled himself on a rosebush, he might pop off a noisy "Goddamn sonofabitch." Just one.

But when he was profoundly distressed, as he was when my brother Mark, upon graduation from college *summa cum laude*, announced that out of a sense of obligation to his peers he had enlisted in the army with the intention of serving in Vietnam, Dad became just awfully controlled and articulate. Scared me to death.

I would far rather have the quick outburst and be done with it than to suffer through logical discourse delivered in complete complex sentences that included a plan to rectify the problem so that it would never recur. Excruciating.

That latter form of angry expression is what I read in his letter. Especially the plan to rectify the problem. As it turns out, some problems—daughter caught with a joint or ditching class—can be dispatched fairly easily with a little application of reason and fear of the consequences. While some problems—adult son volunteers for war, an extracurricular child or two—just cannot.

Based on what he told Isabelle, if DNA testing had been available at the time, Dad probably would have refused to give a sample. He would point out that when legal paternity was established, biological paternity did not matter. Problem rectified. Too bad Isabelle didn't agree.

Does my history get weirder from here, I wondered? Could it possibly? I tucked the letter back under the bundle's blue ribbon and thumbed through to the last note. The date was just about the time that Freddy met Dad in New York—Freddy was about twelve—when Dad had a great argument with Isabelle. After that meeting Isabelle stopped sneaking over to snap pictures of me, but I remained entombed in a convent school, just in case she came for something other than pictures.

The salutation on the last letter was, "Isabelle Martin," and what followed was a flat refusal by my dad to change any part of their agreement relating to the patents or the royalties they earned. Obviously, there had been many letters back and forth while they haggled over the issues and details, but this one was the only one of that sort in the bundle I took from Isabelle's silk treasure box; an odd, random collection, I thought.

Apparently, Isabelle wanted Freddy to be included in the *tontine* that held title to the patents. Taking Freddy, on the cusp of adolescence, to meet Dad may have been part of her campaign to get Dad to finally acknowledge paternity. Without ever mentioning Freddy by name, Dad refused.

Dad reminded Isabelle that the patents were the result of their shared work, and belonged to them equally and solely. However, as I was the result of their sharing of another sort, I, and only I, was the rightful heir of all rights and earnings, and therefore should remain in the *tontine*, as they agreed all those years ago. "Before you and your husband started your family," he said. B.F., Before Freddy, I inferred. I wondered, though; if Isabelle could prove that Dad was Freddy's father—another product of their shared work—could Freddy be excluded as an heir?

For my "protection" I was not to be told about the *tontine*, and therefore about Isabelle, until both Dad and she were dead. For whose protection, Dad? I wanted to ask. But, by design, he wasn't around to answer. I knew that the entire arrangement needed to be looked at by a good lawyer.

Dad used his academic title in his signature, Professor Alfred Duchamps, something he rarely did. There was a handwritten postscript: "It was wrong of you to bring the boy."

I put the letters away, head abuzz with a whole new set of questions. I made one last trip to listen at Casey's door; not a peep. From behind Grand-mère's door I heard some soft snores, so all was well. Last, I peeked in and saw Bébé asleep in his chair, book open on his chest, long legs sprawled out in front of him, mouth open. He looked perfectly comfortable, so I left him, not wanting to wake him. Sleep would be hard to come by in that house on that night, I thought. Let him get what he could.

It was midnight. Except for the wind blowing outside, all was quiet. I climbed back into my own bed, turned off the bedside lamp and pulled the duvet up under my chin. Lying back on the pillows, I kept playing over my father's tortured words and the messages between the lines. Soon enough, the lines overlapped, blurred, and I slipped into the abyss of deep sleep.

— 20 —

MY MIKE, A homicide detective, had spent his days trying to untangle the muddles some people make of their lives and the lives of others. At night their stories and the wild things he had been exposed to all day wove their way through his dreams: crazy, complicated dreams, played out by a random assortment of characters who morphed and merged from one scene and one adventure to the next until the sun came up.

Sometimes, early in the morning before the alarm went off, I would lie next to him and watch him sleep, watch him dream. As he surfaced back to the reality of being in our bed, in our room, sometimes, in his last sleepy moments, he would be confused, not certain that he was awake again. Then he would smile, relieved, I think, to be back.

"Where you been?" I would ask, an invitation for him to tell me about his dreams.

Like any great storyteller, Mike had no qualms about embellishing. I would snuggle against him, wrapped in his arms, and listen as he unwound his strange overnight wanderings. He dealt with stuff during the course of an ordinary day that most of us could never conjure by great feats of imagination. So the exaggerations that are the stuff of dreams were wonderful fodder for a man with bizarre material and a penchant for embroidering tales. I was always sorry when a story ended. I am sorrier still that I will never hear one again.

That night, warm in a bed in my newly discovered grandmother's house—a situation I never imagined until it happened—I dreamed that Mike and I were in bed together and he was telling me a convoluted story about a woman who fell or was pushed or who took off flying—dreams don't need to follow a logical route. We could see her fall through the air from our bed, like watching surround-TV. As the woman dropped through the sky, a terrible storm came up: clashing thunder, bright flashes of lightning surrounded her, tossed her in spiral trajectories with Sergei in his car seat tumbling along with her.

I was afraid of the thunder, but Mike was there. Then he wasn't, and it was me who was falling, not through the sky but down into water, deeper and deeper until everything was black and the weight of the water pressed against my chest. Seaweed covered my face and I couldn't breathe. I clawed at it. Though I couldn't see anything, I could still hear the thunder, great crashes like huge boulders colliding overhead and tumbling toward me. Desperate for air, desperate to get out of the path of the boulders, I fought my way to the surface just as lightning crackled through the blackness.

In this nightmare I ran, crazy with panic, frantic to escape the noise and the blasts of silver lightning. Sharp gravel cut my bare feet. Someone was screaming and would not stop.

"Merde!" I knew the voice and realized that this was no dream, but a nightmare nonetheless. Claude Desmoulins loomed out of the dark and reached for me. A flash of lightning lit the compound and made his sparse hair stand on end; I had seen exactly that happen before. "Marguerite. *Arrête-toi! Chérie*, stop, I beg you."

The screaming stopped; it was me. I was standing in the middle of the compound in my pajamas, barefoot, in a freezing downpour.

Claude grabbed me, threw something around me—a blanket. He gripped my arm in a viselike hold and wouldn't let go no matter how hard I pulled. It was all too familiar, his face, the way my arm hurt, his voice, the storm trying to crush and drown me.

"Let her go you son of a bitch! Let her go!" Max came out of nowhere, made a flying tackle into Claude that dropped both of them to the ground; Claude released me as he fell. They rolled around in the gravel and the muddy slush underneath, each man trying to land blows and dodge them at the same time.

"Stop it, both of you," I ordered, tiptoeing over to them, icy water sluicing over my feet. I reached out of the blanket Claude threw around my shoulders and into their squirming dog pile to grab an arm or a leg, trying to separate them. They wrestled in the muck with the abandon and fire of pissed-off little boys, but with more huffing and puffing. A real brawl is an inelegant, messy affair, not at all like the stand-up punch-outs of the movies.

"Max, Claude, stop it. Right now!" I clapped my hands like a playground supervisor. "Someone will get hurt."

Doors of all three houses flew open and people streamed into the compound draped in hastily grabbed coats: Freddy, Antoine, Kelly, Gérard, Gillian, a couple of the kids. There was a lot of racket all around, great smashing thunder only adding to the noise, flashes of lightning giving random snapshots of the scene, like an old black-out routine. A car drove through the gate and gave steady illumination to Max and Claude trying to pummel each other.

Gérard and Freddy got into the fray but only made the ruckus worse as they tried to separate Max and Claude. They both received a few punches for their efforts. Kelly offered her voice. I no longer had feeling in my feet.

Just as I was about to give up and leave the men to their slugfest, an explosive *Crack!* cleaved the night air. Suddenly, everyone froze in place, like a house party playing statues. Slowly, heads turned toward the source of the great bang.

Grand-mère, wrapped in a full-length mink coat, raised a pistol over her head and let off another round into the black sky. "That will be enough. Everyone go home."

Still holding the pistol aimed upward, she handed me a pair of rubber garden clogs to slip onto my feet, then draped a raincoat over my shoulders.

The car came to a stop, the lights went out, and the compound was dark again—the show was over. The fighters uncoiled themselves from the mud and struggled to their feet assisted by Gérard and Freddy. Inspector Dauvin emerged from the car, looked from face to face with a puzzled expression.

"Qu'est-ce qui arrive?" What is going on? he asked. Everyone tried to answer the question at once, a great babble of voices.

Grand-mère took me by the elbow and marched me toward her open front door. She still held the big pistol, an old Luger, pointing forward, as if she knew what to do with it.

"Grand-mère, where did you get that?" I asked.

"I took it off a dead German," she said with a proud little toss of her head. "Right after I slit his throat."

—21—

"YOU HAVE TO believe me," Claude implored. "I would never harm Marguerite."

He had washed up and changed into dry clothes, like the rest of us; Casey and Bébé had never stirred from their beds. Claude had begged Grand-mère to let him come over and speak with me. Grand-mère thought it would be all right, but Max was a tougher sell. He relented on the condition that he could stay with me during the conversation.

Turns out, Max was on hand when I ran out the front door in a panic because Grand-mère had asked him to stay over, to sleep on the sofa and serve as the downstairs watchman as Bébé was upstairs. Max hadn't brought a bag, so Grand-mère gave him flannel pajamas and a beautiful flowing blue velvet robe that had been my grandfather's to change into because his own clothes were sodden with mud. I put on the sweats I ran in that morning—now yesterday morning—and that had magically reappeared in my room nicely laundered.

Max, Dauvin, Grand-mère and I sat huddled in front of the fire-place in Grand-mère's salon, ready to listen to what Claude had to say.

Both Claude and Max had hatch marks from the gravel on their faces and hands, but neither of them had managed to connect a blow that did any visible damage to the other.

My feet had some gravel nicks, which Grand-mère dressed with antibiotic ointment and covered with thick white cotton socks. Some-where during the course of the evening's events, I had put a tooth into my bottom lip. It bled and swelled, made *M* and *B* words sound a bit distorted, and it was sore. My arm ached where Claude had gripped it.

But I was otherwise okay, except that it upset me unduly to be in close proximity to Claude. His voice yelling at me through the racket of the storm had been familiar in a very scary way.

Claude seemed to be genuinely upset by Max's assumption that he had ever tried to hurt me.

"I was wakened by the storm," Claude said. "Outside the church today, I saw how Marguerite reacted when there was a little lightning. I remember how it was for her in a storm, so I got up and went downstairs to watch for her. I was concerned for her, you see?"

"You bastard," Max said. "You know what else she heard at the church today? She heard what you said, that you should have done away with her when you had the chance, when she was a baby."

Claude flinched, seemed chastened to the point that I expected him to drop to his knees and offer to crawl all the way to Lourdes seeking forgiveness. "I was stupid to say such a thing."

I asked, "Is that how you feel about me?"

"No." He shook his head. "You must know that I was fond of you, Marguerite. I *am* fond of you. I was profoundly sorry when you were taken away. What I said this morning..." He hesitated, distressed by what he was going to say. Finally, he looked directly at me.

"What I said this morning, I said for Freddy's benefit. He was always so jealous of you. And now his mother, who found him imperfect in every way compared to you, is dead, and it is you who carried her ashes home, as if even in death she preferred you. Do you understand?"

"I understand that instead of reassuring him of his mother's love you encouraged his jealousy." I nailed him with a glare that made him look away, flush an unhealthy degree of red. "I've spent some time with Freddy. He's wonderful. He seems to accept me, now that we've finally met. You, however, seem far more upset that I'm here than he does. You have been a goddamn problem for your son all through this difficult day when he needed your support."

"No, I..." He stopped, sort of collapsed in on himself, unable to finish the disclaimer. "Yes. And I am so sorry. But you must understand how it was for Freddy."

"Isabelle didn't know me," I said. "Didn't know what I could and couldn't do. Surely he knew that."

"Would it matter if he did? He was only a boy."

"Poor little bugger," Max said, glancing over at Claude, shaking his head. "Between you and his mother..."

I put my hand on Max's knee, and he stopped. He was still steamed, but he contained it, with effort. I told him when we sat down that I wanted him with me, but that I was afraid that he would stir up something again before I got what I wanted from Claude. He promised he would control himself. Besides, I told him, I needed him to translate for Dauvin. The entire conversation was conveyed to the inspector in a mix of French and English, with hand gestures and facial expressions filling in some of the gaps.

I turned to Claude. "You said I was taken away. But Isabelle had already sent me away. I read that I was here, with Grand-mère, from September until at least mid-December, and Isabelle never visited."

Claude furrowed his brows and wanted to know, "Read where?"

"In a letter my father wrote to Isabelle in the middle of that December, when I was two."

"He wrote to her in December?" Torrid disbelief as he spat out the words. "The sonofabitch promised.... He wrote to her?"

"Claude!" Grand-mère snapped. "That will do. We have seen enough of your temper for one day. You owe our Maggie at least some explanation. You tell her what she wants to know. And I hope you can be civil about it. It's very late and we all want to get to bed. We don't have patience for your outbursts."

He took a couple of breaths, and worked to compose himself before he nodded for me to continue.

I asked, "Why was I left here when Isabelle went back to Paris?"

Claude wrapped an afghan around his thin shoulders, stared off into the fire, sorting out what he wanted to say. And probably what he didn't. After a moment he brought his focus back. In a quiet voice, he began to tell his story.

"For your second birthday, in September, there was to be a party, here, Marguerite. Isabelle brought you early in the week for a visit, but my school term in Chantilly had begun so I wasn't able to join you until the weekend. When I arrived, you and your mother were riding a little pony together, a Norman cob, a sweet-tempered beast you called your little friend. It had been a birthday gift, an extravagant one, so I thought that Élodie had given it to you to ride when you came to visit."

I checked Grand-mère. She was listening as intently as a schoolmarm watching for errors in a student's recitation.

Claude continued. "I took a few pictures, a very charming scene. Later, when the horse was back at the stable, I reached up to help you down and I said, 'Come to Papa.' But you shook your head and told me I wasn't your Papa. You said your Papa gave you the pony for your birthday."

"Two-year-olds say all sorts of things," Max interjected.

"Yes," Claude acknowledged. "But in that case, what she said was true. Alfred Duchamps had been here for the birthday, and my wife hid it from me. I was rightfully angry, I believe. Before we married, Isabelle promised that it was over between them. She told me she would not keep Marguerite from her father, but that she would arrange not to be present when he visited. I trusted her. And I was a fool."

I turned to Grand-mère. "Who gave me the pony?"

"Your father. Out of guilt, I think."

"So." I turned back to Claude. "You were angry with me and jealous about my father, so you—what?—disowned me and left me here?"

"Not at all." A vigorous denial. Finally, he seemed to have some starch, the return of a modicum of the righteous ire he had expressed earlier. "Isabelle and I had a big fight, of course. In the end, we decided that we needed a little time alone to make some repairs to the marriage. Louise and Grand-mère offered to watch you for a week or two—no more."

He begged me, "You must believe I was very fond of you. Your mother was so busy with her work that many evenings it was just you and me for dinner and bedtime. We made a nice little family."

"But you didn't come for me after a week or two," I said. "It was more like three months."

He smiled for the first time, a little rise at the corner of his mouth. "You see, the repairs to the marriage went quite well, and in no time my wife was pregnant with Freddy. From the very first, she was sick, not just in the morning, but all day. She felt very tired, her work was demanding. It was decided that, considering her condition, it was best for you to stay a little longer with your grandmother. So Isabelle could get some rest."

"Three months and not a single visit?" Max wanted to know.

I patted my uncle's knee again. He took a deep breath and leaned back, gazed off into the corner; there was a lot he wanted to say.

"But you did eventually come for me," I said. "Why?"

"Why?" A lift of the bony shoulders, as if to say, who needed a reason? "School was out for the winter holiday. It was almost Christmas. Isabelle was anxious to see you, quite insistent one day that we go immediately. Of course, we wanted our little girl with us. We missed you."

"You came for me just before Christmas?" When he nodded, I said, "My father wrote to Isabelle just before Christmas and told her that he felt she had abandoned custody, and he was coming over to discuss taking me back to America with him."

"Where did you see these letters?" Claude demanded.

"Isabelle kept them."

Claude turned red and started to blow off again, and again it was Grand-mère who cautioned him not to. All she said was, "Claude," in a low but very firm voice.

"I didn't know about the letters," he said, voice reedy with anger.

"So, you took me back to Paris, and a few weeks later Isabelle called my dad and told him to come and get me." I glanced at Max. "I understand that I was pretty battered when Dad and Max got here."

"You bastard," Max hissed.

"Yes, you were hurt." Claude wrapped the afghan tighter, a protective cocoon. "But I never harmed you, Marguerite. I would not."

Clara, in her robe and slippers, hair in a braid down her back, came in carrying a tea tray. She had a fat bed pillow tucked under one arm as she groused about all the mud we had traipsed into the house—mud was even tracked into her kitchen—and don't expect her to clean it until tomorrow. Did people think she had nothing better to do than mop up after them? And who dragged his pillow downstairs and left it in the kitchen? What is she now, the chambermaid?

Grand-mère thanked her for the tea, apologized that all the noise in the house had wakened her, and sent her to bed. Mud on the floors could certainly wait.

When Clara was gone, I got Claude's attention again.

"Go ahead," I said, "you were telling us what happened."

"Isabelle—well, a pregnant woman can be a bit emotional, yes?"

"You're blaming Isabelle now?" Max said.

Grand-mère raised a finger to her lips to stop him from saying more.

Claude resumed: "The three of us were together again in Paris. But Isabelle was having a difficult time—pregnancy, pressures at work, the holidays, a toddler to look after—she was exhausted, I thought. But now that you tell me your father was pressuring her, I understand better."

I wasn't sure why Dauvin stayed to hear about ancient family history. He seemed bored by it all, couldn't understand much of what was being said, and Max was a very inconsistent translator. Idly, he picked up the pillow Clara had left on the footstool next to his chair and turned it over. I thought he might be contemplating a little nap. He caught me watching him, gave me a nod. He asked if the bump on my lip hurt. I told him it did, a little. He asked how it happened. All I could do was shrug: happened somehow in the confusion. Looked worse than it was. Again he nodded.

I turned back to Claude. "You didn't know Dad and Max were here right after Christmas to challenge Isabelle's custody rights?"

Claude sat very still, processing the question. When he spoke, he addressed Max, without open rancor this time, only curiosity. "What did you do?"

"We hired a lawyer to begin the legal process to get custody," Max told him. "Our grounds were abandonment. The lawyer asked Élodie and Louise to sign affidavits affirming how long Maggie had been with them without visits from her mother, or the payment of child support money that my brother sent to her."

Claude asked Grand-mère, interested, not challenging her, "You signed?"

"We considered it, yes. The state Isabelle was in when we saw her at Christmas, we thought it might be best for all to let Mr. Duchamps care for Maggie, at least for the time being. He was from a good French family, and we knew she would be well cared for. Her circumstances would be more stable, though we would miss her terribly."

This time, Max squeezed *my* knee to keep me from saying the wrong thing. We weren't a French family. When my grandfather emigrated from Eastern Europe bearing one of those names without vowels, an immigration officer spelled the name the way he heard it, Duchamps; happened to a lot of people. My grandfather thought Duchamps sounded a little classier than the name he was born with, so he kept it. We wondered if maybe having a new name helped him start over, avoid some issues he left behind in the old country, but he was no longer around to ask.

I covered a spontaneous chortle with a little cough: if my grandfather had kept his Bohunk name, as he referred to it, would Élodie have been so accommodating to Dad?

Claude was thoughtful. "I never knew any of that was happening. But it explains a great deal. As fatigued as she was during the autumn, Isabelle had seemed to be happy, quite content, expectant, if you will, of something wonderful—our baby, of course. But that changed suddenly with the approach of the holidays. She was volatile, quick to tears. I could do nothing to please her. I confess, I was exasperated. When she announced that we had to go and get you right away, we went."

"She wanted to reestablish custody," Max said, "before we got here."

"I understand that now."

"Why did she decide to relinquish me to Dad in the end?" I asked.

"She reached the end of her endurance." An ironic little smile crossed his face. "Forgive me if I say, 'It was a dark and stormy night.'"

Max laughed, a nervous little *Ha!*

Claude continued: "Isabelle and I were in bed. We had not been together as a husband with his wife for a very long time, but that night, a nice meal at a good restaurant, a little wine..." He dropped his eyes as his voice caught, remembering. "There was a storm, and Marguerite, who was always afraid of thunder and lightning, came running into our room, crying."

"As two-year-olds do," Max said.

"Yes, of course," Claude acknowledged. "But well, it was normal that I was a bit angry for the interruption; it was a very inopportune moment. I told her to go back to bed."

"You called me a *petite merdeuse*, a little shit," I added.

His eyes were wide with surprise and mortification. "You remember?"

"I think I do."

"How mad did you get, Claude?" Max wanted to know.

"A bit of a scolding, that was all. I took you by the hand, Marguerite, to put you back in bed, and told you to stay there. But Isabelle exploded. She pulled you away from me and started screaming, saying crazy things."

"Like what?" Max asked.

"Doesn't matter what she said," I said. "What did she do?"

"She twisted your arm to make you stop crying, but you only cried harder. She was thoroughly distraught, out of control. When I tried to take you from her she ran to the window, opened it..." Claude dissolved into pitiful weeping. He finally managed to gasp out, "She threw you out the window."

The rest of the room fell silent. Grand-mère poured tea with shaking hands, something to do. I was worried about her. I took a cup from her hand and met her eyes, deep pools full of grief.

Dauvin rose, muttered something about a glass of water, and wandered off toward the kitchen, taking the errant pillow with him. I thought Claude's show of raw emotion might have embarrassed him.

I asked Grand-mère, "Do you believe Claude?"

She leaned toward Claude. "You would never tell us how Maggie was injured. Were you protecting Isabelle?"

"What else could I do?" He wiped his face with the back of his hand. "You remember how it was for her?"

To me, she said, "Yes, I believe him."

Claude gulped air like a drowning man finally breaking to the surface. But he seemed, in sum, relieved to have shed the burden of this secret. Calmer now, he continued.

"I called an ambulance and ran outside. The neighbors had found you and wrapped you in a coat and called the police. I took you from them, looked you over, fearing the worst. They told me they saw you slide down an awning and land in the chrysanthemum bed. You had some bruises, some scrapes."

"And a broken arm," I said.

Max took my hand. "I think that happened before you went out the window, honey. It was a spiral fracture, a twisted arm." He turned to Claude. "Did Isabelle break Maggie's arm before she threw her out the window?"

"Yes. I heard it." His face went white as he remembered. He glanced at my arm, looking for scars, maybe? "I told the police that you were frightened by the storm and tried to run away from it, and that you must have fallen and hurt yourself. They were skeptical, so they went inside to ask your mother what she knew. When they found her, they didn't ask any more questions."

He lost it again, buried his face in his hands and sobbed.

Grand-mère came and sat beside him, began to gently pat him on the back. "Claude went to the hospital in the ambulance with you, Maggie. Shortly after you arrived, your mother was brought in."

"She tried to kill herself, and our baby," Claude managed to say between gasps. "After I ran from the house, she called your father, Marguerite, and told him that she gave up, he could come and get you. Then she slit her wrists."

"Dear God," Max uttered.

"The police were right there?" I said. "They saved her?"

He nodded.

Grand-mère stopped patting Claude's back and handed him a cup of tea. As she watched him sip, she said, "Claude brought you both here, Maggie. We took your mother back to Ma Mère at the convent, where she had gone for sanctuary before. Ma Mère gave her quiet, watched over her, oversaw the doctors who came to care for her, as before."

"As before?" I asked. "How much like before? When before?"

"Just before you were born."

"That's why she was at the convent when I was born? She had tried to kill herself?"

Grand-mère's answer was the slightest tilt of her head: Yes.

"Some women have a very rough time with pregnancy. We could not risk putting Isabelle through that a third time." Claude made scissors with two fingers. "I got a vasectomy."

Max squeezed my knee: the things Claude did not know. Among them, Isabelle told Dad that Freddy was his child, and she wanted them to run off together with, as Dad said, two babies. That tidbit was better left quiet.

I asked Claude, "Did you ever meet my dad?"

"No."

Probably a good thing, I thought, considering how much Freddy looked like Dad.

"Have I told you what you wanted to know?" Claude asked.

"Yes, thank you. I'm sorry to have brought back bad memories," I said. "If I may, just one more question?"

"Oh dear, oh dear, what now?" but said with surprisingly good humor.

"The pony. Why did Isabelle send it over to me?"

"To punish Freddy for doing something naughty. He loved *Amie* very much."

When he rose to leave, Claude apologized to Grand-mère for being so difficult all day. She let him off the hook, telling him that we all live private lives, and no one can really know the pressures we're under. Then she kissed me and headed upstairs for bed, obviously grateful to have Max's arm to lean on; he did look swanky in my grandfather's velvet robe.

I saw Claude to the door. He embraced me, kissed both of my cheeks before he bade me good night. There was, odd as it is to say, a sweetness in the gesture. I stayed in the open door, watching his back until he arrived safely at Isabelle's house. Freddy had waited up for him. He opened the door before his father reached for the latch, wrapped an arm around Claude's shoulders and took him inside.

For Claude, our conversation seemed to have been cathartic. It was an ugly story to have kept locked up for so long. By the end, we had all learned a great deal. There were still secrets, some of them now mine. Some of them I intended to keep. At least for the time being.

As I turned after closing the door I almost tripped over Inspector Dauvin. He was on his knees behind me looking at the jumble of muddy shoes piled under the coat hooks in the entry. He sorted the wet from the dry, putting Casey's and Bébé's dryish ones aside. There was a pair of muddy prints where Claude's boots had been. The inspector held up the clogs Grand-mère had brought outside to me.

"You wore these?" he asked. When I said I did, he asked about the others: Grand-mère wore the black galoshes with her mink coat, the leather house slippers were Max's. Dauvin acknowledged the rubber overshoes he had worn over his brogans. Who else came inside with us?

"No one," I said, after he repeated the question a couple of times; he was using very elementary French and speaking very slowly for me. I ran through the list of people: After the brouhaha, Freddy took his dad home, cleaned him up and brought him over for our talk, but Freddy did not come inside. I was to have a private conversation with Claude, at Claude's request. Dauvin insisted on staying, and so Max, my lawyer, needed to be there, too. Grand-mère asked everyone else to go home and go to bed.

"The four of you came through the front door?" Dauvin asked.

"Yes."

"No one else came in?"

"The only other people in the house, as far as I know, were asleep in bed," I said. He nodded.

I asked him how he got to us so quickly, and he said he had the compound under surveillance from the *bocage* along the drive. Just to be safe. When he saw me run out of the house with Max following and Claude coming out of Isabelle's, and then a fist fight—actually, a wrestling match—he thought he needed to take a look.

"Tell me again how it all got started," he said.

I tried, but I needed a translator. Max stretched out on the sofa after he tucked in Grand-mère and was nursing a snifter of brandy, looking like the lord of the manor lounging in my grandfather's robe. I asked him to help us. He lumbered to his feet, encased in white socks, and waited for us to come to him; it was warm in front of the fire.

"I was frightened by the storm," I told Dauvin, with Max's help. "I ran outside."

"I heard what Desmoulins said earlier, and I saw you react at the church." Dauvin studied me through narrowed eyes. "Tonight you were frightened and you ran outside."

"Yes."

"But before you ran outside, what happened?"

"I don't know, exactly. I was asleep, having a bad dream, I panicked when I heard the storm, and that was all I knew until I was outside and Claude grabbed me."

Dauvin pointed upstairs with his thumb. "Please show me where you were."

The three of us traipsed upstairs.

Earlier, after the big mud wrestling bout, I was in my room only long enough to pick up clean clothes before showering. When the three of us opened the bedroom door, nothing had changed: the room was still a shambles. During my nightmare I had put up quite a struggle with the bedding. Sheets were in a tangle, pillows tossed here and there. I must have dragged the duvet halfway across the floor as I ran out.

I started to pull the bed back together, but Dauvin stopped me. He asked Max and me to wait by the door while he made a circuit around the room, looking things over. He got down on his knees on the far side of the bed. When he stood up again, he said, "Please tell me what you remember."

"I was asleep, as I told you," I said. I was so tired I was woozy. "Dreaming."

"Un cauchemar?" he asked, a nightmare? When I nodded, he asked me to tell him what I remembered of the dream.

I had to think for a moment. "I was falling through water. It got very deep. I felt pressure on my chest, something was on my face, I couldn't breathe, it was dark."

"Very dark?" Dauvin asked.

"Pitch black. I heard thunder, I fought, I cleared my face, I saw lightning, I panicked, I ran. The rest you know."

"You dreamed for a long time?"

"That part? A nanosecond."

He thought for a moment, looked around some more. He asked me to pass him the box of tissues on the bedside table. As he took it, he said, "Will you please drop by the clinic sometime today to give a blood sample? I will leave the order."

Max translated, but held up a hand and stopped me from responding as he slipped into lawyer mode. I didn't need to say anything; he asked the question I was about to.

"What the hell for?" Max asked loudly enough that a very sleepy Bébé appeared at my door."

"Ça va?" he asked around a yawn: How's it going?

"You were across the hall all evening?" Dauvin asked him.

A moment of confusion before he gave a nod, yes.

"Did you hear anything unusual or see anyone other than Madame Flint in or around this room earlier tonight?"

"Maggie, what's happening?"

"Bébé, please answer," Dauvin said.

"Hear anything, Pierre? Absolutely. It was a bloody noisy night. Big storm, plenty of *kaboom*, a light show."

"You didn't hear people outside?"

Bébé shook his head.

I offered, "His room is on the back side of the house. These walls are thick."

Bébé brightened as a thought occurred to him. "I did hear someone go down the hall toward the stairs. I thought it was probably Maggie or Casey going to the loo."

"Did you see anyone?"

"No. I opened my door and looked out, but no one was there. So I got into bed."

"When did you close your door?" I asked.

He shrugged. "I thought you did it."

Dauvin thanked him and suggested that he go back to bed and close his door again.

"Why a blood test?" Max wanted to know after Bébé was gone.

In lieu of an answer, Dauvin asked me, "How did you hurt your lip?"

I did a full-on palms-up shrug: I didn't know.

"A pillow was found in the kitchen with blood on it," he said. "I would be interested to know whose, Madame."

I went around the room picking up pillows and piling them onto the bed. There were only three, one short. I didn't remember running from my room, but I also couldn't imagine how or why I would have detoured to dump a bed pillow in the kitchen when I was running in panic to get outside.

Dauvin took a little digital camera from his pocket, turned on the Replay function and showed us some close-up pictures he had taken of the muddy shoeprints on the kitchen floor that Clara groused about, a trail that came from the back door and grew fainter as some inconsiderate lout traipsed muck across the floor and into the dining room. What did I think?

"A pillow thief?" I asked.

A small wag of the head was as close to a smile as I had seen the inspector give up. He put the camera away, reached over and pulled up the bed sheet with both hands, held it up to the light one length at a time, as if inspecting dress goods. When he finished, he asked to see my forearms.

I looked at Max, who frowned but nodded assent. I pulled up my sleeves and reached my arms out for the inspector. He took my hands in his, one at a time, looked them over, examined my arms to the elbows. He pointed out a few little cuts on my knuckles and wrists.

"How did you get those?"

Again I shrugged. "Look at Max's face. Gravel nicks. Probably happened when I was trying to separate Max and Claude."

"Your neck, please."

I showed him, he looked. "Good, nothing."

Max took my hands to look at the cuts. "What's this all about, Dauvin?"

"I'll show you."

He pulled a tissue out of the box I handed him earlier, took a plastic bag from his pocket, went around to the far side of the bed again, bent down and picked up an object with the tissue and dropped it into the bag.

"Pruning knife," he announced, holding up the bag for us to see: a wooden handle with a short, curved blade. "I assume you didn't put it there."

"Correct," I said.

"Do you know, madame, what happened on this estate during the war?"

"To the German soldiers?" I pointed my chin at the knife. "Yes."

"This little knife is very useful for getting rid of useless suckers growing from a tree." He gripped the plastic-encased knife handle in his fist, held it near his throat and gave it a quick twist. "And other annoyances. You understand?"

"Like me?" I asked.

"It certainly appears someone feels that way about you, yes."

—22—

I PRESSED THE bandage over the end of my ring finger to make it stick as I walked out of the nurse's station at the clinic. The nurse on duty had pricked the finger to take a blood sample, just a dab on a slide, another on a card.

That morning, Sunday, I was the last one in the house to get out of bed—I managed to get about five hours of sleep after Dauvin left—and the last into the bathroom I shared with Casey and Bébé. I lingered over the shower, the croissants and coffee that followed, and had enjoyed being fussed over by Grand-mère a bit. Bébé and Casey, and various of their cousins, had left for the beach with David to set up for the volleyball game before I got downstairs.

Grand-mère was exhausted that morning, certainly showed the beginnings of the great letdown that morning after the funeral. But more than that, she was burdened by a sort of free-floating remorse about my early life with Isabelle after hearing Claude's account. She should have known, she should have done… It was a long time ago, I reminded her. And what should have been done probably was. In due course. By the time she went upstairs to dress for Mass, she seemed stronger.

When Dauvin arrived to take me to the clinic to give a blood sample, I still wore the sweats I pulled on after my shower, and my damp hair was twisted under an alligator clip borrowed from Casey. I didn't bother with makeup; the face looking back at me from the mirror just wasn't worth the effort. The fat lip from the night before? Not pretty. After the stop at the clinic, Dauvin was to drive me to join the family for the volleyball game at Anneville-sur-Mer. How dressed does one need to be to play volleyball on the beach?

"Not too bad, was it?" Dauvin asked when I rejoined him in the hall outside the nurse's station.

I shook my head as I held up my bandaged finger. Just one more little nick to add to the collection on my feet, hands and wrists from the night before.

Max was there waiting also, along with the old friend he had been staying with in Créances. The old friend, Patricia Dutoit, was a very attractive woman in her late sixties, about the same age as Max. It became obvious right away that she and Max had at one time been more than just friends, and that she wouldn't mind rekindling the relationship.

Patricia's title, she told me, was *notaire*, equivalent to a family lawyer in the U.S. or a solicitor in England. To round out her résumé, she was also a cousin of both the Bretons and the Foullards through separate parents, and had gone to local schools with Isabelle and Louise.

As we walked out of the clinic Dauvin asked me, "Shall I explain to you what I believe happened last night, madame?"

"May I take a stab at it?" I said. "Apologies for the bad pun."

The joke didn't translate, though Max did his best. Or, maybe it did translate and it just wasn't funny. Dauvin, however, did smile a bit when he invited me to offer what I thought happened.

"Last night, when the house was quiet, someone came in through the kitchen," I said, "went upstairs, closed Bébé's door so he wouldn't see anything if he woke up, continued to my room, pressed a pillow over my face to muffle any sound I might make—pushing hard enough that I bit my lip—and prepared to slit my throat in the same way the local women slit the throats of the estate's last interlopers, German soldiers.

"But the pillow over my face and the sound of thunder wakened me in a panic. I bucked free, got a couple of knife cuts in the process, and ran outside screaming. Is that about right?"

"Fairly close," Dauvin said, bowing slightly.

"My screams may have stirred Bébé from sleep enough so that when my attacker later left my room—with the pillow but not the knife, probably dropped in the struggle—Bébé heard him or her and got up to take a look."

He nodded.

"So crazy panic saved my life this time," I said, "though it nearly got me killed when I was two years old."

Dauvin shrugged—who can say? "The important thing to remember is, you woke up, and you fought. Chances are, you would have fended off the attacker in any case."

"Do you know who it was?" Max asked him, hanging on to my arm.

"Someone who was inside the compound before we started surveillance," Dauvin said. "Someone familiar enough with the layout to walk around in the dark. That leaves a large number of people, of course, though I have managed to eliminate a few." He tilted his head toward me. "Your uncle here, for example, and your stepfather are in the clear."

Max guffawed. Was he relieved to be in the clear, or had it never occurred to him that he might be a suspect?

"You looked at the footprints in the kitchen," I said. "What did they tell you?"

"That the intruder wore a rubber boot made in China that is sold at the local market, the feed store, and the *gasoil* station. It is nearly ubiquitous in the region."

"Where is Sherlock when you need him?" I asked. "Don't the footprints tell you height, weight, shoe size, country of origin and stomach contents?"

"They tell us the size of the boot, not the size of the person wearing it," Dauvin said, almost giving away another smile. "What is more important to me at the moment is who was where at the time the mud was left in the kitchen."

"Have you made a chart?"

"Of sorts." His eyes were fixed on me. "You have some ideas of your own, I believe."

I thought about the appropriate shrug to use here. An *of course*, with both palms up? A *perhaps*, a slight lift of one shoulder only? A *not at all*, both shoulders up, chin turned to one side with a moue, the little pouty frown? In the end, I just said, "Yes."

"Yes?" An invitation to continue.

Instead of answering his question, I turned to Max and asked, "As I understand the *tontine*, the last survivor inherits everything. Right?"

He deferred the question to Patricia Dutoit, the expert on such things in France.

"Yes, exactly," she said.

"If I had died before Isabelle, who would eventually inherit the patents from her?"

"Your children, and only your children," Patricia Dutoit said. "In a *tontine* of this sort, arranged to protect the inheritance rights of people *not* related by blood—spouses for instance, or, in this case, paramours—children born to either party outside of their relationship would not be able to claim their *réserve légale*, the legal share all offspring in France are entitled to receive from their parents' estates. So, in the case you mention, your daughter would have become co-owner of the *tontine* with Isabelle, and eventually the sole owner."

I asked, "If Freddy can prove he is the biological child of both my father and Isabelle, does he have a claim on the *tontine*?"

She was nodding before I finished. "Of course. If he can prove he was born within their relationship, he cannot be excluded."

Max dropped his head and let out a deep sigh. "Oh, dear God."

"Inspector," I said, "before we leave the clinic, maybe you should get a blood sample from my uncle."

Three sets of eyebrows rose.

I patted Max's shoulder. "I smell a paternity claim in the offing. You might as well offer up some Duchamps DNA now, before someone comes at you with a subpoena; you are the only male survivor in Dad's bloodline, my dear Max. And as we know, in France inheritance follows blood."

Dauvin frowned as he asked Max, "Have you told her about the letter?"

"What letter?" I asked.

Max said, "A letter dated shortly after your dad died, signed

'Marguerite Duchamps MacGowen,' directing Monsieur Hubert to deposit all patent earnings into Isabelle's account, for starters."

"How could I do that?" I demanded. "I knew nothing about the arrangement."

"Exactly," Max said. "Funds were siphoned into an offshore account; Isabelle, it seems, knew nothing about the scheme. Inspector Dauvin is looking into it."

During the last four or five years, the patents had begun to bring in ever larger amounts of money; solar power applications, and maybe oil shale Hubert told me. We weren't talking about orthodontia payments and college tuition anymore, but something significant enough to tempt someone to commit fraud. If Isabelle had managed to get in touch with me, the scheme could have unraveled in a hurry. And someone's life with it.

———

"It's about time you got here, Mom." Casey held a soccer ball on her open palm, as she would a volleyball, ready to serve it over a fishing net rigged between two driftwood poles driven into the sand at Anneville-sur-Mer.

"Give me a minute to catch my breath," I said, stowing my bag, the one Jean-Paul gave me, against the cottage wall.

Max and Patricia walked together behind me. Dauvin stood watch with some local gendarmes from the end of the beach road, camouflaged by heavy growth like gnomes in the woods.

The beach at Anneville was a beautiful long, broad expanse of golden sand. The tide was out, way out. Along the hard sand at water's edge, cart drivers exercised their trotters, silhouetted black against the silvery water that made up the horizon. A couple of the drivers had ventured up to watch the game, horses tethered to a tree, the drivers lounging against their long, slender sulkies.

The family sat in low canvas beach chairs around a firepit ablaze with driftwood, wrapped in blankets and clutching hot drinks. The storm had blown out, and there were hints of blue sky in the distance, but it was still cold. I took out the digital camera Max had borrowed from Patricia and started snapping pictures of the place and the people, and the game being played on a makeshift court. They had been playing for maybe an hour before we arrived and had mastered, in a rudimentary way, the basics of volleyball.

"Catch your breath, camera lady," Casey said. "You rotate in after this side. We're playing real women against hairy men."

"What does that make me?" demanded Antoine's son Chris, the fifth person on the team of Casey, Kelly, Lulu and Jemima.

"It makes you a real man," said Kelly, "until Maggie gets in here to help the fair sex vanquish the hirsute."

"What's hirsute?" he asked.

"Manly," Antoine answered, making a show of smelling his armpit. The rest of his team were David, Freddy and his sons, Robert and Philippe.

There was a lot of good-natured posturing and bantering back and forth until Casey's serve was in the air, and then all were quiet, focused on the ball. The ball cleared the net with mere millimeters to spare, and when it was clear, sank immediately. David dove under it before it hit the sand, popped it up from underneath with clenched fists, set it for Freddy to smash back over the net.

Lulu crouched under the ball's trajectory and drove straight up with spring-loaded legs and made a gorgeous head butt, sending the ball in a tight arc back over the net and dropping it perfectly into the sand between Robert and Philippe.

"No fair." Philippe scooped up the ball. "Hands only, no head butts."

"Says who?" Lulu demanded of her cousin, coming right up against the net with her hands pugnaciously planted on her narrow hips. "Casey said no feet. I didn't hear no heads."

"We need a decision from the peanut gallery." Casey turned to the bystanders for a decision. The elders among the French cousins only shrugged at Casey's question; volleyball was new to them.

Casey appealed to me: "Mom?"

I said, "That was such a beautiful head butt, I think it should be allowed. Men?"

"I agree," Bébé said, reaching up from his chair to fist-bump me. "Head butts are now in. For both sides."

The ruling: heads and hands were okay, feet still were not. A sort of hybrid volleyball-soccer.

As I passed behind him, Claude leaned back in his chair and reached his hand up to me. I took his hand, leaned forward and kissed the top of his head. There were some surprised looks, but it was Lena who reacted most. She seemed taken aback, but managed to smile up at me and wish me good morning. Her confusion was understandable, I thought. She had probably heard Claude rail against me for years, and here he was all of a sudden reaching out to me, the enemy. Confusing, indeed.

Uncle Gérard got up and offered his chair to Patricia, and fetched one for Max. Then he asked me if I would like for him to show me around. I said I would.

There were maybe a dozen small seasonal cottages along the shore and in the dense gorse beyond. The cottage immediately behind the game belonged to the family, though exactly what "family" meant I wasn't sure. Martins, Bretons, Foullards, Cartiers and collateral cousins all apparently had access.

Gérard told me that Isabelle designed the building, replacing an earlier, primitive, summer beach shack with something more comfortable and more functional for family outings in any season.

It was simple cinderblock construction, basically one big room with a full kitchen and a bath, with a sleeping loft built above the far end. The furnishings were knock-about stuff, cast-offs probably from various of the family's homes. The entire front wall of wood-framed glass panes could be folded open during warm weather to turn the space into an indoor-outdoor lanai. But on that cold day, only one of the windowed panels was open, and then only part-way.

"It's wonderful here," I said.

"You should see it in summer." Gérard handed me a mug of coffee with milk and poured two more to take to Max and Patricia. "But I'm sure you will. Maman hopes you will come back and stay for a very long time. But I think it more likely that you will only visit from time to time. Am I wrong?"

"I have a job, a daughter to get through school, my mother."

"Of course." He put a hand under my elbow. "I remember her, Elizabeth. She is lovely."

"So, you knew her? And my dad?"

"Yes, of course. Quite well. My wife Louise and I spent a good amount of time with him. During the year your family were here together, your mother took the children home to America for Christmas—I believe her father was ill—but your father had work to do and couldn't go with them. So, naturally, we asked him to stay with us for a few weeks. We had a wonderful time; so intelligent and so gracious, what a wonderful guest he was."

"And where was Isabelle?"

"With my parents of course." He lowered his head and winked. "Next door to us."

I had an *aha* moment, a little mystery solved. I didn't know when *l'Affaire Isabelle* began for Dad, but I knew roughly when I was conceived: My namesake Ste-Eugénie's feast day? Christmas. Mom was in the States with Mark and Emily, and Dad delivered a little present to Isabelle: me.

Isabelle obviously attached some significance to the date—ergo and to wit, my name—which made me wonder about the sequence of events that Claude laid out last night. Freddy, little present number two, was conceived at my second birthday, and announced to Dad just before the following Christmas, like a gift. Claude said Isabelle suffered from morning sickness, but that she was very happy during the fall. Then in December, when Dad wrote and turned down her suggestion that they ride off into the sunset with their little family, she went off the rails. Again.

When Gérard suggested that we go back and join the others, I put my hand on his arm to stop him. He looked over at me, brows up, expectant expression on his face.

"Uncle Gérard, tell me about Isabelle."

"You've asked the others, I know. Is there something you think I can add?"

"You're her big brother," I said. "You knew her in a different way than the others. I've heard she was brilliant, eccentric, and absentminded. And volatile. What's missing in the descriptions?"

He cast his eyes down, sighed; obviously a tough question for him to answer. Then he seemed to make a decision, and he brought his eyes back to mine.

"I will tell you something no one else wants to admit," he said. "My little sister was every bit as mentally unbalanced as she was mentally gifted."

When I nodded, he seemed surprised, seemed to have expected a different reaction, some disbelief, a protest. I said, "Please, tell me."

He hesitated. "You have to understand, that for some people, traditional people, there is a greater stigma attached to mental illness than to, say, creating an illegitimate child."

I waited for him to continue.

"Isabelle was far more than eccentric," he said. "From the time she was a teenager, my sister rode an emotional roller coaster, up and down in cycles. Over time, the ups became wilder—more creative and more dangerous, as well—and the downs became profound. My wife, Louise, loved Isabelle very much. She tried to get her into the care of a proper doctor, a psychiatrist. My father, a good man, but…" He shrugged.

"But very traditional?" I interjected. "And maybe stubborn?"

He acknowledged both as understatement. "Papa wouldn't hear of it. And Maman, a strong woman but an obedient wife, went along with his wishes. When Isabelle had breakdowns, do you know where they sent her?"

"To Ma Mère at the Convent of the Sacred Flower."

"Exactement," he exclaimed; we had touched an emotional nerve and apparently he was ready to talk about it. "After one of Isabelle's breakdowns, my Louise persuaded Claude that he should take charge of his wife's care and get her to a shrink."

"And did he?"

"Yes. If he hadn't, Louise would have. The diagnosis: bipolar disorder. There were good medications, not always pleasant for her, and Isabelle resisted them—she missed the creativity of her manic phase—but in time she was able to settle down into a calmer existence. For Freddy, that was essential.

"From time to time, the medications didn't work or she couldn't tolerate the side effects or she forgot to take them, so there were episodes, periods of unpredictable acts, but never again so destructive. After she went through the change, life became smoother yet."

"Thank you for telling me," I said. "It explains a great deal."

"I warn you," he said, wagging a finger, "if you try to talk to Maman or Grand-mère Marie about this, they will deny there was ever anything more wrong with Isabelle than overwork. You see, the culprit was her career, far too taxing for a woman, in their estimation."

Note to self: three things we don't discuss with my grandmother; suicide, mental illness, equal rights for women. What else?

He looked at me closely before he asked, "How was she when you met her?"

"It wasn't much of a meeting. The way Isabelle approached me, jumped out at me, I thought she was a crazy person. I called for Security to take her away."

This was no surprise to him.

I said, "Why do you ask? What do you know?"

"She called me when she was in Malibu," he said, palms up. "Some problem with her medication. I think that's what made her go to California to talk to you, that damn emotional roller coaster. After she got there, she became afraid, knew she needed some help. She called her doctor in Paris, and he gave her a new prescription, but no local pharmacy in Los Angeles would honor it. She asked me if I could do something."

"Could you?"

"Yes. I called my friend Jean-Paul Bernard—you said you met him—and he was able to get a physician he knew in Los Angeles to speak with Isabelle's doctor so he could write the appropriate prescription. She had it filled. But my dear, those medications can take days if not weeks to become effective.

"The way she sounded on the telephone, I knew she was in trouble. I was prepared to go and get her. When I heard that she died in a traffic accident just a day or so after I spoke with her, I thought that she had done something to make it happen."

"Maggie!" Bébé came inside, cheeks pink from the cold. He gave his father a perfunctory nod; clearly, Gérard wanted something more from him. "You're in. Freddy's dumping out to catch his breath and Chris wants to play on the guy side."

I thanked Gérard for his honesty. He kissed my cheek and held my arm, keeping me from running off before he had a final word.

"Whatever else my sister was," Gérard said, looking deep into my eyes to show his sincerity, "she was smart. I should have listened when she told me that my plans for the estate would only cause dissension. The family doesn't need to worry any longer. Except for repaying what I owe them, I'm finished with my scheme for the estate."

"Probably wise," I said.

"Maggie?" Bébé said, urging me to go with him. He heard what his father said. They exchanged a long look before Bébé turned away.

Outside, I kicked off my shoes and socks, rolled up my sleeves and pant legs. I grabbed Bébé by the hand. "If I'm in, you're in."

Casey put me in the middle as setter, Bébé was sent to the back corner for the other team. David served, a fast, low ball. Jemima, playing net, slammed the ball, sending it into Bébé's mid-section so hard and so fast he didn't have time to get out of the way, much less hit it.

"Hey," he shouted, scooping the ball up off the sand.

"Heads up, Chuck," Jemima said; his given name was Charles.

"Don't call me Chuck, Puddleduck." Bébé slung the ball under the net to Casey.

"You're not my baby, Chuck," Jemima said, and turned away. Lulu high-fived her, grinning.

Casey served, another low, fast ball. Philippe jumped, spiked it back over the net. Again, Jemima slammed the ball straight at Bébé. He dove, tried to get under it, landed on his belly in a spray of sand. The ball rolled away.

"Eye on the ball, Chuck," Jemima chided, snapping her fingers. "Eye on the ball."

Bébé got back to his feet, really pissed, thoroughly embarrassed, and side-armed the ball back to Casey.

Casey served, David blocked it at the net. Jemima's hands were there, sent it straight back. Philippe intercepted, sent the ball whizzing toward Kelly. Kelly retrieved it, set it for me. I managed to get the ball over the net, barely.

"Mine," Bébé called, and passed it to David at the net. David slammed the ball into the sand on our side of the net.

"Point for men," Philippe shouted. "Service, men."

"Substitution." Kelly raised her hand. "Thumb jam."

Jemima turned toward the spectators, "Mummy, you're in."

I thought that Gillian, decked out in a pink velour warm-up suit and matching pink sneakers with a Sherpa vest to complete the outfit, would decline. But she jumped right up, shed the shoes and vest, rolled up her trousers, and came in. Surprised us all. Turned out, she was pretty tough, and very quick. Didn't flinch at all when one of her acrylic nails flew off when she hit the ball. And when she hit it, she blasted it.

Jemima kept up the pressure on Bébé. She rotated to the service position. As she bounced the ball on her left palm, she called out to Bébé, "Hey, brother, in honor of our new-found California cousins, I've decided to call you after one of their finest wines, Two-buck Chuck. Cheap generic plonk, I understand. Barely drinkable. Service!"

She smacked the ball with deadly accuracy. He retrieved it this time, but only with heroic effort, wincing as its speed stung his hands. He set it for Robert.

Robert had decided, correctly, that I was the weak man on our team. He hit the ball, I dove for it, got a face full of sand but managed to keep it from touching the ground. Gillian sent it over the net where it landed just inside bounds, a line drawn in the sand.

"Time," I called, getting to my feet. Mouthful of sand, sand in my eyes, I staggered to the sideline. I pulled up my sweatshirt to wipe the sand away, but the shirt was so sandy it only made matters worse.

"Don't rub." One of the men took my hand, wiped it off and put a linen handkerchief into it. I knew the voice, but thought my ears must be full of grit as well. "Lean your head back, let me flush your eyes."

He cupped the back of my head for support as he gently poured water over my eyes. When I could, I squinted at him, confirmed who this Sir Galahad was. When he was finished, I dabbed at my dripping face with his handkerchief and said, "Thank you, Jean-Paul. I didn't see you arrive."

"I've been standing over there trying to figure out the game. What do you call it?"

"We call it rough," Bébé said, panting. "Maggie, you in or out?"

"Out for the moment."

Lulu looked at the spectators. "Who's in for women?"

Robert called to his mother, the only available female, but Lena waved him off. She had no interest.

Antoine rose, and pitching his voice high like a girl, called, "I am."

I took Jean-Paul inside to get him coffee and to get me cleaned up. He looked amazingly well put-together for a Sunday morning: tailored blue jeans, black cashmere polo, brown suede jacket as soft as butter. No question, he was handsome. I assessed myself: hair, still damp from my morning shower, the sweats I pulled on afterward no lovelier, bare face sweaty, lip puffed, and all of me liberally floured with sand.

"I wasn't expecting to see you here," I said after rinsing my hands in the sink. I filled a mug for him and offered him milk.

"I was in the area, I wanted to stop by and give my condolences to your grandmother. She invited me to join the family for lunch and told me where to find you." He stirred his cup. "I hope you aren't disappointed to see me."

"Not at all," I said, holding my arms out to the sides. "I dressed especially for the occasion."

He laughed, brushed some sand out of my eyebrows. "Lovely, as ever. Do you need ice for that lip?"

"No thanks. That happened earlier."

Cradling his cup he asked, "Are you aware that the woods are full of cops?"

"They followed me in."

"I had to show my diplomatic credentials to get past."

"There have been some nefarious goings-on."

"Yes?" He tipped his head toward me, looking at the lip, asking if whatever those goings on were responsible for the bump.

Watching his face, I said, "You didn't tell me that you had spoken with Isabelle in Los Angeles."

One shoulder up, a little frown—the answer should be obvious. "It was a confidential matter."

"Did you mention the matter to the police?"

"I didn't need to," he said, touching his index finger to the tip of his nose and then toward me. "You gave the essential information to the very efficient Detective Longshore, and he made the appropriate inquiries."

I was shedding sand on the floor. I turned and looked at my trail, and then back at the lovely Jean-Paul. He had a goofy smile on his face. I was happy to amuse him, but wished for a slinky black dress and maybe a cigarette in a long holder to magically appear.

"Will you excuse me?" I asked. "I do need to clean up a bit."

He took his coffee and went out to join the others.

I went into the bathroom and surveyed the wreckage. Far more than a little freshening up was needed to transform the creature in the mirror into a glamorous babe, but I did my best. A few minutes later, feeling much better, looking maybe marginally more presentable, I went back outside.

The game was still on, but it had changed in its make-up and character. The teams were now coed. I was told that Bébé, having declared "If you can't beat 'em, join 'em," had selected Jemima first for his team. Jean-Paul was playing on their side. Team Casey was up by one point.

I took the empty chair between Kelly and Freddy and wrapped a blanket around my shoulders. Kelly, jutting her chin toward Jean-Paul, said, "Good for you."

"He has nice legs, doesn't he?" I said, ogling the tanned ankles showing below the rolled-up jeans.

"Among other things, yes." She patted my arm. "Best of luck."

Lena leaned forward, reached past Freddy to catch my eye, and said, "You don't waste much time, do you?"

"Seize the day is my motto," I said. "Because who knows what to-morrow will bring?"

She smiled, uncertain, and sat back.

At noon, the churchgoers arrived: the two grandmothers, Jacques and Julie, Ma Mère the abbess, and her young Chinese assistant. While the game continued outside, the bystanders were put to work inside setting up for lunch. Freddy and Gérard pulled a long table into the middle of the room, and food began to appear out of hampers, buckets, and the refrigerator.

Antoine had gone out early that morning to meet the fishing boats when they came in with the tide loaded with fresh catch. He traded Cal-vados and Camembert with the fishermen for beautiful whole Dieppe sole, Atlantic lobsters and spider crabs.

The seafood was cleaned, drizzled with butter, seasoned with salt and pepper, and arranged in flat wire grilling baskets with thick slices of leeks, cloves of garlic and sprays of fresh fennel from Isabelle's greenhouse, and then cooked over the driftwood coals in the firepit outside. When it was ready, everything was piled onto huge platters and served buffet-style from the kitchen counter with fresh rye bread, sweet butter, and green beans sautéed with butter and tarragon. There was a delicious cream-and-Calvados sauce on the side, and carafes of dry cider and crisp white wine to wash it all down.

Conversation was lively during the meal, full of game replays and joshing about who did and did not do what, but the most interesting exchange was between Bébé and his stepmother, Gillian.

As she pulled a succulent chunk of white flesh out of a lobster shell, Gillian said, "Bébé, the portrait you painted of your mother is lovely."

Bébé flushed furiously, and sat frozen, holding the bread basket, waiting for the punch line. Or, perhaps, the punch.

"I may not admire the reason you painted it," Gillian said in a neutral tone, "or the reason you hung it where you did, when you did. But it is exquisite."

"Thank you?" was the best he could manage.

"I have a favor to ask."

He put the bread down and waited for it.

"Would you paint my daughter?"

Bébé tilted his head, unsure whether she was serious or teasing.

"Nothing as monumental as the portrait of your mother of course—we'd need to erect a cathedral to hang something so large," Gillian said. "But something on a more personal scale."

Bébé recovered himself enough to be snide. "Something to hang over the sofa, perhaps color-coordinated to the draperies?"

"No." She parried his jab. "More like over the mantel. You know, to disguise the retractable panel that covers our flat screen when we aren't watching Ab Fab reruns—they are my style gurus, of course."

Bébé turned to Jemima. "Is she putting me on?"

"Yes, Chuck, she is."

"But not about the portrait," Gillian said.

"Would you sit for me?" Bébé asked his half sister, sounding doubtful, but curious.

Jemima said, "As long as you understand that when Mummy says to paint me, she means for you to create a likeness on canvas, not literally to paint *me*."

Uncle Gérard had been watching this exchange like a spectator at a three-way tennis match, grinning. I wondered when he planned to make a general announcement that he had abandoned his development scheme. At dessert?

Lulu nudged her uncle. "Do it, Bébé."

"I suppose you want one too, squirt," he countered.

"Oh, would you, Bébé?" Kelly chimed in enthusiastically. "I've been waiting for you to offer."

Bébé turned to Gillian and threw up his hands. "See what you've started?"

"So, will you do it?" she asked.

"When's Christmas this year?" he asked.

"When it always is," I said, leaning forward to catch Ma Mère's eye. "On the feast day of Sainte-Eugénie."

Ma Mère nodded, hid a small smile as she said, "To some, a very special day, indeed."

Antoine spotted Inspector Dauvin lurking outside—he was sticking close—and, rising, gestured for him to come in. "Join us, Pierre, eat."

Dauvin looked to Grand-mère for permission. She gestured to an empty chair and then to the spread on the kitchen counter. "Please, help yourself, Pierre."

Dauvin served a plate and scooted Lena and Antoine apart so he could squeeze a chair in across the table from me.

I said, "You look tired. Will you get a break soon?"

A slight leftward wag of his head said not. "And you?"

I imitated his head wag. "After another glass of wine, I think I'll go up to the loft and take a nap."

I saw Jean-Paul drop his eyes, smile; a lovely thought caught him by surprise. And me.

"I will wait until tonight for my nap," Dauvin said pointedly, looking around the table. "But tonight, I expect to sleep better than I have for over a week."

I waited for him to explain. But he didn't. Instead, he asked Lena, sitting next to him, to pass him the bread.

He said to her, "Robert and Philippe have grown like the rest of these weeds we call children since I saw them last."

Lena glanced down the row at her boys, smiling proudly. "They are getting so tall."

"Maggie," Gillian said. "You should have Casey sit for Bébé, too. Maybe we could talk him into painting all of the children. Wouldn't that be wonderful?"

"Dear Lord," Bébé gazed heavenward, "they seem to have me by the balls, these mothers."

"Charles," Ma Mère said, that quiet nun reproach that could shrink anyone's balls to the size of raisins, even if one did not have a pair.

Jean-Paul smiled at me with lights in his big brown eyes. He was having a wonderful time, very comfortable with that particular mob.

I asked, knowing the answer because Gérard had already told me, "Do you have children?"

"One son, he's eighteen," Jean-Paul said. "If I had known there would be so many kids here his age, I would have taken him from school and brought him."

"Next time," Kelly chimed in. Damned American directness, assuming there would be a next time.

"I look forward to it," he said, dipping his head in a gracious little bow to her. Then he smiled at me, and corny as it sounds, he took my breath away.

It was a beautiful feast. In keeping with local custom, there was a break before the cheese was served, the *trou Normand* it is called, the "Norman hole," a rest period, an opportunity for a mid-meal glass of Calvados to perk up the appetite to continue eating.

After lunch, while the youngsters took over cleanup chores, I walked outside with Jean-Paul. He slipped his hand through my arm and asked to be excused, saying he had a few people he needed to see that afternoon.

"Thank you for a most interesting morning," he said. "Do we still have a date for dinner tonight?"

"I'm looking forward to it." I walked with him along the path toward the road's end, leaning a little against his shoulder. "Not black tie, I hope. I left my pearls at home."

"Certainly not black tie," he said with a charming chuckle. "It's Sunday, so there aren't many restaurants open. But I know a wonderful small place called La Neustrie in Pirou. It's very informal, and very good. The food is typical of the region, and Sunday is *poulet-frites*, roast chicken with fries. I'll introduce you to real French fries."

"After the meal we just ate, I'm not sure I'll ever want to eat again, but I'll do my best."

"I will appear on your grandmother's doorstep at about seven." He gave the bottom of his polo a shake, releasing a little flurry of sand. "With a clean shirt. How will that be?"

"Perfect."

As we neared the ragged wall of gorse at the edge of the beach, he leaned in as if to kiss me, and whispered, "Don't look, but you are being followed."

I turned, saw Dauvin about twenty feet behind us, and waved. I hadn't been out of his sight since we left the house that morning.

Jean-Paul said, "Shall I tell the restaurant that we are a party of three tonight?"

"Maybe," I said. "But ask for two tables."

—23—

MAX STROLLED UP to talk to Dauvin while I said good-bye to Jean-Paul. The two of them were deep in conversation when I joined them.

"So?" I said.

Max had a wicked twinkle in his eye. "Handsome fellow, your Jean-Paul."

"Tread gently," I warned him. He could be a terrible tease.

"I just thought it was awfully genteel of him to come by to meet your family."

"Uh-huh." I turned to Dauvin, and with Max's help asked him if there was anything new. There was.

Sergei's telephone turned out to be a little pot of gold, as it were. Connected to Sergei by telephone records, the Russian mechanic in Pacoima with the unpronounceable name began to talk, hoping to make a deal to save his neck.

'Ovich, the mechanic told Rich Longshore that he made a good living off stolen cars, but he was no killer. He was, however, late with loan payments to Sergei's father, a far scarier entrepreneur than the son. Sergei offered him both loan forgiveness and some cash to set up a fatal car "accident": he was supposed to send me over the side of Malibu Canyon Road.

No guns, no personal contact, nothing to tie me to the mechanic, and debt forgiveness in the package—it seemed like a good deal. The man hired one of his stolen car suppliers, the gangbanger Chuy Cepeda, to do the actual deed.

Chuy Cepeda didn't mind the killing part, according to the mechanic. I wouldn't have been his first victim, Rich told Dauvin, though I would be Chuy's first "civilian." Other than the occasional innocent bystander, to that point he had only taken out people from rival gangs, or so it was alleged. The thing about Chuy was, he was a professional car thief, and proud of it. When he got to Malibu and saw that candy store of motorized bling running along Pacific Coast Highway, he got distracted. The mechanic said he could hardly keep Chuy focused on the job at hand. And he admitted to being nervous when he had to actually identify the target, me, to Chuy.

Between nerves, inexperience and language issues, a mistake was made in the identification. Chuy followed Isabelle out of the parking lot instead of me. He waited for her to get into her car, but she was on foot, and instead of driving up the canyon, she walked down PCH.

In the end, having a short attention span and needing a meth hit, out of patience, Chuy saw his chance and just ran her over.

Because of the mistake, the mechanic wouldn't get paid; his loan was still overdue. So, he tried to take care of the problem himself. He brought me a bomb in a FedEx mailer. And failed again, thanks to studio security. He told Rich that without the funds to make a loan payment to Sergei, Senior, he might be better off in prison where he had friends, than out on the loose and vulnerable to the Russian's collectors.

Who shot Chuy? Could have been the Russian mechanic, to shut him up or as punishment for killing the wrong person. Or maybe it was just Chuy's time, and a gang rival took him out. Other than a mother in Reseda, no one seemed too concerned.

"It was a cut-rate deal," Max interjected. "A bargain struck between amateurs; Sergei had no idea how to pull off a professional hit. None of them did."

I asked, "Did the mechanic tell Rich who put Sergei up to it?"

"The guy knew better than to ask a lot of questions," Dauvin said. "He says he doesn't know."

Then Dauvin cocked his head to the side and looked at me out of the corner of his eye. "Do you know, madame?"

"I have a pretty good idea," I said. He nodded when I told him who I thought was responsible.

"It's a long-range plan," I said. "And I'm not the ultimate target, am I?"

He tilted his head to the left: probably not.

I asked, "And Louise?"

Dauvin glanced away, saw the two grandmothers, the abbess and her assistant, and Claude walking toward us on the beach path, headed toward the cars parked at the end of the road. He dropped his head nearer, and in a very low voice, he said, "We conducted a thorough investigation, I assure you. Sadly, the dear woman died by her own hand."

"Yes?" I challenged.

"Yes." His posture, the tone of his voice left no room for uncertainty. "Perhaps, however, that event served as a model for one with very different motives. No?"

The grandmothers and their party reached us just then.

"Here you are." Grand-mère handed me my bag. "I didn't see you. I was afraid you might have left this behind."

"I had my eye on it," I said, slinging the bag over my shoulder.

It was nap time, Grand-mère said, and Claude had volunteered to be their driver. She encouraged me to come with them. When I promised I would be along soon, Dauvin had his hand under my elbow. I wasn't going anywhere until he said so.

Freddy and Antoine were folding chairs and blankets, preparing to close up the cottage. Antoine turned toward the house, responded to someone, and went inside. I was glad that Freddy was alone. He looked up and saw us approach.

"Big day yesterday," he said. "I hope my father didn't keep you up too late last night."

"We had a lot to talk about," I said, picking up a blanket and folding it. Max walked across the sand to join Patricia Dutoit, Jacques and Julie at water's edge, and Dauvin wandered over to watch the kids kick the soccer ball back and forth along the beach.

Though there was some actual sunshine, the day was still cold. I held my hands above the last of the coals in the firepit to warm them.

Clearly, Freddy was curious about my conversation with Claude the night before. I caught him glancing at me, expectant.

"Freddy," I said. "I read some of my father's letters last night."

"Yes?" His brows rose, he paused, and then, trying to be nonchalant, he picked up a chair and folded it.

"You've read them, haven't you?" I asked.

He nodded. "Many times."

"There are some odd gaps in the collection you gave me. Are there more letters?"

"There's a drawer full of them in Maman's Paris apartment. I selected only a few to bring this weekend. I hoped we could talk about some of the things your father said to her, and things she must have said to him."

"All right. I've asked you so many questions, now it's your turn."

Freddy, chair in his hands forgotten, shifted his focus to the sea, seemed to steel himself, struggling with something.

"I lied to you," he said, focus shifting back my way. "I told you I didn't know who your father was when I met him in New York."

"How did Isabelle explain the meeting?"

A frown, let me think, it said. "That day, in preparation for dinner with him, I got a haircut. Maman told me that what happened that night might change my life, might change all our lives. She didn't say how. She was very nervous, and very excited, the way she got sometimes."

"When she was having problems with her medication?"

The question seemed to surprise him, information he didn't know I knew. In the end, he said yes. "That night, whatever she expected to happen, well…"

He cast his eyes down, remembering. "There was an argument—that much was the truth—and your father left. And we went back to Paris; nothing changed."

"Do you know what they argued about?" I asked. He told me earlier he did not, but that was then.

"I heard enough." His glance fell into the empty space between us. "You read the letters, you know what Maman believed. Is it true?"

"You met Dad, you've seen pictures. Have you looked in a mirror?"

He smiled, finally. "I have, and I saw you looking back at me."

"I look at you," I said, "and I see my father looking back at me. Hardly scientific proof, though, is it?"

"More important to me than the science is what your father believed in his heart."

"It seems to me that when Isabelle told Dad she was pregnant with you and wanted him to go away with her, he finally began to think with his head, and not with his heart, or his…" I glanced at Freddy, saw that he knew where that comment was going. "Freddy, there were so many people Dad had to consider. You and Claude among them."

"I," he said, and went no further. He opened the chair and sat, heavily.

"Do you know why Isabelle let Dad take me away?" I asked.

His eyes came up, eager for the answer.

Instead of telling him, I asked, "Did Isabelle ever hurt you?"

He nodded, fought for composure; I thought he was angry more than anything. "Once, a beating, after their argument in New York."

"I'm sorry, Freddy." I knelt on the sand in front of him. "You do know that Isabelle was emotionally unwell, right?"

Again he nodded.

"Sometimes she wasn't responsible for what she said or did."

"Is knowing supposed to make things easier to live with?" His voice rose enough that Dauvin moved in closer. "I was a kid, living with a cyclical lunatic and I wasn't supposed to mention it."

He broke my heart. It was after Dad turned her down another time that Isabelle took out her rage and grief on me. Sick or not, she was consistent.

What did Mike always say? In life there is no re-do. A damn shame.

Freddy reached out, took a piece of my hair that had worked free of the alligator clip and tucked it back in.

"I wrote to your father after I read some of his letters," he said. "After that meeting I snooped around. He wrote back, a short note. He said my father was a wonderful man named Claude Desmoulins. Then he asked the same question you just did, had Maman ever hurt me. I told him what I told you. He never responded to me, but shortly after that Papa had a long talk with Maman, and I essentially went to live with him. I was rarely ever alone with her again until I came back from graduate school. Papa made sure of it."

"Dad must have contacted Claude after you wrote him," I said. "He was concerned for you."

"That's what I thought, too. I wanted to believe that even if he denied paternity he cared about me."

"He was a good man, Freddy." I sat back on my heels, faced him. "Not a perfect man, but he had a good heart. Like Claude."

Casey and David spilled out of the cottage and came over to us, checking in.

"How's the cleanup progressing?" I asked.

"Kitchen's finished," Casey said. "Uncle Gérard and Gillian went up to the loft for a nap. Kelly and Antoine fell asleep watching a soccer match. Lena's catching up on her phone calls. What are your plans now?"

"I want to talk to Freddy for a few minutes," I said. "Then a nap for me, too."

She clicked her tongue. "Get all rested up for the big date, huh?"

"Rested enough so I don't fall asleep in the soup."

They excused themselves, walked down the beach to join the other young people.

Lena came out onto the cottage porch and summoned her sons from their game, giving them instructions. Reluctantly, they began a good-bye round of *la bise* with their cousins. Lena had said earlier that she was driving the boys back to Paris that afternoon. I needed to know something before they got away.

"Freddy," I said, "did you ever tell your wife that you thought my dad was your father?"

"Of course. For a long time, Lena told me not to think about it. But she changed her mind—probably got tired of listening to me. She encouraged me to find out."

"Did you do anything?"

He wagged his head, yes and no. "A year ago I wrote to your father again. But the letter came back marked Addressee Deceased, Return to Sender.

"I planned to contact you." He smiled. "But Lena said it would be better to wait until Maman's illness ran its course, so that we didn't upset her, and then to speak with you."

Lena told him to wait. I said, "Lena is short for Hélène?"

"Yes."

"Hélène *what* Desmoulins?"

"Godard," he said, puzzled by the question.

There it was. The initials at the bottom of the royalty account sheets M. Hubert gave me, HGD, Hélène Godard Desmoulins. Lena.

"How long has Lena been managing Isabelle's accounts?" I asked.

"Oh," a shrug, a moue, thinking back. "Several years. Since Maman's illness; she was having more difficulty keeping track of things. And Lena is wonderful with numbers."

"How many years?"

He shrugged. "Three, maybe four."

Because she audited Isabelle's royalty statements, Lena would have known that Dad was already dead when she suggested that Freddy write to him. I leaned back on my elbows, looked up at the sky and thought that over.

"Freddy?" Lena came off the porch and strode toward us, slinging her beautiful bag over her shoulder. "It's getting late. If I may interrupt your little *tête-à-tête*, the boys and I need to head back to Paris. When will we expect you home?"

I stood, Freddy rose, both blushing as if we had been caught at something illicit. My thoughts were certainly impure at the moment, but had nothing to do with Freddy.

"I don't know yet, I'll call you," Freddy told his wife. "The bank has given me the week, and I'll probably need it. There's a lot to be taken care of."

"Will you remember to go get the dining chairs back from Kelly?"

"All right," he said.

She offered me her hand and her cheek. "I'm glad we met at last. You must come to us in Paris before you leave."

"Thank you," I said. "I plan to be in Paris Monday afternoon. I've been admiring your bag. Maybe you'll show me where to shop. I want to take some gifts home."

"Of course," she said. "How long will you be in Paris?"

"Just the afternoon," I said. "Some business to tend to. It appears that there has been an error in the distribution of royalty earnings since my father died, and Uncle Max and I need to find the source of the problem."

I saw something dark cross her face before she smiled. A pale smile. "I'm sure Monsieur Hubert will clear up any issues," she said.

"We'll see on Monday," I said. I hadn't mentioned Hubert. "I'll call you when I'm free."

She turned from me to Freddy, offering her cheek. He took her upper arm in his hand, an automatic gesture, but he didn't lean toward her. Freddy had caught something in the exchange between me and Lena, reacted to the mention of royalties. He said, "You never mentioned anything to me about the royalties, Lena." His glance shifted to me. "From the patents, right? *La tontine?*"

"You know about them from the letters," I said.

He looked into his wife's face, puzzled. "Who is Hubert?"

"For God's sake, Freddy." Lena gave her husband a perfunctory kiss as she gestured for her boys to come with her. "He's just one of your mother's accountants. I don't bore you with your mother's mundane household matters any more than we bored her with ours. Shall I show you her grocery bill next?"

"But you knew I was curious about the patents. More than curious."

"I doubt Hubert can tell you much about the technicalities of the devices—I certainly can't." She called for the boys to hurry. "All he does is keep records and write checks, and all I do is make sure his columns tally. Now, we're going or we'll hit traffic."

With an annoyed toss of her head, she set off toward the cars parked at the end of the road. She called back. "We'll expect you by Thursday, Freddy."

Dauvin, with a flick of his hand, summoned a gendarme out of the watch post in the gorse near the cars. When Lena hit the remote to unlock her green Jaguar, the gendarme moved in to intercept her.

Philippe had just come up to Freddy to say good-bye when Lena began to argue with the gendarme. Dauvin walked briskly toward the scene unfolding beside the Jaguar.

I exchanged glances with Freddy, tipped my head toward his son. Freddy was upset, but he was coherent enough to hold his son Philippe by the arm to keep him from running over to his mother.

Freddy narrowed his eyes at me, confusion, a challenge behind them. Still holding on to Philippe, he ordered Robert to come to him, *now*.

When he had both of his boys in hand, he shushed their questions about what was happening with their mother.

"Routine," he said. "You know what happened to your grandmother. The police are merely conducting their investigation. Now, please, carry these chairs inside and put them away in the cupboard."

When the boys were gone, he turned back to me, trying to form the words for the right question.

"Lena injured her left arm," I said. "I saw the bandage when she passed the bread to Pierre Dauvin at lunch."

"She cut herself cooking last night," he said, seeming to be confused—who cares about a cut on her arm? "A knife slipped. That's why she missed dinner. She showed me this morning."

Dauvin and the uniformed gendarme walked Lena away down the road. We lost sight of them as they moved behind the heavy gorse.

"Excuse me." Freddy started to follow. I went after him, stopped him.

"Freddy, be very careful what you say and do here."

"But my wife." His face was white; I was afraid he was going to faint. I took him by the hand and walked him toward the water. The tide was coming in. The trotters had been driven home and we had that part of the beach to ourselves. Except for the pair of uniformed gendarmes who stepped out of the gorse in front of us.

"Last night," I said, pulling his attention away from the road. "I was attacked in my bed by someone with a knife."

He snapped his head toward me. "When?"

"That's why I ran outside."

"We all thought it was the storm."

I shrugged, moved past complicated explanations. "In the struggle, I got some little cuts." I showed him. "But my attacker was cut more seriously. A slip of the knife."

"Did you see who it was?"

"No. It was dark. Whoever it was took a pillow from my room and tried to stanch the blood with it on the way out of the house."

"You think it was Lena?" He was incredulous.

"Dauvin does. He has the bloody pillow," I said. Then I tapped my fat lip. "Actually, he has two bloody pillows, one from the kitchen, one from my room. He'll know soon enough whose blood ended up where."

"Why weren't we told about the attack earlier?"

"Dauvin asked me to keep it quiet." I touched his arm. "What I said to you earlier I'll repeat. Be very careful what you say and do here."

"You don't think I...?"

I shook my head. "Not you. I lost one brother. I don't intend to lose another."

"Promise me you don't think Lena had anything to do with Maman's death."

"I can't make that promise," I said. "Isabelle's death was a mistake. Lena meant for *me* to die. And Freddy, if she had managed to pull off her plan, I believe that you would have been next."

—24—

"BECAUSE HER HANDBAG was counterfeit you decided your sister-in-law hired a hitman?" Jean-Paul set his cheese plate aside. "Is this an example of female intuition?"

"No," I said. The beautiful bag Jean-Paul had given me was on the floor, resting against my leg; Grand-mère had insisted that I carry it. "How about an example of brilliant investigative work?"

"Dazzle me further." He took a sip of the after-dinner drink the restaurant proprietor brought us, lager with a shot of Picon, a sweet and bitter orange liqueur.

"When we were at the hospital last night my cousin Antoine told me that at Easter Sergei, Junior, tried to sell designer handbags, cheap, to family members. No one accepted any that day, but he handed out his card in case anyone wanted something later. Lena wanted a bag, but that contact wasn't all she wanted from him."

"But how did you know your sister-in-law's bag was, as we say, *contrefaçon*, a fake?"

"Detective Longshore gave me a Web site that helps the customs people spot fakes. The stitching that attached the handle of Lena's bag was wrong. Besides, her bag was very new, the real thing would have been extraordinarily expensive, and they were so broke they were living with his mother." I sipped the bitter beer concoction, made a face, made the handsome Jean-Paul smile. "By the way, in case you were wondering, the bag you gave me is authentic."

He laughed. "I am relieved to know that."

I skipped saying anything about why I asked Rich about identifying counterfeits in the first place. Why risk ruining a lovely evening? And it was a lovely evening. The restaurant was as promised, small and informal. We were seated at a long table, family style, with two other couples. The meal was delicious. Simple food, expertly prepared. By the time we got around to cheese, we were the only diners left, though there were some locals at the bar in front, talking with the proprietor and his wife over nightcaps.

"The truth is, though I hate to share credit," I said, "Inspector Dauvin was onto Lena long before I began to wonder about her. He was happy to hear about the handbag because it makes a connection between Lena and Sergei, Junior that can be taken into court. But with bank and phone records—she transferred a small down-payment to Sergei's account—he already has plenty. And, of course, they have the text messages Lena sent to Sergei that made him so angry."

"What did she text?"

"He asked for cash to cover expenses so far. Besides the Russian mechanic in LA—twice a failure—there were those two attempts in France to run me down, the cost of an assistant, the stolen van," I said. "Lena's first response was, 'Incomplete, no pay.' When Sergei, Junior begged for one more shot at me, she responded, 'Drop dead.' And within a couple of hours…" I shrugged.

"Fait accompli." He covered my hand, aimed his big brown eyes at me. "We are fortunate that the man she hired to, if you will, terminate you, was such an idiot. Tenacious, but an idiot."

A mere four days ago, I asked Jean-Paul how an upstanding citizen would go about finding a hit man. Therein lay the crux of Lena's downfall.

When Lena met Sergei, Junior, a boaster, a braggart, a wannabe hood whose startup was selling knock-off designer handbags out of the trunk of a borrowed Lamborghini, she decided she had her man. How many street thugs does an insurance executive meet in a day? She made him an offer and, full of himself, he accepted. Evidence of Lena and Sergei's actual criminal naïveté was the mess they made of things.

Each mistake created new problems. Lena wouldn't pay Sergei, Junior unless he finished the job. 'Ovich was demanding that Junior live up to their deal, though 'Ovich had screwed up twice, or he'd go to Ludanov, Senior and snitch on the kid. The mechanic's loan payment was due. Sergei, Junior had to find a way to make it before his father found out what he'd done. The consequences for him wouldn't be deadly, but they would be dire.

For Lena, I was not only still a problem, I became a more immediate problem once I had spoken with Monsieur Hubert. Lena, of course, had redirected my dad's share of royalties, in effect stealing from Mom, for over a year. If I died before Isabelle, the flow of those funds would remain unaffected. But I didn't, and Lena knew that her tidy row of financial dominoes was going down. And her with it.

Lena gave Sergei another chance to earn his money. Actuary that she was, she still insisted that I go out in an automobile "accident," the most common way for a healthy woman my age to die in France. Again Sergei hired an amateur to help him, the man with the foul vocabulary, but they were foiled first by David's skill as a driver and next by Jacques Breton's watchfulness. And then, on Saturday when I identified him from the airport, Lena knew he needed to go.

"You have to give Lena credit for one thing," I said. "She knew car wrecks. But that was her business. She knew where to drive a knife into a tire to make the steel belt separate, the tire to shred. And that's what she did to the Lamborghini on her way out of the house."

"How is your brother handling the situation?" he asked.

"He's stunned," I said. Freddy looked shellshocked when I left him with Max and Claude at Patricia Dutoit's office in Lessay. He asked the *notaire* to begin divorce proceedings, and to rewrite his will, right away. In the original, he had left all of his legally disposable assets, one-third of his estate—two-thirds by law would go to his sons—to his "beloved wife." An affectionate generosity that damn near got him, and me, killed. "His wife sits in the local jail, waiting to be arraigned for murder, murder-for-hire, attempted murder, embezzlement.... Poor man doesn't know what hit him."

"I am sorry for him, and for his boys. For them, a nightmare begins." Jean-Paul covered my hand, looked into my eyes. "But for you, I am more than relieved that the threat is..." his free hand swept the air "...*fini.*"

He caught the proprietor's eye and signaled him with a lift of the chin. After some apparently complex computations, a handwritten bill, folded, on a saucer, was set next to Jean-Paul. He gave it the barest glance, and placed a stack of euros on top.

"Thank you," I said, rising. "You're good company."

"My dear Maggie," Jean-Paul said, holding my coat for me. "Now that *l'Affaire famille Martin* is resolved, how am I to entertain myself? I have a lovely title, but what the consul general actually does is, frankly, quite dull: receptions, funerals, lost passports, occasional mischief by my countrymen abroad. The events of the last week have been more interesting than all of the last two years combined."

"Maybe we'll think of something," I said, slipping my hand through his arm. I had several fairly interesting ideas.

We walked out into a cold, clear night, a sliver of a moon, a few clouds in the distance. Except for the light coming from the restaurant's windows, and the occasional burst of laughter from the patrons still standing at the bar inside swapping their stories, the night was black and silent. Could have been any small town on a Sunday evening.

As we drove out of the restaurant lot, Jean-Paul asked, "How long will you be staying in France?"

"I'm not sure. Depends on how things go tomorrow in a couple of meetings. Casey has a flight out of de Gaulle Tuesday morning, and I would like to be on the plane with her. I need to get back to work." I looked at his profile, lit only by the dash lights. "And you?"

"I have the horse auction in St-Lô tomorrow and then I'm in Paris until Wednesday. If you're staying over in the city, please call me."

We settled into an easy conversation, the sharing of life stories that comes early in a new friendship. I felt comfortable with him.

He took a shortcut, turned into a dark lane, shielded on both sides by heavy *bocage*, the hedgerow. The only light came from his wide beams.

"This is a beautiful car," I said, running my hand over the burlwood veneer on the glove box. It *was* a beautiful car, an older model Mercedes S-class, a stately vehicle powered by a thrumming diesel engine.

He patted the steering wheel. "This fine lady is the same age as my son, just a youngster." That made the car eighteen.

I asked about his son, and the conversation naturally segued into a discussion between two widowers, both emerging in fits and starts from under the cloud of grief, both with children on the threshold of adult-hood. Clearly, this shortcut was the long way around, a ploy to give us more time together.

Jean-Paul was telling me about his son's plans for college, when I felt the first bump. Something in the road? I thought, startled.

"Merde," Jean-Paul swore, eyes on the rearview mirror. When the second bump happened, he jammed down on the accelerator, pushing

the big diesel Mercedes forward. I turned, saw the profile of a black Range Rover, lights out, riding our bumper. The Range Rover hit us a third time, an assertive thump.

I pulled out my phone, saw there was service, dialed 17, Police emergency. I asked, "Where are we?"

"Road between Pirou and Créances."

When Emergency picked up, I couldn't understand the operator's questions. I held the phone against Jean-Paul's ear, and he gave our location, explained what was happening, listened, told me to keep the line open, told the operator when we turned, all four tires squealing, onto the road toward Lessay; I could see the spires of the abbey, black against a night sky.

The Range Rover stayed with us, occasionally dropping back to make some space to build momentum so he could bump into our rear again, jerking us against the seat belts. The old Mercedes took the abuse like a tank.

Ahead, I saw the lights of Lessay and, approaching fast, the flashing blue lights of a police car. As quickly as it appeared, the Range Rover was gone, turned down a side lane, slipped off into the night.

Jean-Paul spoke rapidly into the phone, told the operator where the other car went. The police car passed us with a flash of its headlights. Following Jean-Paul's information, it turned.

Shaken, Jean-Paul pulled to the side of the road. He turned to me. "Who knew where we were going tonight?"

"My uncle, my daughter, my grandmother."

"I'm sorry, a silly question to ask." He took my hand. "We were easy to follow. But who?"

I shook my head, dialed Uncle Max. Jean-Paul put the car in gear and drove on toward the village of Lessay. Max answered, but the signal dropped. I said my usual prayer to AT&T and dialed again, reached him again.

"Honey, where are you?" Max demanded, voice gruff.

I checked the dash clock. "Did I wake you?"

Like a black bat out of hell, the Range Rover came out between the hedgerows, clipped the back corner of our car, a perfect maneuver that sent us into a spin. Jean-Paul fought to steer into the spin, to regain control. As I braced, I dropped the phone. I could hear Max calling my name. Maybe I answered, but I was trying to see what we were going to hit, to prepare for impact.

Jean-Paul jockeyed the car, got it straight, still moving fast, but on the street. The Range Rover came back for another go at us. The air was full of noise, Range Rover revving, Mercedes roaring, tires scudding sideways along the pavement, the crash of metal on metal.

We saw him coming at us yet again, this time aimed at my door.

Jean-Paul managed to swerve, avoided impact, but only by jumping the stone curb and driving on the lawn. The convent was straight ahead and there wasn't time to stop the car before it collided with stone wall.

"I'm braking hard. Get set to bail," Jean-Paul said.

"Ready." I gripped the door handle with both hands, braced; he stomped the brake, both doors flew open.

"Now," he said.

I hit the lawn tucked and rolling. The empty Mercedes collided with a corner of the stone building and stopped dead no more than five yards from me.

"Jean-Paul!" I heard him groan, found him piled against the base of a marble fountain. The Range Rover squealed into a U-turn. It was coming back. I thought the hesitation was the driver deciding which of us to go after first.

In the distance, there were sirens. Help wouldn't get there in time.

I scrambled to the Mercedes, found my bag, and ran toward Jean-Paul. The Range Rover's big V-8 motor revved, laid rubber as it surged toward us.

I stood in its path, put my hand in my bag and pulled out the German Luger Grand-mère forced on me as I left her house that morning—the one she took off a dead soldier—aimed into the approaching windshield and pulled the trigger twice as Mike had taught me. Then I shot out both front tires. As the Range Rover hit the stone curb it cartwheeled, ass over teakettle, and landed on its roof.

Nuns in their white nightclothes began to pour out of the convent, Ma Mère in the middle of the pack, like a flock of angels in the night. Several of them went straight to Jean-Paul, rendering aid.

Luger held in front of me, ready to fire again, I went over to the upside-down beast, which was groaning and leaking fluids. The driver was slithering out a broken window when I got to him. He, also, was groaning and leaking fluids. I had winged him. His right arm hung limp from a shattered shoulder.

"Who the hell are you?" I demanded. The young man wearing a dark hooded sweatshirt was no one I knew.

"Don't shoot, lady." He held up his one good arm. I recognized the voice, Sergei's buddy who was swearing the whole time that he chased me across a carrot field the day before. "Jesus, don't shoot, lady. Where you think you are, Texas?"

Ma Mère reached over and put her hand on my right wrist. I lowered the Luger and gave it to her. It disappeared somewhere into the folds of her gown.

The driver managed to sit, back against the wreckage. Several of the nuns fluttered to his side, expertly assessing his injuries.

"Who hired you?" I asked the driver.

He squinted at me with one eye while a sister of mercy sponged blood from a cut above the other one. He was pumped on adrenaline and probably a few other mood enhancers. Hyper at the moment, he started rattling off his tale of woe.

"That bitch who hired Sergei," he said, as if I should have known. "I called her. Sergei was dead, and I never got paid. I wanted my money. No one else was going to give it to me except her. So she says, finish the job tonight. I'll pay you tonight."

"When did you talk to her?"

"This afternoon. What's it to you?"

"Not a lot, except it's me she hired you to kill. And I'm taking that fairly personally."

Any number of car doors slammed at once. I heard Dauvin giving orders, turned, found him among a clutch of emergency responders and uniformed gendarmes.

"What kept you?" I asked him.

I have no idea what he was saying to me, though I got the gist: What the hell was I doing with a gun?

I said, "I just got real tired of car chases and decided to put a stop to it."

I walked off to check on Jean-Paul. Behind me I heard Ma Mère laugh heartily.

Jean-Paul wanted to sit up, but the nuns wouldn't let him. Paramedics were right there, got his head and neck into a brace, got a board under him and lifted him from the ground.

He managed a smile as he reached a hand out to me.

"Hey, Jean-Paul," I said as I took it. "What should we do for our second date?"

fin

Stephanie Jacobs

ABOUT THE AUTHOR

Wendy Hornsby is the author of eight previous mysteries, six of them featuring Maggie MacGowen. Hornsby won an Edgar Award for her story "Nine Sons," which appeared in *Sisters in Crime IV*. Her books have won the Grand Prix de littérature policière, and readers' and reviewers' choice awards, as well as nominations for the Prix du Roman d'Adventures and the Anthony Award.

Hornsby lives in Long Beach, California, where she is a professor of history at Long Beach City College. She welcomes visitors and e-mail at www.wendyhornsby.com

MORE MYSTERIES
FROM PERSEVERANCE PRESS
🔮 *For the New Golden Age* 🔮

JON L. BREEN
Eye of God
ISBN 978-1-880284-89-6

TAFFY CANNON
ROXANNE PRESCOTT SERIES
Guns and Roses
*Agatha and Macavity Award
nominee, Best Novel*
ISBN 978-1-880284-34-6

Blood Matters
ISBN 978-1-880284-86-5

Open Season on Lawyers
ISBN 978-1-880284-51-3

Paradise Lost
ISBN 978-1-880284-80-3

LAURA CRUM
GAIL McCARTHY SERIES
Moonblind
ISBN 978-1-880284-90-2

Chasing Cans
ISBN 978-1-880284-94-0

Going, Gone
ISBN 978-1-880284-98-8

JEANNE M. DAMS
HILDA JOHANSSON SERIES
Crimson Snow
ISBN 978-1-880284-79-7

Indigo Christmas
ISBN 978-1-880284-95-7

JANET DAWSON
JERI HOWARD SERIES
Bit Player *(forthcoming)*
ISBN 978-1-56474-494-4

KATHY LYNN EMERSON
LADY APPLETON SERIES
**Face Down Below
the Banqueting House**
ISBN 978-1-880284-71-1

**Face Down Beside
St. Anne's Well**
ISBN 978-1-880284-82-7

Face Down O'er the Border
ISBN 978-1-880284-91-9

ELAINE FLINN
MOLLY DOYLE SERIES
Deadly Vintage
ISBN 978-1-880284-87-2

HAL GLATZER
KATY GREEN SERIES
Too Dead To Swing
ISBN 978-1-880284-53-7

A Fugue in Hell's Kitchen
ISBN 978-1-880284-70-4

The Last Full Measure
ISBN 978-1-880284-84-1

WENDY HORNSBY
MAGGIE MacGOWEN SERIES
In the Guise of Mercy
ISBN 978-1-56474-482-1

The Paramour's Daughter
ISBN 978-1-56474-496-8

DIANA KILLIAN
POETIC DEATH SERIES
Docketful of Poesy
ISBN 978-1-880284-97-1

JANET LAPIERRE
PORT SILVA SERIES
Baby Mine
ISBN 978-1-880284-32-2

Keepers
*Shamus Award nominee,
Best Paperback Original*
ISBN 978-1-880284-44-5

Death Duties
ISBN 978-1-880284-74-2

Family Business
ISBN 978-1-880284-85-8

Run a Crooked Mile
ISBN 978-1-880284-88-9

HAILEY LIND
ART LOVER'S SERIES
Arsenic and Old Paint
ISBN 978-1-56474-490-6